ABSOLUTELY AND TOTALLY SMITTEN

DEBBY MELTZER QUICK

Also by Debby Meltzer Quick

May I Have Your Attention Please
I Just Can't Say I Love You

ISBN: 979-8-9871874-2-5
Cover and interior design by: Jai Design
Author photograph: Milana Gilligan Photography
Printed in the United States of America

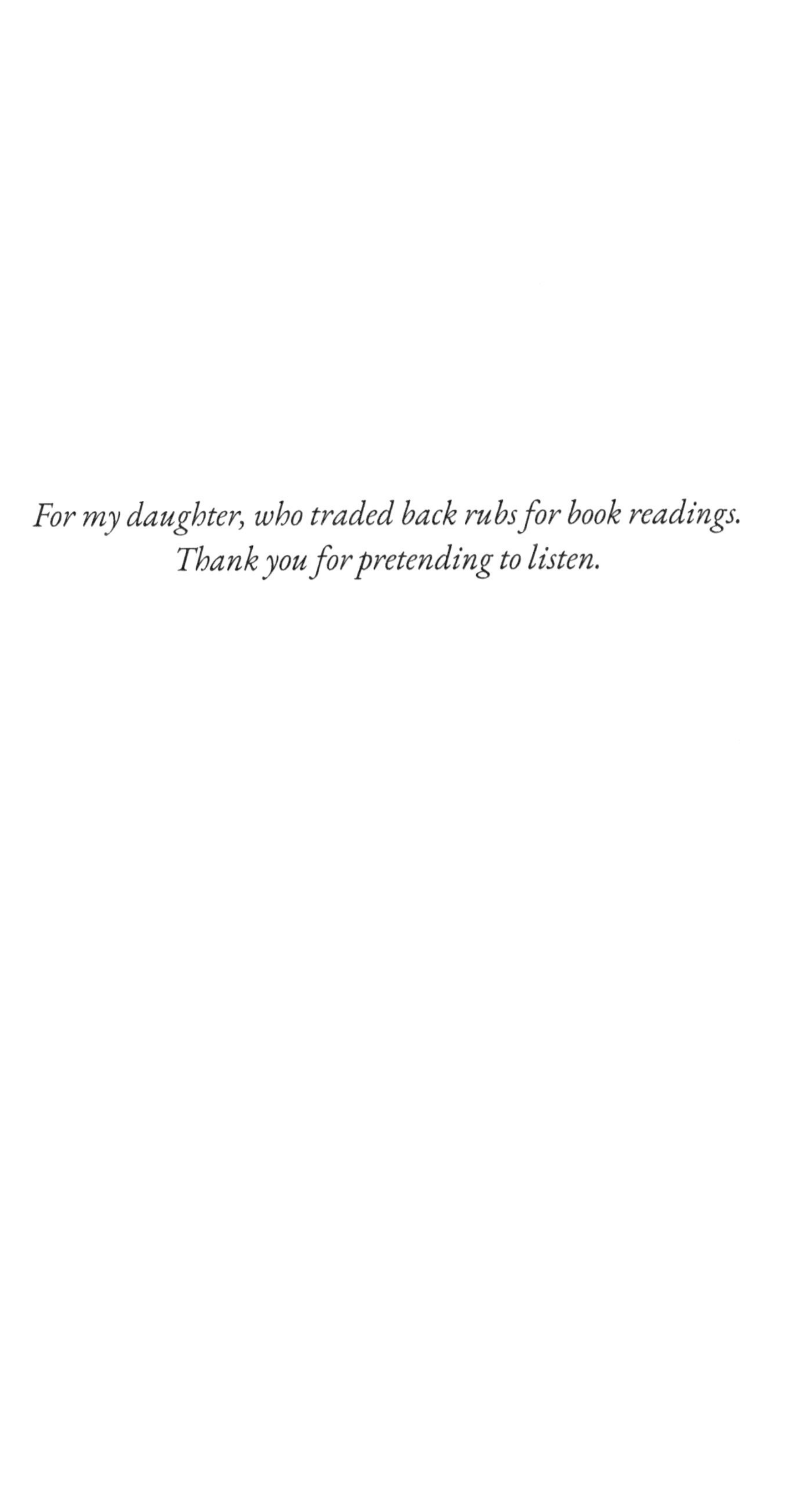

*For my daughter, who traded back rubs for book readings.
Thank you for pretending to listen.*

PROLOGUE

I DO, DO YOU?

They had all wondered who among their friends would be the first to get married. Everyone had a pretty good idea. They were all, of course, wrong. At a beautiful outdoor venue, with flowers in large vases and lining the aisle, they had a view of a small pond with swans and geese flying above and ducks floating on the water. The sun was shining bright between a few fluffy white clouds, and a light breeze blew through the seventy-five-degree afternoon. Dozens of guests sat ready and waiting as violin music filled the air.

Two identical twin grandmothers, wearing fancy dresses and ornate corsages, one carrying an almost six-month-old baby in a tiny tuxedo, made their way down the aisle and sat in the front row. Thirteen-year-old Stella Drake and her ten-year-old sister Sophia walked down next in matching dresses, carrying small bouquets of spring flowers. James Newell and Sally Bachman walked down the aisle holding hands. They both spent a moment imagining this was their wedding. Then they dropped their hands. James went to the right to start the line of groomsmen, and Sally to the left to be the first of the bridesmaids. They were followed by Pete Cooper and Michelle Gorman, then Chris Mahoney and Darlene Feinman, the best man and maid of honor.

The music stopped. Everyone stood. A string quartet started playing "Pachelbel's Canon," and everyone watched the back of the aisle in anticipation. Slowly, they were rewarded with the vision of a beautiful, brown-haired woman in white. Grasping her arm on one side was a sandy-haired man looking dapper in a black and white tuxedo, and on the other, another woman with a corsage, talking softly to the man as they walked. He smiled brightly as he escorted his daughter, his wife continuing to coax him along with her soft words. The bride was radiant.

Mr. and Mrs. Drake stopped at the foot of the aisle, and both gave Kim a kiss on the cheek. Then they took their seats next to the Grams and baby Drake. Kim's face was already wet with tears. Carl Bishop took a step closer to her, took her hand with a smile, and together they stepped up to the officiant to speak their vows of everlasting love, for the second time.

Chris Mahoney could not remember another moment in his life when he felt so proud and so happy for someone he loved. For two people he loved. This was their moment to shine, their moment to show the whole world how their love conquered everything. But this was not the story of Kim and Carl. Or of James and Sally. This was the story of why, at that moment, Chris turned his attention to the girls he knew in high school and smiled warmly at one of them. And she smiled back. And he felt something new inside of him stir.

PART ONE

OUR TRUE BROTHERS

Bad Boys Are Made, Not Born

"He has Farmer eyes," Kate Bishop Mahoney said sleepily as she gazed at her newborn son's face.

Her husband Ken nodded. "He does," he agreed. "And if he has even a tenth of the intelligence, compassion, and charisma of Jerome Farmer, he'll do really well in the world."

Chris Mahoney was born into an Eastboro legacy. His maternal great-grandfather, Jerome Farmer, was the mayor of Eastboro, Massachusetts, many, many years before Chris or his mother were even born. He was considered a brilliant man before his time and beloved by the people. He even had his own statue downtown in front of city hall. Chris had inherited three things from his great-grandfather: his eyes, Jerome as his middle name, and his overpowering charisma.

Chris was not the only one in Eastboro with the legacy. The Bishops and the Farmers were prolific breeders, and there were three generations of cousins in every nook and cranny of Eastboro and surrounding towns. There were cousins at school, cousins in the government, cousins working at the auto repair shop, cousins in the police force. And even cousins in jail. Anywhere you went in Eastboro and met a Bishop or a Farmer, you could be assured they were part of Chris's famous family.

In the middle of all the pomp and circumstance was Chris's grandmother, Cecelia, and her identical twin sister, Melissa. The Farmer girls. They were affectionately known as Gram Cissy and Gram Missy by their grandchildren. They were made famous countrywide for their storybook double-wedding to handsome and charming brothers, the Bishop boys, Cecil and Clyde, thus securing the Bishop-Farmer legacy for further generations.

Chris seemed to know from the time of his birth in March of 1968 that he was destined for some sort of greatness. He was a charming baby, and people gravitated toward him. As he grew, Chris got to know his cousins, aunts, and uncles, their habits, and their quirks. As a small child, he knew who kept candy in their pocket or on their coffee table. He learned which cousin got a discount at the toy store, or who could set him up with free samples of new sneakers or demo music tapes from the radio station. In junior high, he knew beyond any doubt who could hook him and his friends up with joints or six packs of beer, or free tickets to R-rated movies. The cousins didn't need much convincing to do these things for Chris. They liked him. He took them seriously. He listened to their stories, and he told them his tales, both true and farfetched. He was interesting and friendly. It was all about the Farmer charisma.

Chris developed a group of school friends in second grade, and they were his troop, his posse of bad boys. He was their unofficial leader, and he made his second cousin, Carl Bishop, Gram Missy's grandson, his righthand man. Carl was a lost little boy with no sense of confidence and neglectful parents. Chris liked having a lieutenant, but he also knew instinctively that Carl needed protection from the world. He needed Chris to help him navigate through social situations, and to keep him safe. Chris was not sure back then why he needed to keep his cousin safe. It would not be clear to him for years why he made Carl come to his house several times a week, made sure he was invited to stay for dinner when he was there, and included him in everything he did. He made sure the posse was tight. They were a team, Chris, Carl, James Newell, and Pete Cooper. And Chris ensured that nobody, *nobody*, messed with Carl.

They made it through elementary school and most of junior high before the walls started to crumble in on their bad boy careers. Chris, James, and Pete were caught sneaking out of school to go smoke a joint by Carson Lake in ninth grade. It wasn't their first time sneaking out, but it was their first time getting caught. Chris was holding the joint. He was suspended from school for three weeks, his friends for three days each. Their parents began to tighten the reins. The boys endured tense meetings with their parents and the principal. There was talk of Chris being expelled if anything even similar to this ever happened again. James and Pete were grounded after school for a month and kept away from Chris's influence. Chris had to beg his parents, with promises of being good, to help him to please get his friends back. Eventually things settled down, and his friends were allowed back into his life, but they had already changed. They had lost some of their recklessness, their good-natured bad boy innocence. They had become more careful, more mindful of the rules. And that was the incident that led James to decide to live the sober life that would later help define his character.

But all along, Carl was always there. Carl had not attempted to go with them to the lake that day, had not gotten in trouble, and had not had any of the consequences. Even if he had been with them, his neglectful parents were not too interested in his bad boy ways. They probably wouldn't have cared. He probably would have still been free to do as he pleased. He was always still up for trouble. He was still Chris's loyal sidekick. They still engaged in harmless mischief, just not enough to get in trouble at school.

In tenth grade, Pete went to Murphy High, while Chris, Carl, and James all went to McKinney High, thus breaking up the quartet. The latter three started high school as a close-knit trio. Carl and James turned to Chris for guidance on what to do, how to act, and how to fit in. It was a role Chris was born to play and had provided to them for years. But soon after their first year of their high school career began, Rhonda Jenkins made her first move.

Help Me, Rhonda Jenkins

Chris knew of Rhonda at Randall Junior High. All of the boys were aware of Rhonda from a distance. She was the first of the girls to experiment with tight sweaters, sexy bras, and lavish makeup. She had a very fortunate growth spurt between seventh and eighth grade and came back on the first day of school tall and curvy, dressed in brand-new designer jeans and a halter top. Chris was sure all the boys in his class had similar sex dreams about Rhonda that night. They never talked much about girls, and especially their sex dreams, but their eyes drifted down the hallway when Rhonda passed by. She was like something you'd see on a movie screen but was way too far away to touch.

On the first day of sophomore year, their first day at McKinney High, Rhonda closed her locker door, turned to look at Chris standing nearby, and smiled.

"Hey, Chris," she said, and then started to walk away.

Chris dropped his thick math book on his foot. He waited until she disappeared around the corner to wince, curse, and pick up the book. Chris was too cool to show his pain in front of Rhonda. Carl, who witnessed the whole event, laughed heartily.

"Dude, I wish you could see the look on your face," Carl told him. Chris wrote off Rhonda's smile as a fluke and went on with his life.

There were other small signs throughout the fall and early winter months that Rhonda might be interested, and Chris stowed them away in the back of his mind, one by one.

"Hey, Chris," she said before the bell rang in history class. Chris looked up. "I can't find my pen. I have more in my locker, but I don't have time to go back there before class starts. Do you have one I could borrow?"

Chris quickly dug through his own bag. He found a stubby old pencil with no eraser at the bottom. He kept that for himself and handed his good pen to Rhonda.

After class, Chris was walking toward the cafeteria when he heard Rhonda calling behind him. He stopped and turned around.

"Chris," she said, scurrying up to him. "You forgot to get your pen from me. Here." She handed it to him with much ceremony and a smile.

"Thanks, Rhonda," Chris said. "You could have given it back to me tomorrow, you know."

Rhonda shrugged. "But you might need it before then." She gave him a little wave and turned to walk away. Chris watched as she moved down the hall.

After that, Rhonda's friends started saying hi to him when they passed him in the hallway, which they had never done before. Rhonda complimented him on his baseball shirt in the cafeteria, even though it was almost exactly the same as his other four baseball shirts. His friends were starting to notice the attention, too.

"She's totally into you," James told him as they hung out in the crisp mid-November air at Store 24 after school. "She's always looking at you and turning away when you look at her. She doesn't have a boyfriend. You should ask her out."

"You should," Carl agreed. "She's hot, and she's popular. And I bet she's experienced. Maybe she could hook us up with her friends."

"I don't know, maybe," Chris said with a shrug. He wasn't going to tell his friends, but he was worried that if he asked Rhonda out, she would say no. No one had ever said no to Chris before. Most girls were impressed with his confidence and surety. He may have only gone out with most of them one time, but he never got an initial no. Rhonda was in a whole different league, though. One of the differences was that he hadn't cared if those other girls said no, so there was never anything to lose. But if Rhonda said no, he would feel it. And people would know. It was a calculated risk. He kept it in the back of his mind.

It wasn't until after Christmas break that they finally connected. They had to choose partners for a project in history class, and Rhonda turned to Chris. "Hey, Chris, wanna be my partner?" she asked. Then she gave him *the* smile.

He knew he had a golden opportunity at that moment. He could say no. He could publicly turn down Rhonda Jenkins. He could show her who was in control. Then later, he would ask her out and not care if she said no, and she would be unable to say no. But the smile turned his brain to mush.

He nodded. "Sure," he answered as nonchalantly as he could manage.

"Great," she said, and then turned back to the front of the room. Chris realized at that moment that Rhonda knew all the same tricks he did. Just throw it out there like it doesn't really matter if they say no. And they never say no. It was the first sign that he didn't have all the control in his relationship with Rhonda. It wouldn't be the last.

Their schoolwork relationship morphed quickly into a romantic relationship. While they worked on their history essay in her bedroom the first day, she shoved aside their books, pushed him backward on the bed, and kissed him.

"My parents won't be home until five," she whispered to him. Then she started to pull his shirt up over his head.

Their relationship was largely physical at first, because it could be, and they wanted it to be. But as the weeks went by, Chris realized that he really liked Rhonda—a lot. She was funny, and interesting, and she liked heavy metal and rock music. She was also smart and had nice friends who really seemed to like him. And she seemed to like him, too. The sex became more intimate as they talked more, and asked questions, and cared about the answers. They started to spend more and more time together after school and on weekends, until Rhonda clued him in on a problem.

"Chris," she told him, "you're neglecting your friends. Your posse. Especially Carl. Carl seems lost. I've seen him standing there in the hall sometimes just looking around. And something's going on with James. I don't know what, but he seems so angry all the time. Haven't you noticed that something's off?"

Chris had to admit that he hadn't. He'd been completely swallowed up by his relationship with Rhonda and only really thought about his friends when they were right in front of him. Even then he was likely thinking about Rhonda. He felt a pit develop in his stomach. He thought about Carl being alone and lost and suddenly wanted to go find him. He wanted to know what was up with the normally agreeable and amicable James that was making him so angry. But he also wanted to be with Rhonda. She understood.

"Chris, I'm not gonna just disappear if we're not together all the time," she assured him. "I mean, you know I still spend time with my friends. You just need to make some time for yours. I'm okay with that. I actually respect that."

Chris liked the idea of Rhonda respecting him. It felt good. He wanted her to respect him, even if it meant doing things that made him feel uncomfortable. Even if it meant he could no longer actively pursue the bad boy lifestyle.

"I'll talk to them," he told Rhonda.

Later that day, Chris found Carl in the hallway, standing alone and looking lost, just like Rhonda had said. Chris approached his cousin.

"Hey, Carl," he said as he leaned up against the wall next to him. "I was thinking we should head over to Store 24 after school. We can grab James and just go hang out for a while."

Carl nodded. "I'd be up for that," he agreed. Carl's expression was flat. Chris hoped he hadn't waited too long to re-engage with him. He'd have to work on getting him to joke around later. Carl was usually happiest when he thought he was being funny. And sometimes, he actually did make Chris laugh.

He saw James last period in Spanish class. "Wanna go hang out at Store 24 after school today?" he asked him. "Carl's coming. Maybe we can ask Pete to meet up with us next time."

James nodded. "Yeah, man, that would be good."

"Is something going on with you?" Chris asked him, noticing James did seem all tensed up. "You seem kind of off lately. What's up?"

Much to his surprise, James appeared to relax a bit in response to Chris's question.

"Yeah," he said. "There's some stuff going on at home with Howie and my parents that's really bumming me out. I haven't really had a chance to talk to anyone about it yet, but I think hanging out today would help a lot. Y'know, just getting away from it all for a while."

After talking to his friends, Chris was feeling even better about his relationship with Rhonda. She was insightful, and kind, and tuned in to what was going on with him and his friends. Their romance had grown comfortable over summer break, and Chris had become very skilled at managing his time so he could see his friends and Rhonda on a regular basis. When junior year started, James quickly fell into a serious relationship with Sally Bachman, an old friend from Randall Junior High who had just come back to public school after a stint at the private school, Gearhart Prep. As their relationship progressed, James spent less and less time with the group, except lunch four days a week, which Chris and his friends had declared sacred. Soon, Sally was friends with the girls they had gone to elementary school with, and they all ate together. Things were changing, but they all agreed it was definitely a change for the better.

That Thing About Kim

When Chris looked back on his life as an adult, he would always remember junior prom as the day when his life changed forever. It started off well enough, except a nagging feeling he had about Carl and his prom date, Kim Drake, one of the girls they had known since kindergarten. Kim and Carl had gone to the prom as friends, but the two friends had a very strange dynamic. Chris could not interpret what drove Kim and Carl's friendship. Sometimes, Kim was possessive and protective of Carl, and others, she was downright mean to him and called him a moron. Sometimes over the years since they were kids, Chris felt a sense of contempt from Kim when she was near him, and he had no idea why. She'd had some tragic things happen to her as a kid, but as far as he knew, Chris had never done anything to offend her, at least not on purpose.

And then there had been his huge mistake. Chris and Kim had gotten high with a group of friends at a Christmas party sophomore year and ended up having sex in the host's bedroom on top of the guests' jackets. Kim quickly informed him that it was her first time.

"Please, Chris, don't tell anyone about this," Kim had begged with tears in her eyes.

Chris didn't think that the sex was that bad and had wondered why Kim was so upset. "Not even Carl?" he'd asked. "He's my best friend. We talk about everything. He wouldn't tell anyone."

Kim had given him a pleading look. "No, especially not Carl. Chris, I'm begging you, please don't tell Carl. Or anyone." Now she was sobbing.

"Okay, okay, I won't tell anyone, I promise."

Chris had been baffled. It wasn't like he was going to broadcast to the whole school that he'd had sex with Kim Drake, but he also wasn't ashamed that he had. He didn't want to do anything to ruin her reputation. But then, even in his intoxicated state, it clicked. Kim didn't want Carl to know. *Because Kim likes Carl,* he thought. Chris had had no idea. If he told Carl about their night together, that would sabotage any chance that Kim and Carl would ever get together. He knew Carl. It would make a huge difference to him. Chris didn't want that kind of responsibility to be on him. So he reluctantly agreed to keep the secret for Kim. He had never kept anything from Carl before, but he had promised Kim, and he'd meant to keep his word.

The encounter with Kim had not been Chris's first time. His first time had been the summer between freshman and sophomore year, when the Bishop clan had a big family camping trip in the woods of New Hampshire, and his fifteen-year-old cousin Sarah Bishop from Sudbury had invited her best friend, Randi, along as her guest. Chris didn't even know Randi's last name, just that it wasn't Bishop or Farmer, and that she definitely wasn't his cousin. They were sitting by the campfire after the adults had gone to bed when Randi had turned to him.

"Hey, Chris," she said. "Do you want to go for a walk with me?"

Chris had felt his heart start to pound. He knew what going for a walk meant. Maybe some making out, maybe a little under-the-shirt action. But Randi wasn't having any of that. They'd found an old, secluded clearing, and she kissed him.

"Take off your pants," she whispered in his ear, and he complied.

They went back to the same place the next day for one more round before leaving. He never saw Randi again. Sarah had never been able to look Chris in the eye at family events again after that trip. But then there was no more sex for Chris until the night with Kim. And then the many times with Rhonda.

Then at junior prom, Carl lost his virginity and his whole heart to Kim, and Kim told him the truth about what had happened with Chris at the Christmas party. Later that night, Carl informed Chris that he knew the truth. He assured Chris that he knew he hadn't done anything wrong, but despite that, the dynamic of their relationship had changed. For the first time ever, Chris had kept something important about his life from Carl. And it had been about Kim, who was not only their mutual friend, but someone that had been very special to Carl since kindergarten—something that had belonged to Carl alone. Chris knew his friendship with Carl would never end, and they would always be closer than just cousins, but Carl knew a truth about him now, a weakness he never wanted to expose, a lack of good judgment on his part. Their power differential shifted immediately. Carl no longer looked to Chris for all of life's answers. This was just the very beginning of Chris's ultimate slide from the top of the world.

Our Love's in Jeopardy

He never saw the breakup coming, and even looking back, he couldn't find the warning signs. Maybe as a teenage boy in love, he was blind to the signals, or maybe there just weren't any there. Or maybe it was something else. He would probably never know.

It was the first day of senior year. It all started like normal. He was hanging out with his crew and talking about being back in school and about the coming year when Rhonda approached and told him she needed to talk. He excused himself and they walked down the hall to the empty auditorium. They stood in the back. The room had an ominous echo when empty that Chris had never noticed before.

"What's up, babe?" Chris asked, smiling at her.

Rhonda grimaced. "Chris," she started. "I'm so sorry to have to tell you like this, but .. . I'm breaking up with you."

Chris was sure he hadn't heard her right. "What?" he said, a hollow feeling in his stomach. He knew what she had said, but he repeated herself. He felt his spirit rip from his body.

"Chris, I'm sorry, but this just isn't working for me anymore," she said. "I thought if I gave it some time, and just waited, things might change, but that's not gonna happen. I mean, we're starting our senior year. We should be spending all our time with our friends, and doing stuff for the last time, you know? I just don't want to be tied down anymore. I just want to be able to decide to go do stuff, and go do it."

"I . . . Rhonda, I don't get it," Chris said, completely forgetting his promise to himself to never plead with a girl about ending a relationship. He had made that vow before he had even met Rhonda. Just say goodbye, good luck, and walk away. "I mean, things were really good this summer. We had so much fun. We were together all the time. I thought things were good."

Rhonda shook her head. "Like I said, I'm sorry, Chris, but it's over. Yeah, we had some great times together, but this isn't what I want anymore. I don't think we need to stand here and keep rehashing it. It's not gonna help anything. I've already made up my mind. I'm sorry. I need to get to class. Goodbye, Chris. I hope you have a great senior year. Really, good luck."

She had just said exactly what he would have said to her, had he been the one to be initiating the breakup. She had his number. She had all the power, and he had none.

She started to walk away, and Chris could hear the *click-click* of her heels echoing throughout the auditorium. "You told me you loved me," he said toward the door, but she was already gone. Chris looked up and saw a custodian in front of the stage, looking at him from across the vast room, having witnessed the whole interaction. The man looked away, and then pushed his garbage bin up the ramp and onto the stage. The first bell rang for the first period. Senior year was beginning.

Chris didn't know what to do. He couldn't go to class. He wanted to go to his car, start it up, and just drive. He would drive all day and night on the highway, and when the car ran out of gas, he would just get out and walk. But he still wouldn't be far enough away. He couldn't go home. His mother would be there, and his sisters didn't start school until the next day. He didn't want to tell them what happened, and he didn't think they would believe him if he said he was sick. He walked out the side door and toward the parking lot. He unlocked his car and got in the driver's seat. He turned the engine. The air vents started to blow. He got a whiff of Rhonda's perfume, and he started to sob.

Finding Things That Help

Chris found out the true meaning of friendship that year. It wasn't about being in control in a relationship. It wasn't about being the leader of his posse of friends. It was about caring for someone when they were hurting. His friends—James, Carl, Kim, Sally, Darlene Feinman, and Michelle Gorman—rallied around him. They took care of him at school. They looked after him. They kept him safe and barely ever let him be alone. Carl was watching out for him, even though he was the one that needed protection. He felt loved, but he also felt every ounce of his confidence being strained to the max. He'd once had charisma. Now he didn't even know if he could spell the word. He had been so wrong about his relationship with Rhonda, thinking that it was good, thinking that she loved him. Now he didn't trust his judgment or instincts at all.

He thought about going to see a therapist, but he didn't know how to even ask without letting on that he was lost. He didn't want people to worry about him. He didn't want to cause his family distress. But finally, he found something to give him direction.

Chris liked physics class, but he couldn't always understand how physics worked. He went to his teacher after class one day to ask for some help.

"Come back at lunchtime," Mr. Jackson instructed him. "We can go over the material and figure out where you're getting stuck."

That one lunch changed the focus of Chris's life. Not only was he able to improve his physics grade over time, but he also made a new friend. Mr. Jackson had taught five years earlier at Randall Junior High, and Chris had been in his earth science class. He remembered Chris from back then, and his role as leader of the bad boy posse. He remembered his confidence. He remembered his drive. He remembered sending him and his friends to the office for mouthing off. They had a good laugh about these memories. But Mr. Jackson, with all of these memories from back then, noticed the changes in Chris, and he asked about them.

"We all thought of you as being the leader of your pack. Even after Mrs. Fox busted you for that joint, she still always saw you doing big things someday, maybe even becoming a politician like Jerome Farmer. But you seem so different now. So much more subdued. Did something happen?"

Chris thought for a minute before answering. "I guess you could say that. Things have changed a lot. And I really don't know how to deal with it."

For once, Chris opened up and made himself vulnerable to someone else. He talked about losing Rhonda and how empty it made him feel. He talked about his concerns about Carl not having any direction. He talked about his famous family and the expectations of its members. He talked about his group of friends. And he finally talked about the biggest issues: His loneliness, even in a room full of people. His lack of drive to try to re-create the life he had before Rhonda, the life that he knew no longer worked for him. His fear of what would happen to him in the future, when he and his friends finished high school and everyone moved on and said goodbye. His fear of being left all alone and doing nothing to stop it. His complete loss of confidence and charisma.

"I don't know who I am anymore," he confessed. "It's like I'm walking around every day in someone else's body. I don't even know how to talk to people. I think there might be something wrong with me."

Mr. Jackson understood. "I was a high school student myself once, Chris," he said. "And I've taught hundreds of students, and many experienced the same feelings that you're describing right now. I'm gonna assure you that no matter how alone you're feeling, you are not alone. There are many, many teenagers going through it, too, even if they aren't talking about it. As time goes by, things *will* get better. But it might take some work and effort on your part, Chris, and some acceptance that things have changed, and that you've changed, too."

"I think I can do that," Chris said.

When Chris left Mr. Jackson's classroom after lunch period that day, he felt lighter. He didn't feel that all his problems were resolved, but he felt they could be someday. Mr. Jackson had also offered to help him work out how to get to therapy if that was what he decided to do. He still wasn't sure if that was the path he wanted to take, but at least now he felt much less alone and afraid.

He started attending Mr. Jackson's office hours at least once a week, and if no one else was there, they talked. They talked about science, change, and the future. Pretty soon, Chris started to develop a new idea of what he wanted to do after high school: he wanted to be a teacher. And he wanted to be a teacher like Mr. Jackson, a teacher who listened to his students, who asked them the questions that mattered. He wanted to work with kids who needed a teacher like that. Like himself. And like Carl. And this decision became his new driving force.

Chris worked harder in school. He improved his grades. He asked his parents if he could enroll in an SAT prep class, and they agreed. He scored 1140 on his SATs, and he felt that might be enough. He filled out his college application. He only applied to one school: Eastboro State College, which had the most comprehensive teaching program in New England.

He worried over Carl, who had scored very high on the SATs and was on the honor roll but didn't seem to have applied for any colleges. He was baffled. Carl had all the brains, but none of the drive. He didn't know how to help him without pissing him off. But he did know one thing: Carl's parents had taken off. They had abandoned him, and his older brother, Scott, was never around. Carl was on his own at his house. Chris would continue to protect Carl with his life if he had to. And he would make sure Kim did the same.

Chris got into Eastboro State College. His parents were ecstatic and respected his need to move into the dorms, even if he would be only two miles away from home. Chris knew it was the only way he could put himself out there, to make new friends, to not isolate himself. Maybe at some point he could even meet a girl. The thought seemed so foreign to him now. He hadn't been with anyone since Rhonda, and he wasn't sure if he even knew how to be with someone anymore.

How Do I Say Goodbye?

Chris's friend group decided to go to the prom together rather than with dates. Three of them—Chris, Darlene, and Michelle—didn't have dates, and no one wanted to go if everyone wasn't going. They went in a limo, ate a fancy dinner out, and all danced together as the night went on. The girls looked out for Chris, and Darlene even gave him a big kiss right on the lips when Rhonda danced too close to Chris with her date. Then they had an afterparty at Chris's house. Chris went to sleep in a sleeping bag on his rec room floor that night, drunk on beer, surrounded by friends, and feeling secure that his friends were the best friends that anyone could ever have.

After prom, Chris and his friends were preparing for finals and graduation when Chris got a call from his Aunt Missy, Gram Cissy's identical twin.

"Chris," she said, "I'm planning on having a very serious talk with Carl after graduation, and I need for you to back me up."

"What's up, Aunt Missy?"

"Well, Carl has not budged at all this year about making plans for what he's going to do in the future, Chris, and that worries me. He hasn't applied to any colleges, and he's not even considering any type of job or training. I feel like he's just standing in the middle of the street, waiting for a bus to come along and hit him. And I also worry that he's holding Kim back from making any decisions for herself, because she doesn't know what he's gonna do, and that's just not fair to her."

"I agree with you, Aunt Missy," Chris told her. "I'm worried about him, too, but I don't know how I can help."

Aunt Missy sighed heavily. "Chris, I have a plan, but it won't work without you being on our side."

"I'll help any way I can," Chris assured her.

"You remember my brother Rolland Farmer's son, Laine Farmer?"

"Of course," Chris said. "I remember all of my cousins. He used to hang out at our house when I was little, and I think he might have babysat for me a few times. Didn't he and his wife move to California?"

"Yes, six years ago," Aunt Missy confirmed. "A small town out there called Seska. He has his own business. He's an electrician. Well, the thing is, Laine wants to help us help Carl. Laine's a pretty smart guy, like Carl, and Rolland and I thought that Laine would make a great mentor for Carl. Now the way I want to present this to Carl, and this is actually true, is that Laine wants him to come out to California to be his apprentice, to become a licensed electrician. But the deal is, in reality, Carl could also do a similar apprenticeship right here in Eastboro with any other licensed electrician willing to have him, so we need to convince him he can only do this in California. The thing is, Chris, we need to get Carl out of Eastboro."

Chris felt his heart sink. "Why does Carl need to go?"

"Chris, Carl's not like you, or his other cousins," Missy explained. "Carl has certain gifts. I think you know that. He can figure things out that other people can't figure out. He can fix broken things with no instructions, just by taking them apart and putting them back together. He can remember things, like words, numbers, conversations, and diagrams, that he shouldn't be able to remember."

"So, what, he has a photographic memory or something?" Chris asked.

"Chris," Aunt Missy said, "you don't know this, and Carl doesn't know this either, but when Carl was very young, he showed some exceptional skills at school, and they had him tested in first grade. Carl has a very, very high IQ, Chris. Genius level. His parents didn't want him to know, so no one ever told him. He still doesn't know. His teacher begged them to enroll him in a school where he could learn how to use his gifts, but they refused. They didn't do anything to nurture his talents and gifts. It was tragic. Carl doesn't really fit the stereotype people think of when they imagine a child genius. He's always seemed very happy to be the second banana to you. He's never seemed to get bored in school. He might not have been challenged, but he wasn't bored. And he started to really thrive in high school, especially after Kim became a regular part of his life. But he can't go on like this anymore. We can't just let him stand there and do nothing with his life. He needs guidance. He needs someone with patience to show him his potential. And that's where Laine Farmer comes in."

"So you want to send Carl to California to be Laine's electrician apprentice, but really, you think what he needs is to apprentice Carl to learn how to live his life?"

"It's kind of like that, Chris," Missy said. "We're not gonna lie to him. A few months ago, Laine was actually able to propose a pilot project to the city meant to lure intelligent and driven young men and women out to the small towns in California to work in the trades. It's a real issue out there. They need people. So he proposed that the city offer a scholarship to pay for the classes and part of the required work hours. And his proposal was actually accepted. Carl would be the first participant, like a test case. The only thing that Carl won't know is that the project was developed with him in mind. It's not just a random thing. Chris, Laine knows that Carl got a lousy set of parents. He remembers Rosa and Jack. He knows that Carl has had no guidance for years. He knows that Carl has been pretty much left on his own since he was sixteen. And he wants to help. He has an apartment unit where Carl can live, and he can help him build a nest egg for his future. Carl will get a skill and get paid for his work. And he'll have a guide and a friend to be there with him on his journey."

"What's in it for Laine?" Chris asked, thinking that he himself had always wanted to be Carl's guide and friend but knowing he couldn't offer him what Laine probably could. Laine would be Carl's Mr. Jackson.

"Well, I guess Laine would have the satisfaction of helping someone thrive," Missy responded. "And he would have a new family member nearby. Maybe a built-in babysitter for his kids. But Chris, Laine has a special gift like Carl does. He's not a genius like Carl. He's smart, but his gift is that he has an overwhelming sense of compassion, justice, and kindness. People are drawn to him. They really like him. You must remember that from back then, even if you were very young."

"I do remember a lot of good things about Laine," Chris admitted.

"The way I see it," Missy went on, "is that if you take Carl's smarts, and you take Laine's kindness and patience, and you put them together, you get my father, Jerome Farmer, who was an extremely gifted man. Together, Laine and Carl can do some pretty amazing things, like my father did."

"But you're saying you want me to help you convince Carl to go to California," Chris said. "Why would I want Carl to go to California? Why would I knowingly want to do something that would take my best friend three thousand miles away from me?"

"Because you love him as much as I do, and you know it's the right thing to do." He could hear the sadness in Aunt Missy's voice.

Chris could feel his heart starting to break, both for him and Aunt Missy. "But what about Kim?"

"Yes, what about Kim," Missy said. "Well, we'll give Kim a little space. Just a little. Kim will go with him to California. I know she will. But she has to think it's her idea. And maybe, just maybe, she'll get just a tiny little nudge from her mother, if needed. It's possible Mrs. Drake already thinks that Kim needs a new start in a new place. Maybe she thinks Kim being stuck in Eastboro helping her take care of her invalid father is really holding her back from her true potential. Maybe her mother would miss her terribly, but still thinks she'll be happier if she's with Carl. I'm just saying, maybe that's the case."

"Wow, Aunt Missy, you've really thought of everything, haven't you?"

Aunt Missy sighed again. "I owe it to Carl to make things right," she told him. "He's already been let down by so many people, so early in life, and one of them was my son. But the one thing I haven't figured out in this whole scheme is what to do about you, Christopher Jerome Mahoney. How do I take away your lifelong best friend, and make things right for you at the same time?"

"Maybe," Chris told her softly, "that's not for you to figure out. Maybe that's for me to figure out. I'll help you, Aunt Missy. We'll make sure that Carl goes to California. And we'll just have to hope that Kim figures out the right thing to do."

Road Tripping

Carl did decide that going to be Laine's apprentice in California was the best choice for him, and Kim ultimately decided to go with him. And to ease the separation, the Grams arranged it so Chris would be delivering Kim's car to their new door along with their friend Pete, so the cousins could have one more adventure together before a long time apart.

Still, the goodbyes were hard. The friend group was moving apart. Carl and Kim would be in California, and James, Sally, Darlene, Pete, and Michelle would all be off to college. Chris would also be in college but still so close to home. It was reassuring to be so close to family, but there would be many reminders and memories of those who had moved on. He knew there would be visits, but they would be rushed so his friends could see other friends and family while they were home. It would be a new kind of life for all of them. Different places, different friends. They all promised to stay close, but only time would tell.

Chris and Pete left for California in mid-August in Kim's blue Chevette. They made stops each night for food and lodging and took in some sights along the road. They played loud music and sang along. They drank coffee in the morning and beer at night before bed. They watched bad movies on motel television, and repeats of M*A*S*H. They ate M&M's and Doritos from the bag in the car. They took turns driving and managed to avoid any speed traps, which was good, as they were smuggling alcohol to their friends across multiple state lines. They figured they were both too good looking to make it unscathed in prison.

Chris was nervous as they approached Seska. He drove twenty miles per hour above the speed limit down I-5, bringing them to Laine's house earlier than expected. Kim and Carl weren't even home. They approached the house and surprised Laine's wife, Beth, who wasn't expecting them until later that night. But soon Kim and Carl arrived home, and they were all off to get some takeout for dinner.

While Pete and Carl went to pick up the food, Chris and Kim talked. They even talked about their sophomore year encounter at the Christmas party. She asked him questions about his plans to be a teacher. He confided things to Kim that he had never told anyone else, including about his relationship and breakup with Rhonda. Chris felt a new closeness to Kim, and for the first time, he felt complete peace at the idea of Kim being able to take care of Carl in his absence.

Later, Chris went to visit Laine and Beth while Kim and Carl visited and caught up with Pete. Chris had been hoping to have time with Laine on his own. After they caught up on their lives, Chris told him about his conversation with Aunt Missy.

"I know why Carl is really here," he told him. "I know it's for the apprenticeship, but it's also so you can help him with all his other stuff."

Laine shrugged. "Carl is here to be with family and learn some new skills. Now, a lot of them are gonna be electrical skills. But some of them are gonna be about life, and about being part of a family. I'm hoping these things happen organically, without any assistance, but I'll do whatever I can to help him feel at home with us. Chris, no one's trying to give Carl a free ride here. He'll be pulling his weight. He'll be learning about a real job, so he can support himself. But we're just trying to level the playing field a little bit for him. You get that, right?"

Chris nodded slowly. "Laine, you gotta remember, I was there the whole time we were growing up. I know firsthand what Carl went through. And I've been there for him the whole time. I won't be able to be there anymore. I'm just checking to make sure he's gonna be okay. You get that, right?"

Laine smiled. "I see what you just did there. Yeah, you're right. It's up to me to let you know that we'll make sure he's okay. And he will be. He's been here a week now, and I can already feel we have a connection. It will never be the same as the connection that he has with you, no matter how long he stays here. I know that. But it'll be good, I promise you. I'll make sure Carl's okay. But Chris, who's gonna make sure you're okay?"

Chris looked at his shoes. "I-I guess I will, but I promised my mentor, Mr. Jackson, that if I needed help, I would find it. I have my parents, and my grandparents, and I can call my friends. And I know I'll make friends in school. There's bound to be someone there that's never heard of me and is willing to give me a shot."

He smiled at Laine to show he was joking.

Laine smiled back. "I know you'll be okay, Chris," he said, "but would it be okay if I just checked in with you every now and then? You know, just to give you an update on how things are going?"

Chris was beginning to understand more about Laine's gift of compassion. Just sitting with him for a short time made him feel at ease. He wanted the calls from Laine more than anything.

"Okay," he agreed. "My mom can get you my phone number after I move into the dorm next week. You can call me."

Beth walked into the room with a plate of apple pie. "I brought you some dessert," she told him, putting the plate down on the table in front of him. "It's to make up for not feeding you guys earlier. Do you want some vanilla ice cream on top? Laine always takes it with the ice cream. I'll just get the ice cream." She stepped back into the kitchen and moments later came back with a carton of ice cream and a scoop.

When Chris headed back to Kim and Carl's apartment a half hour later, he was feeling good about Carl's move and felt that Carl was in the right place with the right people. Now he could enjoy his visit and his time with Carl, his only remaining worry being how he would face their last goodbye.

After a fun two-day visit with Kim and Carl, the time finally came. Chris and Pete were leaving from their motel in San Francisco, where the four friends had spent the previous day as sightseers. Chris woke Kim to say goodbye, and then approached Carl, who was still lying in bed. It was 5:30 a.m. He kneeled next to the bed.

"Don't get up, man, you need to go back to sleep after we leave," Chris said quietly.

Carl had his eyes open but his head on the pillow. "I can't believe we're saying goodbye," he told his cousin. "We've never said goodbye to each other. When are we even gonna see each other again?"

Chris shook his head and tried not to let tears fall from his eyes. "I dunno, maybe at someone's wedding. Maybe one of us. You'll need to come back with Kim to visit her family. Just promise me, bro, that you won't forget about me, okay? You're starting this exciting new life out here. Just, please, stay in touch. Call me. Don't just disappear."

Pete was done saying goodbye to Kim, and it was time for them to go. Carl sat up and embraced Chris tightly.

"Chris," he said, "you're my real brother. You're more than my brother. I know it was you that was looking out for me all those years. I know what you did. I'll never have the words to tell you how much I appreciate everything you've done. I'll never forget about you. You'll get tired of me calling you all the time." He released his embrace. "You're gonna be a great teacher someday. The kids are gonna love you. Take care of the Grams, okay?"

They both had tears on their faces, but they resisted the urge to acknowledge them by wiping them away.

Chris sniffed. "I will," he promised. "See ya later, man," he said, and he picked up his bags and walked to the door.

The door closed, and Chris and Pete were gone. "Goodbye, Chris," Carl said to the back of the door.

In the hallway outside the room, Chris turned back to the closed door. "Goodbye, Carl," he said, and he started down the hall after Pete.

Leaving on an Airplane

Chris got the window seat on the first flight, and Pete would get it from Minneapolis to Boston. He put up the shade and looked down at the Earth below him. Things got smaller and smaller until they went above the clouds. Then he looked down at a carpet of white. He tried to imagine that he was flying toward his destiny, and in a way, he was. He had already registered for classes, which would start on Tuesday. He would have a few days to settle into his dorm, to meet his roommate and the people on his floor. Later that week, he would get his school observation assignment, and he only hoped he wouldn't get McKinney or Murphy High. Anywhere else would be fine. Even Randall, where he might see his sisters, or Michelle, Pete, or Kim's little brothers or sisters. They all still thought he was somewhat cool.

In the early evening, they touched down at Logan Airport after cruising over Boston Harbor. They deplaned and made their way to baggage claim. Chris saw a Gram waiting for him by the turnstile, but for the first time in his life, he had to try to figure out which one she was out of context. A few seconds later, the second Gram appeared by her side. The comparison made it clear who was who. He reached Gram Cissy and gave her a hug, then moved on to Aunt Missy. Aunt Missy looked sad. The Grams hugged Pete, and then they all went to find their luggage.

The Grams dropped Pete off at home and then brought Chris to his house. They thanked him again for all he had done for Carl and Kim, said good night, and left him to his family. His two sisters, Melanie, who was fourteen, and Scarlet, twelve, greeted him.

Chris hugged them, then pulled back and gave them a baffled look. "What was that all about?"

Melanie blushed. "You were gone for a long time," she said. "We missed you."

Mrs. Mahoney smiled at Chris. "They've gotten a small taste of what it will be like when you leave for college," she explained, "and they didn't like it. Are you hungry?"

He was starving. His mother warmed up dinner for him, and the family sat around him and listened to the stories of his trip while he ate. His mother sighed when he talked about Laine.

"He's always been one of my favorite cousins," she admitted. "It was so hard for me when he moved away with Beth. Maybe not as hard as it is for you with Carl, but goodbyes are the worst."

"Yeah," Chris agreed. He suddenly lost his desire to finish his dinner. "Thanks for making me food, Mom," he said. "I think I've had enough. I'm gonna go unpack, and then maybe listen to some music for a bit before bed. Good night, you guys."

Mr. and Mrs. Mahoney glanced at each other briefly before looking back at Chris, who was heading for the stairs. They called out good night.

Chris threw all his dirty clothes in a pile on the floor, went to brush his teeth, and then lay on his bed, blasting heavy metal albums with his headphones on. He woke up the next morning with the headphones still in place, fully dressed, the dirty clothes from this trip still sitting in a mournful pile. He shook the cobwebs from his brain and sat up slowly. He put his legs over the side of the bed and his feet touched the floor. He felt the carpet beneath his feet, between his bare toes. He tried to let it ground him.

It was Friday, his last day at home before he, like Carl, would start a new life, and he wanted to start it with a good attitude. If Carl could go three thousand miles away to start over, he could go two miles and do the same. He got out of bed, put on clean shorts, grabbed his pile of laundry, and headed for the basement.

When he moved into the dorm, he endured a brief but tearful goodbye from Scarlet and Melanie. "I'm gonna miss you so much, Chris," Scarlet wailed as she hugged him tightly.

"Can I have Chris's room?" Melanie asked their parents as she wiped the tears off her cheeks. "It will ease the pain of our separation."

They would see each other the next weekend at Gram's for Grandpa's birthday, but he let them have their dramatic farewell. After they left, he unpacked his belongings alongside his roommate, Grant Adams, who had arrived that morning from Pawtucket, Rhode Island. They got to know each other as they filled their closets and dressers and rearranged their furniture in a way they both agreed made more sense.

"I want to be a Spanish teacher," Grant said as he lined up his shoes under his bed. "I've been taking Spanish classes since seventh grade, and my parents took me to Mexico last summer so I could practice with the natives. I want to teach high school kids."

Chris recalled that they had both been high school kids just three months earlier. "I went to high school here in Eastboro," he said. "My Spanish teacher was old when my mother went to my high school. Maybe you'll get lucky, and he'll retire in the next couple of years."

Grant laughed. "If that's the only way I can get a job when I graduate, I'll go down there and help him pack his boxes."

They agreed to go to dinner together. When they got to the cafeteria, Chris was surprised to see someone he knew.

"Chris Garcia?" he asked the guy standing in line in front of him.

Chris Garcia turned to look at him. "Hey, Chris Mahoney, of the Randall Junior High Bad Boy Posse," he said, reaching out to shake his hand. Chris Garcia had gone on to Murphy High after Randall. "You're much taller now, man. This is my roommate, Liam."

Everyone introduced themselves, and they all sat together at a round table. Chris Garcia and Liam were on the third floor, and Chris Mahoney and Grant were on the fourth.

"We're gonna have to come up with nicknames for the two of you," Grant announced halfway through dinner. "It's gonna be too confusing to tell which Chris is which all the time."

"My middle name's Jerome," Chris Mahoney said. "I've had cousins call me C.J. before."

From that day forward, Chris's dorm friends referred to him as C.J., and Grant dubbed Chris Garcia "Jerry" after the Grateful Dead frontman, Jerry Garcia. Both nicknames stuck. Eventually, Jerry appropriately became obsessed with the Grateful Dead and obtaining bootleg albums. The four dormmates became fast friends, and Chris stopped worrying about having someone to eat dinner with. Things looked like they were starting out surprisingly well.

College Days, College Haze

Eastboro State College had an innovative teaching program that placed students at a local school for observation as early as their first semester. Chris was assigned to Mrs. Long, an English teacher at Fremont Middle School, a slightly more affluent school than Randall Junior High. In the second week of classes, he drove to Fremont, which wasn't too far from Eastboro State, and met his new teaching mentor for the semester. She was about thirty-five years old and primly dressed. She wore glasses and kept her long straight brown hair in a ponytail.

She told Chris never to wear any type of jewelry that the students could get their hands on. "It's something they don't teach you in school," she told him. "If you ever get stuck in the middle of two students fighting, the first thing they go for is the face. If you're wearing a chain around your neck or earrings, they'll rip them right off your head."

"Yikes," Chris responded.

Mrs. Long nodded. "Yes, yikes indeed. I've never seen it happen, but it's not going to happen to me." She picked up a piece of chalk. "You know all the different forms of the words 'your' and 'there,' correct?" She wrote them on the blackboard for him to see. "I expect you to use correct grammar and spelling in my class, just as much as I expect it from my students. You're, that's y-o-u apostrophe r-e, their, t-h-e-i-r, role model now."

Chris nodded. This was going to be a very interesting semester.

And it actually was. It turned out the kids loved Mrs. Long and responded to her very well. She got them very excited about reading and writing, and she pulled Chris into all of their ongoing projects. Within the first two weeks, two of his eighth-grade students had noticeable crushes on him.

Carl's eighteenth birthday passed, and Chris wasn't able to reach him by phone. He left him a message, and they talked the next day after Carl's first day of work with Laine. They gave reports on their progress and their plans. Carl already loved working with Laine and living with Kim, and Chris was enjoying his classes and making new friends.

The first semester passed quickly. Chris studied for exams, completed papers and projects, and wrapped up his time at Fremont. Now it was Christmas break. Grant, Jerry, and Liam were all picked up by their families for vacation, and Chris drove the two miles back to his parents' house. It was good to settle into the quiet of his own room, but he missed the activity of the dorm and the nightlife he had enjoyed with his new friends. Now it was time for his old friends to come home for the break, and he looked forward to seeing them all together soon. With two important exceptions. Everyone coming home reminded him of who wouldn't be there: Carl and Kim.

As was her way, Sally organized all the group's social activities. They went to see *Star Trek IV: The Voyage Home*. They joked for days about humpback whales flying through space. Chris went to Pete's house to hang out and play video games with him and James and Pete's girlfriend, Carolyn. Sally, Michelle, Chris, Pete, and Carolyn went to Luigi's Restaurant, where James had returned to work during the break, just to annoy him and make outrageous requests while he worked. Then they gave him a huge tip. On Christmas, they spent time with their families and then all met up after at Michelle's house.

"Pete promised Carl and Kim we'd all call them on Christmas," Sally reminded them. "It's their first Christmas away from home."

"Let me call," Darlene insisted. "Then we can pass the phone around."

Chris stood by the phone like a hungry puppy until it was his turn. Carl and Kim were both on the line, and he had so much to say to them that he could barely say a word. He let them talk, and then he promised to call them later. It was so good to hear their voices and to be with everyone else. But them being gone still made his heart hurt with emptiness.

The last big hurrah of the season was the First Night celebration in downtown Eastboro. They all went, dressed for the frozen tundra. The temperature was 22 degrees when they left home, and it only got colder in the wind. Chris watched James and Sally prepare to kiss at midnight. Pete and Carolyn were poised to do the same. That left Chris, Darlene, and Michelle with no one to kiss. Chris knew Darlene was not seeing anyone and had not seen anyone since she broke up with Charlie after junior year. But from what he could gather, Michelle was still involved with Joey Cafaro, who had gone off and joined the Marines the day he turned eighteen. He didn't know when she had last seen him, or if she had at all since he'd left. He looked at her, watching the clock hands turn closer to twelve, and she looked so forlorn. She had her mittened hands stuffed in her pockets, and her winter hat on her head made her appear as young as his preteen sister.

The seconds were ticking closer to midnight. Chris grabbed Darlene by the arm and pulled her toward Michelle. He put one arm around Darlene's shoulder and the other around Michelle's as they counted down the seconds. When midnight struck, he pulled them both in close and then kissed each of them on the cheek.

"Now kiss each other," he instructed. They gave him a look, and then they kissed each other on the cheeks. They joined in a three-way hug, laughing and jumping up and down in the cheering crowd. The fireworks erupted.

Michelle looked up at Chris and smiled. "Thanks, prom buddy," she said. "I needed a group midnight kiss."

Chris smiled back.

"Yeah, thanks prom buddy," Darlene echoed. "You're a good man, Charlie Brown."

Winter Term Blues

In January, the snow seemed to fall daily but barely accumulated. At the beginning of February, it dumped from the sky. Then there was the winter thaw, and everyone emerged from their dorm rooms, stepped outdoors, and squinted in the sun. Students "borrowed" trays from the cafeterias and used them to sled down slushy, muddy hills. There were icicles falling from eaves, threatening to impale passersby through the tops of their skulls. Chris was assigned to Lincoln Elementary school, Mrs. Black's third grade class. Sally had gone to Lincoln, along with many other classmates at Randall and McKinney. He wrote her a letter, filling her in on all the details of his placement and telling her which teachers were still around. He received an excited letter back from her, so thrilled that he had written, and that he was at her old stomping grounds.

Chris had not met any girls during his college experience, either of interest for romance or just friendship. Now that he had settled into school, he tried to be more aware of his surroundings. He observed like a scientist. There were two girls in the cafeteria who were looking at him at different intervals. He checked the next night. They were both looking again. There was the blond girl in his Teaching Practice class who sat next to him on the first day of the semester and had made her way back to that seat every class, rushing before anyone else could hijack her space. She dropped her pen a lot. Sometimes Chris would pick it up for her, and she would smile at him. There was the sophomore girl who did work-study in the library who always asked him if she could help him find some reference material. Lastly, there was the girl in the bookstore who gave him an extra five percent off the top of all his purchases.

Most of them were cute, albeit not quite his type. Most of them were petite, and maybe a bit preppy, but the one in the bookstore wasn't preppy at all. She wore tight jeans, black concert T-shirts, and black boots that went up to her knees. She had black hair, which she wore in a punk style, kind of spiky with a lot of gel. She wore black eyeliner and mascara and shiny red lipstick and nail polish. Yeah, not his type. Not his type at all.

She was still not his type when he saw her at the bar one weekend night in early February. So not his type, in fact, that after he'd had a few beers, he approached her, pretty much to tell her he wasn't all that interested in her in a romantic or sexual way. Ten minutes later, they were against the back wall near the bathrooms, making out. Forty-five minutes later, they were in her private suite bedroom in her dorm, with their clothes off, comparing closely how much they weren't attracted to each other. Eight hours later, he woke up next to her, face down and naked on her messy bed, taking a few moments to remember where he was.

Her name was Amanda. She was from Framingham. She was a sophomore. She liked Frank Zappa. That's about all he knew about her, except that she was ticklish inside her right thigh. Oh, and he remembered a small mole on the left side of her neck.

She woke up when she felt him stir. "Good morning, Kafka," she croaked.

"Why did you call me Kafka?"

"Last book I sold you at the store," she said. "*The Trial*. For your lit class. A little light reading for your evening pleasure."

Chris smiled. "You got anything to drink in here?" he asked. "I'm parched."

"I have some berry wine coolers in the mini fridge, but I don't think that's what you're hoping for."

Kim loves berry wine coolers, he thought. This popped into his mind unsolicited. "Yeah, I was thinking more like water. Where are we?"

Amanda laughed. "We're at Eastboro State, Kafka."

"I meant which dorm. And you do know my real name, don't you, Amanda?"

She raised her eyebrows. "Ah, impressive, Christopher J. Mahoney," she said. Seeing the look on his face, she laughed. "It's printed on your checks, Kafka. The bookstore, remember?"

"Oh, right," Chris said. He looked around. "So which dorm?"

Amanda stood and pulled a T-shirt over her lean naked torso. It was a Van Halen Diver Down tour shirt. "Vickman," she said. "On west campus?"

Chris nodded, then stood and looked for his clothes. He pulled on his briefs. "Is there a cafeteria here?" he asked, turning his jeans right side out. "I could really use some coffee."

"Coffee addict, huh?" Amanda said, stepping into her own jeans. "Yeah, there's a cafeteria. Wanna head over with me for some breakfast?"

"Okay," Chris agreed.

He put on his socks and shoes and felt his back pocket for his wallet. It wasn't there. He lifted the edge of the comforter off the floor beside the bed and discovered the wallet underneath. The emergency condom he had stowed inside was gone. He really needed some coffee.

"So what's your story, Chris Mahoney?" Amanda asked as she looked for her shoes. "You were the popular kid in high school, weren't you? I can just tell. Did you have a popular girlfriend? Was she the prom queen?"

Chris watched her tie her sneaker laces. "Uh, no, not really," he told her. "I was one of the bad boys up until junior high, but we all kind of grew up a bit in high school. I had a pretty steady group of friends. Not popular. I had a girlfriend until senior year, but we broke up."

She was taking a long time to tie her shoes.

"She broke your heart, huh?" she asked, standing up. "Take your jacket. We have to go outside to get to the cafeteria."

Chris slid his arms into his navy blue down jacket. "Yeah, she broke my heart. I got over it, though."

"Where are you from?" Amanda asked as she walked toward the door. "Oh, by the way, this is a suite, so my roommates might be out there. Get ready for your walk of shame."

"I'm from Eastboro," he told her and crossed the threshold. Two girls sat on a dorm-style couch, eating toast and watching *Star Trek* on a portable TV.

"Shatner, Nemoy, meet my friend Kafka," Amanda called out, still walking toward the door.

"Hi, Kafka," both girls called to him, barely looking up. *They've done this before,* Chris thought.

"Kirk, Spock," Chris said back. "Nice to meet you. Bye."

He followed Amanda out the door.

"From Eastboro, huh?" Amanda said. "Close to home. Got a good family to go home to?"

"Very large family," Chris revealed. "Famous Eastboro family."

He followed her through the hallway, out the door, and down some concrete steps. The chill in the morning air helped with his alertness.

"Famous Mahoneys?" Amanda asked, now walking up another set of concrete steps.

"No, just regular Mahoneys," he told her, following her through a set of double doors into the cafeteria. "Famous Farmers."

Amanda grabbed two trays and handed one to Chris. "As in, Jerome Farmer, former mayor of Eastboro?"

Chris stopped short and looked at her. "How do you know that?" he asked.

He was used to Eastboro residents knowing about his famous great-grandfather, but so far no one at school had seemed aware.

"The guy has a statue downtown," Amanda told him while waiting for the cafeteria lady to call on her for service. "I'm a history buff. I looked him up. He was a pretty decent guy from what I can see."

Chris nodded. "He was a very decent guy," he said. "Jerome is actually my middle name."

"Cool," Amanda said. Then she addressed the server. "Scrambled eggs, toast, hash browns, please," she said. She turned to look at Chris. "So how are you related to the famous identical twins?"

Carl shook his head and laughed. "I thought I escaped all of this after high school," he said. "Cecelia Farmer Bishop is my grandmother. Her sister, Melissa, is my great-aunt."

"Cissy and Missy, right?" Amanda had reached the coffee service and had grabbed two cups. She poured one for Chris as he got his food.

"Yeah," Chris told her, accepting the cup of coffee gratefully. He added some cream and sugar and sucked it down. Then he refilled his cup. "My Gram and her sister are extremely close. Gram lives not too far from here, and Aunt Missy lives about ten minutes away."

Amanda laughed. "Gram Cissy. I can't believe I picked up a Bishop-Farmer grandchild at a bar!"

"There are 28 of us, so it could happen again if you're not careful." Chris looked at her and shook his head. "And if I remember correctly, it was me doing the picking up last night."

Amanda snickered. "Okay, Kafka, we'll remember it that way if you want. We won't remember the little bookstore discounts, and the complementary beer that was being fed to you at the bar all night."

They sat at an empty round table. "That was you?" Chris asked. "I thought the bartender was just giving them to me by mistake. Oh, okay, then, thanks for the beer. And the pickup, I guess."

They started to eat their food. "Yeah, well, you're welcome," Amanda said. "Do you live in the dorms?"

"Yeah," he told her. "I'm in Douglas, on the east side. Are you in the teaching program?"

"Library Arts," she replied. "Do you have a car?"

"Yeah," he said. "Do you like Italian food?"

"Love it," she said. "Do you like to dance?"

"If there's alcohol involved," he said. "So next Saturday night then, Italian food, I drive, dance club and drinks after?"

Amanda smiled. "We seem to speak the same language, Kafka."

The Biggest of All Newses

Amanda was fun, sexy, and smart. That seemed like a lot at face value, but it wasn't enough. Chris started to feel lonely again, even when they were together. He couldn't understand the logic. It seemed that being with someone should make you less lonely than not being with anyone. But this didn't seem to be about logic. And it didn't seem to be about control, either. Neither Chris nor Amanda seemed to really care about control in their relationship. They cared about having fun. And about having sex. The sex was good, but it wasn't *really* good.

Chris spent much of his time with Grant, Jerry, and Liam, hanging out, eating, going to movies, and going to bars. They all had procured decent fake IDs, so getting in was no issue. They could choose for themselves if they wanted to drink once inside.

Chris called Kim on her birthday but ended up speaking to Beth.

"Kim's really sick," Beth told him. "Poor thing, she got a bad stomach virus for about a week, and just when she was starting to feel the slightest bit better, she got socked with strep throat. Her birthday is canceled, and Carl is beside himself taking care of her. Chris, you would be so proud of him. He's taking such good care of her. And he's keeping it all together. He's just so smitten with that girl. He would throw himself in front of a train for her if he had to."

"I know he would, but I hope it never comes to that," Chris said. "Just have Carl call me when he can, okay, and tell Kim I'm thinking of her and I hope she feels better soon. And happy birthday. And oh, Beth, have Laine give me a call soon, okay?"

"Okay, Chris. I will. And I'll catch up with you soon, too, to see what you've been up to. But now I'm gonna go give Kim some tea. Love you, Chris. Take care."

"Love you, Beth. Bye." Chris hung up with mixed emotions. He was worried about Kim, but happy Carl was there for her, caring for her. He hoped Carl was taking care of himself, too. But maybe Carl didn't need to be taken care of quite so much anymore.

He put the thought behind him and picked up *The Trial*. He had some chapters to read. *Way to go, Kafka*, he thought.

On spring break, Chris and his dorm friends took a package trip to Daytona. Chris had been saving his summer earnings from the yard crew the last two years and figured he needed to use some of it for something fun. They went to the beach, went to clubs, drank in their hotel room, and took a bus trip to Disney World. Chris had never been there before. He had fun, but the whole trip seemed like a fever dream after all of the alcohol and late nights. It was almost a relief to get to the airport to head home. Until the flight was delayed for six hours, and there was nowhere to wait but the gate at the airport with hundreds of hungover spring breakers waiting to head home. The food lines were long, the bathrooms got gross, and everyone got cranky. Chris tried to lay down on the floor against the wall and take a nap, but he was kicked three times in the shins for his trouble.

Eventually, they made it back to Boston, and his parents were there to pick him up. He fell asleep in the quiet, cool car, and slept in his own bed that night. He let his mother serve him breakfast the next day and then watched movies with his sisters through the afternoon. That twenty-four-hour period was the most relaxing and enjoyable time of his whole break.

He called Carl before heading back to the dorm. "How was Kim's rescheduled birthday?" he asked.

"It was great," Carl told him. "We checked out Modesto, which was fun but not much more interesting than Seska. But we want to try everything at least once. We found this great Italian restaurant in Carsonville on my birthday, and we went back there for her birthday. If you come back here sometime, we'll take you there. And things are so good for Kim right now. She loves her internship, and she's so good at public speaking. I'm so proud of her. She's really gonna do something great with this someday."

"That's so great," Chris agreed, thinking, *They're never coming back. I'm gonna have to accept that.* "You guys are both doing so great out there. I talked to Laine recently and he said that you're doing a great job at work. He's kind of blown away by you."

"So I've heard," Carl said. "He makes stupid jokes to me all the time about electricity." He laughed. "And I guess he is pretty funny. He's a really good guy, Chris. You were so right about him. So how was Daytona?"

"Hot, humid, and crowded," Chris said. "It was fun, but it's one of those things you really just need to do once in your life for the experience. I don't think I'll take another spring break trip like that."

"Was Disney World fun?"

"It was good," Chris said, "but it probably would have been better if I was ten and you had been with me at age ten, too. We would have had so much fun. Maybe someday, we'll take our kids there together."

Carl laughed. "What a thought, huh?" he said. "You and me with kids. Can you even imagine?"

Chris thought about it. "The next generation of Bishop-Farmers. It's up to us to repopulate our clan, man. Better get used to the idea."

"How's it going with Amanda?" Carl asked.

"Y'know, alright," Chris said blandly. "I haven't seen her since before break. I guess I'll call her tonight to see what's up."

"Doesn't sound like much is up," Carl said. "You just don't seem that into her. I hope she's not keeping you from meeting someone else you might be into."

"Nah, you know, I'm just not that interested in being into someone right now. I'm okay with it. Amanda is a distraction. And she doesn't mind, so it's kinda the best of both worlds."

Chris could sense Carl shrugging. "Okay, man, whatever works for you," Carl said. "I just want you to be happy. It's been a while."

"Yeah, I'm okay," Chris said. "I like school, I like my classes and my friends. I mean, I guess I'm happy enough right now."

"Okay, I believe you," Carl said.

They agreed to talk again soon and got off the phone.

School started back up. The semester would be winding up quickly. Chris worked hard in his placement and classes and spent a lot of his time on homework and studying. He and Amanda were focusing on their schoolwork and didn't see each other often. Chris realized he didn't really miss her. He found himself avoiding walking by the bookstore and spent more time in the library. He started flirting back with the work study girl, who he'd dubbed Library Girl, but never took it further than that.

As April passed, he talked on the phone with Amanda but found reasons not to come over. On April 21, a call from Carl changed everything for Chris.

"So Kim's pregnant," Carl announced.

"Oh my God," Chris responded. He had to sit down. Carl was going to be a dad. Carl was going to have a baby. With Kim. In California. With Laine and Beth. And not with Chris. Carl was moving forward. And Carl was happy about it.

"Congratulations," he said at the end of the call.

When he hung up, he sat and thought for some time. Then he called Amanda. He knew exactly what he needed to say. *This isn't working for me anymore. There's really nothing to discuss. I've made up my mind. It's time to move on. Goodbye, Amanda, and good luck with your finals.* End of call.

The phone rang twice, and Amanda answered.

"Amanda, listen," Chris started. "There's some stuff going on in my family that I need to deal with, so—"

"Oh, okay, that's good," Amanda interrupted, sounding relieved. "Because I was gonna suggest that maybe it's time for us to, you know, give this thing a rest. You know, it just doesn't seem like we're going anywhere, and I really think I want to see other people, you know?"

Chris felt confused. This was not the way it was supposed to go. Should he wish her luck on finals now, or was that what she was going to say next? Did the whole control thing just shift hands?

"Well, then, I don't really need to say anything else. It sounds like we're both speaking the same language. So, I'll let you go, then."

"Okay, Chris. Well, it's been fun. Good luck with finals, and I hope you have a great summer." She hung up.

Damn, Chris thought. *She got there before me.*

He breathed a sigh of relief. *Why did I break up with her?* he thought.

He knew why. Because he didn't want to do it anymore. He couldn't just be with someone without emotion. He couldn't bear touching someone without feeling anything. He couldn't make that work. He wanted something real. He wanted Carl and Kim back. He wanted to be there for this baby. He wanted what they had, and he couldn't have it. And until he could have it, he would rather be alone.

Summer Break

Summer break started, and Chris moved out of the dorm and back home. He and his three friends had already registered to live together in a four-bedroom suite in a different dorm for sophomore year. Chris would be going back to his old summer job at the medical center on the lawn crew.

All his friends who had gone away to college had come home for the summer, and Chris knew that it was the last year that this would be the case. James would be getting his associate's degree in culinary arts after his second year, and he would be able to get a job as a sous or line chef after that. He and Sally were planning on getting an apartment together in Providence. Pete would be doing a summer internship for his sports management major with a New England sports club. Michelle would be taking summer classes toward her RN degree in Amherst, and Darlene was planning to go to Europe for the summer. But for now, they all had the summer of 1987 to be together, to have fun, and to talk about their disbelief that two of their own were going to be parents in December.

"Kim's had a rough time with being so sick back in February," Darlene said as they all sat around the clearing in the woods behind her house on a warm early-June evening. "Things were going so well for her in school and her internship, and then she got so behind. She's really excited about the baby now, but I hope it doesn't set her back too far."

"Do you think they'll stay in California?" Michelle asked. "I mean, she's still so young, and she's so far away from her family. She's got to be thinking about coming home."

Chris's ears perked up. He looked at Michelle. "Do you think they'd come back?" he asked her. "I mean, like Darlene said, she's doing so well with stuff out there, and Carl really likes his apprenticeship. Do you think they'd want to come back here and give all that up?"

"I would," Darlene admitted. "I don't think I would want to be so isolated with a new baby. And I know they really like Carl's cousins, but will they be enough for them? They can't be making much money out there. If they come back, their families can help them with all that."

"I don't know," Sally put in. "Kim and I have been writing to each other the last few months, and she just seems so excited about what she's doing at that head injury agency. They love her there, and they keep giving her more responsibility. She's like a rock star there. I don't know if she'd find something like that here. I just worry that she would miss out on an opportunity that she wouldn't be able to get back."

"I hope they come back," Chris admitted. "I miss them. I would love to be around for them with the baby. And I know Aunt Missy and Gram would love it. They would help them. Everyone would help them. That would be one spoiled little Bishop baby. I mean, I'm not gonna try to talk them into it or anything, but if they decide to come back on their own, I'm okay with that."

Sally reached out and put her hand on Chris's arm. "I know you miss them," she said softly. "I know you miss Carl. I hope whatever they choose to do, it's the right move for them. I want to see the baby too. I just worry, though. Will Carl's parents surface and want to see the baby, too? I wonder how Kim and Carl would feel about that."

Pete shook his head. "If I was Carl, I wouldn't let my parents within two miles of my baby," he said. "They're toxic people. They've lost their right to have access to their grandchild."

Chris nodded. He agreed. He would make sure that Carl's parents knew their place if they ever showed up again. No one even knew where they were these days, and no one was trying to find them. But despite his feelings about his older cousins, Chris was feeling a ray of hope. Carl and Kim might, just might, decide to come back to Eastboro. And that was hope he could hold on to.

The days on the lawn crew were hot and long, but they still passed quickly. The friend group did their annual trek to the airport for July Fourth fireworks and followed up with late breakfast at Denny's. Pete had gotten some news he wanted to talk about.

"Carolyn called me from her grandmother's house in New York last night," he said. "She's been accepted to a German college exchange program. She's going in September, and she'll stay until May."

"That's the whole school year!' Darlene exclaimed.

"Yeah," Pete confirmed. "I supported her in applying. You know, her grandparents are from Germany, and she's been taking German classes. She wants to become fluent. She wants to be a translator for the government in DC someday, which is really pretty cool. But the other thing we talked about was what would happen to our relationship when she goes."

"What did you decide?" James asked.

Pete sighed. "Well, we kinda said if she went, we would take a break. I mean, we figured it would be better for both of us if we didn't have the attachment. Now that it's happening, it's kinda unreal, but I think we're sticking to it." He paused. "I love Carolyn," he said, "We've been together since sophomore year, and we've both really never been with anyone else. At least in a relationship."

Sally and James felt their friends look at them "It's not for everyone," Sally said. "You don't always meet your soulmate on the first try. Some of us do, but not everyone."

Pete made a sound that sounded like a laugh. "I'm sad, but in a way, ending it like this is sort of a relief. I mean, this is like a natural way to move on, no bad fights or messy breakup someday. And maybe when she comes back, we can be friends. It just depends on what's going on then."

"It sucks, but it does almost seem ideal," Chris agreed. "The worst thing is breaking up with someone and then having to see them every day, or worrying about running into them somewhere when you're not expecting it."

"That's where your friends come in," Darlene said. "That's why they give you a big smooch at the prom when your ex-girlfriend is dancing with her prom date right in your face."

Chris rubbed his lower lip. "I think you actually bit me at prom," he joked. "I still have the scar. But Pete, really, man, you're not that far away. If you need to ever get away from Boston and hang out, you can come hang with me this year. I'll have my own room. I can show you a side of Eastboro nightlife you've never experienced before."

Pete smiled. "Sounds enticing, Chris, I might take you up on that sometime this fall. And it would be good to hang out with Chris Garcia. What do you call him, Jerry? I haven't seen him since we graduated."

"Yeah, Jerry's a good guy," Chris replied. "He's getting a bit shaggy these days and he wears a lot of tie dye. He's really gotten into his new role."

"Ooh, a shaggy guy in tie dye?" Michelle piped up. Chris didn't think she had been following the conversation. She had been peeling polish off her nails onto a napkin quietly for some time. "Is he single?"

They all laughed. Michelle had finally ended things with Joey the Marine in the beginning of the summer when she realized he would not be coming to see her at all for the break, and she was depriving herself of any kind of meaningful relationship and missing out on most of the fun in college. But Michelle was not one to date a deadhead. She had certain romantic standards that she insisted on adhering to, and patchouli and body odor were not exactly on her list.

"Do you guys think Kim and Carl will get married?" Sally asked the group after a short silence.

Chris almost slid off his seat. He hadn't even thought of that possibility.

Darlene shrugged. "I don't know," she said. "Kim has some weird issues about love and commitment. I know that she and Carl are doing great and are so right for each other. I just hope they can get past their demons and just dive in headfirst. Especially for the baby's sake."

Everyone nodded. Chris sat very still. He knew that Carl and Kim should be together. They were the ideal couple. But they had both been so broken by childhood tragedy, Kim with her father's accident and subsequent disability, and Carl with his parents walking out on him. He wished he could call Carl and tell him what to do. Or ask Aunt Missy to give Carl one of her little nudges. But this wasn't their place, or their business. Chris would have to sit on his hands and wait like everyone else. Or he could ask the universe to help them to do the right thing and just hope that someone out there was listening.

When Things Change

The end of summer was nearing. The August days were hot, the nights sticky, and anxiety was up. Carl and Kim had been talking about moving back to Eastboro to have their baby, and the decision would have to come soon. Carl called Chris to ask what he thought he should do, and Chris told him to do what was right. But he did tell him he would be happy if they came back.

By the end of the month, they had decided. They were coming back. They would fly back in November and have their cars and belongings shipped. They would live with Aunt Missy until they were settled in, and the Grams would support them until they were able to figure out how to support themselves. Chris was ecstatic. He felt like he was the one coming home. He would have his sidekick back. It wouldn't be exactly the same. Things had changed, for both of them. Carl would have more responsibility. He had grown up a lot in the past year. He was a working man, and nearly a father. But he was still Carl Bishop, Chris's other half. Things would be better with Carl back, he knew it.

Less than three weeks later, on Carl's nineteenth birthday, these ideas were all blown out of the water. Kim and Carl had changed their minds. They were going to stay in Seska after all. They were having the baby there. And beyond all that, they finally admitted to each other that they were in love, and they were going to get married. They sounded happier on the phone than Chris had ever heard them. They had finally opened up to each other about their feelings. Chris hid the fact that he felt like he had been stabbed through his gut with a pitchfork and congratulated the couple, and told them they had made the right choice. And in that moment, he knew that they had. Their choice was about their happiness, not Chris's. It was their lives, their baby, their decision. They didn't even have to take Chris into account when making up their minds.

Chris had just moved into his new dorm days earlier. He sat on his bed now, feeling numb. For some reason, he had expected that Carl and Kim coming home was going to solve all his problems. He had been depending on Carl, the lost little boy, to find Chris now. He couldn't figure out how things had gotten so turned around. It was like they had switched places now. Carl had it all together, and Chris was just . . . lost.

He knew it wasn't just junior prom that had made things go awry. And it was no longer the breakup with Rhonda. Now he wondered if perhaps the life he had before then had just been unsustainable, no matter what had happened at prom. Maybe you just can't be in control of so many things, for so many years, and expect it to go on forever. The mighty will fall. Maybe sayings like that were a warning to people like him. Be confident, but just don't let it go to your head. The mighty had fallen.

But now it was time for the mighty to rise back up. He had also read about the Phoenix, who rises out of its own ashes and once again feels the glory. Maybe he could be the Phoenix now. Maybe he could start anew. Not totally anew, but with a new attitude. He didn't have to depend on anyone to make him happy. He would have to figure this out himself, and he couldn't just give up because things didn't go the way he wanted them to. He would be the Phoenix.

But first he needed to learn how the Phoenix did it.

He decided to go to the library. His new dorm was much closer than the last. The sky was starting to darken, and a light breeze blew. Soon, it would be Fall, and the leaves would drop from the oaks and maples on campus onto the sidewalks, and students would kick them up or crunch them down as they walked back and forth to class. Some more industrious classmates would sweep them up onto the quad and leap into the piles, like they had done when they were small. College was a place like that, a place where you could experiment, be playful, learn to be who you're going to be in the world. An artificial bubble of safety where you could make mistakes, one a day if you had to, and be forgiven and given another chance.

Chris walked into the library and checked the time. It was 6:30, and the library closed at 8. He had time. He approached the desk.

Library Girl was there. The little preppy girl he had seen last year. The one he had innocently flirted with before ending things with Amanda. She had her dirty blond hair up behind her head in a French braid. She was wearing minimal makeup and a polo shirt and jeans. He stepped up to her at the desk.

She smiled. "Hi."

He smiled back. "Hi."

"Did you have a good summer?" she asked. She said it in a way that made him think she really wanted to know.

He nodded. "Yeah," he said. "I did. It was good to see my friends." Then he said something that surprised himself. "So how was your summer?"

He really wanted to know.

She glowed a little. "It was good. I worked here and stayed in town," she said.

Chris nodded and waited.

"Do you want me to help you find something specific?" she asked. She always asked. He always said no thank you.

"Yeah, actually, I do," he said. "Can you help me find anything about the legend of the Phoenix?"

"Of course," she answered. "I know exactly where those books are."

"Can you show me?" he asked. Chris knew how to navigate the library, but Library Girl didn't need to know that. She was happy to take him back.

They entered the mythology section, and she moved right to the correct area. She pulled out two books and walked a bit further to retrieve one more. She went to hand them to Chris, but he didn't make a move to take them just yet.

"I've been seeing you here for a year now, and I don't think you've ever told me your name," he said. Then he took the books.

She smiled. Her smile wasn't at all shy like he thought it would be. It exuded confidence. "It's Alison," she told him. "And I know you're Chris from your student ID."

"That ID is always giving away valuable information," Chris said with a smile.

She laughed. Just a small, appropriate laugh for a silly joke. "I don't remember every name on every ID," she told him. "No one could."

"No, that would be a lot of names, wouldn't it, Alison," he said, trying her name on for size. He could tell she liked it.

It's not about power, he reminded himself. *I'm just a guy talking to a cute girl. And she is pretty cute.*

"So Chris, do you need any other books, or do you want to go back and check these out?" Alison asked, always the professional.

"I think checking out is a good idea," Chris said, knowing it was a corny thing to say but trusting his wit.

She smiled. "Good, because I'm off at seven tonight, and it would be a shame if I didn't get to check you out before I go."

Yikes. Chris got a wave of something through his body that he hadn't felt since high school.

"Okay, then. We'll go check out. Hey, maybe we're heading in the same direction. Do you live in the dorms?"

"I live in Phillips," Alison told him.

"Cool. I'm right next door, in a suite in Jefferson," he told her. "Our cafeteria snack bar is open until eight. Do you like industrial chocolate cake and slushy coffee?"

"Those are my favorites," she revealed with a grin.

"I was thinking about stopping by the caf. Would you be interested in coming with me?"

"I would," Alison replied. "Let's just go take care of your books, and I'll sign out and get my purse from the back room, then we can go."

"Okay," Chris said, and he followed her back to the desk.

Twenty minutes later, they were sitting at a table with two pieces of cake. Alison had herbal tea, and Chris had grabbed a decaf coffee. It was awful.

"Every time I see you, it's in the library," Alison said, "and they have me wearing this stupid uniform. There are rules on what we can wear and how we do our hair. It's primitive. But this is not really how I look."

"I think you look great," Chris said truthfully.

Alison chuckled. "Thanks, but I wasn't compliment fishing. But we should hang out some day when I'm not working and you'll see. Everyone thinks I'm all preppy and highbrow, but I'm not."

"I didn't think that at all," Chris said. "I've always just noticed your eyes. They're such a light shade of blue. I've never seen other eyes like yours, and I know a lot of blue-eyed people."

She looked closely at Chris's eyes. "Yours are what, hazel?" she asked. "They go well with your brown hair."

Chris laughed. "Thanks. I got them from my grandmother. She really wants them back now."

Ugh, lay off of the Farmer humor, he warned himself, but she laughed.

"You make jokes like my dad," she said. "He's always trying to make us laugh."

"Where do your parents live?" Chris asked.

"Right outside of Hartford," she said. "I grew up in Bristol. What about you?"

"Born and raised and will probably die in Eastboro," he admitted.

"Ha, you're a townie!" Alison said.

Chris shook his head. "Nope, you can't call me that. I don't commute. I live in the dorms, like you."

Alison laughed. "Townie," she said under her breath as she sipped her tea.

Chris smiled. He felt this was going well. He'd never imagined when he woke up that morning that he would be eating cake with Library Girl. He never would have believed it. But now it seemed kind of normal.

"So are you taking a mythology class this term?" Alison asked, looking at the three books on the table.

"No," Chris admitted. "It's a bit of personal reading. I've always been interested in the myth of the Phoenix. Tonight it just occurred to me that maybe I could learn more about it."

"There's a lot to be said about rising from the ashes, Chris," she said. She had finished her cake. She reached across the table and snagged a bite of his with her fork. "Or the crumbs, I guess."

"Do you want to meet my roommates?" Chris asked her impulsively. He was going to ask if she wanted to see his room but remembered quickly enough that it might be too forward to ask that this early on. But the cake and hot drinks were almost gone, and he wasn't quite ready to say good night.

She thought about it. "Sure," she said, "I'll meet your roommates. But just for a bit, then I have to get back to my room." She stood. Chris followed suit. "But maybe you could walk me home after that."

Chris introduced Alison to Jerry and Grant. She was confused, because she'd had a class with Jerry before and thought his name was Chris. She was reassured that she was not incorrect. The four of them sat in the suite lounge, chatted, and watched TV. After two hours, Alison realized how late it had gotten. She jumped out of her seat.

"I have class early tomorrow," she announced. "I have to go."

The guys all stood. "I'll walk you home," Chris offered.

Alison said good night, and they headed toward the exit. They walked quietly the short distance to her dorm, both wondering what would happen when they got to the door. When they arrived, they both stopped. They faced each other. And then came the kiss.

It wasn't a sensuous kiss. It was tentative. It was gentle, and timid. Then Chris wanted to see what would happen if he touched her. He put his hands on her waist and pulled her slightly closer. The kiss continued, with slightly more pressure, and a bit more hunger. Then Alison pulled away.

"I have to go in," she said. "You know, class tomorrow and everything."

Chris held his right hand to the back of his head and stepped back. "Yeah," he said. "Class in the morning. Me too."

"Okay, well, good night, Chris," she said, and she reached up and gave him a chaste kiss on the lips.

"Good night, Alison," he said, taking another step backward.

She went inside. He took one more step back and waited.

Ten seconds later, she came back out and he smiled. He had called it.

"I have class every morning," she said. "What's one sleepy morning?"

Then she threw her arms around him, and the sensuous kissing began in earnest.

They went back to her room and kissed frantically but quietly, lying on her bed. Then suddenly Chris realized he wasn't prepared for this.

"Alison," he said breathlessly, "I don't have anything with me, you know, protection. Do you . . ."

"Crap," she said quietly. "No, I don't. Ugh. I'm sorry. It's been, eh, a while for me and I got off the pill. What should we do?"

Chris considered their options and realized they only had one. "We kiss some more," he said, "and then we sleep? I have friends, my best friends actually, who were always really careful, but now they're expecting a baby in December. Yeah, I'm not ready for something like that just yet."

"Me neither," Alison said. "Yikes for your friends, though. Maybe this is a sign. Maybe we're supposed to wait. I mean, maybe we're supposed to get to know each other more first, you know?"

Chris nodded. "I mean, that wouldn't be the worst thing, right?" He sat up uncomfortably. "There are some ways we can get to know each other, though, you know, without having to wait." He smiled at her.

She smiled back. "I think I might have heard of those things, too," she said coyly, "but you might have to show me again. Just to remind me." She pulled her braid out and shook her hair loose. Then she took off her preppy polo shirt and revealed a black lace push-up bra. She had transformed from preppy and cute to sexy and hot in seconds flat. It was every boy's librarian fantasy.

Chris gave her a refresher class, and she was a quick learner. Then she educated him. This was all accomplished with a snoring roommate twenty feet away. They stuffed their noises inside of them, but sometimes giggles escaped. Chris realized this was the most fun he'd had in years, and there was no alcohol involved. No struggle for control. This is how he expected it would be with a girl when he was younger, but it never had been. When they were done with their lessons, they lay still on the bed, catching their breath.

"I liked that a lot," Alison whispered. "That was the most fun I've ever had not getting fucked."

Chris laughed out loud then put his hand over his mouth. "You did not just say that," he whispered back.

"But I did," Alison said with a smile. "Shocking?"

"A bit," Chris admitted. "But like, sexy shocking. Are you a secret bad girl?"

"Maybe I was at one point," Alison admitted. "Turn on, or turn off?"

"Alison," he said, turning on his side to face her. "I started my own bad boy posse at age seven. You might not know it to look at me, but I was on a first-name basis with my junior high principal, I saw him so often. I was suspended for three weeks at age fourteen for possession of drugs with intent to use on school property, and a threat of being expelled. So definitely turn on."

"Oh my God, Chris," Alison said, her eyes rolling back. "I would have been so hot for you in junior high. We would have been expelled for possession of sexual desire with intent to orgasm if we had been in school together back then. There wouldn't have been a supply closet we hadn't checked out."

Chris looked into her light blue eyes and kissed her, moving his hands back down her body with intent to start another lesson. He had seriously misjudged her by her polo shirts.

Breaking Up Is Hard To Do

After class the next morning, Chris went directly to the drugstore and bought a large box of condoms. He stowed a few in his wallet and the rest in his underwear and sock drawer. He was not going to be caught unprepared again. He thought about Alison throughout the day. She had told him about her bad girl ways. She had been a junior high bathroom smoker. She had frequently challenged the school dress code by wearing too short skirts and halters and had gotten called out and sent home. She had a healthy contempt for authority, which often landed her in trouble with those same authority figures. She was grounded frequently by her parents. But she had pulled her act together senior year, when she realized she needed to get serious about her schoolwork so she could get into college with a scholarship. She wanted to teach elementary-level science. She wanted a classroom full of fish tanks and gerbils. She wanted to make the water cycle seem exciting to small children. She had been placed at DeMarco during her first placement freshman year and loved it. She was excited to learn that this was the school where Chris's bad boy career had begun.

"I can just picture you standing at the top of that wobbly play structure on the playground with your group of baddies," she said with a smile.

After two weeks, Chris invited Alison to dinner at Luigi's, which was his group's go-to date spot. It wasn't the same without James as their waiter, but they enjoyed their meals and the romantic atmosphere.

"I get to see the seamy underside of Eastboro culture," Alison said as she took a sip of wine. "It's a bit more cultured than I thought."

"You want culture, you should come with me to my Gram's house sometime," Chris said. "You'll get more Eastboro culture than you can handle."

Alison smiled. "Okay," she said. "Let's make plans to go visit your Gram."

Chris was slightly thrown by this response. "Are you serious? I mean, because if you are, we can make it happen."

The next weekend, they drove to Gram Cissy's house and arrived at her door for dinner. Alison handed her a bottle of wine as a thank-you for having them. Gram immediately gave her a hug. Chris had prepared Alison for what to expect, so she was not surprised when a second identical Gram appeared and she got a second embrace. The Mahoneys were also present for dinner, and Chris's sisters teased him mercilessly about being there with a girl.

Chris rolled his eyes. "Oh, grow up, you two," he said. "Just not too fast, though, okay?"

Gram broke out the photo album after dessert and showed Alison pictures from the Bishop-Farmer wedding. Then she showed her baby pictures of Chris. Soon after, there were pictures of Chris and tiny baby Carl. Almost every picture of Chris from that point on also included Carl, all the way up to high school graduation.

On the drive back to school, Alison asked him about Carl. "You've mentioned him a lot, but you two must be even closer than you sound. You've always been together. It must be so hard with him moving away."

Chris nodded as he drove. "You have no idea," he said. "It was always like we were physically connected in some way, so when he left, it felt like I lost a major part of myself. It's hard to explain to people who have never had a relationship like ours what it means to feel like you're even closer than brothers. There's no word for it."

"This might sound weird," Alison said, "but I wonder if you can have a person who's not your partner but is still your soul mate. I mean, totally not romantically, of course."

Chris shrugged. "I guess it's possible. I mean, I've had a hard time connecting with people since he left, like I don't know how to connect anymore. I mean, it was like that, up until recently. I guess I finally realized I had to move on. You know, like pull myself up out of the ashes."

"Ah," Alison said with realization. "So that's the deal with the Phoenix. But you're doing great now, though, right? I mean, your roommates are really cool and you're all so tight. And you and I, well, let's just say you're doing a good job!"

Chris laughed. "Well, that's good to know. Did you like the Grams?"

"I did," Alison replied. "They're adorable! So is the rest of your family. They were trying to act like they were not totally excited that you brought a girl home, but they totally were. Your sisters are funny. And your grandpa is so cute."

"He's the king of the Bishops," Chris told her. "That's the side where I got my bad boy traits. The other side, the Farmers, they're the sensitive ones with all the corny jokes."

"All the things I like about you, Chris," Alison said. "You got the best of both worlds."

Chris smirked. "Grandpa Clyde is a hot sexy player, too, and I'm pretty sure that passed directly to me. I think you like that, too, don't you?"

Alison laughed. "Yeah, I was gonna say, he's a hottie. Gram Cissy is a lucky lady."

"I'll take you back to my room and you can be a lucky lady, too," Chris told her.

"Hey, it's not luck, it's skill," Alison said smugly.

Chris laughed. "You are a very talented young lady, Alison. I'm looking forward to once more being wowed by your skills."

After they compared skills and techniques, they lay still on Chris's bed on their backs, cuddled together.

"How long was your longest relationship?" Alison asked. She was proficient in pillow talk.

Chris did the math in his head. "One year, nine months," he said. "In high school."

"Was that Rhonda?" she asked.

"Yeah, we started going out sophomore year, and then broke up the first day of senior year. She didn't want to be 'tied down' for her last year of high school. She kind of caught me off guard."

"Yikes," Alison said sympathetically. "That's kinda cold. I'm sure she could have done it in a way that wasn't so harsh. I mean, almost two years together. It's like she owed you more than that."

Chris shrugged. "Yeah, well, I was a lot different back then, and she's probably a lot different now. But yeah, it might have been better if she had been a bit more, well, kind, I guess. What was your longest relationship?"

"Two and a half years," Alison told him. "Senior year in high school until the end of my sophomore year, last year."

"Why did it end?" Chris was curious to know.

Alison sighed. "Well, he's studying to be a marine biologist," she said, "and he got an opportunity to go on a research study in Alaska. He was going to be gone all summer, and maybe longer, depending how things worked out. I just couldn't see having to maintain a long-distance relationship. I mean, it was gonna be over three months, and he would only have limited access to a phone. So we talked about it, and we decided to just say goodbye. It was hard, but it was the right thing to do. I would have been miserable all summer if we stayed together. I probably would have gone back to Bristol and just sat around, waiting for him to call. We did the right thing. And last I heard, he's still in Alaska, so, yeah, we did the best thing by moving on."

"Wow," Chris said, holding her closer. "That's really sad. I mean, it sounds like it was the grown-up thing to do, you know? But still so hard. My friend Pete is going through something like that now. His girlfriend went abroad to Germany this year, and they thought it just made more sense for both of them if they went their separate ways. But you get so used to people in your life. And their friends and family. Breaking up is hard. I think there are more humane ways to do it than what Rhonda did to me, but breaking up is still breaking up. It hurts."

Alison nuzzled her cheek against Chris's bare chest. "It does," she said. Then she smiled. "But moving on, meeting new people, and doing new things, that's a really good thing. If Brett and I had never broken up, you and I would still just be flirting at the library desk until I graduated!"

"Yeah," Chris agreed. "Moving on is good."

He kissed the side of her head and then stared at the ceiling. Moving on really did seem like it was gonna be good.

Kind Can Be Cruel

The following Monday, Carl and Kim got married at the Seska Courthouse. Chris knew it was coming, but with all of the excitement with Alison, he had forgotten that was the day. Gram Cissy called to remind him.

"Don't forget to call them tonight," she urged him. "It's a big day. They'll be coming home to have a real wedding sometime after the baby is born, but this is still a huge deal. Missy and I sent them some baby supplies, and Missy sent Carl her own engagement ring to give to Kim. I hope everything gets there on time. How are you doing with all this?"

Chris paused. "I-I mean I'm happy for them. This all just happened so fast. I wish I could have been there with them."

"I'm sure Carl wishes that, too," Gram told him. "It's so hard to live so far away. Call them. Just don't forget the time difference. And remember this is their wedding night. Plan accordingly."

Chris had class to distract him until mid-afternoon, and then he walked to the library, just to be able to study near Alison while she worked. He sat at a table on the first floor and took out his early childhood development textbook. He started to read chapter five.

Half an hour later, Alison took her break and plopped down next to him at his table. "Everything okay?" she asked.

He looked at her. "Carl and Kim got married today."

"Oh," she said. "Well, you knew that was coming. Wanna go for a quick walk?"

Chris stood. "I do."

Alison laughed. "That's what they said."

They went out to the quad and walked around. Alison reached for his hand.

"They're coming back in the spring to have a wedding, right?" she asked.

"Yeah," Chris confirmed. "But I should have been by his side. I'm supposed to stand up for him at his wedding, and him at mine. It just wasn't possible. I'll be the best man at the wedding, he told me. But I'm just missing so much." He stopped for a minute. "We talked about bringing our kids to Disney World together someday."

"That can still happen, Chris," Alison said. "You'll have kids, and he'll probably have more than just this kid. And kids of all ages like Disney World."

"That's true," Chris conceded. "I'm just thinking in extremes today. It's like if I miss anything going on now, I'll miss everything. I might not. But it's still hard."

"Did you call him yet?"

Chris started walking again, still clutching Alison's hand. "Not yet. My Gram made a reference to them consummating their marriage, so I have to work that out with the time difference."

Alison laughed. "Oh my God," she said, "that sounds like something your Gram would say. Kim's like seven months pregnant, right? I don't think they'll be spending a great deal of time on the consummation."

"True, but these two would figure out how. Trust me." He sat on a bench and she sat down next to him. "But after I get you back to the library, I'll go back to my room and try to call. Can you come over tonight?"

Alison smiled and squeezed his hand. "I can be there by 7:15."

When Chris got back to his room, he checked the time: 5:30. It was 2:30 on the west coast. He picked up the phone and dialed.

Carl answered the phone. "Hey, Chris," he said. "I'm so glad you called. Kim's taking a nap right now. I just brought in a bunch of packages from the Grams. They sent us like an entire nursery. I don't know where we're gonna put everything."

"Hey, man, congratulations!" Chris said with enthusiasm. "I can't believe you're a married man now. You're like a real grown-up."

"Thanks, man, but I think knocking up my girlfriend made me a grown-up seven months ago. Getting married just makes it official. Kim changed her name. She's Kim Bishop now."

"Wow," Chris said, sitting down hard on his bed. "That's unreal. Remember that time when Kim told the Bishop-Farmer story after the junior prom? Now she is one!"

"I know!" Carl replied. "She's kinda blown away by that. Pregnancy's made her so emotional. We need to buy stock in Kleenex for all the crying she's been doing. At least it's happy crying."

Chris paused. "I wish I had been there."

Carl hesitated. "I know. Me too. Laine's great, but it still wasn't the same. Just know you're my best man, okay, even if you can't stand up for me until our real wedding."

"I know," Chris told him.

"So how are you doing? We haven't really talked much lately."

"I'm seeing someone now," Chris told him. "Alison. Do you remember me telling you about Library Girl last year?"

"You're going out with Library Girl?" Carl laughed. "I hope it works out better than Bookstore Girl. You're gonna run out of places to get books if you're not careful."

"Well, I actually like Library Girl," Chris said. "She's awesome. And she's already met the Grams. She may be around for a while."

"She met the Grams?" Carl asked. "Sounds serious. Hold on to this one. Maybe she can be your date at our wedding."

"I'll do my best," Chris promised.

"I'm gonna crawl into bed and take a nap with my wife for a bit. But call me this weekend? We can talk more."

"Yeah, I will. Give Mrs. Bishop my love, okay? Talk to you soon."

"Bye, Chris."

On Halloween, like they did every year, Sally and James came back to Eastboro to give out candy. They didn't like the party scene, and always found it best to avoid their campuses on the rowdy holiday. This year, they invited Chris and Alison to join them at the Bachmans' house. Sally's parents would be at their other daughter's house for the evening, and the friends would have the house to themselves. It was the first time Alison got to meet any of Chris's high school friends. Alison and Sally took to each other instantly.

"Are you into sports at all?" Sally asked almost immediately.

"Not many," Alison said. "The only sport I really like is baseball, and really only the Red Sox. I get a lot of grief from the Yankee fans back in Connecticut. "

The joy on Sally's face could not be hidden. "Do you want to see my signed Red Sox program from August? It was my birthday, and my dad was able to get someone in the dugout to pass it around to the players. I also have a signed Oil Can Boyd foul ball that my brother-in-law caught two years ago. I mean, it was a ball he pitched that the other team hit as a foul, but he still signed it because my brother-in-law's in the Army."

"Oh, my God, yes!" Alison said, and Alison followed Sally up the stairs to her room. They were gone for a while.

"Well, that worked out pretty well," Chris said to James.

"Yeah, Alison seems pretty great." James took two Reese's Peanut Butter Cups out of the candy bowl and handed one to Chris. "Have you spoken to Carl lately?"

"Yeah," Chris said as he chewed his candy and swallowed. "They're doing great and trying to spend their time wrapping things up before the end of the school year and the baby coming. I guess Kim is huge now, which has got to be weird, since she was always so small. I picture her like the big blueberry girl in *Willy Wonka*, but don't you dare tell Sally I said that!"

James laughed. "I won't say a word. I miss those guys. The group always seems incomplete without them."

"Yeah," Chris agreed. "It makes me feel better to know they're happy out there, but I wish they could be happy like 2,500 miles closer, you know?"

"That would be nice," James agreed.

They went into the den and switched on the TV, found a channel playing Halloween movies, and settled in. Eventually, Sally and Alison came back down.

"Chris," Sally said, settling in next to James, "why didn't you tell me that Alison has a neighbor whose cousin actually knows Carl Yastrzemski? Didn't you think that was something I'd want to know?"

Chris's mouth dropped open. "Uh, I don't think that's come up at all, Sally," he told her. "If it had, I would have run to the phone and called you immediately, I promise."

Alison sat down next to Chris. "Now that I know how crucial things like that are," she said, reaching for Chris's hand, "I'll make sure I don't keep anything like that from you ever again."

"Better not," Chris said, and he leaned over for a kiss.

"James and I are going to Maine this year over Christmas to visit his Nonno and Nonna," Sally reported, "since we won't be able to go on Thanksgiving. Darlene and her dad are going skiing in Vale. Has anyone heard if Pete's coming home?"

"Pete's going home with his roommate to Texas," James said. "He didn't really feel like being around Eastboro and having to be all cheerful this year."

"Is that your friend whose girlfriend went to Germany?" Alison asked.

"Yeah," Chris replied. "So that means it's just gonna be me and Michelle in Eastboro over break?"

"Who's Michelle?" Alison asked.

"Remember that picture I showed you upstairs of all of us at the prom?" Sally asked her. "Michelle was the one with the bright red hair."

"Oh, the tiny little girl in the green dress?" Alison said.

"That's the one," Sally said. "But we won't be gone all break, just like four days around Christmas. Just no one will be here for the actual holiday."

"Maybe Michelle and I can hang out," Chris said. "We haven't hung out for a long time. It would be nice to catch up. And Alison, if you're around at all, you can meet her too."

"Didn't you go to prom with her?" Alison asked.

James, Sally, and Chris all laughed simultaneously.

"I guess technically," Chris responded. "Me, Michelle, Darlene, and four other people. It was a group date. But Michelle, Darlene, and I danced together because we were single. But honestly, Alison, she and I are totally just friends."

"Oh, I wasn't worried about that," said Alison, sounding clearly worried. Chris put his arm around her shoulder and pulled her closer to him.

"Alison, one thing I can assure you of going forward is my fidelity," he said. "I have a huge distaste for the idea of cheating. I wouldn't tolerate it in a girlfriend, and I wouldn't tolerate it in myself. It's one of my stricter values."

He could feel Alison's shoulders relax under his arm. "That's good to know," she said. "I feel the same way."

"Good," Chris said to her with a smile.

They all turned back to the TV to watch *Poltergeist*. Next would be *Poltergeist II*. The doorbell rang, and Sally jumped up to go pass out candy.

Alison went to Bristol for Thanksgiving, while Chris spent the holiday with his parents, aunts, uncles, and first cousins at Gram Cissy's house. His mother, Kate, had four siblings, all married with teenage or adult children of their own. Some even had small grandchildren. Some years, they combined their holiday with Aunt Missy's clan, too, but this year, too many people were attending both gatherings to fit them all in one house. Gram had considered renting a hall, but she and Aunt Missy were budgeting for Carl and Kim's wedding in the spring and needed to be frugal.

Chris was able to escape the noise and commotion of the day to go outside, where luckily, the weather was mild and only a light jacket was required. He brought Gram's cordless phone outside and dialed Carl and Kim. They didn't answer, so he left a message. They were most likely with Laine and Beth for the holiday. Then he dug Alison's parents' phone number, written hastily on a scrap of paper, out of his pocket, and dialed.

"Hey, Chris," Alison said when she got to the phone. "How's Thanksgiving at Gram's?"

"Good," he told her. "Noisy as always. Lots of food. I'm gonna have to help with the dishes later. Oh, and lots of little kids this year. It seems like having babies is the fashion these days."

"Not in my closet it's not," Alison responded, and Chris laughed. "Yeah, things are okay over here. I ate too much, but that's what holidays are for, right? So Chris, I just have to tell you something, in the interest of our being open and honest with each other."

Chris sat down on the deck stairs. "Okay, what is it?"

He could hear her sigh. "So my cousin Rob? He lives in Bristol, too, and he was friends in high school with Brett."

"Your ex-boyfriend?" Chris clarified.

"Yeah, that Brett. Anyway, he talked to Brett's sister the other day, and it turns out that Brett's gonna be home from Alaska by Christmas break."

"Okay," Chris said. "So what does that mean?"

"Nothing," Alison said quickly. "It means absolutely nothing, but now that I know, I thought I should tell you, since I'm also going to be in Bristol for break. I just thought it would be better if I let you know now, when I found out, so it wouldn't be weird, you know?"

"Yeah," Chris answered, already feeling weird. "No, I get it. I think it's great that you're telling me right away. But I mean, so he's coming back. That's no big deal, right?"

"Yeah, I agree," Alison said. "We broke up, so it's not like there's anything going on. I just didn't want any, you know, future misunderstandings."

"Thanks, Alison, I appreciate that."

Alison paused. "Good. Now that we've gotten that out of the way, what does the rest of your weekend look like?"

Chris mulled over the idea of Brett coming home from Alaska. The more he thought about it, the less it bothered him. Alison and Brett had broken up. It had been six months since they had even spoken. Chris and Alison were doing really well. And Chris had made that big speech about fidelity at Sally's house on Halloween. Alison was just respecting his desire for them to be straightforward and honest with each other. It wasn't her fault that Brett was coming home. He trusted Alison. He just hoped he could trust Brett.

Thanksgiving break ended, and the crunch to prepare for the end of the semester started in full. Alison and Chris satisfied their need for time together by studying in each other's rooms or meeting up in the library. The days leading to break went quickly. Papers were turned in, last-minute homework and extra credit completed. Exams were approaching.

On December 10, Carl got a call from Aunt Missy. She was the designated baby informant, and she needed to report that Kim was in labor. They were on their way to the hospital in Seska, and the baby should arrive soon. Chris instructed Aunt Missy to keep him up to date on any changes and went back to his studying. But he couldn't sit still. He paced his room. He imagined himself pacing around the waiting room at the hospital, waiting to find out that the baby had arrived. He imagined Laine and Beth, and Kim's mother, Mrs. Drake, sitting around, waiting, drinking coffee, reading magazines, watching the door for any news.

The evening went by with no news. Chris went quickly to the cafeteria and ate his dinner. When he came back, there were no messages on his answering machine. He tried to study again, knowing it would be no use. Finally, he went out to the suite lounge, pulling the long phone cord behind him, and turned on the TV. Soon, Jerry, Grant, and Liam came out of their rooms, and they all watched TV together.

At 11 p.m., Chris needed to get ready for bed and get some sleep. He called Aunt Missy, and she still hadn't heard a word. She promised she would call him, any time, day or night, as soon as she heard.

Chris called Alison quickly to say good night, and to let her know he was on baby watch. She wished him luck and promised to come over the next day to find out the news and to hang out. They got off the phone and Chris went to bed. After what seemed like hours tossing and turning, but was probably less than one, he fell asleep.

The phone started to ring at 3:45 a.m. Chris reached for the phone in the dark room and made contact. It was Aunt Missy. The baby had been born, at 12:11 a.m., Pacific time. 12:11 on 12/11. It was a boy. His name was Drake Pedro Bishop, and he was perfect. And Kim had come through it like a trooper.

Drake Pedro. *Well at least his middle name isn't Jerome,* was all Chris could think before falling back into a restful sleep.

He got up at 10 a.m. on Friday. Alison would be coming over soon, and he had to get ready. He took a shower, cleaned his room, and made his bed. Then he went into the suite lounge, straightened up, and threw out the trash. He called his mother to make sure she had heard the good news. Then he turned on the TV and waited.

At 11:30, Alison arrived. He let her in, and they went into his room. He went to kiss her, and she put out her hand. "Was the baby born?" she asked.

Chris smiled. "He was." He filled her in on all the details, and she nodded.

"That's awesome," she said, sitting down on the edge of the bed.

Chris knew immediately something was wrong. "What is it?" he asked her, although in his heart he already knew.

She looked at him sadly. "Brett called me this morning. He just got in from Alaska. We talked."

"You're getting back together, aren't you?" Chris asked, looking right at her.

"Chris," she said, tears springing from her eyes. "I didn't know this would happen. I didn't plan it. But he's back, and he wants to see me. He missed me, and he wants to see if there's still something there. I think this is just something I have to do. I didn't know it until he said it, but I know it now. I really don't want to hurt you."

"I don't think you have any choice in the matter of whether or not I feel hurt," he said, not unkindly.

Alison nodded, the tears now running down her cheeks. "I know. It's like you said that one time, there's no good way to break up. No matter how it goes, it's gonna feel bad. I don't want you to feel bad, Chris. I really care about you."

"Then why, Alison? Why can't you give us a try instead?"

"Think about it," she said. "Think about your friend Pete. Think about his girlfriend coming back from Germany and wanting to give it another try. What would you tell Pete to do?"

"If he was seeing someone new?" Chris asked. "I'd tell him to think about why they broke up in the first place, and why he'd moved on to someone else. And I'd tell him to think about that new person."

Alison nodded. "But now think, Chris. Remember that Pete had been with his girlfriend for two and a half years and they loved each other. He'd been with the new person for three months, and even though they care about each other a whole lot, they never talked about love. Now what would you tell Pete to do?"

Chris sat silently, thinking about it. "I'd probably tell Pete to go back to Carolyn," he said softly. He looked back up at Alison, tears now forming in his eyes. "You're probably right," he said. "It's probably the right thing to do. If I try to talk you out of it, you'd only resent me."

"You're not gonna talk me out of it, Chris," she told him. "I'm so sorry. I really am. I keep thinking about Rhonda, and how she hurt you, and I so don't want to be a girl that hurts you, too. I don't know what I can do to not be that girl."

"Don't go," Chris whispered, the tears starting to roll down his cheeks.

"I can do one thing," Alison told him, putting her hands on his shoulders. "I told Brett about you, Chris. I told him that I was coming to talk to you. And he knows everything. And he and I are not back together yet. I don't know if this will help or not but . . . did you ever have that time when someone broke up with you, and you thought that if you had known the last time you were together was going to be the *last time* you were together, you might have paid more attention, or you might have done it better? Chris, if you want that closure, it's here for you. I'm here for you. All of me."

He put his hands on her shoulders. Then they both grabbed onto each other and started to kiss and undress each other. They went through every move, every trick they had used on each other the past three months, touched every part, caressed every inch of skin, until at last Chris reached into his dresser drawer and withdrew from the box . . . the last condom.

After, they lay next to each other, both with tears running down into their ears. "So this is really goodbye then," Chris said.

"I hate that we have to say goodbye," Alison whispered. "We can say 'see you around the library' instead."

Chris nodded quietly. Alison got up and started to dress. She found a Kleenex and blew her nose. She put on her shoes and turned back to Chris. "See you around the library some time, okay?"

Chris watched her but didn't move. "See you around the library," he said back.

And then she was gone. And in that moment, baby Drake's birthday became the worst day of Chris's year.

Christmas Breakup

Christmas break started, and Chris went home. The first time anyone asked about Alison, he asked them not to and went to his room. No one mentioned her name again.

Friends were coming and going during the break, and Chris met up with them mechanically. They understood he'd had a breakup, but no one knew what had happened, and they waited for him to want to talk about it. They all remembered the time after the breakup with Rhonda, and they worried.

Mrs. Mahoney talked to Gram Cissy about her concerns about her son. Gram Cissy talked to Gram Missy, who called Kim, who talked to Carl. Then Kim and Carl had a serious conversation. And then Carl called Chris.

"Chris, you wouldn't believe this baby we have," he told him. "He's already doubled in size. He's like a truck. And he's really strong. He's already lifting his head. You know, you need to be able to lift your head to do a lot of things, so he's in pretty good shape so far."

Chris laughed lightly. "Yeah, he sounds pretty amazing."

"Kim and I were talking, and we had to make a bunch of decisions about Drake. You know, like if anything ever happens to us or anything. I mean nothing's gonna happen, but you have to think about it, you know? So he'd either go to Kim's mom or Gram. So we got that figured out, but we also have to give him godparents."

"What do godparents do?" Chris asked.

"Well, they kind of look out for you, like, spiritually and stuff? Like, some religions make them responsible for the kid's religious training, but we're not looking for that. We want a godfather who will teach Drake about life, and values, and shit like that.

Someone who will show him the ropes, and maybe teach him kung fu if he needs it. Maybe teach him some bad boy skills. Alright, Chris, I'm gonna stop talking now because you already know I'm talking about you."

"Me?" Chris said in disbelief. "You want me to be Drake's godfather. Carl, are you insane? I mean, you just told me this kid can hold his head up. You know that sometimes I can't even do that, right?"

Carl laughed. "Dude, shut up. You're gonna be Drake's godfather. We don't want anyone else. Do you even know who your godfather is?"

"I have a godfather?" Chris asked.

"Yeah," Carl told him. "It's Jack. My father. Your parents made Jack your godfather. Do you want Drake to have someone like Jack as his godfather?"

"Who in their right mind would make Jack their kid's godfather?" Chris asked in amazement.

"Your parents," Carl said. "Remember? Kate and Jack used to be best friends before my dad became, in Laine's words, a total fuckwad."

"Okay, okay," Chris said, giving in. "I'll be Drake's godfather. It would be an honor. By the way, who's your godfather?"

"Fuckwads never gave me one," Carl said. "That was why I grew up with no values. Or just the ones I learned from you."

Now Chris's laugh was heartier. "Yeah, you're a soulless vessel," he said. "So who's gonna be the godmother? Do we become like, some sort of spiritual partners?"

"No, Chris, you don't," Carl told him. "It's Darlene."

"Oh, okay, then, no," Chris said. "Darlene and I are fine with just being friends!"

Carl laughed. "But hey, man," he said. "If you're gonna be all responsible for my kid, you're gonna have to unburden yourself about what's going on with you. Everyone back home is worried about you. Tell me what happened with Library Girl."

Chris sighed, started to protest, but then agreed to unburden himself. He told Chris the whole account of Library Girl.

"Oh, man, that sucks so bad," Carl said. "She sounded so great. I hate that Brett guy."

"He's probably a really nice guy," Chris said diplomatically. "But yeah, I hate him too."

"I can't believe she offered you closure," Carl said. "Who even does that?"

"Really nice girls who you try to hate after they dump you but you can't," Chris explained. "She was so worried about hurting me. But it's like that hurts even more, you know? If she cared about me that much, how could she even think about ending it? Relationships make no sense to me."

Carl was quiet. "I know, Chris. You know what hell Kim and I went through before we were finally able to be honest with each other. I'm talking about years of being unsure and scared. Love is so stupid. Why does it have to be so hard?"

Hearing Carl say this made Chris feel better. Carl got it. He knew what Chris needed to hear. "I don't know," he answered. "But you guys give me hope that maybe it's all worth the trouble, you know?"

Chris could hear Carl's smile. "Yeah, man, I totally know."

As Christmas got closer, Chris's group of friends started to disperse to pursue their holiday plans. Chris and his family were going to have a Mahoney family Christmas, which consisted of two grandparents, one aunt and uncle, and two female cousins around the same ages as Melanie and Scarlet. Gram and Grandpa Bishop would come by later for dessert after the hordes of guests left their house. Chris was relieved everything was lowkey, but after dinner, his sisters and their cousins disappeared into their rooms to do whatever girls their age do behind closed doors, and Chris began to crave company his own age. He remembered that Michelle was still in town and gave her a call.

"Hey, Michelle," he said. "It's Chris."

"Chris?" she said. "Chris Mahoney?"

"Yeah," he said with a laugh.

"Wow, Chris," she said. "I don't think in the fifteen years I've known you that you have ever called me. I didn't even know you had my number."

"Really? That's weird," Chris said. "We've hung out so much, I guess I've never even really thought about it. I guess Sally pretty much arranges everything for all of us."

"That's true," Michelle agreed. "What's up, Chris?"

Chris sighed. "I don't know, not much, really. I just wanted to see if you were still around, and maybe wanted to hang out or something."

"Hang out?" Michelle asked. "Like just you and me? Where would we hang out?"

Chris shrugged. "I don't know. I could go over there, or you could come over here, or we could go somewhere else? Where do you usually hang out?"

"Amherst," Michelle said. "Or Sally's house."

"You want to come over here? Or you know what? My dorm is actually open for the holidays. We could go hang out in my suite."

There was a brief pause. "Okay, I guess that would be cool," Michelle said. "I've never been in a dorm at Eastboro State. It might be interesting. Can you pick me up?"

"Yeah," Chris said, looking for his shoes on the floor. "I can be there in about fifteen minutes?"

"Sounds good," Michelle said. "Come to the door, okay? I won't be able to hear you if you beep."

"Okay, see you soon, Michelle."

It was about seven o'clock when they headed back to Chris's dorm. Michelle was wearing her big knit winter hat and mittens and a long down jacket. He could barely see her under all of her accouterments. Chris had the radio tuned to the local rock station, and a Def Leppard song came on.

"Remember when Rick Allen lost his arm in that accident when we were in high school?" Chris asked.

"Yeah, I remember you telling us about it at lunch," Michelle said. "It was one of those moments that sticks with you, you know? Like when someone asks you where you were when the space shuttle exploded."

Chris nodded. "Yeah, it's weird how that happens. Where were you for the space shuttle thing?"

"My mom and I had driven out to UMass that day for my admission interview. I decided I wanted to go back to school when we got back because I didn't wanna miss art class. We were glazing our ceramics that day. So my mom pulls into the parking lot, and the radio's on, and all the sudden the DJ guy says, 'Well, by now everyone has heard about the space shuttle tragedy,' and my mom and I were both like, 'What?' So we parked and listened until they told the whole story. It was so unbelievable. How about you?"

Chris thought. "I'm pretty sure Principal Catalano came over the loudspeaker and made an announcement right after it happened. I was in Mrs. Foster's class. She actually cried."

"Mrs. Foster?" Michelle asked. "Really? She doesn't strike me as the emotional type."

"It was the whole Christa McAuliffe thing," Chris explained. "It could have been any teacher in the shuttle. I don't know, maybe Mrs. Foster had applied for the astronaut gig too."

"Poor Mrs. Foster. I wonder if she's still at McKinney."

"She is," Chris told her. "One of the guys in my teaching practice class was placed at McKinney last term. He told me the names of the teachers he met. A lot of our old teachers are still there." Chris pulled into the parking lot at Eastboro State and parked. He and Michelle got out of the car.

"It would be pretty cool if you got placed at DeMarco or Randall," Michelle said as they walked to west campus toward Chris's dorm.

"My ex-girlfriend got placed at DeMarco," Chris said, and he sighed involuntarily.

Michelle grimaced. "Alison?" she said softly. Chris nodded. "I'm so sorry, Chris. I really am. Sally told me about Alison. She really liked her. It's totally her loss, by the way. I think she made the wrong choice."

Chris turned to look at her. "You do?" he asked. "Why do you say that?"

Michelle smiled. "You forget I spent a year and a half in a long-distance relationship with a Marine. I spent a lot of time thinking about this stuff."

They walked up to the front door of the dorm, and Chris unlocked the door with his keycard. They stepped inside. "Yeah? What stuff?"

"Okay," Michelle started. "So this guy breaks up with this girl so he can do whatever he wants the whole time he's gone, and not feel guilty about it right?" Chris nodded. "So he does whatever he wants, comes home, wants his girlfriend back, gets her back, and now he's not guilty of cheating on her while he was gone. If she says no, he gets the consequences of his actions. He sees he can't just do whatever he wants anytime he wants, just because she's not there."

"How do you know he feels that way?" Chris asked. "What if he was really pining away for her the whole time he was gone?"

"If he was pining away for her, then why didn't he call her at all the whole time he was gone?" Michelle said knowingly. "Why did he wait until he was back? No excuses, like he didn't have access to a phone. He could have written! So in the meantime, this girl goes on with her life, feeling like she did the right thing by letting him go. Maybe she ends up with a great new boyfriend, right? Her life is going well. Then, on a whim, this guy is back, on his own schedule, not caring a whit if she's moved on. Just trying to get his needs met. She is so moved by his reports that he's missed her so much, and just needs to know, just needs to try one more time . . . she knows that she needs to give him another chance. I actually feel sorry for her. She just walked away from the good guy, and right back into the arms of the guy who left her without a second thought. Poor Alison."

They had arrived a few minutes before at the door to Chris's suite, but they just stood there in the hallway while Michelle completed her soliloquy. He was blown away by what she said. She was completely right. He and Alison had been totally played. Poor Alison.

"I hate that guy Brett," he said, and he unlocked the door to his suite.

"I do too," Michelle agreed, walking into the lounge area. "He gives all guys a bad name. But you know who's even worse?" Chris shook his head. "The guy who joins the Marines before prom, doesn't break up with his girlfriend, and then just never comes home."

Chris looked at her and nodded. She understood his pain. They were kindred souls. Then he heard a noise. Someone else was in the suite.

"Hello?" Chris called out.

Jerry stepped out of his room. He smiled. "Hey, C.J."

"Hey, Jerry," he said. "This is my friend Michelle from McKinney High. Well, from UMass Amherst now."

"Hey, Michelle," Jerry said, looking at her as she removed her coat and hat. Her long red hair spilled out. "Oh, Michelle, hi!"

Michelle looked at Jerry carefully. His hair was now down his shoulders. He was wearing a multicolored tie-dyed Grateful Dead shirt and baggy jeans. He was barefoot.

"Wait," she said. "Aren't you Chris? Chris Garcia? Why did Chris call you Jerry? Oh, wait. Jerry Garcia? And you called him C.J. I get it. You're both Chris. You needed nicknames."

Chris Mahoney looked perplexed. "How do you know Jerry?" he asked Michelle.

"Uh, *Jerry* went to Randall, remember? And then he was at Murphy. We had some friends in common."

Jerry nodded. "Yeah, Michelle went out with Joey Cafaro for a long time. Didn't you go to the homecoming dance with him at Murphy senior year?" Michelle nodded. "What ever happened to Joey?"

"He joined the Marines, remember?" Michelle said. "He dropped out of school when he turned eighteen and took the GED. Then he went off to boot camp."

"Wow," Jerry said. "That's intense. So you guys split up?"

"Not until this past summer," Michelle admitted, "but it's much longer since I've actually seen him."

"Man, that's such a bummer," Jerry said, shaking his head. It was at that moment that Chris noticed the smell of incense wafting from Jerry's room.

"You been toking up in there?" he asked.

Jerry shrugged. "A bit," he admitted. "My friend Dave is in there. I think he's taking a snooze. You guys want a hit or two while you're here?"

Chris looked at Michelle, and she looked back at him. She shrugged. That was as close to an endorsement as he would get.

"Okay," Chris told Jerry. "Maybe just a hit or two."

They all went into Jerry's room. The lights were off, candles and incense were burning, and live recorded Grateful Dead music played softly from the boombox on the shelf. The walls were decorated with tapestries and posters covered with peace signs. Chris could tell that Michelle was amused. It seemed like every dorm had at least one guy like Jerry, completely immersed in the Deadhead culture. They were harmless, but it all got pretty boring after a while. Chris couldn't differentiate one Grateful Dead song from another.

In the center of the floor, Jerry had spread a ragged old towel, and in the middle of that was a tall and well-used bong. Jerry sat on the floor, and Chris and Michelle joined him.

"I've never done bong hits in a boy's dorm room on Christmas night before," Michelle admitted.

"Really?" Chris said, smiling at her. "Oh, I do it all the time. You're really missing out."

Michelle laughed.

They each took a drag from the bong. After Michelle took a hit, she started to cough.

"Sorry," she croaked. "Tiny little girl, tiny lung capacity. First one's always the hardest."

Chris laughed, then took one more hit. Michelle took one more, and they were both done. Jerry took a few more, then sat on his chair.

"If Dave doesn't wake up before bedtime," he told them, "I'm gonna go sleep in Grant's room. He and Liam won't be back until after break. As a matter of fact, C.J., I'm kind of surprised to see you here. Aren't you staying at your parents' house for break?"

"Yeah," Chris said, suddenly aware of his eyebrows over his eyes, and started to raise and lower them. "But it gets kind of crowded over there sometimes. I just needed to get a break, you know? So I called up Michelle to see if she wanted to hang out. I thought you were going home, too, Jerry."

"I was at home," Jerry revealed, "but my parents weren't too thrilled with my recent lifestyle choices and were giving me grief, so I bailed. Picked up Dave on the way."

"What's Dave's last name?" Michelle asked.

"Bernard," Jerry said.

"That's Dave Bernard on the bed?" Chris said, propping himself up a bit higher to see. "Wasn't he our class president in ninth grade at Randall?"

"Oh yeah, I forgot about that," Jerry said. "Yeah. He goes to Boston University now. He's gotten into the Dead, too. I don't think he aspires toward politics much anymore."

Michelle stood and walked over to the bed. She leaned down and took a closer look. "Yeah, that's Dave, alright," she said. "His hair is longer and he has a shaggy beard. And I think maybe he has a beer belly? Wow, I had a little bit of a crush on him in like, eighth grade. Yeah, he's changed a lot."

Chris laughed. "Who else did you have a crush on in junior high?" he asked. "Were you one of the thirty girls who had the hots for Pete? Everyone thought that James was pretty cute, too."

Michelle looked at her feet. "I'm not telling," she said. "That's private. But I know who Sally had crushes on."

Chris snickered. "Michelle, everyone knows that Sally had crushes on me, Carl, James, and Pete. That's no secret."

"Oh, that's right," Michelle said. "I forgot. But it's kind of concerning that I was about to sell out my best friend to protect myself, don't you think?" She started to laugh.

"Oh my God, Michelle," Chris responded, and he started to laugh. He and Michelle continued to set each other off in laughing fits.

"You two are totally lightweights," Jerry said, shaking his head. "Do you wanna see what's on TV?"

Chris and Michelle pulled themselves together and followed Jerry out to the lounge. He flicked the on switch and turned the dial. He settled on the black-and-white Christmas movie *It's a Wonderful Life.*

They all watched quietly for several minutes. Finally, Chris turned to Michelle. "Is this supposed to be a comedy?" he asked. "Because it's pretty damn funny!" Then he started to laugh as Jimmy Stuart's character was planning to jump off a bridge to his death. Michelle started to laugh with him.

"Okay, you two," Jerry said, pointing at them. "You're banished from the lounge. This is not a funny movie. It's very serious, and very touching. If you can't take it seriously, you need to go to your room."

Chris stood, still laughing. He had to wipe his eyes. Michelle was doubled over. Chris grabbed her arm and pulled her toward his room.

They both fell onto his bed and rolled onto their backs. They stopped laughing as they watched the action on the ceiling.

"I never noticed that paint pattern before," Chris said, pointing to a spot near the light fixture. "Do you think maybe someone painted it with a squirt gun? Isn't that what it looks like?"

Michelle giggled. "So you think they had the painters lying on the floor with squirt guns, squirting the ceiling to get that pattern?" Chris nodded. "I can see that," Michelle agreed. "It's actually a genius idea. I might try it in my dorm, but like, with black paint. Or purple."

"That would be so awesome," Chris agreed. "If you do it, take lots of pictures, okay?"

"Okay," Michelle promised. She looked at him. "I love that you and Jerry have nicknames," she said. "Especially Jerry. It fits him so well!"

"I know," Chris said. "In high school, the only nickname I had was Chris. I don't even think anyone knows my real name is Christopher." He considered for a moment. "What's even a nickname for Michelle, anyway?"

"Some people go by Missy," Michelle told him, "but I never liked that. But when I was really small, my family called me Chelley, with a C. My mom liked it before I was even born. But I put a stop to that. I like my full name. So yeah, no nickname for me. Just the full name."

They lay still and quiet for a long time, lost in their own thoughts. Finally Chris spoke. "It was me you had a crush on in junior high, wasn't it?"

Michelle laughed. "No, Chris, it wasn't you. I swear. I really wasn't like Sally. I didn't go for the bad boys. And I had known you guys forever. Remember, we all used to chase each other around at recess when we were young. No, my schoolgirl crush was on Mr. Russo."

Chris burst out laughing. "Mr. Russo? The music teacher? The one with the Fu Manchu mustache? Wasn't he like forty? And married? To Mrs. Russo from McKinney?"

Michelle looked at Chris with a very serious face. "He was soulful, Chris. Soulful. He understood the music. And he played the piano. It was magical. Well, when I was thirteen, it was magical. Now it's kind of gross to think of, but what did I know back then? I thought for sure that someday, I would marry a musician. Like Paul McCartney."

"Who was also an old man by the time we were in junior high," Chris said. "The Beatles were pretty much done with their band by the time we were all even born."

"Hey, a girl can have dreams, you know," Michelle said, and she sighed. "And then in high school, I guess I started to like guys who were attracted to the military. Barf. Never again. I need someone who will stay in one place, who wants to be with me, who will put me first above everything else."

"Yeah, Michelle," Chris said. "You deserve that. None of that waiting around for him to come home. I'm so sorry you ended up wasting so much of your time waiting for that guy. I don't get why anyone would choose the military over you. That's crazy."

Michelle laughed. "Oh, Chris. I needed to hear that. Thank you. I learned a lot from all of this. I learned not only what I want, but also what I don't want. So I won't make the same mistakes again." She paused. "I hope that happens for you, too, Chris."

He reached out for her hand. "We'll both be okay," he promised. "And we have the best friends anyone could ever have to back us up. We'll be okay in the end. I know it."

They were quiet again, lying on the bed, still holding hands, watching the ceiling. "I probably need to go home at some point," Michelle said. "What time is it?"

Chris let go of her hand and checked his watch. "It's about eight thirty."

"How is that even possible?" Michelle said, sitting up. "I feel like we've been in here for like four hours. Ugh, I hate it when time gets all distorted!"

Chris laughed. "I'm not ready to be able to drive you home yet," he admitted. "Let's see if Jerry will let us watch TV again." He stood up.

"Jerry," Michelle said, shaking her head as she stood. "We could totally take Jerry."

Chris chuckled. He opened his door. Jerry was asleep on the lounge couch. Chris stepped up to the TV and changed the channel. He found the movie *White Christmas.*

"Is this good?" he asked Michelle.

"Good with me," she said. "How about you, Jerry?" Jerry continued to sleep. "Jerry's okay with it, too."

They watched the movie and drank large glasses of water. When the movie ended, it was ten thirty, and Chris was okay to drive. He had Michelle call her parents to say she was on her way home, and then they headed out. They took deep breaths of the cold winter air to refresh their lungs.

When they got to Michelle's house, Chris walked her to the door.

"Thanks so much for hanging out with me tonight, Michelle," he said. "It really meant a lot. I hope we have another chance to do it again someday. Don't be a stranger, okay?"

Michelle hugged him. "It was fun," she said. "I haven't laughed so hard in a really long time, and usually it involves something like dirty word Mad Libs with James and Sally. I hope everything works out for you, Chris. I'll probably see you on New Year's Eve. Merry Christmas."

"Merry Christmas, prom buddy."

Chris headed back to his car and turned around to make sure that Michelle got in safely. Then he drove home, confident in the thought that he really did have the world's best friends.

New Year, New Problems

Chris would be lying to himself if he said he was not feeling anxious about returning to campus and seeing Alison. Her dorm was right next door to his, and there would be times that he would have no choice but to go to the library to do research for classes. But he couldn't transfer schools, and he couldn't upend his life by avoiding routes or places he needed to go. He would keep his regular routine, and if he saw her, he would deal with it.

The two times he saw her in the first two weeks, it was from afar, and she didn't see him. He pretended not to have seen her and just kept going. He went out with his friends on the weekends and ate with them in the cafeteria. He was starting to hit his stride again.

He got his assignment for his last semester of observation: Randall Middle School. He was placed with Mrs. Fox. She was the teacher who had busted him and his friends in ninth grade when they were sneaking out. She was also the one that Mr. Jackson said thought he was destined for big things. One way or another, he hoped he had not disappointed her, and he looked forward to being back on his old stomping grounds once more.

His sister Scarlet was stunned. She was an eighth grader at Randall, and she was also in Mrs. Fox's science class. She didn't know whether to be excited or horrified that her older brother would be observing her class.

"Just don't embarrass me," she begged him. "I have friends in that class."

Chris laughed. "Don't worry about me," he told her. "I bet within a week all of your friends will have a crush on me. It's a curse. Just don't *you* do anything to embarrass *me*."

"Chris!" Mrs. Mahoney chastised him. "Don't tease your sister. And Scarlet, just be on your best behavior for Chris, okay?" They both nodded to their mother, then made faces at each other.

On his first day, Chris parked in the Randall teacher parking lot, which was surreal in itself. Then he went into the building and presented himself to the office. The office staff had changed since his last day of ninth grade, but when he announced his name at the counter, a familiar face stepped out from the back offices to greet him. It was Mr. Jackson, his old mentor, and he was wearing a suit.

"Chris Mahoney!" he said. He came around the counter and shook Chris's hand. "I heard you were coming, but I'm glad to see it with my own eyes. My goodness, you've gotten even taller since graduation. Are you over six feet now?"

Chris grinned. "I think I topped out at six-foot-one," he told his mentor. "Are you principal here now?"

Mr. Jackson laughed. "No, not yet," he told him. "Mr. Jeffries is still here. Or Sean, as I think you used to call him inappropriately! Oh, he will be excited to see you! No, there was an opening for vice principal this year when Mrs. Coleman retired, and I took a shot. I always wanted to come back to Randall. I like the middle school atmosphere. So you'll be working with Mrs. Fox, then, huh?"

"Yeah," Chris said with a grimace. "I hope she doesn't hold my past against me."

Mr. Jackson laughed. "No, Chris, trust me. You are not the first delinquent Angela Fox ever busted, and you won't be the last. She will be thrilled to see you. Just be on your best behavior, and you'll do fine. Listen, I have to go deal with a situation, but let's plan to catch up soon. Oh, but before I go, how's your cousin Carl been doing?"

Chris smiled. "You want to feel old?" he asked. "Carl and Kim Drake moved to California after high school. Now they're married with a one-month-old baby."

Mr. Jackson raised his eyebrows. "Oh, my goodness," he said. "That's not at all what I expected to hear, but congratulations to them and your family! Wow. A baby. That's amazing. Okay, Chris, I'll catch up with you later. It's so good to see you!"

"You too, Mr. Jackson."

Mr. Jackson laughed. "Chris, I'm not sure if you knew this, but I have a first name. You can use it now. Just not in front of the students. It's Dante. See you later, Mr. Mahoney." He turned back toward his office.

"Bye, Dante," Chris called out. It felt weird to call his old teacher Dante.

Mrs. Fox arrived at the office and walked him back to her classroom.

"Chris, I was thrilled to see your name on my schedule last week," she told him. "I consider any of my old students ending up in a teaching program a big success. I am very happy for you. When we have more time, I would love to talk to you all about how things have been going for you the last several years, and all about your old friends. But first off, we have to address one small rule I have for my observing students."

She sat down at her desk and directed him to sit in the chair next to it.

"Mr. Mahoney, I will have no tolerance for my trainees sneaking out of the school at lunchtime to go smoke joints by Carson Lake. Otherwise, we will get along just fine."

She smiled.

Chris laughed. "Mrs. Fox, I can assure you, beyond a shadow of a doubt, that will never happen again. I've grown up a lot since ninth grade. I can be pretty appropriate when I need to be."

"Mr. Jackson thinks very highly of you," Mrs. Fox told him. "I would not be surprised if your name ending up on our shortlist had something to do with him." She handed Chris a packet of stapled papers. "This contains the outlines for my lesson plans, my schedule, and any important notes you'll need to read about events and student needs. This stays locked in my desk when you leave for the day. I am very excited that you will be here for our science project fair. You'll be able to help my students develop ideas in class when we break into groups. Oh, and one more thing," she said. "A Miss Scarlet Mahoney is in my fifth period class. I assume you know that I expect more discretion from you than I do from Scarlet during class time. Understood?"

"I will leave my big brother persona at the door when fifth period starts," Chris promised.

"Very good. First bell is in five minutes. We can talk more over lunch in the teacher's lounge. Are you ready for this, Mr. Mahoney?"

He nodded. "Yes, Mrs. Fox."

Mrs. Fox nodded. "Very well. I am very happy you are here, Chris."

Soon, the students began to filter into the room. Chris watched them come in from behind Mrs. Fox's desk. They looked so small, even though he knew they were the same age as Scarlet. He didn't recognize any of them, but he also didn't know Scarlet's friends from school. When everyone had arrived and the bell rang, Mrs. Fox got the class to settle down.

"Everyone," she said, "I'd like you to meet Mr. Mahoney, our student teacher observer for the term. I expect you will listen to his instruction and treat him as you would any other teacher in any of your classes. Mr. Mahoney, will you tell the class a little bit about yourself?"

Chris smiled, remembering when Mrs. Fox made the class do this on the first day when he was in eighth grade. He had probably said some snarky thing and gotten in trouble immediately. Now he cleared his throat.

"Hi," he said. "I'm Chris Mahoney, and this is the third school I've been assigned to for observation. I actually went to Randall years ago when it was seventh, eighth, and ninth grade, and we were the last ninth grade class. I had Mrs. Fox for science like you do. I want to be a teacher because I've had some great teachers who have taught me some great lessons, including Mrs. Fox, and Mr. Jackson, your vice principal. I hope I can learn to teach kids not only what's in the books, but also about things that are important in life. So I look forward to working with you all." The students applauded.

"Does anyone have any questions for Mr. Mahoney?" Mrs. Fox asked.

Several girls raised their hands. Chris smiled. That's usually how it went. He called on a girl with long brown hair in the second row.

"Miss Hampton," Mrs. Fox told him.

"Mr. Mahoney," she said sweetly. "Are you related to Scarlet Mahoney?"

Chris hesitated. He cleared his throat again and glanced at Mrs. Fox. She nodded.

"Yes," he told the girl and the rest of the class. "I am related to Scarlet, and please don't hold it against her." He heard some laughter.

Miss Hampton spoke again. "Scarlet said her brother used to get in trouble all the time at Randall, and almost got kicked out. Was that you? I think Scarlet only has one brother?"

The class started to mumble. Mrs. Fox nodded again.

"Yes, that's true," Chris said. "I got in a lot of trouble when I was at Randall. Lots of times. I won't lie to you. I got called to Sean—I mean, Mr. Jeffries's office all the time, and one time I got in a ton of trouble with my friends. To be honest, it was Mrs. Fox who caught us."

Now the mumbling got louder. Chris laughed.

"Yeah, I was a troublemaker back then. But I want to tell all of you a secret. Sometimes, it takes people a long time to find themselves, to figure out who they want to be. Back then I was so sure I had it all figured out, and that everyone else had it wrong. That attitude worked for me for a long time, until the day it didn't anymore. Getting caught that day and getting in trouble was one of the main things that led to me changing my perspective, and seeing that getting in trouble wasn't going to get me where I wanted to go in life. It took some time, and sometimes it was really hard, but I did change, and now, instead of getting in trouble, I want to work with kids the same age as I was then, to help them to figure stuff out, so they don't have to go through what I went through, and they don't end up hurting other people or hurting themselves. So yeah, I'm Scarlet's troublemaker older brother. But I hope maybe you might learn something from me while I'm here."

When he finished his monologue, Chris took a deep breath and then exhaled. He looked up at the class and realized they were all staring at him. And some of the girls were smiling.

Mrs. Fox stood. "Thank you for that, Mr. Mahoney," she said. "Any more questions?"

A few girls raised their hands.

"Any questions not related to Mr. Mahoney's troubled past or his relationship to Miss Mahoney?"

All of the hands went down.

"Very well then. Let's proceed with our lesson."

After the class ended and the students walked out, Mrs. Fox turned to Chris.

"Chris, what you said to the class earlier was wonderful," she said. "I'm impressed. I think some of them might have even heard what you said. You were very eloquent, but you also spoke their language. I think you won them over. Especially the girls."

Chris laughed. He knew that he had gotten past his first obstacle at Randall.

He was returning to his dorm from Randall two weeks later when he saw her there. She was sitting on the bench between their dorms, facing his, and when she saw him, she stood and started to walk over. His heart rate shot up. He stopped to wait for her.

"Hi, Chris."

"Hi, Alison."

"How are you?"

He shrugged. "Okay, you know. How are you?"

She shrugged. "Okay," she said. "Can we talk in your room?"

Chris thought about it. "Can we talk out here?" he asked.

She nodded. They walked back to the bench and sat down.

"Chris," she said. Then she stopped as if she didn't have any other words.

"So you saw Brett over break," he said, trying to help her get started. "I'm guessing you slept with him."

Tears immediately sprung to Alison's eyes. "Chris, I know. I made a huge mistake."

"I know that," Chris said, looking right at her. "It was a mistake. You chose the wrong guy. I figured that out with a bit of help from my friends."

Alison nodded. "I did. I was wrong. I am so sorry, Chris. It was like I was possessed for a while. Maybe I should have spent more time thinking about it. I was thinking about the past, not about now. I was thinking about the time before he left, not the time he was gone."

"He never called you, Alison. He never wrote."

"No, he didn't," she agreed. "He lied to me. He didn't want to see if there was still something there. He wasn't thinking of me at all. He was just thinking about himself and what he wanted."

"I know," Chris said, feeling sadness for her rising in his chest. "He played you, Alison. And in a way, he played me too, through you. It would have been different if you were both still single, but you weren't, and he knew it."

"He did know," Alison said. "But what I didn't know was that he had a long-term relationship with a girl in Alaska, someone on his research team. I mean, that's okay, we had broken up. But what wasn't okay is that they hadn't broken up when he came back, and he didn't tell me about it. He didn't give me a choice, until it was too late."

"Oh, Alison," Chris said, shaking his head.

He resisted grabbing her hand, and he could sense that's what she would want. He wanted to. He wanted to take her in his arms, and hold her, and tell her that all was forgiven, that they could go back to where they were on December 10, the day before Brett called and it all went to hell. But he couldn't. He wanted to so badly, but he couldn't.

They sat in silence. Then Alison spoke through her tears. "I just wanted you to know that I realize I was wrong. I just wanted to apologize to you and let you know. I never, ever, wanted to hurt you, Chris, and it kills me that I did. I'm not even sad about Brett. It's over for good with us now. I'm not asking you for anything, but I just wanted you to know."

"Okay," Chris said softly. "Now I know. And it's okay, Alison, you don't have to apologize anymore. I forgive you."

"You do?" Alison asked, looking up at him.

"Yes of course," Chris said. "I know you're sorry for hurting me. I know you're a good person, Alison. I know you got played, and Brett sounds like he knows how to play. I forgive you."

He could sense relaxation in Alison's shoulders. "Thanks, Chris," she said. They sat quietly for a bit longer. "Do you think, maybe, we could—"

"No, Alison, I can't," Chris interrupted. "Whatever it is you're gonna say, I can't. I mean, I forgive you, I promise, but I don't think I can ever forget that you chose another guy over me. Even if it was a mistake. I wasn't enough for you in the moment, and I don't think I will ever be able to forget that. I don't think I could ever trust you again to not hurt me. I'm sorry, Alison, but you really hurt me pretty bad. I don't ever want to feel that way again."

New tears came to Alison's eyes, even as she nodded. Chris tried to blink his tears back.

"Okay," she said, standing up. "Fair enough. I understand. I can just be happy knowing you forgive me, Chris. And maybe someday, after some time, we can be friends. I miss you. I might not deserve your friendship now, but maybe someday I can earn it back. Bye, Chris."

She started to walk toward her dorm.

Chris watched her walk away.

"Bye, Alison," he called after her. And quietly to himself he said, "See you around the library."

How We Help Ourselves

That night he went out with his friends and drank too much beer. They walked home from the bar, and when they got to the dorm, Chris sent his friends ahead and stood outside, looking at Alison's dorm, willing her to come out the door. But she didn't. He considered seeing if someone would let him in, and then knocking on her door, but he didn't. He turned around and went into his dorm. When he got to his room, he picked up the phone and started hitting the buttons. He got the number right the first time. Carl picked up on the second ring.

"She made a mistake, Carl," he said after Carl said hello. "He lied to her. And I forgave her. Why why why couldn't she have known she made a mistake before she made it?"

"Chris, man, have you had a few beers tonight?" Carl asked.

"A few," Chris admitted. "I forgave her. I had to. She was so hurt. She was crying. But I can't forget what she did. Forgive and forget they say. But how could I *forget*?"

"I'm so sorry, Chris," Carl said.

"Me too," Chris said. "I think she wanted to be friends, but how can I ever even trust her?"

"What do you want to do, man?" Carl asked.

"Go to her room and knock on her door and grab her, and, you know, just be with her."

"What happens after that?" Carl asked.

"I haven't thought that far," Chris admitted.

"Can you trust her any more tomorrow than you can tonight?" Carl asked.

Chris sat and thought about it. "No," he finally said. "I keep thinking it would be closure, but we already had that, didn't we? Why does it feel that not trusting her makes me the one who's doing the hurting, instead of the one who was hurt?"

"Chris, maybe it's the beer that's doing the thinking right now. Maybe you should wait until you've sobered up before you make any big decisions about your life, okay?"

"Okay, Carl." He wondered when Carl had gotten so smart, and then he remembered that Carl had actually tested as a bona fide genius. He laughed. "What time is it there?"

"Uh, almost eight thirty," Carl told him.

"Oh, so it's only late here. Is Drake awake? Oh, that rhymes!"

Carl laughed. "Man, it seems like Drake is always awake. Kim's feeding him right now. Then we're hoping he'll go down for a few hours, so we can chill for a bit. Chris, man, are you gonna be alright?"

Chris nodded in his room three thousand miles away and then realized he needed to answer out loud.

"I don't know, bro," he said. "But if I'm not okay for a while, please don't judge me, okay?"

There was a pause. "Chris, please, just don't do anything you'll regret. Everything's gonna be okay. You just need to give it some time. It's gonna be okay. Just go to bed, man. Get some sleep. And call me tomorrow night, okay? When you're not intoxicated."

"You know, Carl," Chris confided, "I've never been with Alison when I've been drunk. I mean never. I don't know why. I just think that's interesting, don't you?"

"Yeah, Chris, it is interesting."

"Okay, Carl, I'll let you go so you and Kim can have your chill-out time. I'll try to remember to call you tomorrow. I'll go to bed now. Good night, Carl. Kiss that baby for me."

"I will, Chris. Love you, man."

"Love you too, man, and Kim, and Drake. Bye."

Chris hung up and fell flat on his bed, and he cried. Then he fell asleep.

The next day, after a breakfast of Pepto Bismol and coffee, Chris was feeling better physically, but he still didn't feel settled. He wanted Alison. He couldn't stop thinking about Alison. He wanted to call her or go to her door. He wanted to hold her, console her, and make them both feel better. But he was confused, and after what he had said to her the afternoon before, he knew she would be, too. He decided to wait.

He was able to wait until the next day. Finally, the urges overwhelmed his common sense, and he called her. He met her outside the door of her dorm, and they fell into each other's arms.

"I don't know what I'm doing," he told her as he kissed her face, then her neck, and she threw her head back. "Alison, I don't think this changes how I feel. But I can't deny that I want to be with you, right now."

"Let's just be in this moment for now," Alison agreed. "Let's not even think about what comes next, okay? Let's just go inside. My roommate is gone for the weekend. We have the room to ourselves." She paused. "And I've been back on the pill for two months now, Chris. We don't need to worry about that anymore."

"You got back on the pill when you were still with me," he stated.

He didn't know why, but this made him feel good. Maybe it meant that before everything fell apart, she was thinking about their future. They went inside and into her room.

They stayed in her room the rest of the afternoon. They followed their urges and satisfied their needs. They touched each other in many ways and whispered to each other. Chris still felt the ache in his heart, but he pushed it aside, willing it to leave him alone until he needed it to come back, and he willed that to be never. They stayed in bed, rested when they needed, cuddled together, limbs entwined. They made love when they had the energy and finally knew they needed to eat. They dressed over their unshowered bodies and walked to the cafeteria, ate what they needed, and grabbed some loose apples for later. Then they went to his dorm and started all over again in his room. Finally, as the hour got late, they fell asleep in each other's arms and slept through the night until Monday morning. Then it was time for their fragile bubble to pop.

"We need to say goodbye again, don't we?" Alison asked when they woke.

Chris had felt the heartache arise as soon as he opened his eyes, and he knew what she said was true. "I think so, yeah."

"We're not going to be able to be friends, are we," she asked, but it came out more like a declaration.

"No, I don't think we can, Alison," Chris said. "I don't think I'll get to a place where that can ever be enough for me with you. But I also don't think we can be more. This is gonna sound weird, but I'm kind of hoping that if someone ever hurts me again, that they don't do it kindly. I hope they are so harsh that I never want to see their face again. I want them to just shut the door. In a way, I think that maybe that's more kind. Maybe just a clean break. It might take some time to get over, but at least it's over, no doubt about it. With you and me, if I let it, it will never be over, and just a few weeks ago, that would have been okay, but now, well . . .

"In the past few weeks, I became a godfather to this tiny little baby, and I was told I need to teach him my values someday. And I've started teacher observation in a class where I see my sister, an eighth-grader, and I'm told I need to be a role model. This is at a school where I once got in so much trouble, I almost got expelled. Now they're trusting me in a classroom with my very own sister. I have to take this stuff seriously, you know? I have to start living my own values before I can pass them on. If I feel my heart aching when I'm with someone, I need to listen to it, to figure out how I'm not living my own truth.

"Alison, I feel like I need to apologize to you now. I feel that me calling you yesterday was a mistake. I feel like I did exactly what Brett did to you. I took care of my own needs, and I didn't think ahead to how this would affect you. I am so sorry."

Chris stopped speaking, and he and Alison looked at each other.

"Chris," she finally said, "I forgive you. The difference between you and Brett is that you realize that what you do can affect someone else. You realize that your actions are not without consequences. But to be honest, I wanted last night just as much as you did. It's what I was going to ask for when you interrupted me on the bench the other day. So what do we do now?"

Chris shrugged. "We go our separate ways, and we both feel like shit for a while. Hopefully at some point, we start to feel better, and we move on. And we know that we had someone in our lives that was this amazing person, a person we had potential to love. And we hope we meet someone else someday, someone who we can love with no reservations, and maybe sometimes we think of each other and we remember feeling good, or we remember feeling sad, but at least we remember."

Alison nodded. "I can do that," she said. "I don't feel like I want to right now, but I will."

"I will too," Chris promised. "Saying goodbye to you hurts so much each time, so let's have this be the last time, okay? If we see each other, we can smile, or say hello, or maybe even ask each other how we are, but let's never have to say goodbye again, okay?"

Alison squeezed her eyes shut, and again there were tears. "Okay," she agreed.

They embraced one last time, and then Alison got out of bed and got dressed. The scene was far too familiar, but this time, they said goodbye.

"Goodbye, Chris."

"Goodbye, Alison."

And this time, it was really over.

Chris noticed his answering machine light blinking, and he knew who it was before he even listened. He had forgotten about calling Carl back the night before, and now he had made Carl worry. It was only six in the morning on the west coast, and Chris had to go to class. He got up, got ready, and then called Aunt Missy. He asked her to call Carl at a reasonable time and tell him he was okay and would call him that night.

Then he assured Aunt Missy that he really was alright. And then he went to class and pretended it was a normal day.

Looking Ahead

The days flew by, going to classes, going to Randall, spending time catching up with his old teachers. There were times he could not avoid the library, so he tried to go on Alison's days off, but when they did see each other, they both tried to smile and move on. Chris went to the cafeteria with his friends and even found reasons to laugh sometimes. They went out on weekends, and sometimes on weekdays, but Chris was careful not to overdo it. He wanted to keep his wits about him. He didn't want to make any more mistakes.

After talking to his academic adviser, Chris decided to apply for the five-year program at Eastboro State so he could start taking master's level classes in his junior year. He would be able to work as a teacher with a BA, but he would be much more marketable if schools saw he was close to getting his master's degree. He felt good about this decision. Grant had also decided to do the master's program, so Chris wouldn't be alone. The four friends were starting to talk about getting an off-campus apartment for their junior year and looking into their options. Chris was looking forward to living off-campus. There would be much less temptation away from the dorms.

Soon, it was the end of February, and it was Kim's twentieth birthday. Chris called to wish her a happy day and got a chance to talk to Carl, as well. They were both very excited to be planning their wedding celebration, and they were planning it for Memorial Day weekend. Carl, Kim, and Drake would be coming home. Chris would finally get to hold his godson. And their friends would all be there, including Traci, who had moved to Detroit with her family at the beginning of their senior year in high school. Carl wanted his brother, Scott, to come to the wedding and to meet his nephew, and Chris decided he would find Scott and let him know. Kim offered for Chris, the best man, to bring a date to the wedding, but he knew he wouldn't. A few months earlier, he imagined himself at the wedding with Alison, and if that wasn't going to happen, and it wasn't, then he just wanted to go alone.

Gram Cissy called him the next day and asked him to come check out a possible wedding venue. It was a beautiful outdoor spot on a pond, and they could accommodate a ceremony and a reception. In Kim and Carl's absence, she wanted to make sure it would be appropriate for their needs, and she trusted Chris's judgment when it came to these things. Chris agreed, and the Grams picked him up later that afternoon.

The location was perfect, and Chris assumed Kim would cry when she saw it. It was a storybook setting. There were swans and geese in the pond, and in May, the host told them, all of the spring flowers would be in bloom. It would not only be a feast for the eyes, but the aroma would be strong with floral blooms. In case of rain, they would be able to do the ceremony inside the building, which was a large Victorian bed-and-breakfast, and have the reception outdoors under a large tent. A few lucky guests would be able to reserve rooms in the B&B for the night, and the honeymoon room would be reserved for the bride and groom.

Chris gave his blessing for this location, and Aunt Missy wrote a check on the spot.

"Kim's father will be walking her down the aisle," she told Chris. "I hope he's able to understand what's going on. But from what I hear, he adores Kim, no matter what stage of life he understands she's in. Oh, this is really going to be a lovely wedding. I can't wait until they're here and I can meet my newest great-grandchild!"

Chris smiled. "It will be pretty sweet," he agreed. He was counting the days.

Darlene, Pete, and Michelle came home for spring break. They all spent time together, talking about their lives at school, but inevitably, the conversation went back to the upcoming wedding.

"Sally's coming up this weekend," Michelle said with a smile. "We're all going to the bridal store to try on bridesmaid dresses. Kim's gonna let us make a choice for the group with some guidelines, but there's no way we can get pictures to her fast enough for her to choose. It's pretty cool that she trusts us so much."

"So Laine and Beth aren't gonna be in the wedding?" Pete asked.

"No," Chris said. "Since they got to go to the courthouse with them for the first wedding, they thought they'd sit this one out. And the big news is that Beth is pregnant! I guess this one was a big surprise for everyone. But it's pretty cool that Drake will have a little cousin."

"Just like you and Carl," Michelle said, grinning.

Chris smiled back. "Yes, exactly. I hope."

Darlene sighed. "I can't wait for the wedding," she said. "I'm so psyched to be maid of honor. And I can't believe Traci will be here! She is so stoked to see everyone. And her new, well, new to us, boyfriend Paul will be coming with her."

"She's going to Michigan State, right?" Pete asked.

"Yeah," Darlene responded. "And she's in a sorority. She's made a lot of good friends. But we still talk and write, and I know she and Sally write."

"Sally writes so much, she's got to have hand cramps," Chris mused.

"Are you guys wearing tuxes?" Michelle asked. "God, this really feels like prom!"

"Yeah," Chris said. "The Grams are taking care of renting us tuxes. We'll have to do all that pre-wedding stuff. I guess the guys will take Carl out, and you ladies will have to do something with Kim."

"Can you imagine," Darlene said, "that these guys are getting married, but they still can't drink in a bar? That's kind of nuts."

"I think they'll get some champagne for toasts at the wedding," Michelle said hopefully. "I really hope no one comes over to card them at their table!"

"We'll need sparkling cider for James and Sally anyway," Pete said. "We can always make it a dry wedding."

"No way," Michelle and Darlene said at the same time, then laughed.

"Yeah, I'm with the girls," Chris agreed. "There will be Bishop-Farmers as far as the eye can see. I'll need to drink. Especially if I'm gonna go out and dance."

"Chris, you'll need to do a toast," Pete reminded him. "Maybe hold off until after that."

Chris suddenly flashed to the memory that he'd had sex with the bride in high school and realized that Pete was right. He could see himself getting tipsy and making some stupid comment about Kim. Or crying about Alison.

"Yeah, okay, you guys, keep me sober until after my toast," he said. "Then once I'm out of the spotlight, all bets are off."

Counting the Days

The best part of wedding planning was the calls from Carl and Kim. They were excited, but also stressed out, being so far away and having to decide things over the phone. They also had to deal with the Grams and Mrs. Drake footing the bill and were feeling guilty over choosing anything that cost too much. Kim had already purchased her dress and was awaiting alterations. She knew what type of flowers she wanted to carry. She and Carl had strong preferences for what food was served. They were looking forward to their wedding night in the B&B and had reserved all the other rooms for anyone in the wedding party who wanted to stay. So far, Michelle, Darlene, Traci and Paul, and James and Sally had committed to rooms. Chris didn't see a reason to stay since he lived in town. If he was too drunk to drive, he would have a family member bring him back to his new apartment after the reception ended and come back for his car the next day. He and his roommates would be moving into the place one week earlier, between their final exams.

May finally arrived, and the wedding was just weeks away. Chris wrapped up his placement at Randall and made the rounds to say goodbye to all of his old teachers. Mr. Jackson gave him his home phone number, and they agreed to arrange to have lunch over the summer. Chris said goodbye to the students in his classes, and even Scarlet seemed sad to see him go. He had been right; at least two of her friends now had a crush on him and wanted to be invited for dinner at Scarlet's house on a night when he was there. Chris picked up his tux and also those for Carl, Pete, and James to stow until the weekend of the wedding.

The day of the move arrived, and Chris brought his boxes and suitcases to the new apartment, which was six blocks from campus, in a three-decker that rented to students on each floor. He and his roommates all chose bedrooms and started to unpack their belongings. After Chris went back for his last haul of things, he spent a moment outside of the dorms, sitting on the bench, remembering the year. Finally, he got up, looked toward his dorm, then toward Alison's, and then walked away for the last time.

Carl, Kim, and Drake were flying in with Laine, Beth, and their two children, Benjamin and Claire, on the Thursday before the Sunday wedding. Both couples were renting cars for their stay, as they all would not be able to fit into one. Carl and his family would be staying with Aunt Missy, and Laine and his would be staying with his father, Rolland Farmer.

The Mahoneys were at Aunt Missy's house on Thursday when the Bishops arrived. When the car pulled up, Chris was outside, and as soon as Carl was out of the car, he was by his side. The two best friends embraced. They held on for several seconds before letting go and looking at each other.

"I can't believe you guys are actually here," Chris said with a smile.

"Yeah, I know," Carl replied. "It's so weird to be back. So much has changed since I left, but Gram's house is the same. You actually got taller."

Chris laughed. Aunt Missy came running out of the house and grabbed Carl in a bear hug without speaking. Then she let go. "Where's Drake? Where's that baby?" She went to the car and found Kim unstrapping the baby from his seat. Kim held the curious and confused baby in her arms, as Missy embraced them both at once and then reached for Drake.

"That's the last time we'll see him on this trip," Carl quipped. Chris nodded.

Kim came around and hugged Chris. "Carl's right," she said. "You've grown! Aren't you twenty? Shouldn't you be done growing by now?"

Chris smiled. "I'm done," he said. "I was done last year, you just haven't seen me."

"So I need to go see my family," Kim said. "But first I need to feed Drake, and I also want to see the venue. Do you want to come with us?"

"Yeah, that would be great," Chris said. "I'm all yours for the whole weekend. Whatever you need."

"So," Carl said, "has anyone heard from Scott? He's supposed to come on Sunday, but I don't know any more than that. Oh, he chose chicken for his dinner. But that's all."

"If Scotty said he'll be there," Aunt Missy said, "he will be there. We just need to take his word."

She turned to walk toward the house, and everyone else followed her in. The Mahoneys greeted Carl and Kim at the door with hugs and kisses, and the girls fawned over the baby. Kim sat on the couch, and Missy handed Drake back to her. Kim lifted her shirt discreetly, and Drake began to nurse. It was one of the most wholesome and touching things that Chris had ever seen. Carl sat down next to her, and Chris could not remember the last time he felt such relief to see an old friend. And Carl looked so happy.

Missy reappeared and put two jars of baby food on the table. "I hope these are okay," she said to Kim.

Kim nodded. "Yeah, that's the stuff we use. He's basically just eating baby food for practice at this point. He still gets everything he needs from me."

"Carl," Missy said, "your aunts and uncles and cousins will be stopping by to say hi over the next few days, but no one wants to overwhelm you too much with the baby. Everyone will be at the wedding, and you'll see them there."

"That's fine," Carl replied. "We're just gonna let everyone except Kim's family come to us. We'll just let you know when we're planning to be here so you can let them know." He turned to Chris. "We're staying with Gram tonight and tomorrow night, and then on Saturday, after the rehearsal dinner, Kim will be staying at the B&B and hanging out with the girls, and I'm on my own. I figure we'll do something with the guys that night. And then on Sunday, we'll be staying over at the B&B. Drake's gonna stay with Gram for the night."

"It will be our first night away from him ever," Kim said. "But it is our wedding night, so it makes sense."

"I'm pretty sure the girls are planning something for you on Saturday night, Kim," Chris told her. "You might want to make arrangements for some babysitting, because we've already made plans for Carl. And Carl, we'll either get you back to Aunt Missy's and I'll stay over to make sure you get up and get ready in the morning, or you can come stay with me for the night at my new apartment."

"No getting him wasted," Kim commanded. "I really don't care about strippers, but I need him to have his full wits about him for the wedding. I mean, a girl only gets to get married to her true love twice, right?" She smiled.

Chris returned the smile. "No drunk or hungover groom, I promise,"

Drake had pulled his face away from his mother and started to look around. He smiled and babbled. Everyone laughed. Kim brought him to the table, tied a bib around his neck, and sat him on her lap. "Would you like to give it a try, Gram?" she asked, offering her the spoon. She opened the jar of squash and set it on the table. Missy came over and began to feed him the strained vegetables.

After Drake was done eating and cleaned up, Kim, Carl, and Chris went with him to the rental car and headed for the Drakes' house. This would be his first time meeting his young aunts and uncles. Mr. Drake was now living in a nursing facility, and Kim and Carl would be going over another time to introduce him to his grandson.

After an emotional reunion with Kim's family, and promises to spend more time together later, they all headed for the wedding venue. Chris directed them on how to get there, and when they arrived, he led them around back. Just as he expected, Kim had an emotional response.

"Oh, my God, it's so beautiful!" she exclaimed. "There are swans! And it smells like flowers! It's so perfect!" She rushed around the grounds, checking out the area, and brought Drake closer to the pond to see the geese and ducks.

"Wow," Carl said. "The Grams really scored with this place. It's awesome. And look at Kim! She's ecstatic! She's right, it is perfect."

"We can go look inside when Kim's ready," Chris said. "It's not supposed to rain, but that's where they'd do the ceremony if it does for some reason. I can't wait to see how this all looks when it's set up with tables and chairs and flowers."

"This is a world of difference from our first wedding at the city courthouse," Carl said. "I mean, it was nice, but this is amazing. I really can't believe it's even all for us, you know?"

Chris clapped his hand around Carl's shoulders. "Get used to it, buddy," he told him. "The next four days are all about you two. People are flying in to see you and to celebrate you. Just enjoy it, man."

Carl shrugged. "I'll try," he said. "I'm doing all this for Kim. She deserves her fairy tale wedding."

Chris had forgotten about this part of Carl, the part that thought he didn't deserve good things and didn't expect them to happen. He had hoped that once things had solidified with Kim that this trait had gone away. He had made a lot of progress.

"Yeah, well," Chris said to his cousin, "you deserve it too. You're my best friend, cousin, and brother, and you're doing it for me too, because I think you're worth the effort. And I'm never wrong about these things."

Carl smiled. "Okay, okay, I promise, I will enjoy myself at my wedding. I will let people celebrate me, and I will just say thank you. I will be a gracious groom. But on Tuesday, I'm going back to being my regular self, feeling sorry for myself, putting myself down, and having low self-esteem. I won't take no for an answer."

Chris laughed. "Okay, deal. We'll work on that stuff later."

Kim came back over to them and handed Drake to Chris.

"Let's go look inside," she said, taking Carl's arm and walking toward the back entrance.

Chris looked at baby Drake. Drake looked back at him. He smiled, cooed, and reached up to grab Chris's nose.

"Hey," Chris said softly, pulling his nose away. "I might need that nose later!"

He made a funny face at the baby, and Drake laughed. Then they followed his parents into the B&B. Chris had made his first meaningful connection with his godson.

Friday was a whirlwind day with relatives stopping by, and last-minute plans being solidified. Carl and Chris's friends would be making their way back to Eastboro before the start of the evening, and they would all get together at Chris's apartment before the night was over. It would be their only time together alone for the whole weekend. Chris spent the afternoon finishing his unpacking and making the apartment clean enough for a baby to be on the floor.

At seven, the friends started to arrive. First was James and Sally, always the first to every event. Next was Pete, and soon after, Michelle. Darlene arrived along with Traci and her boyfriend Paul, who she had picked up at the airport. They were staying at Darlene's mother's house with her for the night. The girls got up to say hello and give her hugs. Pete, James, and Chris all looked back and forth at each other. Traci had always been cute in high school, but now she was outright beautiful. Her skin had cleared up from her teenage acne, her hair had gotten long and silky and was fixed in the latest style, and her face had taken on a more mature shape. She had also become more proficient in her use of makeup, and her cheekbones looked sculpted. She had gotten hot. But she was still the same Traci.

"Oh my God, I can't believe we're all together again!" she exclaimed. "I have missed you all so much. It was so hard to leave everyone that day we left, but just knowing that someday I'd see you all again . . . oh my God Chris, you're so tall! You all look so good!"

"So do you, Traci," Chris responded. "You look great! You certainly don't look like a high school girl anymore."

Traci laughed. "Yeah, it's rough in Detroit," she said. "I had to learn pretty quickly how to do my hair and makeup when I got there. And luckily, the benzoyl peroxide finally started to kick in. Oh! Everyone, this is my boyfriend, Paul! Paul, this is Chris, Pete, James, Sally, and Michelle. And of course you already met Darlene. Where are Carl and Kim? And baby Drake?"

"Good question," Chris said. "I'm guessing they got stuck at his Gram's house with some good-intentioned relative that came to meet the baby. They should be here soon. Everyone, sit. I got beers and wine coolers in the fridge. Anyone want anything?"

Carl, Kim, and Drake arrived just as Chris came back with the drinks. "Sorry, everyone," Carl said as they settled down on the couch. "My uncle Ted showed up late, and he insisted on having a full visit with Drake, even though we told him we were on a schedule. People just don't get that the schedule is about the baby, not them."

Kim had greeted Traci and met Paul and now sat next to Carl. "I've got to feed him, guys, sorry," she said as she automatically lifted her shirt. Soon, Drake was nursing away, and everyone tried to pretend that this wasn't weird for them.

They talked about the schedule for the wedding and how things were going for the Bishops in California. Then Traci told them about Michigan State and how she and Paul had met. Everyone talked about what it was like to finish their first two years of school, and James and Chris told them about their plans for master's degrees. The whole time, Drake was passed from friend to friend, until eventually he fell asleep in Michelle's arms.

"I used to always lull my brothers to sleep when they were babies," she told everyone. "My mom would hand one to me when she was dealing with the other. You learn the skill pretty quickly when you're dealing with twins."

Pretty soon, the friends broke off in groups and caught up with each other. The volume in the room got louder, and Michelle brought the baby into the kitchen where it was quieter. Chris went in to sit with her and check if she was okay with continuing to hold him. They sat at the small kitchen table and talked quietly.

"So how did things ever end up with Alison?" Michelle asked. "Did you ever talk to her about getting back together with Brett?"

"I did," Chris admitted. "You'll never believe what she told me."

"He used her?" Michelle guessed.

"He used her so badly, Michelle," Chris said with sadness still present in his voice. "He had a girlfriend in Alaska. He came back for the break, and wanted Alison to jump through his hoops, but he never broke up with the Alaska girl. Everything you said to me at Christmas, everything was spot on. He made her feel like there was still something with them, and she had sex with him. And he couldn't fool her for long. She figured it out. And then she dumped him, for good. She made a mistake. She knows it now."

Michelle looked at him carefully. "You didn't take her back, did you, Chris?"

Chris shook his head. "No. I wanted to, so bad. I did forgive her. We did have one last night together. But Michelle, you just can't go back to someone after they pass you over for someone else like that. I would never be able to entirely trust her feelings for me again. I almost gave in. But I didn't. And she respected that. But I never, ever want to have to walk away from someone like that again. Next time I love someone, it's gonna have to be for keeps. I just can't handle the goodbyes."

Michelle gave him a look of strong compassion. "Oh, Chris, I'm so sorry," she said. "I wish there was some way you could have worked it out with Alison. I wish we could go back in time and tell her what was going to happen, to make her make the right choice. I wish I hadn't been right. But I knew I was."

"You were, Michelle, and it helped me. I understood what had happened, and it helped me forgive her. It meant a lot to be able to do that, for both me and for her. I totally owe you for that."

They had several seconds of eye contact, both knowing what that type of loss felt like and understanding each other's pain. Then they both smiled. Kim came into the room.

"Oh, there he is," she said when she saw her sleeping baby. "Would you mind if I take him, Michelle? We're gonna spend some time apart in the next couple of days for the first time, and I just want to hold him. I don't get to watch him sleep too much. You know, you need to sleep when they do, or else you don't get too much sleep."

Michelle stood slowly and passed the snoozing baby back to his mother. Then she shook out her arms. "He's a sweaty sleeper."

Kim laughed. "He is," she agreed. "He drools, too. I think he might be getting an early tooth. Let's go back out there. Hey, did you guys notice? Traci's totally hot now! What's that all about?"

Getting Up To Speed

The next day was devoted to last-minute wedding details. Everyone tried on their tuxes and dresses one more time to make sure they didn't need any final adjustments. The Grams did a final guest list review with the caterers for a head count. Guests from out of town began to arrive and stop by for quick visits. Carl, Kim, and Chris made the rounds to the various hotels and met with aunts, uncles, and cousins in the lobby to welcome them to Eastboro. As the afternoon ticked on, it was soon time to head for the B&B for the wedding rehearsal.

Everyone showed up dressed for dinner. It was reminiscent of the homecoming dances at McKinney. Everyone cleaned up nicely, and now that they were older, they looked more like elegant adults at a grown-up occasion. Although Traci was not in the wedding party, she and Paul came to the rehearsal with Darlene after checking into the B&B. Chris couldn't help but notice Traci, in a tight blue dress stopped above her knees and had a plunging neckline. This wasn't lost on his friends, either.

Michelle stood at Chris's side. "She's a lot different, huh?" she said. "She definitely changed a lot when she moved to Detroit. I think she had to, to fit in. But I spent some time with them last night. She's still the same person. She's just hot now. Can you imagine? Hot and nice. Strange combo."

Chris snickered, still looking at Traci. "What's the story on the boyfriend?"

Michelle shrugged. "He seems kind of dull," she admitted. "Or maybe he's just not comfortable around all the new people. He's a finance major. He's in a fraternity. He's a big football fan. The Spartans. They won the Rose Bowl this year."

Chris turned to look at Michelle. "Wow, you found out a lot in just one night."

Michelle smiled and shrugged. "Hey, I'm Michelle Gorman. If I can't find out, no one can. But I guess they seem happy enough. They've been going out for about six months. It's kind of a big deal to bring a date to a wedding, you know."

Chris nodded. "I notice that you and me and Darlene and Pete are still the group singles."

"Darlene's actually seeing a guy at Ithaca," Michelle stated. "His name is Phil. She met him in math class at Ithaca last year. She hasn't mentioned him to me lately, though. I think it's pretty casual."

"Oh," Chris said. He crossed his arms. "So you and me and Pete are the last three standing." He turned back to look at Traci, who was with Darlene and Kim.

Michelle crossed her arms in front of her. "Looks that way," she said.

They started the rehearsal soon after. The Grams and Drake would be walking down the aisle together. Mr. Drake would be walking Kim down the aisle, and it was decided that her mother would join them to make sure he didn't get confused or disoriented during the walk.

When everyone felt that they had their route down the aisle down to a science, they all headed over to Luigi's, where they would have the rehearsal dinner for the wedding party and out-of-town guests in the banquet room. They were met at the door by Lou, the owner. James and Sally greeted James's former boss warmly.

The party was escorted to the banquet room, and out-of-town guests started to trickle in over the next half hour. Everyone was seated at long tables, and Chris ended up with Traci on one side, Carl on the other, and Michelle across the table from him. The room became noisy with everyone wanting to be heard at once. Traci turned to Chris.

"So Chris, I heard that you and I both had pretty shitty first days of senior year. Sounds like we ruined the fun for everyone else back then."

That first day had been when Traci had announced she was moving immediately to Detroit with her family while Chris was sitting out in his car sobbing over his breakup with Rhonda.

"Yeah, that wasn't one of my favorite days, or years, for that matter," he admitted. "Sorry I never had a chance to say goodbye to you that day."

"That's okay," Traci said. "I was so overwhelmed, I can't even remember half of what happened. It was so hard to leave my friends and everything I knew behind. I was most upset about Dougo."

Chris remembered Traci's boyfriend Dougo. He had left for college the year before the rest of them, but he and Traci were still trying to make things work when she had to move away.

"What ever happened to Dougo?" he asked her.

"Strangely enough, we're still in touch, but just as friends. We write, and he's still friends with my brother, Bobby. But you know, we've both moved on. Sally writes to me too, which is great. I knew she would. She told me that you've been through the ringer a couple times since Rhonda."

Chris shrugged. "Yeah, well, I met a couple of girls. It didn't work out. It's all good now, though. What about you?"

Traci glanced over at Paul. He was engaged in a conversation with James and Sally that looked pretty animated.

"I've dated a few people over the last few years," she said. Then her voice became lower and more discrete. "But nothing really serious, though."

She made eye contact with Chris.

Oh my God, Chris thought. *She's flirting with me. Traci Walsh is flirting with me, and her boyfriend is sitting right next to her.*

"I was actually glad when I heard that Rhonda broke up with you," she went on. "I mean, I never thought she was right for you anyway."

Chris looked at Traci with curiosity. "Why did you think that?"

"I dunno," Traci started. "She just seemed, well, almost overconfident at times. Like she had the whole world at her command. Sometimes, she seemed like she just didn't give a shit about what happened, as long as she came out smelling like roses. I mean, she was always nice to me and everything, but sometimes I didn't think she was so nice to you."

Chris raised his eyebrows. "Really?"

"Yeah, it was like she had conquered the mighty Mahoney and now he was hers to lead around by the snout. I didn't know you for very long before you started dating her, but you were like the lead man in a teen movie, you know? Handsome, confident, smart, lots of friends . . . but even though you were still a lot of those things after Rhonda came along, it's like your volume got turned way down. When I heard she broke up with you out of the blue, I wasn't really surprised. But I was mad. She just decided she was done, no conversation, no real explanation, just done. Who even does that?"

I would have back then, Chris thought. *At least I thought I would. But would I really have ever done it?*

"If you had been my boyfriend, Chris," Traci went on, "you would have known you were special. I would have made sure of it. I never would have made you feel insecure or sad. We'd probably still be together now."

Chris was speechless, but the gears in his brain were twirling around. *She had a crush on me in high school,* he thought, *and I had absolutely no idea.* He wondered what it would have been like if he had been with Traci instead of Rhonda back then.

"Hey, guys," Michelle said across the expanse of the table. "It looks like Gram Missy's about to make a speech or a toast. That is Gram Missy, right?"

Chris nodded and then turned to face Aunt Missy along with everyone else. But his mind was on what Traci had just told him. Rhonda had controlled him for her own selfish purposes? How did he miss that? Looking back, it all seemed to make sense. But why? Then he realized she might have liked it that she broke him. They were both wild horses, and only one could prevail. And she was obviously the stronger of the two. For all of his confidence, charisma, and bad boy ways, she had won. But what he couldn't understand was, what did she win? Had she been hunting for food, or just to mount his head on her wall? The way it had felt that day, and the rest of that year, he would suspect his head had been a mighty trophy for her. He wondered if she still felt she carried it around with her to this day.

But then there was the other issue: Traci. Traci had liked him in high school. Traci had moved away, and he never knew. But in all the time he had known Traci, he'd had a girlfriend or she'd had a boyfriend, so would she ever have told him, or would he have left McKinney after senior year none the wiser?

But Traci had a boyfriend now. And even though she was hot, that was not cool. Chris had ended the best and healthiest relationship of his life because he couldn't stand the thought of being hurt again if she left him. And he had no patience for cheating. But no one was asking him to cheat right now. No one had asked him to compromise his values. And he didn't even really know if he was attracted to Traci. She was definitely nice to look at, and she still seemed really nice, but she lived in Michigan, and he hardly knew her, even back in high school.

Chris had seen Carl shake thoughts out of his head in the past, and now he tried to do that himself. All he did was get hair in his face. But he brought his attention back to Aunt Missy in time to hear her thanking everyone again for coming to this blessed event and then toasting the happy couple. Everyone applauded, and glasses clinked together. Chris picked up his water glass and clinked it with Carl's, then Traci's. Then he looked at Michelle and they both lifted their glasses to each other across the table. Then she turned to talk to Pete.

Traci leaned in closer to Chris as if to tell him her deepest secret. "You know who's gotten really cute since I left?" she confided. "Michelle."

Chris looked at the side of Michelle's face as she listened to Pete talk. "You think so?"

Traci nodded. "Yeah, you just don't see it because you see her all the time. I haven't seen her for three years. I mean, look at her hair. It's gorgeous. And so thick and shiny. She must have found the right product for it at some point. And she styles it so nicely. She used to just comb it or put it in a ponytail. And she started to wear her contacts after junior prom, and her eyes just sparkle now. And she still has that cute little spattering of freckles across her nose. But she's also, you know, got the whole body thing going on. Did you see her in that dress she's wearing tonight? She's totally curvy now."

Chris looked at Traci. "Really?" he said. "I'll have to take a closer look when she stands up. I mean, I guess I just haven't noticed, but again, I haven't been looking. Maybe I can't see her as well as you can because she's like three feet shorter than me."

Traci laughed. "Chris, she's about five feet tall. Just because you're like seven feet tall now does not make her four feet tall."

Chris laughed. He was enjoying this conversation. The only thing that would have made it better was a glass of wine with dinner. But the booze would come later. The Grams would have a fit if he tried to order a glass of wine with a fake ID.

Salads were delivered to the table, and they all started to eat. Chris turned his attention to Carl. "Are you having fun, man?" he asked.

Carl shrugged. "Yeah, for the most part," he said. "I keep looking to see if Scott shows up. Do you think he'll be here?"

Carl really wanted to see his brother, to reconnect as adults, to introduce him to his nephew, Drake.

"I don't know," Chris said truthfully. "I think he'll be there tomorrow. He said he would."

Carl sighed. "I'm glad I only have to do all this once," he said. "This takes a lot of energy. After we got married at the courthouse, we had soup and took a nap. That was nice."

Chris looked over at Kim. "But look at your bride," he said.

Kim was radiant, with Darlene and Sally now standing around her and laughing. Michelle came around and joined them, and then Traci got up. Kim took Drake from Aunt Missy and showed him off on her lap to her friends. They all made noises at him.

"She's having the time of her life, being the center of attention with Drake."

Carl smiled. "She is," he admitted. "That's what this is all about, really. This is for Kim."

After dinner was over, guests were invited to come to the front of the room and make toasts. Laine, Mrs. Drake, Mr. and Mrs. Mahoney, Gram Cissy, and Laine's seven-year-old son, Benjamin, came up one at a time to say touching and sweet things about the happy couple. Chris knew what was coming next. He felt something bounce off his arm and saw a straw wrapper fall to the table. He looked up to see Gram Cissy, motioning for him to get up and speak. She had good aim for an old lady. So he stood and walked to the front of the room.

"I guess as the best man, I'm obligated to say something," he started, "even though this means you'll have to hear me two days in a row, saying nice and sappy things about Kim and Carl."

The group laughed.

"But I think most of us don't mind hearing good things about these two. Carl is my first friend, my best friend, my cousin, and my brother. We don't technically even know what our exact genetic relationship is due to all the sibling marriages in our family . . ."

At this, he glanced at the Grams and Grandpa Clyde, and everyone laughed.

"But sometimes I think that things got shaken up somewhere, and somehow, Carl and I are supposed to be the identical twins. Maybe even Siamese twins. We've always been attached at the hip, and I'm pretty sure we have twin telepathy, just like our Grams. We've been apart now for almost two years, and I have to say, at first it was like someone had removed a vital part of my body and taken it three thousand miles away. It was a huge adjustment. But I went to see Carl and Kim in California right after they moved into their tiny little house in Laine's yard, and I got to see them in action, as a couple. And I knew after that that they were in the right place. It didn't matter where that place was, as long as they were together."

Chris heard some people saying "awww" and realized one of them was Kim.

"So that was when I knew we would all be okay. Carl and Kim were a team, they were happy, and ever since then, I've led their biggest cheering section. Now they've come home to celebrate with friends and family, and introduce Drake to his enormous clan, and we've got the band back together. I never want to let them go again, but when they do go, I know this: they are always with me in my heart, and I'm a better person for that. I love you guys so much. To Carl, Kim, and my godson, baby Drake."

Chris lifted his glass.

"Hear, hear!" several people shouted out, and then there was applause. Carl and Kim got up, and with Drake in Kim's arms, they both hugged Chris at once. Chris could see tears in both of their eyes, and he cursed his own Farmer sensitivity as he felt his tears wash down his cheeks.

When he went to sit down, Traci smiled at him. "That was really nice, Chris," she said. "You brought tears to my eyes. I didn't know that you and Kim had gotten so close."

"It didn't really happen until after they went to California," Chris explained. "You know, she makes Carl happy. That's what matters."

Traci gave his arm a squeeze. "You're a good guy, Chris Mahoney," she said softly, and then she turned to speak to Paul.

Darlene made the final speech, and then dessert was served. It was the famous Luigi's chocolate cake. Chris dug his fork into the cake, and suddenly remembered his cake date with Alison and her reaching out to take some of his cake when she had finished all of hers. He chuckled out loud. Then he looked up and realized that Michelle had witnessed the whole thing. She smiled kindly at him, and he smiled back.

Finally the event was complete. Now it was time for the bride and her maids, and the groom and his men, to go separate ways, and Kim and Carl said their good nights. Kim handed Drake to Gram Missy and went off to ride with Sally in James's car.

Carl turned to James. "Do you still have the Cruiser?"

"Yup, she's still all mine," James replied.

"Is the heating fan still busted?" Carl inquired.

James sighed. "Yeah, I've just never had that thing taken care of. I'll probably get a new car before I get it fixed."

Carl nodded. "Can I take a look at it sometime before we leave? I might have some ideas on how to make it work."

James looked at him. "Yeah, sure," he said. "That would be great! I wish you would have done that three years ago, but there's no better time than the present, I guess."

Carl laughed. "Back then, I might have been able to figure it out at some point, but basically it would have looked like Greek to me. Now I can read the Greek. The electrician training might be the key factor."

Chris, Carl, James, and Pete all piled into Chris's car and headed out for their bachelor night of fun. Chris had picked up some snacks, some beer, and some movies, and they were headed back to his apartment. He also had Liam's video game console. His roommates were all gone for the weekend and would not be officially living there until after all the wedding festivities were completed. The guys would hang out at Chris's, and then Chris would drive Pete and James back to their parents' houses. Then Chris and Carl would stay overnight at Gram Missy's house, so Carl could be there when Drake woke up in the morning. It would be a relatively mellow night.

They settled in with their drinks, ate snacks, and started to watch a semi-racy movie.

"I promised Kim that I wouldn't let Carl get wasted," Chris told them all. "And I'm driving you home and James doesn't drink, so Pete, it's really just you. Have at it. Drink as much as you want. As long as you're not late for the wedding tomorrow or barfing on the bride."

Pete laughed. "That's okay," he said. "I'll just keep pace with you guys. I'm okay with a mellow night. Hey, maybe someday one of us will get married, and we'll go to a strip club or a bar or something, but there's not a whole lot you can do when the groom is only nineteen years old."

"Hey, easy now," Carl warned. "I'll be twenty in September."

"It's only May," Chris reminded him.

"I have a wife and a child," Carl stated. "I think that buys me a few extra months."

They all laughed. They all still felt like high school kids. The phrase *a wife and a child* took some getting used to.

Pete took a swig of his beer and turned to Chris, the movie quickly forgotten. "So, Traci was laying it on kind of heavy with you tonight at dinner, Chris," he said. "I could have sworn you guys were flirting with each other, right there in front of her boyfriend."

"Yeah, I was kind of picking up on that from her, too," Chris admitted. "It was kind of weird. I got the impression from what she said that maybe they're not that serious. Maybe she just wanted to have someone come to the wedding with her, since the rest of us are gonna be so busy being in the wedding. But yeah, she also said some things that made me think she might have been into me in high school."

"Really?" James asked. "I never would have thought that."

"Yeah," Chris said. "Me neither. She had some definite feelings about Rhonda. Not good ones. She told me she would have treated me much better than Rhonda did."

"Dude, anyone would have treated you better than Rhonda did," James said.

Chris turned to face him. "Really? I mean, I was thinking about it, and I could see that maybe her being with me served her in some way, and the way she broke up with me was pretty lame, but I thought things were pretty good with us most of the time."

James shook his head. "Maybe, but I always had the feeling like she was running things, you know? Like if you were doing something, and she didn't like it, you would just stop, even if it meant you had to give up something you liked. She really seemed all about appearances. You're right when you say your relationship served her in some way. I think it helped her reputation for a long time, but then you mellowed out a lot junior year, and it changed for her."

"But she's the main reason I mellowed out," Chris protested at the same time realizing James was right. "Why didn't you say anything to me back then?"

James shrugged. "You wouldn't have listened. And even if you did, Rhonda would have denied it, and then she would have found some way for you to not hang out with me anymore. It was best for me to just leave things alone and let you work it out for yourself."

Chris nodded. "I guess so. I probably would have stopped talking to you on my own if you had said something to me. I wasn't ready to hear anything like that."

I'm not sure I am now, either, he thought.

Carl glanced around the room. "Hey, you know who I think looks really good now?" he said in a hollow attempt to change the subject. "I mean, I've been gone a while, but it seems like Michelle has really gotten pretty hot. It's like she's not that little girl from school anymore. I mean, maybe I thought of her as a little girl because she's so small, but she's really grown up now."

"Yeah," Pete agreed. "That hair. I wonder what it would be like to grab onto that."

Chris shook his head. "I feel like I'm missing something," he said. "Traci said the same thing at dinner tonight, and it kind of threw me. I mean, I know we always used to think of the girls as our sisters, but especially Michelle. She was always just there, kind of in the background. I'll have to take another look tomorrow at the wedding."

"Didn't the two of you hang out over Christmas?" Pete remembered.

"We did," Chris said. "We hung out in my dorm room. We had a good time, actually. She was funny, and we had a lot to talk about. I can't remember ever talking to her like that before."

"She was in your dorm room?" James asked. "And nothing happened with you two?"

Chris shook his head. "It was Michelle! We did a couple of bong hits with my roommate, and we laughed a lot. We were lying on my bed talking about patterns on the ceiling and about our relationships. God, I think we might have even been holding hands at some point!" He laughed.

Carl looked straight at Chris. "You were lying on your bed with her? And holding hands? You didn't tell me that. And you didn't even notice that she's hot now. Man, Alison must have really messed with your head. It sounds like you might have missed out on something there."

Chris couldn't believe what his friends were suggesting. "You guys are whacked," he said. "You're talking about Michelle Gorman. Even talking about this is making me uncomfortable. I don't know. Maybe I should ask Traci about her relationship with Paul."

"I was thinking of inviting him here tonight," Carl said, "since Traci is with the girls and he doesn't know anyone else. But then I thought that we don't know him either, and it might have kinda messed up the dynamic. It's a good thing, since we're talking about you and his girlfriend possibly hooking up."

"Oh, no," Chris said. "I wouldn't hook up with her. That's against the rules, and you all know that. I'm just sayin', you know, keeping my options open for the future, especially if they're not serious."

"Chris, you've gotta leave someone for me," Pete said. "You can't have all of our high school friends. Maybe I can have Darlene."

"They're not trading cards," James scolded. "These are our friends. Maybe neither of you get any of them."

"You and Carl did," Chris reminded him. "It's not too far-fetched an idea."

"I wanna play some video games," Carl said, reaching for the box on the table. "I don't get a lot of time to play at home since Drake, and these are much more sophisticated than mine."

The conversation about their female friends ended as they started to play video games. They played, ate, and talked, taking occasional drinks of beer until midnight, and then Chris drove everyone home.

Going to the Chapel, and...

Carl slept in the make-shift nursery with Drake so they wouldn't risk waking everyone in the morning or during nighttime feedings. But everyone was up by seven thirty. Gram made breakfast for the boys, and some of their aunts, uncles, and cousins who had also spent the night. Kim called at eight to check on her baby, and Aunt Missy assured her that he was fine and happy, as was Carl, and she would see her husband after she walked down the aisle. The wedding ceremony would be starting at three o'clock, so they had a lot of time to fill. James and Pete came over at noon with their tuxes. Gram Missy had arranged for a limo to bring them all to the venue. James's car would already be there with Sally, and Chris and Carl had dropped Chris's car off earlier in the morning. They were due at the venue at one o'clock for pre-wedding pictures. The bridal party would have theirs taken earlier.

The groomsmen and groom changed into their tuxes and fixed their hair. Aunt Missy fussed over them all, fixing hems and seams, and licking her finger to push down cowlicks. Gram Cissy, who had arrived with Grandpa Clyde, snapped pictures of the group as they prepared. When the limo arrived, she lined them up in front of it and had them pose some more.

Before they got in the car, Aunt Missy approached Carl and straightened his white bowtie one more time. "Carlos Jerome Bishop," she said softly as she put her hand on his cheek. "You are so handsome. Almost as handsome as my Cecil on our wedding day. I am so proud of you, Carl." She held him in a long embrace and then shooed everyone into the limo.

As they pulled into the parking lot, Chris could see the girls on the grass, finishing up with the photographer. Aunt Missy noticed, too. She reached up and covered Carl's eyes with her hand. "No peeking at your bride," she warned him. "It's bad luck."

Carl laughed but obeyed. Chris looked over at the girls. They were all there. Kim, the bride, stunning in all white. Sally, Michelle, and Darlene, in off-the-shoulder royal blue taffeta dresses that ended right below their knees, and elegantly coiffed hair and fancy makeup. And Traci, in a low-necked red silk dress, a sequined purse, and black high heels. His friends were a beautiful sight. He took a second look, and his eyes settled on one particular girl. And they stayed there. The girl looked up at the limo, made eye contact through the window, and smiled. Chris smiled back.

The limo stopped. "You gonna get out, man?" Pete asked him. He hadn't realized they had parked, and he was at the end of the row.

"Oh, okay," he said, and he slid out toward the door and his friends followed. They filed into the building to wait for their turn with the photographer.

They stood milling around in the lobby, Carl yanking at the neck of his shirt with nervousness. "Shouldn't we be out there by now?" he asked Chris. "He's not running late, is he?"

Chris put his hand on Carl's arm and was about to say some soothing words when the door opened from the front of the building and a man stepped inside. Carl and Chris turned to look.

"Scott!" Carl exclaimed. He rushed over to the door to his brother. "You made it!"

Scott smiled and pulled at his tie. It was a very old, wide tie, one not currently in style. "I see you're still a genius," he said. "I'm right here, man." He stuck out his hand, and Carl grabbed it. He shook his hand, then pulled his brother into an embrace. They clapped each other's backs with their hands a few times, then let go awkwardly.

"Hey, let me go find Drake," Carl said. "He should be with Gram. You need to meet your nephew." He rushed off toward the back of the building.

Scott looked over and saw Chris standing there, watching him. He reached out his hand. "Hey, loser," Scott said. "Good to see you."

Chris shook Scott's hand. "Hey, Scott," he said. "You're looking good. Carl was worried you might not make it. I'm glad you're here."

"Yeah, you know, Carl's my bro. I had to be here for his wedding. I wouldn't have missed it. You doin' okay over at Eastboro State?"

"Yeah, it's great," Chris started, but then Carl was back with Drake.

"Scott," Carl said proudly. "This is my son, Drake."

Chris had never heard Carl use the word *son* before, and it gave him chills. It seemed to have a similar effect on Scott.

Scott smiled brightly. "Hey, little dude," he said softly. "Man, he looks just like you," he told Carl. "Just like Grandpa Cecil. Poor guy!"

Carl laughed. "Do you want to hold him? He's pretty easygoing."

Scott held out his hands, and Carl handed Drake to him. Drake looked back over at Carl, and Carl smiled at him encouragingly. Drake looked at Scott, who arranged him in his arms and smiled at him.

"Hey Drake," he said softly. "I'm your Uncle Scott."

Drake reached up and grabbed Scott's nose. Chris laughed.

"He did that to me, too," he told Scott. "It means you're in."

Chris looked back at Carl. He was watching the scene wistfully. Scott was his closest biological relative, and he was at the wedding, and holding his baby. Chris noticed Aunt Missy out of the corner of his eye and turned to look at her. She was standing still, just observing, with tears running down her cheeks. She saw Chris looking.

"Damn these Farmer sensitivities," she mumbled, and then reached into her purse for her handkerchief.

The photographer came in looking for the groom and groomsmen. Carl looked around thinking quickly. "Scott," he said, "why don't you and Drake hang out for a bit, and then you can hand him back to Gram to bring to Kim. They haven't seen each other since last night, and Kim's probably going nuts. Then, in about fifteen minutes, come outside, and we'll grab a few pictures together, okay?"

The photographer snapped a few candid pictures of Scott holding the baby, and then asked Carl to put his arm around his brother. One more snap. Then Carl went outside with his friends in tow.

The girls were still milling around on the lawn. *The Girls*, Chris thought. *I'd better not say that out loud to them. They'd insist on being called The Women.* They all looked so nice in their wedding garb. He thought back to prom senior year and their kindness to him when he didn't have a date. They were all his date. And Traci, who was always kind and compassionate and listened to them all without judgment. It was amazing that she was there. He had never thought he would see her again.

The girls started to walk toward the back door en masse so the boys could start their photo session. One of the girls looked up at him as she passed and smiled. He smiled back. She looked so good. She was so close, he wanted to reach out and touch her dress, in a non-sexual way, but instead he held his hands behind his back as she passed by. Soon, the boys were alone on the lawn, and the photographer started to arrange groupings.

Scott came out for pictures, then the Grams, and all of the aunts and uncles from the groom's side. After the photos were done, the caterers cleared the yard to do last-minute preparations for the ceremony. The bridesmaids and groomsmen were given snacks and non-alcoholic drinks inside to get them through the ceremony. Kim was in the bridal parlor with her mother and sisters, and Darlene left to join them. There was a medical attendant sitting with Kim's father, Mr. Drake, in a quiet corner, and his two young sons sat beside them, talking softly to him.

Soon, a woman in a navy-blue dress, tall dark hair, granny glasses, and a clipboard came in and signaled Chris and Carl. The guests had all arrived. The seats were full. The quartet was playing soft classical music. It was time for Carl to walk to the front of the aisle to wait for Kim.

"Ready for this, man?" Chris asked him, feeling a surge of nerves himself.

Carl nodded, a bit too vigorously. "Yes, I am ready to marry my wife. In front of my son. Can't we just skip all this and go right to the wedding night?"

Chris smiled at his cousin and best friend. "You're living the dream, man," he told him. "Now go, get yourself double hitched."

He embraced Carl, and they held on for several seconds.

"I love you, man. You're like my brother," Chris whispered.

"I love you, too, Chris, and we *are* brothers." Carl put on a smile. "Will this do for the crowds?"

Chris nodded. "Knock 'em dead." And with that, Carl walked out the door.

The woman with the clipboard came back and arranged the wedding party by couple and then released them, couple by couple, to walk down the aisle as they had rehearsed. Chris and Darlene were the last of their friends to go. Chris looked back and waved at the Grams. They smiled and waved back, and he was out the door.

Chris took his position next to Carl and watched Kim's sisters and the Grams make their entrance. Once everyone was at the proper end of the aisle, the music stopped, everyone stood, and the music began again. Now Kim started down the aisle with her parents on either side of her. Kim was aglow with happiness, and she smiled brightly when she saw Carl waiting for her at the front. Carl looked at Kim, seeing her for the first time in her lacy white dress, and his jaw popped open. He was stunned. Chris could feel it, too. It was like their love was tangible. He watched as they neared each other and then clasped hands. He could see the relief on their faces, to be together again, after a long night apart.

Chris had to turn away from them for a moment to compose himself. That's when he saw her looking at him. That's when they made eye contact, and that's when she smiled. And he smiled back. And then he felt his knees go weak.

PART TWO

WHAT MAKES THE GIRL

A Girl is Born

She was born in March 1968, two days later than Chris Mahoney, in the same maternity ward, in the same hospital. She was born with a long, thick shock of hair in the middle of her head, and it reached straight up for the sky, making her look slightly like a troll doll. While her mother slept, she was placed in the glassed-in viewing area, where she drew attention from the gawking eyes.

"Look at that redheaded baby," viewers would say to other grandparents, aunts, and uncles who were grabbing peeks at their family's newest arrivals. "How much do you wanna bet that kid burns easily in the sun? And she'll probably freckle like a pear!" "A redheaded St. Patrick's Day baby! I wonder if the parents are Irish." "Someone needs to return that troll baby to its parents under the bridge." She was so unique that strangers snapped pictures so they could show their friends later. There was even a set of identical twin grandmothers fawning through the window for the baby's attention and taking snapshots of her newborn ginger head.

Mr. and Mrs. Gorman brought their tiny baby home when she was four days old, and they named her Michelle after the Beatles song. They introduced her to her older sister, Stephanie. Within one week, three-year-old Stephanie had gotten her hands on a pair of scissors and managed to cut three quarters of Michelle's red shock of hair right off the top of her soft, fragile head. Mrs. Gorman almost had a heart attack.

"She could have killed her!" she yelled in terror. "Or poked her eye out! Frank, what are we going to do? We can't let something like this happen again!"

Stephanie had been diagnosed with Down syndrome at birth. She had poor muscle tone and a heart defect. She had her first major heart surgery at age two. She met developmental milestones late. But her smile lit up her parents' hearts.

She had mastered hugging before she learned how to crawl, and her strawberry blond hair grew beautifully, straight down her back, just like her mother's. When she was born, her parents were both twenty years old and had been McKinney High School sweethearts. They didn't know exactly what to do with her, so they just did the best they could.

Frank and Gloria Gorman loved their firstborn daughter. They bought her cute, stylish clothes and new toys, brought her to doctors for treatment and out to dinner to show off her smile. They fed her and changed her and waited for her to learn new things. But she was extremely slow to learn. Then she got sick and stayed in the hospital for days, weeks at a time. They met with social workers and were offered help at home. They readily accepted the help, learned to better care for their child, and started to accept the inevitability that her future would not be the future they had imagined for her before her birth.

And they grieved that future. They'd had certain expectations when they started their family. They'd had an image of their perfect child. And although Stephanie was perfect in their eyes, they still craved a different kind of perfect. They longed for a child who would share their values and their dreams, someone they could teach their skills to, who would get excited about their passions. A child who would one day fall in love, get married, give them grandchildren, and possibly care for them in their old age. Michelle would become that child for them.

Mrs. Gorman started to fear for her baby's safety. She knew Stephanie meant no harm when she cut Michelle's hair, that she thought of her baby sister as a doll, a plaything, and maybe was trying to make her look pretty. But as much as she tried to teach Stephanie to be gentle with the baby, Stephanie did not comprehend. She would try to pick her up out of her bassinet by her feet and would pull her around by her clothes. She attempted to push cookies into the infant's mouth. She threw toys at the baby when she was placed on any surface or was being held by visiting relatives.

Mrs. Gorman was going to Eastboro State College to get her teaching degree. She had always dreamed of teaching elementary school children. She had completed three years of training and classes, and was coming close to the finish line, but after the birth of Michelle, changes needed to be made. She asked her parents and her husband what they thought she should do. She talked to her academic adviser about her options. And her decision was made. She withdrew from college and started her new career as a full-time housewife. She had to do whatever she could to protect her children.

The Gormans lived in a two-bedroom apartment by the Eastboro State College campus. They had been saving money for a house. They had been waiting for Mrs. Gorman's teaching income to start coming in so they could start shopping for their dream four-bedroom colonial home, near the city's best schools and in a safe and pretty neighborhood by a park. But now that dream was put on hold. They needed more room for their growing family, but they started to look into rentals instead. It made sense to look closer to Aries Corp, where Mr. Gorman was a junior manager in the parts department, so they found an old two-story house near Carson Lake, close to DeMarco Elementary School and Randall Junior High, just a bus ride away from McKinney High School, and they moved their young family in. Michelle got her own room, and Mrs. Gorman installed a chain lock high on her bedroom door to keep little hands from getting in during naps or after lights out at night.

Michelle grew but not a whole lot. She was a tiny little girl, and she looked fragile, but she was not. By the time she turned three, Mrs. Gorman was teaching Michelle to be gentle with Stephanie. She was training her to use her quiet voice indoors and sending her outside to run laps around the house for thirty minutes before dinner each night to give her mother some peace. Michelle adored her big sister and tried to engage her in her games and viewing her picture books with her. Stephanie became interested in the things her little sister could do, and tried, but often failed, to imitate her skills. But now she had a drive, a mission. She wanted to do what Michelle could do. It was time for her to start school.

Stephanie loved school and made lots of friends. She got stronger, and her speech improved. She showed interest in new skills and activities, and she started to thrive. And Michelle was thriving, too. They were best playmates. Michelle couldn't wait to start school like her sister and have as much fun and learn new things.

It wasn't until her first day in kindergarten that Michelle realized that she would not be going to the same school as her sister. She walked into her classroom in her pigtails and short plaid jumper and did not see Stephanie. Her sister was not at DeMarco Elementary. There was no one there at all like Stephanie. Her sister would not be her best school friend. In fact, Michelle didn't know anyone at all. She sat frozen in her seat in Mrs. Storm's kindergarten classroom and barely spoke a word the whole first day.

Michelle came home and cried to her mother. "I hate kindergarten!" she moaned. "No one likes me! I don't know anyone! I don't want to go back there. I want to go to Stephanie's school!"

Her mother hugged her and wiped away her tears. "I know, baby," she said. "I know you miss your sister. But Michelle, you can't go to Stephanie's school. It's a special school. It's only for kids with special needs, like Stephanie."

Michelle sniffed. "But I thought I was special!" she protested. "Grandma told me I'm a special little girl!"

"Oh, Michelle," Mrs. Gorman told her, "of course you're special. You're smart, and full of energy, and you're as cute and sweet as a little bug. But Stephanie needs a different kind of school, where teachers can help her learn things that don't come easy to her. Stephanie wants to learn like you, but she has to work so much harder to learn to do the things you can do without hardly even trying. She needs teachers who can spend extra time with her and friends who learn the same way she does. And she's doing so well there. But you, Michelle, you wouldn't be happy learning that way. You want to learn to read, write, and do math and science. And you will. You'll learn all the things you need to be able to do the things you want when you get bigger. Stephanie needs to learn skills to help her to do things now. Like tying her shoes by herself. And making herself a snack. See? Those are things you already can do yourself!"

"But who will be my friend?" Michelle cried.

Mrs. Gorman nodded. "Baby, you'll make friends very soon," she promised. "But I'll tell you what. Tomorrow, I'll give you an extra cookie in your snack. You look around your class, and you find one little girl that you might want to be your friend. Maybe pick someone who looks like they don't know anyone, too, and they need a friend. And then walk up to her and say hi and offer her your extra cookie. Will you try that?"

Michelle nodded. "Will they be chocolate chip cookies?"

Mrs. Gorman laughed. "I will give you chocolate chip cookies. Maybe you, Stephanie, and I should bake some when she gets home from school. What do you think?"

"Okay, Mommy," Michelle agreed.

The next day, Michelle looked around her classroom to try to choose someone to receive her extra cookie. She remembered Jamie, because that was her girl cousin's name, even though the Jamie at school was a boy. And Chris, because of Christmas. There was Stuart, Joann, Pete, Susie, and Fred. And then there was the girl with the beautiful long brown hair and the exotic name. She tried to remember her name. It was Darlene. Darlene. It sounded like a song. Darlene would get her extra cookie. Darlene would be her new friend.

Darlene was alone but didn't look like she felt lonely. In fact, Darlene looked like she heard music playing in the room when there was none. She swayed back and forth, and she bounced on her feet like she was dancing. Michelle removed her snack from her bag and shyly inched toward Darlene. Darlene looked up at her as she approached.

"Hello," Darlene said.

"Hi," Michelle said back.

"You're really tiny," Darlene said. "Are you four?"

Michelle gave her a look of disgust. "No way!" she protested. "I'm five! My mommy says I just grow slow."

"Oh," Darlene said. "My friend Kim said there's a boy in her class who's still four. Are your parents divorced?"

"No," Michelle answered. "I don't think so. What's divorced?"

Darlene looked at her and shrugged. "I'm not sure," she said. "But if your parents are divorced, your daddy moves to a new house and you get a new bed and you get to paint your new room pink. And sometimes you get a new puppy."

"Are your parents dehorsed?" Michelle asked.

"Yeah," Darlene said. "But I didn't get a puppy. I got a stuffed turtle."

"Oh," Michelle said. "Do you want a cookie? Me and my mommy and my sister made them."

"Okay," Darlene said. "Are they chocolate chip?"

Michelle went home after school and had a lot to tell her mother. "Darlene doesn't have any brothers or sisters. If you and Daddy get dehorsed, can I get a puppy or a stuffed turtle? Did you know there's a boy at my school who is four? Can Darlene come over and play tomorrow?"

Mrs. Gorman smiled. "It sounds like today was a good day. So kindergarten is getting better?"

"I love kindergarten!" Michelle exclaimed.

Mrs. Gorman laughed. "I'll see if I can find out Darlene's mother's phone number," she promised. "And Daddy and I are not going to get a divorce, but maybe we can still find you a stuffed turtle for your next birthday."

The Posse

Michelle and Darlene went out to the playground together. Darlene told Michelle everything she knew.

"See that boy over there? His name is Charlie. He goes to daycare after school. That's where you go after school if no one is home to take care of you. Sometimes he goes to his grandma's house, and other times he goes to the YMCA, and they give him crackers and apple juice. I've had to go there a few times. It's not that bad.

"That's my friend Kim over there on the swing. The boy that's pushing her is Carl. He's her hall buddy. Carl is the boy that is four. He's going to be five next week. Kim lives with her mom. Her mom and my mom are friends. Kim doesn't have a daddy."

Michelle was confused. "She doesn't have a daddy? Everyone has a daddy!"

"Not Kim," Darlene said with authority.

"Are her mommy and daddy div-horsed like yours?" Michelle asked.

"No," Darlene said. "She just doesn't have a daddy. She doesn't even have a daddy that lives in another house. She just lives with her mommy. Her mommy is really pretty. She has long brown hair and she wears dresses that look like shorts."

"Does Kim go to daycare?" Michelle asked.

"No, her mommy brings her to work sometimes. Or else she goes to her grandma's house."

"Why don't you play with Kim at recess?" Michelle asked. She suddenly worried that Kim would come and want Darlene to play with her and leave her all alone outside.

Darlene shrugged. "She wants to play with Carl," she explained. "He's her new friend."

"Oh," Michelle said, feeling relief.

Kim was pretty and was wearing a pretty dress. She had a ribbon in her hair. She was smiling at Carl. Carl was smiling back. Michelle didn't know any boys. She thought Carl looked nice.

They walked on. Darlene pointed. "Chris is in our class, and Carl is his cousin. And Jamie and Pete are best friends."

Michelle didn't understand how Darlene knew all of this information. They had only been in school for three days.

As the weeks passed, Michelle and Darlene played together on the playground at recess every day. They enjoyed the swings and the jungle gym and waited in line for the slide and the seesaw. Sometimes, they played with other children, as well, but Michelle stuck close by Darlene's side. Sometimes Mrs. Storm would bring balls outside, and they would all play together. Chris liked to kick the ball really hard, and this scared Michelle. Every time he got near the ball, Michelle would duck. The other boys were rough in their play as well, but they seemed gentle in class.

The weather got colder, and then came the rain. Recess would be inside in the rain. That meant they all played together in their classroom. Mrs. Storm entertained them with circle games and singing. Darlene always squeezed in next to Michelle in the circle, but Michelle would also sit next to other classmates. Her favorites were Jamie and Pete. They had known each other for a long time and were best friends. They pushed and shoved each other around in fun and made silly jokes. They would try to pull Michelle into their antics, and sometimes she felt silly enough to join in. Now on days when the sun shone on the playground, sometimes Jamie and Pete would run around near Darlene and Michelle. Darlene would roll her eyes at them and continue to play with Michelle, but Michelle could tell she liked the boys, too.

The winter passed quickly, and the snow around the jungle gym started to melt. The playground became a muddy mess, and the children waited for the sun to bake the ground dry and clean once more. The fifteenth of March arrived, and Chris's mother brought the class homemade cupcakes to celebrate his sixth birthday. Two days later, on St. Patrick's Day, Michelle's mother arrived to bring in cupcakes to celebrate her special day. She had decorated them with frosting and candy shamrocks. Mrs. Gorman stayed in the classroom for the celebration.

Chris came up to Michelle, with green frosting smeared above his lip. "I'm older than you," he said.

Michelle made a face and then took a dainty bite of her cupcake. "Only two days," she said. "That's not very much."

"Why does your mommy have such a big tummy?" Chris asked, wiping his mouth with the back of his hand.

"She has a baby in there," Michelle explained. "It's my baby brother or sister."

"I've seen people with babies in their tummies before," Chris told her. "I have a lot of baby cousins. I've never seen any mommies with such a big tummy. Maybe your mommy has more than one baby in there."

Michelle squinted at Chris. "More than one baby?" She shook her head. "Mommies don't have more than one baby."

Chris nodded. "My Gram has a dental twin."

"What's a dental twin?" Michelle asked.

Chris looked at her with authority. "Well, there are regular twins and dental twins. Twins are when the mommy has two babies at the same time. Dental twins are when the babies look zactly the same. Sometimes, the moms and dads can't even tell which baby is which. They go to school together, and share a room, and then sometimes they even get married together, like my Gram and my Aunt Missy. Aunt Missy is my cousin Carl's Gram."

Michelle shook her head. "No, we're not getting dental twins at my house. My mommy would have told me. And I have a sister, and we share a room, and we're not dental twins."

Chris shrugged. "I dunno. Your mommy is really big. Maybe she's having puppies instead."

Michelle's mouth dropped open. "Is not!" she protested. But Chris had already gone off to play with the other boys. "Hmph," Michelle said, folding her arms in front of her.

Michelle's mother did give birth to twins, and they were clearly identical, with fuzzy red hair and dark green eyes. They had strong lungs and sharp cries, and they needed a lot of attention. Michelle begged Darlene to invite her to her quiet house to play in the afternoons. Sometimes, Kim was there, too, and they all played together. Other times they played by themselves. And now Michelle had a new sort of respect for Chris Mahoney's insight about pregnant mommies.

In first grade, Michelle was still in class with Darlene, and Kim and Carl were in the other class. Most of the same kids from kindergarten were together, and Michelle was glad. She liked Darlene, and she was becoming friendlier with Jamie and Pete. She was even learning to tolerate Chris, who was also growing closer to Jamie and Pete. The class didn't feel so big and scary, and Michelle enjoyed the year. Kim and Carl still played together in the playground every day and walked down the hall hand in hand, even though no one told them to do that anymore. Michelle's twin brothers, Stevie and Sam, got much bigger and didn't cry as much. Michelle started to invite Darlene, and sometimes Kim, too, to come over after school, but never just Kim by herself.

Her friends had never met Michelle's big sister, Stephanie. Then one day in the winter of their first-grade year, Stephanie's school was closed for the day for teacher training, and Stephanie was home all day. Michelle brought her friends to her shared room, and Stephanie was there, sitting on her bed, looking at a First Words book. She looked up when they came in and smiled.

"Chelle," she said. "You have friends. Can we play?"

Before Michelle could respond, Darlene turned to her. "Is that your sister Stephanie?" she asked. "Why does she talk so funny?"

Michelle glared at her. "She does not talk funny," she protested. "She just talks like Stephanie. She just wants to play with us."

"But she's a lot older than us," Darlene protested. And then she whispered. "And she's reading a baby book."

"She looks kind of funny," Kim added. "Is she dopted?"

"No!" Michelle exclaimed. "She's my sister and she's my best friend. And she has red hair like me. And she's special, right, Stephanie?"

Stephanie nodded. "Yeah. I'm special, and I go to special school. Michelle is special too, but not the same special."

"See?" Michelle said. "Let's just play and she can watch, and maybe she can play too. And Steph likes to hug, too."

Kim shrugged. "Can we talk to her?"

"Of course you can talk to her," Michelle responded. "She's a person!"

Stephanie laughed. "I'm a person but I want to be a princess."

"A princess?" Darlene asked. "You can't be a princess if your daddy isn't a king."

Kim glared at Darlene. "So I can't be a princess because I don't have a daddy? That's not fair."

"You can marry a prince!" Stephanie said with glee.

"I don't know any princes," Darlene said, "and I know my daddy's not a king. He's an underwear writer."

Michelle laughed. "There's no such thing!" she said knowingly.

"There is so because my daddy said it," Darlene insisted.

No one mentioned Stephanie's differences anymore that day.

Two months later, Darlene told Michelle Kim's big news. "Kim's mommy is getting married, and Kim is getting a daddy, and a little brother and sister who are already born, and they're all moving to a new house that's right near mine."

"You can get a new daddy?" Michelle asked.

Darlene grunted at her. "Michelle, it's not a new daddy, it's her first daddy. I told you she didn't have a daddy at all. And the daddy's gonna dopt her. She loves him. They're gonna have a big wedding and her mom is gonna look like a real princess in a white dress."

"Wow," Michelle said.

"And Kim gets to wear a fancy dress and carry flowers, and my mommy and I get to go watch."

"Can I come?" Michelle asked.

Darlene shook her head. "I don't think so. I'm going because I'm Kim's best friend. But you aren't her best friend, so I don't think you're invited."

"I thought you were my best friend," Michelle said.

Darlene sighed. "Michelle, I'm your best friend, but Kim is my best friend, and I'm her best friend. I've knowed Kim longer."

"So I'm not anyone's best friend?" Michelle asked sadly.

Darlene shrugged. "I don't know, maybe Stephanie?"

"She's my sister," Michelle responded, feeling deflated. "I want a school best friend."

"Maybe Jamie or Pete will be your school best friend," Darlene suggested. "But I'm still your recess best friend. Let's go down the slide." She ran off toward the play equipment. Michelle stood still a few seconds, then ran after her.

Second grade was when everything started to change. Michelle was not looking for change, but she still found it at school. She and Darlene were still in the same class, but now, Jamie, Chris, and Pete were in the other class with Kim and Carl. She was glad to have Darlene with her again, but she missed Jamie and Pete. They were fun, and they could be sweet. And they always invited her to play with them, even when she didn't want to. Now all the boys she knew were gone.

Michelle and Darlene still played together every day, but then something else changed. Chris was in class with his cousin Carl now, and he became different. He gathered the other boys and directed them at playtime and in the playground. Carl would follow Chris around like a puppy, responding to his every word. The boys would run around together in a tight little pack. But the strangest thing was what happened to Kim. When Carl started to follow Chris, Kim started to follow Michelle and Darlene. Not only follow them, but chase them angrily, insisting that they wait for her and let her play with them at recess. At first, they resisted. Kim seemed different. She didn't seem so happy anymore. She wasn't smiling like she did when she was with Carl. And Carl didn't even seem to notice that his friend was so upset.

After some time, Michelle, Darlene, and Kim became a threesome on the playground. And in no time at all, Kim was directing their play. She told them where they were going to go and who they would be talking to. She told them whose house they should go to and who they should be friends with. And then one day, there was a new word. Chris told the boys that the girls had cooties. Michelle had no idea what cooties were, but she knew she didn't have them, and she didn't like being told she did. And neither did Kim. Kim just kept getting angrier and angrier, until one day, she pushed Carl over in the sandbox. She walked away smiling, until a teacher led her inside to have a little talk with the principal.

As the next few years went by, they were all in different classes, at different times, but the groups of friends stuck together. Chris started calling the boys his posse, and the name stuck. So Kim dubbed her group a posse, too, and told her friends that the posse boys were off-limits as friends. But sometimes, when Kim didn't know she saw her, Michelle saw Kim staring at Carl and looking sad. Michelle still said hi and smiled at Jamie and Pete, and they would smile back, but things had clearly changed. It was always the boys against the girls, or the other way around, and they even played a game with those names on the playground. It was the whole third grade playing the game, but the posses would focus on chasing each other. And Kim took her role seriously. One time, she actually caught Pete, knocked him over, and he got hurt. Kim laughed. Pete cried. For the first time, Michelle felt disgust toward one of her friends.

Darlene still considered she and Kim to be best friends. And the boys were gone. Everyone else seemed to avoid the posse girls because they were slightly afraid of Kim's wrath. Michelle remained in the posse, because she was too afraid of being left alone to walk away. She never wanted to be left alone.

The Accident

During the summer of her tenth year, Michelle went to sleepover camp for two weeks. She went swimming, jumped on a trampoline, and sang songs around a campfire with groups of other girls. She had fun, but was happy to be coming home, to sleep in her own bed, and see her family.

But when she and her father arrived home and finished unpacking her belongings from the car, her mother and father sat her down at the kitchen table for a serious talk.

"Michelle," her mother started, "while you were away, there was a bad accident over at Kim's house, and her father was seriously hurt."

Michelle gasped. "Oh my God, her dad? Mr. Drake? He didn't die, did he?"

Mr. and Mrs. Gorman glanced at each other, and then looked back at Michelle. "No, baby," Mrs. Gorman said. "He didn't die, thank goodness, but right now, he's in a coma. Do you know what that means?"

"Does it mean he's asleep and he can't wake up?"

Mrs. Gorman nodded. "Yes, he's at the hospital, and they're taking good care of him, but he's not waking up. They're pretty hopeful that he will wake up again, but they have no idea what he'll be like when he wakes up. Like if he'll be able to walk, or talk, or be able to do other things he could do before without help. We just need to wait and see."

Michelle sighed. "Poor Kim!" she said. "Did she get hurt in the accident too?"

"No," Mr. Gorman told her. "Mr. Drake fell off a ladder and hit his head on the concrete patio floor. He also broke several bones. Kim was in the yard with him, but she didn't see it happen. And you know that Kim's mother was expecting a baby. Well, she's had the baby, and things are really hectic for their family right now. Everyone's trying to help by watching the kids, and Darlene has been with Kim most of the time. Her mom is helping by going to the hospital with Mrs. Drake when she can. And your mother has been bringing them some meals when she can."

"Michelle," her mother said, "things are going to be really hard for Kim and her family for some time, and we're all going to have to do what we can to help. How would you feel about going over to spend some time with Kim before school starts back up, just to keep her company?"

Michelle hesitated. "Would Darlene be there, too?"

"Well," Mrs. Gorman said, "it would make more sense for you to be there when Darlene wasn't there, so Kim wouldn't be alone. Is there a problem with that?"

"Oh, no," Michelle said quickly. "No, it's not a problem. I can do that. Just let me know when."

Mrs. Gorman stood and kissed Michelle on the head. "You're a good girl, Michelle Gorman. We really missed you when you were gone. Why don't you go upstairs and say hello to Stephanie. She'll be so happy to see you. And we can talk more about this later, okay? Let me know if you have any questions about Mr. Drake, and we'll let you know if we get any news."

Michelle stood, too. "Okay, Mom. Thanks."

She headed for the stairs and to go see her sister. Her heart was pounding fast, and she wasn't sure why. She felt sad for Kim, but she also had a healthy fear of being alone with her. But she had no idea what Kim would be like now. Things might be changing drastically again.

Michelle went to Kim's house on Thursday. Kim was home with her Grandma Susan, and her four-, three-, and one-and-a-half-year-old brothers and sister. The newborn baby was with her mother. Kim was in the den watching TV with the older two kids. Her grandmother was giving the toddler his lunch.

"Hi Kim," Michelle said as she walked into the room.

Kim looked up at her. "Oh, hi," she said. Kim reminded Michelle of a balloon that had been left out overnight in the heat. "Thanks for coming, Michelle. My mom doesn't want me to be alone, I guess. I didn't realize you were back from camp."

Michelle walked quietly across the carpet and sat down next to Kim on the couch. She held her hands together on her lap. "Kim, I-I'm so sorry about what happened. I—"

Kim put her hand on Michelle's knee. "You don't have to say all the things the adults say," she said. "It's okay. I'm okay." She had tears in the corners of her eyes, but they didn't fall. "He's gonna be okay, I know he will. And hey, we have a new baby, that's pretty cool, huh?"

Michelle gave a timid smile. "Yeah, that is cool. What's the baby's name?"

"Sophia," Kim answered. "Like Sophia Loren, the actress." She gestured at the other small children in the room. "I don't think you've met Chip and Stella. My brother and sister. And the little guy with my grandma is Zachary. They're all pretty much clueless about what's going on. They keep asking where Mommy and Daddy are, and we just keep telling them they'll be home soon."

"This is all so awful, Kim," Michelle said.

"Yeah," Kim agreed. "It is. They won't let me go see him in the intensive care unit. No kids. Even though Sophia is there with Mom. So I just have to sit here all the time and wait. And play with the kids. And wait some more."

"Um," Michelle started, "do you want to do something while I'm here? Like go for a walk? Or play a game or something?"

"Do you know how to make cookies?" Kim asked. "We don't have any cookies, and people keep forgetting to get any. We have tons of tuna casserole, but no cookies. And the kids love cookies."

"I can make cookies with you," Michelle said, "if you have the right stuff for them, and your grandma can turn on the oven. In my house it's grown-ups only to touch the oven because of my sister, you know?"

"Yeah, I know."

They made the cookies quietly, eating the dough along the way, and then they shared them with the kids.

The next week, Kim met Michelle at the door.

"He woke up," she said. "Not all the way, but at least he's not asleep anymore. Let's make brownies."

They made the brownies, and Kim told Michelle a story. It was a true story about her mother and how she got pregnant when she was nineteen years old. How her biological father got mad when he found out, slammed things to the floor, and then walked out the door and never came back.

Suddenly, it made sense to Michelle. *It's not that she didn't have a daddy,* she thought, remembering what Darlene had told her when they first met. *It's just that she's never met her dad.* In a lot of ways, Michelle thought maybe that could be worse.

The next week, Kim was out in the yard playing with Stella and Chip.

"He's been talking! Well, not very well, but if he keeps improving, they're going to move him to a rehab place next week so he can get better. Grandma got out the special tools. Let's go make a cake with fancy frosting."

This week's story was about Chip and Stella's mother and how she decided she didn't want to be a mother anymore. Kim told Michelle all the details of what happened in the hospital after Stella was born and how Mr. Drake took control of the situation and made it through. "Next week, I'll tell you what happened next."

They finished the cake, and Grandma Susan took a picture of them in front of it. Then they all had a piece to celebrate Mr. Drake's continuing recovery.

Michelle started to look forward to the visits to Kim's house. The baking was fun, the snacks were delicious, and she loved to listen to Kim tell stories. Her stories came alive with her words. Michelle couldn't wait to hear what came next.

The next week, they were back to cookies, this time with peanut butter, and the story of how Mrs. Drake and Kim met Mr. Drake, and it was love at first sight. It was so romantic. Michelle wanted to applaud when they got to the part about the wedding, but she didn't. She remembered that she hadn't been invited to the wedding, and she still harbored a small grudge. But the story was wonderful, just the same.

The next week was the last week before school started, and they would be in fifth grade. When Michelle got to Kim's house, Mrs. Drake was there, and Kim was on the couch in tears.

"Michelle, I'm so sorry," Mrs. Drake said when she opened the door. "I meant to call your mom to cancel today, but I just . . . listen, we got some discouraging news today about Mr. Drake, and Kim's feeling sad. We all are."

Michelle felt a rush of dread. "Is he gonna be okay?" she dared to ask.

Mrs. Drake smiled at her. "We just don't know everything yet. He's doing much better in a lot of ways, but he's struggling to remember some things. Kim saw him this morning, and he had forgotten who she was for a little bit. Then he remembered, but it was very hard for Kim. I think maybe we should just call your mom and ask her to come back to get you. I'm so sorry, Michelle."

"It's okay," Michelle said as Mrs. Drake went into the kitchen to the phone. Michelle walked slowly over to Kim. "Are you okay?"

Kim looked up. Tears streamed down her face. "No, not really," she said. She sniffed. "But I will be. I need to help my dad get better, so I have to be strong. I have to learn to take care of him when he comes home, to help my mom. Look, my sister Sophia is here. Come see her."

Michelle eased over to the bassinet near the couch. Inside, she saw a tiny little baby that looked to be made of porcelain, but she could see her stomach rise and fall as she breathed. She was asleep and her mouth formed a perfect "o" shape. She had very short, sandy brown hair covering her head.

"She's so beautiful," Michelle whispered.

Kim nodded. "She looks just like Dad," she said. Then she started to sob.

Mrs. Drake came back in from the kitchen. She went to Kim and wrapped her arms around her and made soothing sounds. Then she said, "Michelle, your mom will be here in a minute. Would you mind waiting outside?"

Michelle nodded and gave a little wave. "Bye Kim," she said. "I guess I'll see you at school next week." She stepped outside to wait for her mother.

When school started, Kim was there, but she was subdued. She went to class, and she sat with Michelle and Darlene at lunch, but she didn't say much. She didn't mention her father or make any plans for what they would be doing at recess. When recess time came, they all went outside and sat on the grass by the backside of the playground under the big oak tree. Then Kim started to tell a story about her Grandma Susan and her Grandpa Joe, who had died when she was four. She told them about how they bravely made the decision to move from Wisconsin to Massachusetts as a newly married couple so Grandpa Joe could find work in the factory to support their family. She remembered Grandpa Joe as a jovial man with a soft and squishy lap, who always gave her caramels.

As the days went by, there was more of the same. Kim was present, but she wasn't always alert, and Michelle and Darlene didn't dare go off and leave her alone. Sometimes, the posse boys would come by and taunt them, but even they could tell when enough was enough and went away. Michelle could often see Carl glancing back at Kim with concern as they left, but Kim didn't seem to notice.

Then, right before Christmas break, the news was good.

"He'll be home for Christmas!" Kim exclaimed.

"He's all better?" Darlene asked.

"Well, as better as he can get at rehab, at least," Kim answered. "They're gonna have people come over to help us at first and teach us what to do. But he'll be at home, and we can see him whenever we want!"

All of the girls smiled. Michelle wondered if Mr. Drake could remember things now. That would be so great! She would love to get back to baking at Kim's house and hearing her stories and maybe even playing with the kids. Or maybe they could all go to her house again and include Stephanie in their fun.

But that's not how things turned out. While Kim was finally happy at school, and the girls could talk and be active on the playground again, Kim spent all of her time away from school helping her mom with her dad and taking care of her siblings. Michelle and Darlene went back to going back and forth to each other's houses, and Darlene was not too interested in baking. But she did like to gossip. She seemed to know everything, so soon Michelle knew everything, too. She noticed that sometimes, when they were out on the playground, Darlene would be talking to her, but she would have her head pointed in a different direction. She soon figured out that Darlene was directing her ear toward other peoples' conversations, in attempts to hear what juicy tidbits of gossip they could offer. Michelle tried it too, but there was too much background noise to distract her from the gossip. She had to depend on Darlene to keep her in the know.

"I heard my mom talking to Mrs. Daniels on the phone last night," Darlene told her. "She said that Kim's dad can only remember things that happened before the accident. Sometimes, he can remember for a few minutes, but then he forgets again. He can't even remember that they had their baby!"

"That's so sad!" Michelle said.

"And people come to visit them, and he doesn't know who they are. I can't imagine."

"Me neither." Michelle thought of what it would be like if her dad couldn't remember her anymore. Even the thought made her want to cry.

Darlene went on. "And I heard Theresa Gallo telling Mary Sumner that Johnny Stoner's parents are getting a divorce."

"Johnny Stoner? Oh no! He's so close to his dad. I wonder if he'll go live with him."

Darlene shook her head. "Theresa said the mom's not gonna let him have a thing. I guess they're really mad at each other."

"Yikes!"

Michelle noticed something interesting about people when they gossiped. They tended to lean in close to the person they were talking to and hush their voices. Her mother even did it on the phone.

"Did you hear about what happened at Grace's party last weekend?" she heard her mother saying to her friend Mary on the phone. Her mother leaned away and cupped her hand over the mouthpiece. "Chuck Waterman got a little tipsy and gave up some private details about his wife's father's financial situation. Gina Waterman was not very happy, to say the least."

Michelle noted that cupping her hand over the phone receiver did nothing to mask what her mother was saying. She took mental notes. She might not be good at getting the gossip, but she could be a pro at passing it on efficiently.

Fifth grade ran into sixth, and life went on. The girl posse was still together, and the boy posse was still running wild through the hallways and playground, but they all assumed a cool air of tolerance for each other. Darlene and Kim started to grow taller and leaner, and Kim started wearing a bra. One week later, a bra magically appeared under Darlene's white shirt as well. Michelle wanted one, too, but when she looked down at her body, there was nothing for a bra to hold up. Michelle was the shortest, smallest girl in the whole sixth grade. And the freckles on her nose made her look about eight years old. It wasn't helping that the boys looked older, too. Soon, they would all be starting junior high, and Michelle worried that people might stop her in the hallway to ask if she was in the right place and try to direct her back to elementary school. She protested to her mother.

"I'm tiny!" she pouted. "Everyone else is growing! Pretty soon, even Stevie and Sam are gonna be taller than me."

Mrs. Gorman shook her head. "Stevie and Sam are five, Michelle. Don't be so dramatic. You're just a bit behind with growing. You'll catch up to everyone else."

Michelle rolled her eyes. "When? When I'm thirty? Can't we do something?"

Her mother made her an appointment with the pediatrician. She ran labs and took measurements. "There's nothing wrong with you, Michelle," Dr. Chen told her. "You're on the very low end of the normal growth chart. Your bones look good, and you are very proportional. You're a very healthy young lady."

Michelle sighed. "Isn't there something I can do to make myself grow more?" she begged. "Like a stretching machine? Or a special vitamin?"

Dr. Chen smiled at her. "No, nothing like that exists. But you can make sure you eat lots of protein and fruits and vegetables. And drink your milk. It won't make you tall, but it will make you strong."

So Michelle focused on strong. Strong body, strong opinions, and strong attachments. If she was going to be small, she was going to be outspoken. She would be heard and understood. She lifted phone books up and down over her head to help grow her muscles. She read books to expand her mind. If she disagreed on a topic, she debated. And if she made a friend, she made one for life.

And the Child Shall Grow

During the summer between sixth and seventh grade, Michelle went back to camp, this time for a month. She ran and she played tennis and rode on her first horse. She swam and she canoed and excelled at Capture the Flag. She made friends and did crafts and wrote letters home to Stephanie. When she came home near the end of August, she was feeling confident and strong. She was ready for the new year, at a new school. There would be new kids to meet, along with her old and faithful friends. Her mother took her shopping for clothes and shoes, and even brought her a pint-sized training bra. She picked out the outfit she would wear on the first day and waited.

On the first day of school, she walked for the first time around Carson Lake and went in through the front door of Randall Junior High. The first boy she saw in the hallway had a tiny, fuzzy mustache on his upper lip. He headed down the hall toward what appeared to be the office. A teacher was directing new students into the auditorium to wait for further instructions. Michelle walked in and looked around. She couldn't find Kim or Darlene, but she did see Jamie. He was standing up against the side wall with his foot propped up, chewing on a bent straw. She approached him.

"Hi Jamie," she said timidly.

Jamie took the straw out of his mouth. "Hey Michelle, what's up?" he said, smiling down at her. He had grown a little bit over the summer, but he was still one of the smaller boys. He looked relieved to see someone he knew.

"Have you seen Darlene or Kim?" she asked.

Jamie shook his head. "Nah, no one's here yet. I haven't seen my friends, either. I have no idea what we're supposed to do. I mean, do you know where to go when the bell rings?"

Michelle shook her head. "I didn't get a letter in the mail this year like we did at DeMarco. I think we get assigned to a homeroom, but I don't know where they are."

Just then, Kim and Darlene walked through the auditorium door. Michelle felt relief, but then the girls took a right turn away from where she was standing and headed for the other side of the room. They sat down in the seats. Kim said something to Darlene, and Darlene covered her mouth and giggled. They didn't even look around for her. She and Jamie looked at each other. Jamie gave her a look of sympathy. Michelle shrugged. She was strong; she could handle anything. These were her old friends.

"I'm gonna go see my friends," she said to Jamie, starting to walk away. "Good luck with junior high, Jamie. See you around." Jamie gave her a wave and put the straw back in his mouth.

Michelle walked around the back of the auditorium and approached her friends. "Hi guys," she said.

They both looked up. "Oh, hi Michelle," Kim said. "We were wondering where you were."

Michelle squinted at Kim through her glasses and then sat down in the row in front of her. She turned around to look at her friends. "Yeah, I was over talking to Jamie," she said. "Did you guys walk here together?"

Darlene nodded. "We've been doing everything together," she said. "Kim slept over my house the other night, and we went shopping for clothes together at the mall. By the way, I like your shirt."

Michelle looked down at the loose floral-patterned smock she was wearing over her jeans. Then she looked at her friends. They were both wearing tighter-fitting solid-colored shirts tucked into their jeans, with belts around their slim waists. Michelle could feel herself turning red in the face. She was not only tiny, but it appeared she was also dressed like a third grader.

"Thanks," she said graciously. "I like your hair."

Darlene and Kim now both had layered bangs, and they had them combed back stylishly. Michelle hadn't gotten a haircut in years, except a trim here and there to even things out.

"Thanks," Darlene replied, touching her head. "My mom brought me and Kim to her hairdresser to get new school hair. She even put us under the big hair dryers! It was pretty awesome."

"It was wicked awesome," Kim corrected, and Darlene giggled.

Michelle smiled at her friends. "Cool," she said. "When I was at camp, we sometimes had to wash our hair in these huge trough sinks. It was kind of fun, but you'd always end up getting your clothes all wet."

Kim looked at Michelle. "Wow," she said. "That's kind of gross. Everyone washed their hair in the sink? Didn't they have showers at your camp?"

Michelle looked right back at Kim. "Of course they had showers!" she retorted. "But sometimes, you'd want to wash your hair after swimming in the lake, or sometimes your hair would smell like campfire smoke, and you didn't want to wait until your shower time."

Darlene smiled at her. "It sounds great," she said. She turned to Kim. "Speaking of showers, remember that night my mom dropped us off at Friendly's, and we got Fribbles, and we saw Mike Franco, and his little sister knocked over that big glass of ice water onto his lap?" She grabbed Kim's elbow, and they both laughed. "The look on his face was awesome."

Michelle rolled her eyes. "Yeah, wicked awesome," she said under her breath. She sat there for five more minutes listening to her friends talk about all the great things they had done together without her while she was off at camp. Then the bell rang.

A tall, slim woman with cropped gray hair had positioned herself in front of the auditorium, and now she grabbed a microphone and said, "May I have your attention, please!" Everyone hushed and looked up front. "I'm Mrs. Coleman," she told them. "I am the downstairs vice principal, so I'll be in the downstairs office, and I will be responsible for you seventh graders through the year. When you get called to the office, that means you are getting called to me. Right now, we need to get you all sorted and to your new homerooms. Then your homeroom teachers will give you further instructions."

She put reading glasses on her nose and picked up a piece of paper. "I will read the list of class assignments now. Please stay in your seats until I complete reading the list, and then you may proceed to your groups. Students with last names beginning with the letters A–C will be in room 101 with Mrs. Lopez. Teachers, please raise your hands so the students can see where you are. Last names D–F, room 102 with Mrs. Fox. G–J, room 103 with Mr. Harris."

Michelle closed her eyes. *Darn it!* she thought. Kim and Darlene were in the same homeroom. She just missed their classroom by one letter. It was so unfair! She quickly went through the last names of the boy posse members in her head. Not even one of them would be in her homeroom. Carl and Pete would be together, and so would Chris and Jamie. Everyone got to be in pairs with their friends. Except Michelle.

She looked over at Mr. Harris. He was a short, stout, balding man of about forty, wearing a bright yellow short-sleeved button-down shirt with pens and pencils in the front pocket and tan pants. Michelle had never had a man for a teacher before. She hoped he was at least friendly. He must have liked kids if he became a teacher. She just hoped he was nice to tiny little redheaded girls with freckles and an attitude.

Michelle said goodbye to Kim and Darlene and was actually slightly relieved to get away from their annoying giggling and all the bragging about how close they had gotten over the summer. She walked over to the group surrounding Mr. Harris, who had started to count heads.

"Twenty-three," he said. He looked at his roster. "I should have twenty-four. Maybe someone's not here today or moved away. Let me count again." He lifted his right hand and moved his lips as he pointed to each student. He stopped when he got to Michelle. "Oh, there you are," he said with a chuckle. "Number 24. I couldn't see you at first behind everyone else because you're so tiny. Okay, everyone, follow me. Stay together. No wandering away in the hallways."

Michelle stood frozen in her spot. A few of her homeroom classmates glanced at her with grins as they passed by. One boy looked her right in the eyes and snickered. "Hey there, Tiny," he said, and the students walking near him laughed.

Michelle sulked alone at the back of the group. She couldn't believe she had started the day in a good mood, feeling optimistic about starting the new year. Now she wished she had never gotten out of bed.

When they got to the classroom, they were seated in rows in alphabetical order. Then they were handed personalized daily schedules. Michelle noticed that she had Mr. Harris for math, first period. She heard the other students talking and found out that they all seemed to have the same schedule for their first four classes. Mr. Harris for math, Mrs. Fox for science, Mr. Crisp for English, and Mrs. Lopez for social studies. The classrooms were all at this end of the hall, and the students rotated from class to class in a circle. Kim and Darlene would have the same teachers, just during different periods. They wouldn't be in any of their main classes together.

Michelle saw she had art class after lunch, and that was the first thing that day that excited her. After that was French with Mrs. Baird, and then home economics with Mrs. Lamb. Once a week she would have gym class and also music with Mr. Russo. Maybe she would know *someone* in one of her afternoon classes. Or else she would be forced to make new friends. And she didn't have any extra chocolate chip cookies this time.

She sat with Kim and Darlene at lunch, and they were a bit more inclusive than they had been that morning. Michelle figured maybe they had just been nervous for their first day but were now feeling more settled in. They asked Michelle about camp, and they filled her in on other fun things they had done. Michelle asked about Mr. Drake, and for the first time that day, she felt she saw the old Kim.

"He asked me who Sophia was the other day," she said. "She's two now. He has no idea who she is. And he asked Stella where Stella was. He asked *her* where *she* was. That was so weird."

Michelle gave her a look of sympathy. "Wow, Kim, that's intense. What did Stella say to him?"

"She said, 'I'm right here, Daddy,' and he smiled and said, 'Oh, okay.' Then she just went away to play. She doesn't get it yet. But she will when she gets older. Poor kid." Kim took a bite of her mashed potatoes. "I have gym class next. I hope they don't make us actually do anything today. What do you guys have?"

"I have art," Michelle said.

"I have Spanish," Darlene said. "I wanted French. Maybe they'll let me take it next year."

"It would have been nice to have you in French class," Michelle said sincerely. "It would be nice to know anyone in any of my classes."

Darlene smiled. "You'll meet people quickly, Michelle," she reassured her. "You're a nice person. People will like you."

Michelle smiled back, grateful for Darlene's kind words.

When Chelley Met Sally

After lunch, she found the art room. It was a large, messy classroom close to the cafeteria. Mrs. Darcy was standing by an easel in a paint-covered smock, hands together in front of her, watching the students file in. "Take a seat, girls and boys," she said as the second bell rang. "You can change seats later if you would like, but for now just be seated."

Michelle sat down at a table near the door, and three other students rushed into the other seats at the table. "Welcome everyone," Mrs. Darcy said. "Welcome to art class. Art class is not about having talent in art. It's about putting your heart into what you make and working hard. As long as you complete your assignments and do your best, you will do well in art. Today, we're going to do a self-portrait in paint, including objects and people that represent you."

She held up a piece of paper.

"Here is my self-portrait. As you can see, this is me in the middle. In my hand is a paint palette. At my feet, there are cats and squirrels. And over here is a red Ford Mustang convertible. I don't own one, but I dream that one day I will. After everyone is done, you will each use your work to introduce yourselves to the class, so keep that in mind while you're painting. I would like one person from each table to come up and pour some paint for your group, and another to come rip the paper off the roll. When you are all back in your seats, you will work quietly, and I will put on some music for you to work by."

Michelle stood up to get the paint, and another girl from her table went for the paper. When they returned to the table, they each spread the paper out in front of them, and everyone grabbed a paint brush. Mrs. Darcy walked over to a radio and hit a button. Music filtered into the room.

A girl sitting next to Michelle perked up with the music. "Oh, I love this song," she said. "'Tainted Love!'" She started to sing along. Michelle recognized the tune and started to sing along too. "You know this song, too?" the girl asked.

"Yeah," Michelle said. "We used to hear it at camp this summer. All the girls would sing it. It was like our theme song."

"I heard it at camp too!" the girl told her. She smiled. "My name's Sally. I went to Camp Larson in New Hampshire."

Michelle smiled back. "I'm Michelle," she said. "I went to Camp Newsome in New Hampshire. Was your camp on Lake Winnipesaukee?"

"No, mine was on Lake Ossipee," Sally said. "Did you love camp? I did. I had my birthday there. They actually had a cake for me! And I got to ride a horse named Princess."

Michelle was slightly taken aback by the force of Sally's verbal output. "Yeah," she said. "I loved camp. I rode horses too. I liked playing tennis."

The song on the radio ended, and a new one came on. The two girls looked at each other and spoke at once. "'Flock of Seagulls'!" They both laughed.

"You like new wave music?" Sally asked. "It's my favorite. Well, after classic rock. I love The Beatles."

"I do like new wave," Michelle said. "And I love The Beatles. I was named after one of their songs!"

Sally laughed. "I was going to ask if you were, but sometimes, my mom says I can talk too much and tells me to slow down so I don't scare people away, so I decided to wait to ask you. But that's so cool!"

Michelle started to paint her picture and took quick looks at her new art friend. Sally was taller than Michelle, but that wasn't anything new. She had dark brown hair that fell long down her back. She had long bangs held back from her face with gold barrettes. Her beautiful blue eyes matched the oversized blue shirt she was wearing. She wore baggy jeans and sneakers. She had perfect, straight white teeth. Michelle ran her tongue enviously over the braces on her own top teeth. Someday, she would have perfect teeth, too. She looked at Sally's portrait. She had drawn herself larger than life with a giant smile and a big nose. By her feet were two Siamese cats. She was starting to add more people.

"Do you have brothers and sisters?" Michelle asked, as she drew in her own twin brothers with bright red hair.

"I have a nineteen-year-old sister, Andrea, and a fifteen-year-old brother, Nate. He goes to Gearhart Prep. Andie goes to Eastboro State College. She wants to be a therapist. How about you?"

"I have identical twin brothers named Stevie and Sam," Michelle told her. "They're six. And my sister Stephanie is fifteen."

"Did she go to Randall?" Sally asked. "Maybe she knows my brother."

"No," Michelle answered cautiously. "She goes to Johnson Learning Center. It's a school for kids with special needs. She has Down syndrome."

"Oh, really?" Sally said. "It's just as well. My brother's kind of weird anyway. Your sister probably wouldn't have liked him much."

"You'd be surprised," Michelle replied. "My sister is pretty good at making new friends." This made Michelle think of making new friends when she was in kindergarten. "Do you like chocolate chip cookies?" she asked Sally.

"I love them!" Sally answered with enthusiasm. "I love anything chocolate. I especially like to bake cookies with my mom and grandma. My grandma makes the best chocolate cakes. Why do you ask?"

Michelle smiled. "Do you wanna have lunch with me and my friends tomorrow?"

The next day, Sally joined Michelle, Kim, and Darlene for lunch. Kim showed off for Sally by telling her a story. It was the story of the Bishop-Farmer clan, and how Chris and Carl's identical twin grandmothers became society celebrities by marrying brothers in a double wedding.

Sally was fascinated. "Kim, you're a really good storyteller," she said. "If I close my eyes, I think I might be able to picture that wedding. It's so romantic! I can't believe that you went to school with their grandsons!"

Kim shrugged. "Well, now you do, too."

"Carl is in our French class," Michelle told Sally. "He's the one in the back of the room looking like he's lost at sea. He has dark hair and kinda tan skin?"

"Oh, that guy?" Sally asked. "I did notice him. He's in my homeroom, too. He does seem kinda lost, like he doesn't know what to do with himself. I can't believe he's in that family!"

Kim looked at Sally. "Carl's okay," she said defensively. "It's his cousin Chris that you have to look out for. He gets them all in trouble all the time. He's like their leader. That's why Carl seems so lost sometimes. If Chris isn't around, he's not sure what to do with himself."

"Is Chris like, a bully?" Sally asked.

The DeMarco girls all looked at each other. "No," Darlene answered. "I've never thought of him like a bully. More like just a troublemaker. And he has his little posse of boys that follow him around and do whatever he does."

Sally laughed. "Posse? You mean like in the old west? I've watched old western movies where the sheriff pulls together a posse to try to run the bad guys out of town."

Michelle nodded. "I guess that would make Chris the sheriff," she said. "And Carl, Jamie, and Pete are his deputies. It's kind of cute when you think of it that way. Too bad they can be so annoying."

"Jamie and Pete aren't as annoying," Darlene said. "They can be kinda sweet. But when you get all four of them together, it can be a lot."

"Maybe they won't be as bad now that we're in junior high," Michelle suggested. She pointed to a table at the far end of the cafeteria. "That's the little posse right there," she told Sally.

Sally turned to look. "Oh my gosh, they're kind of cute," she said. "I pictured them all looking like big thugs, but they're just little like all the other seventh-grade boys. I hope *they* don't end up getting bullied by the older kids. That little blond one is adorable. Which one is he?"

"That's Jamie," Michelle told her. "He's probably the nicest one of all of them. I don't think he has a mean bone in his body. I just hope Chris doesn't corrupt him now that they're in a bigger school with more ways to get in trouble."

Kim laughed. "They'll all be fine," she assured Michelle. "Can you imagine anyone trying to mess with the mighty Chris Mahoney? He wouldn't even have to get in a fist fight. He could just charm them to death with his words. It's a Bishop-Farmer thing!"

Sally pointed discreetly. "The one on the left with the light brown hair is also in my homeroom. That must be Pete. Which makes the dark-haired one Chris. He does look kinda like Carl, only Carl with an attitude."

Kim laughed. "That's what I want to call Chris from now on," she said. "Carl with an attitude!"

That afternoon, Darlene and Michelle walked home together. It was still warm and comfortable outside for wearing summer clothes, but soon, the chill air of Fall would be moving in, and eventually Carson Lake would go through a deep freeze. Michelle was looking forward to taking the shortcut home across the ice when that happened. It always looked so cool when she had seen the older kids doing that when she was younger. Now she was one of the older kids. It was a rite of passage.

They walked quietly for several blocks. Then Darlene spoke. "Michelle, I'm sorry I was so rude to you yesterday morning."

"Yeah," Michelle said. "That was weird. You guys made me feel so left out just because I went to camp. You really hurt my feelings."

"I'm so sorry," Darlene said. Michelle thought she sounded and looked sincere. "It's just . . . Kim was having a hard time with all the stuff at home, and she wanted to keep busy. So we did a lot of stuff together. It was nice. We haven't done anything like that for a long time. And then school started, and I knew everything was going back to normal again, and I just kind of freaked out. And Kim's gonna have to go back to doing all that stuff for her dad to help her mom while she works. So, I don't know. I guess I just wanted to make sure she wasn't gonna all the sudden be gone again, like she was right after the accident. Kim's been my friend for a long time. We've been through a lot together." She sighed. "Michelle, I don't want you to feel left out or hurt your feelings, but I might be hanging out more with Kim now, since we're in the same classes, and we live so close to each other. But I just wanted to make sure you knew that you're still my friend. I still want to eat lunch with you and hang out with you. But sometimes, it's just gonna be me and Kim. She just needs me more."

Michelle nodded slowly. "Okay," she said. "I understand. So I guess I need to make some new friends in my own classes now."

Darlene gave a weak smile. "Sally seems really nice," she said. "And Kim seemed to like her, too."

"Yeah, I can see me and Sally being friends," Michelle said. "But I am still gonna eat lunch with you guys, and maybe Sally will want to, too."

Darlene's smile grew. "Okay," she said. "We'll eat lunch together, and maybe we'll still hang out on the playground together sometimes. Or we can do something after school. I'm sorry I hurt your feelings, Michelle. That's not like me. I won't let that happen again."

"Thanks, Darlene," Michelle said. They had arrived at the other side of the lake, and now they needed to go in different directions. "Thanks for the talk. I appreciate you telling me all this. I'll see you tomorrow."

"See you tomorrow," Darlene replied, and she turned to walk away.

Michelle stared after Darlene until she turned the corner. Then she turned to walk toward her own street. She remembered the time she thought that Kim looked like a deflated balloon. Now she knew what that felt like.

Sally and Michelle became fast friends. They both looked forward to art and French class, where they could sit together and do projects, or just be silly together. Sally introduced Michelle to her friend Laurie from Lincoln Elementary. Laurie was a tall, shy girl, who always carried a book around with her with a tassel bookmark sticking out of its pages. She and Sally had known each other as long as Michelle had known Kim and Darlene. Sometimes, she would join all the girls for lunch, but most often she opted to sit with a group of girls from Lincoln, who all sat quietly and read, or studied their textbooks during lunch.

Sally invited Michelle to her house after school, and they had to take the school bus to get there. Michelle met Sally's older brother Nate and saw what she'd meant. He was awkward and sloppy and quickly retreated to his room and closed the door. Sally and Michelle giggled after him. Sally showed Michelle her room and introduced her to the world of Boston sports teams. Sally had posters of her favorite players on the wall. She also had tons and tons of books on her shelves. Sally showed her a Mad Libs book.

"Have you played this before?" she asked Michelle.

Michelle took the book and looked at the pages. "No, I've never seen this before."

Sally showed her. "There are little stories, and they take out words. One player asks the other player for certain kinds of words, like a noun or an adjective, and fills in the blanks. Once they're all filled in, you read it out loud. It's so funny. Wanna try?"

Michelle shrugged. "Okay."

Michelle and Sally played Mad Libs for over an hour. Michelle was good at coming up with silly words, and when the stories were read out loud, both girls would laugh uncontrollably. Nate knocked on Sally's door to tell them to keep it down, he was trying to study, but that just made them laugh louder.

After they were done, Sally turned on the radio, and they talked. "What kinds of things do you like to do?"

Michelle thought. "I like to hang out with my sister," she said. "And I like to make cookies. And eat cookies! I love music. I can't wait until I can go to concerts. I want to go see everyone! I like to listen to stories, like Kim tells, and I like to gossip with Darlene, although she does most of the gossiping, and I just like to hear it. I'm not very good at finding things out."

"Do you like to go to parties?" Sally asked.

Michelle wrinkled her nose. "Sometimes I do, but only if I go with someone. I don't like big, crowded parties too much."

"Me neither," Sally said. "I'd much rather just hang out with one or two friends. But it seems like everyone is having parties now in their basements. Maybe we can go to one together sometime."

"That would be alright," Michelle agreed. "But I don't want to play any kissing games or anything."

Sally tilted her head. "I don't know if I do either," she said, "but it might be fun to see what it's like to kiss a boy. You know, just for the experience of doing it."

"Who would you kiss?" Michelle wondered.

Sally pursed her lips in thought. "I don't know, maybe that guy Greg in art class?"

Michelle thought about it. "He seems like he might be okay to kiss," she agreed, "but his lips look kind of squishy. There's this guy Freddy, in eighth grade, who's tall and looks like his lips might be soft but not too soft."

Sally laughed. "I guess I haven't really been looking at lips," she said. "I look at eyes. I love eyes. But then, after you kiss a boy, you'd have to talk to him, and they all seem so dumb."

"Yeah," Michelle agreed. "Maybe we could just kiss them and then walk away."

"My sister says that's what some boys do," Sally said. "She tells me a lot of things about boys. She's had a boyfriend since she was in twelfth grade, Derrek, and he's awesome."

"But is he wicked awesome?" Michelle asked with a grin.

Sally nodded. "Yeah, he's totally wicked awesome."

Sally and Michelle spent a lot of time at each other's houses but still spent time with their grade-school friends. They went together to a Halloween party at a house belonging to a girl who went to Lincoln Elementary. There were mostly girls at the party, including Kim and Darlene, who were more social with the others. Sally and Michelle watched from the side, eating candy, drinking punch, and listening to music. They danced a little when the other girls danced and talked to Kim and Darlene when they approached them. They had a good time but were relieved when it was time for Mrs. Gorman to pick them up.

"Did you have fun, girls?" she asked them.

They both nodded. "It was okay," Michelle told her, "but I think I would rather have gone trick-or-treating with Sam, Stevie, and Stephanie. Did they get a lot of candy?"

"They did," Mrs. Gorman said, "and Stephanie is looking forward to sharing with you two. But I want you to remember, this is a sleepover, not a stay-up-all-night over, so don't go overboard, and don't let Stephanie eat any candy after she brushes her teeth."

Christmas break came and went, and school continued. Everyone got in the groove of moving around the school every fifty-two minutes to get to their next class, and the boy posse started to feel comfortable enough to express their true colors. First it was the time that Chris didn't do his homework, and his teacher asked him why. He told her to mind her own fucking business, and Chris got his very first visit with Vice Principal Coleman in the first-floor office. Then Pete was caught throwing wadded-up paper at the back of his classmates' heads, just to see if he could hit them. And that was how he explained the reason for his behavior to Mrs. Coleman. Carl told off the French teacher after he said he didn't know how to say bathroom in French. He was asking to go to the bathroom and the teacher would not let him go until he tried, so Carl told him to piss off in perfect French and went to the bathroom anyway. Michelle was horrified at Carl's behavior, but she also thought the teacher was unfair and deserved it. After he came back to the class, he was sent to the office. Jamie was disorganized and flighty, and often daydreamed in class. His teacher caught him drifting one time and came over and tapped him on the shoulder. Jamie had amazingly quick reflexes and automatically slapped the teacher's hand away without any thought. Jamie was not in school the rest of the day or the next day. Other events occurred, and the boys were back and forth to the office on various occasions.

"They should change their name," Sally said to Michelle, Kim, and Darlene one day when they were talking about the boys getting in trouble. "I think they should be called the Bad Boy Posse." The other girls loved that suggestion, and the name stuck for years.

Summer came, and Sally and Michelle both went back to their camps. When they got back home after a month, Kim invited them both to join her and Darlene at the community pool one afternoon. Sally's mother, Mrs. Bachman, dropped them off with cash for admission and snacks, and they went to find their friends. They pulled up lounge chairs and all sat down. Kim took her shirt off to reveal that she was wearing a black bikini with blue stripes. Michelle and Sally gaped at her. She had actual breasts and a curvy waist. She had her hair pulled back, and sunglasses on her face, and to the unknowing eye, she looked like a high school student. The girls looked down at their own one-piece suits. Sally had a bit of activity going on up front, but Michelle was as flat as the prairie. She was relieved to see that Darlene, who was also in a one-piece suit, was not too far ahead of her in the growth department, but having been around Kim all summer, she seemed used to her sudden grown-up appearance.

When they jumped in the water soon after, the Kim they all knew reappeared. She got hold of a beach ball and started swatting it volleyball-style at her friends' heads. They all batted it back and forth for some time before the lifeguard told them they were playing too rough around the smaller children and confiscated the ball. They played Marco Polo, then competed to see who could do the most somersaults in a row without coming up for air. Then they all felt dizzy. They decided to get out of the water and go to the snack bar.

If Michelle could mark the moment in time when Sally became completely boy crazy, it would have been that very moment. As they were approaching the snack bar, towels wrapped around waists, the front gate from the parking lot opened, and Freddy Pierce walked inside. More like Freddy Pierce glided inside, followed by two of his ninth-grade friends. They were all wearing long swim trunks and T-shirts. They approached a group of chairs and spread their towels across the tops. But Freddy remained standing and started to remove his shirt. All four girls stopped in their tracks as Freddy peeled the white T-shirt from his body in slow motion. Then he slipped sunglasses onto his face. He looked back, saw the four girls standing there looking, nodded his head, and then straddled the chair and leaned back to bask in the sun.

While the act of Freddy disrobing seemed to take forever, it was most likely a matter of seconds. And the nearly perceptible nod was the way the girls would always remember it, but no one could confirm later that it had actually occurred.

"Oh my God," Sally mumbled to the group. "He is absolutely perfect."

"He is," Kim agreed. "I hear he's really nice, too."

"He plays basketball on a team at the YMCA," Darlene told them, "and I hear he's their best player."

"Look at those lips," Michelle said.

"And did you see his eyes?" Sally asked.

The spell was broken quickly for the other three girls when the snack bar attendant asked if they were going to stand there and gawk all day or if they want to order some food. But Sally did want to keep gawking. She had been struck by her first schoolgirl crush, and it hit her like lightning.

When eighth grade started a few weeks later, Sally had changed. She had gone out shopping and bought designer jeans. She had found shirts that didn't look like they were her father's gardening rejects. She washed her hair more often and started to adorn it with prettier barrettes and bows. And she talked about Freddy. A lot.

"Do you think his hair is like that naturally, or do you think he has to put stuff in it?" she asked Michelle as they passed him in the hallway.

"Oh, definitely stuff," Michelle said. "No one has natural hair like that."

"Look how the green in his jacket brings out the green in his eyes," Sally said one day when she saw Freddy wearing a green jacket while walking into school.

"Yeah, it's a nice shade of green," Michelle agreed.

One day, they were doing their homework in Sally's room when she suddenly sighed. "Do you think Freddy even knows I exist?"

Michelle shrugged. "Maybe," she said. "I mean, you're not invisible, so he must see you when you're there."

Sally laughed. This was why Michelle was not driven crazy by her friend's obsession. Sally had a good sense of humor. She could laugh at herself, and she could see how ridiculous she was being over a boy.

The ridiculousness came to a head on one early spring afternoon. Michelle and Sally were walking toward Sally's school bus to go to her house, when Sally spotted Freddy walking up the sidewalk toward the street. She grabbed her friend's sleeve. "Let's follow him and see where he goes."

Michelle's mouth dropped open. "Are you nuts?" she asked. "I'm not even sure that's legal! And how would we get back to your house after?"

Sally had already made up her mind and walked past her bus. "We'll take the city bus," she called behind her. "I have the money for the fare."

Michelle stood still for a minute, considering ditching her friend and just walking back to her own house. But she didn't really want to. And suddenly the adventure bug hit her. She wanted to know where Freddy was going, too, although she didn't know why. Freddy was cute, and it was a daring thing to do. Maybe someday it would make a good story to tell their friends. She chased after Sally.

"Okay," she said, "we follow him, but we stay really far behind. And if he sees us, we turn around and head back. And then if he says anything to us later, we say we were walking to my grandmother's house and took a wrong turn."

"Doesn't your grandmother live near East Firehouse?" Sally asked, eyes locked on the back of Freddy's perfect head as she speedwalked after it.

Michelle shook her head. "That doesn't matter," she said. "It's a lie anyway. We can say whatever we want."

"Oh," Sally said. "Well, I'm not very good at lying. Can't we just say something that's not as confusing? Like we were just out for a walk or something?"

Michelle thought about it. "Yeah, I guess that works too. I just like to make things more complicated. It's more fun. And you totally owe me after this. These are definitely *not* walking shoes. Slow down!"

After a half hour, they were in downtown Eastboro, and Freddy was showing no signs of slowing. Sally finally gave up when they reached City Hall. "Well, at least we're at a bus stop," she said. "It lets off right in front of my house."

"And here's the infamous Jerome Farmer statue," Michelle said, pointing to the front of the building.

Sally approached the eight-foot-tall statue of Carl and Chris's great-grandfather. "You know, I've seen this thing a million times, but I've never actually stopped to look at it." She read the plaque, then looked up at the famous mayor's copper head. "Do you think that Chris and Carl look like him at all?"

Michelle looked closely. "Well, they didn't when we were younger, but they might look more like him now."

Sally stood on her tiptoes. "Maybe the eyes? It's hard to tell when the whole thing has turned green, but I think they could be similar. They're kind of soulful."

Michelle sighed. "Kind of like Mr. Russo," she said softly.

Sally turned her head to face her friend. "Mr. Russo? The music teacher Mr. Russo? Oh my God, Michelle, do you have the hots for him?"

Michelle turned back to look at the plaque. "Well, maybe not the hots," she said. "I mean, he's a grown man and I'm a kid. But he just plays piano so beautifully! It makes me feel like I could fly! I wish I could be as good at something as that. And he has a very sweet smile."

"How can you even see it under that big floppy mustache, Michelle? Besides, he's married. Isn't there anyone in our grade that plays piano that's more appropriate for you?"

Michelle grimaced. "Calvin Baskin," she said and shook her head.

"Oh, no, Michelle," Sally agreed. "I don't care if he played piano for The Beatles. You can't go out with Calvin Baskin. That is just wrong on so many levels."

Their bus pulled up, and Sally deposited the fare money in the slot. The girls sat down in the back of the bus. Sally sighed. "Thanks for going on this adventure with me, Michelle," she said. "You're a good friend. Freddy will be going to McKinney High next year, and I won't see him again until tenth grade. So I guess this was my last big hurrah about Freddy. And you're right, I totally owe you one."

Michelle smiled and nodded. "Oh, I'll find a way for you to pay this back someday," she said. "I promise."

Lost in the Crush(es)

Freshman year arrived, and the freshmen ruled the junior high. Michelle found her new homeroom, which contained almost exactly the same students as it had the last two years. She saw Tommy Griffith give her an impish grin. "Hey, Tiny," he said.

Michelle shook her head. "Tommy, will you just let that go?" she begged. "That was two years ago. I've grown since then."

Tommy chuckled. "Not much," he said, and his friends laughed.

Michelle rolled her eyes. Tommy lived on the other side of the lake from her. He would be going to Murphy High next year, and she'd never have to see him again if she was lucky. She could put up with him for one more year. Just one.

Michelle met up with Darlene, Kim, and Sally at lunch. Sally was distraught. "What's wrong?" Michelle asked her.

Sally sighed. "Now that we're considered to be in high school," she said, "apparently some kids have been assigned to honors classes. So Laurie and all the other girls I was in class with last year from Lincoln Elementary are in honors classes now. I'm not. I mean, I am completely and totally fine with that, but now I'm gonna have to start all over. I'm not gonna know anyone in my classes."

"You'll know people," Darlene told her. "You probably know more people than you think. You've probably been in classes with a lot of the kids you're in with now, but you just didn't pay any attention to them."

Sally shrugged. "And it's weird having the earlier lunch period and having our core classes after lunch. I'm not even hungry now."

"It's gonna be okay," Michelle assured her, although she knew exactly how it felt to be facing a friendless classroom. "I know it's hard for you to talk to new people, Sally, but you're just gonna have to do it. Just pick one person you want to talk to and ask them if they like chocolate chip cookies."

The girls all laughed. "Okay," Sally agreed. "I will speak to one person. But no one gets access to my cookies."

Michelle and Sally met outside after school. "So how did it go today?" Michelle asked.

Sally allowed herself a small smile. "I did what you said," she told her. "I talked to one person. You'll never guess who that one person was."

"Who?" Michelle was stumped.

"Pete Cooper!" Sally disclosed. "He was sitting behind me in history class, so I turned my chair around, and I swear, I asked him if he liked chocolate chip cookies. And you know what he said?"

"Yes?" Michelle guessed. Everyone she knew liked chocolate chip cookies.

"No!" Sally responded. "He said, 'Why, have you got one for me?' And then I noticed, Michelle. They're all in my core classes. All four of them. The Bad Boy Posse. And I talked to them. And I made them laugh! And they all knew my name. I don't know how they all knew my name. It's the first time I've ever seen them all so close before. And they are wicked cute, all four of them. And Chris and Carl? They do have Jerome Farmer eyes. They are totally soulful!"

Michelle was at a loss for what to say. The Bad Boy Posse. The boys from DeMarco Elementary. The boys she had known for ten years. They were all in Sally's classes, and she had a crush on all four of them. And they were "wicked cute"?

Oh no, she thought. *This is going to be four times as bad as Freddy Pierce!*

It wasn't nearly as bad as Freddy Pierce, much to Michelle's relief. Sally got to know the boys, and she talked to them every day. And after some time, she settled on one boy to like. It was Pete. And then after Pete, it was Carl. Then Jamie. And lastly Chris. She was able to spread them out through freshman year, and her crushes always seemed to coincide with some bad boy activity.

Sally had a thing for bad boys. She felt they were misunderstood. If they acted out, it only meant someone should listen harder to them. So she assigned herself as their pre-class sounding board. Pete told her it wasn't fair that Mr. Jackson gave him a C on his science test, so it justified his mouthing off to him. Carl was pretty sure that his shirt wasn't offensive or out of dress code, even if it did have the word *shit* printed on it. Jamie couldn't help it if he forgot to turn in his homework four days in a row; he had a bad memory. And Chris thought all the teachers were giant losers and deserved to be treated with disrespect, just to show them they couldn't beat the students down. He even called their principal by his first name, Sean. Mr. Jeffries was not amused.

Michelle would sit and listen to Sally's stories about the boys while they did homework or listened to music. She quietly doodled in her notebooks while Sally wrote in her journal or wrote love poems that no boy would ever see. She stood by as Sally watched the boys go into the bathroom to smoke or sneak out the stairwell door at lunchtime. She told Michelle what she said when she made them laugh and how they worried when she came back from being out sick for two days. She almost swooned to Michelle on the day she came in with a short new haircut with stylish bangs, and the boys were knocked for a loop. They all told her it looked good, and she soaked in every word.

And then one day, three of the boys disappeared. They were just gone. For three days in a row, there was no Bad Boy Posse except Carl, and he wasn't talking. Sally panicked. She worried they might have been in a horrible accident. Then she worried they might have been expelled. Michelle tried to console her, but it was no use.

Finally after three days, Pete and Jamie reappeared in class like they had never left. But Chris did not come back. Even Michelle was concerned by now. Rumors were flying around Randall Junior High about what the bad boys might have done to get in trouble, but none of them could possibly be true. Sally dared to ask the boys.

"They all got suspended," she told her friends at lunch, glancing at the boys' somber lunch table. "Pete and Jamie got three days, but Chris got three weeks. They wouldn't tell me why. They just said they got caught in the act of doing something and got in a lot of trouble. They all seem so bummed out. Pete said their parents aren't even letting them talk to Chris. They're both grounded for a month. Chris is grounded, too, so Carl couldn't even talk to him. Somehow, Carl wasn't there when they got caught. What could they have done?"

Kim shrugged. "I have no idea," she said, "but it must have been pretty bad for a three-week suspension. Maybe it will finally teach Chris a lesson."

"What kind of lesson can you learn if you're not in school?" Sally demanded to know.

Michelle thought she made a fair point. All suspension would do was put Chris three weeks behind in his classes. It seemed like there should be something better in situations like this.

At the end of the three weeks, Chris returned to school. After school, Sally told Michelle that he was really subdued. "He was friendly and everything," she said, "but all of them were quiet all afternoon. It was like they'd been beaten by the system. They're all still grounded. What a drag."

Michelle tried to distract Sally. "Let's take Steph to Twin Bridges Park to see the ducks," she suggested. So they did. It was the spring of their ninth-grade year, and the flowers were starting to bloom. The park was full of mothers with strollers and toddlers running around on the grass. Stephanie loved to run up to the top of the bridges over the pond, look down at the ducks, and then run down the other side.

Stephanie would be turning eighteen soon. She would be considered an adult. Mr. and Mrs. Gorman were talking to the school, trying to come up with options for the next year. One of the choices was for her to continue at school until she was twenty-one, but the Gormans worried that she had learned what she was going to learn in that setting and would start to get bored. The other option offered was independent living, and that meant Stephanie would move out of the house and into a supported shared apartment. That would mean no more sharing a room with Stephanie. That meant Michelle would be left alone in her room for the first time since she was a baby. But the decision hadn't been made yet. It might all turn out okay.

"I have to tell you something," Sally said as they sat on a bench and watched Stephanie run around.

Michelle felt a cold chill go down her back. "What is it?"

Sally looked into her eyes. "So my parents told me I can decide if I want to go to McKinney High or to Gearhart Prep next year. They had me take the scholarship test, and somehow I managed to qualify. So my tuition would be covered. I think I'm probably gonna end up going to Gearhart."

Michelle's mouth dropped open. "Sally!" she said. "You have to go to McKinney! We were going to start high school together next year. We were going to graduate together. We were going to go to proms together! If you go to Gearhart . . ."

"I know, Michelle," Sally said. "I've been thinking about it a lot, and I really feel I'll have a better chance of getting into a good college if I go to Gearhart. They have a really good record of their students getting into their first-choice school. And there's other stuff, too. They have a big focus on writing, which you know I love, and they have a good art and music program. And they have smaller class sizes. You know how I get so easily distracted in class, especially in the bigger classes. I always have to be part of what's going on around me, and I lose track of what the teacher's saying. And at Gearhart, I won't be as distracted by the bad boys. I mean, I don't even know if there are any bad boys there. You have to wear a uniform, so at least it's harder to tell them all apart, I guess."

"But Sally, you love the bad boys!" Michelle protested.

Sally sighed. "I do," she admitted. "But I really can't imagine that it's gonna be that way forever. I mean, do you think the Bad Boy Posse is ever going to settle down and get married? Or have kids? I mean, in that order? Michelle, I think it's a good idea for me to have a fresh start with a new group of kids. The only bad part is that I won't be seeing you every day, but we can still see each other. We don't live that far apart."

Michelle realized at that moment that nothing she could say was going to change what was happening. Sally, her best friend of three years, was leaving. She wouldn't be at lunch every day or by the door after school. They wouldn't be able to talk about the same boys anymore or complain about the same teachers. Michelle would be back at the starting line, yet again. And without Sally to back her up.

"Yeah," she said. "Sure. We'll still see each other. Yeah, maybe it won't be so bad. There'll be a lot of new kids to meet at McKinney from other junior highs, and you'll be making new friends at Gearhart. But we'll always be friends."

Sally smiled. "It will be okay, Michelle. Plus, we still have two months left of ninth grade, and the whole summer to hang out. At least, after we get back from camp."

"Chelle!" Stephanie called out. She was on the top of the bridge, waving down at Michelle and Sally. "Come up!" she said. "There's so many ducks!"

"Be right there, Steph!" Michelle called out. "C'mon," she said to Sally, starting toward the base of the bridge. "Let's go get Steph and then walk to Scoops to get some ice cream cones. Steph will love that. My treat," she added.

Sally looked at Michelle warmly. "Thanks, Michelle," she said. "Thanks for understanding."

Everything Changes

Francis McKinney High School was huge, and classes were scheduled all around the building. There was no homeroom in the morning or afternoon, so students were expected to make it to their first-period classes on time. There were no more core class groups, and everything seemed to be more random. Pete was now at Murphy High, but Jamie, who was supposed to join him there, had transferred to McKinney. Only now, he was insisting that everyone call him James. The dynamic of the Bad Boy Posse was changing.

Michelle had some classes with Kim and Darlene, which was nice. They sat together when they could and continued to eat lunch together in their new cafeteria. Michelle noticed that Kim, who continued to mature physically, but stayed the same Kim emotionally, deliberately sat down next to Carl on the first day of history class. They didn't really talk to each other much, but when they did, Kim had a tendency to refer to Carl as "moron." It didn't really seem to bother him that much.

The boys in the Bad Boy Posse seemed physically smaller in their new school, even as Chris started to grow taller and passed his two friends in height. There were plenty of former bad boys and cool kids in high school, and they were no longer the big fish in the small bowl. Michelle thought it humbled them, and she never once saw them engage in troublesome behaviors. Carl actually started to engage more in classes, and strangely, he suddenly seemed to know quite a bit about a lot of subjects. Michelle liked this version of Carl. He seemed slightly more confident, even when Chris wasn't around.

Michelle found her classes challenging but not too hard if she did her work. She missed studying with Sally. It had made the time go faster, and sometimes they helped each other out when they got stuck on a homework problem. Now Michelle's room seemed so empty as she sat on her bed poring over her textbooks.

Stephanie had moved out in August. They had moved her into an apartment on the west side. She was with three other young women with similar intellectual capabilities, and they had support staff with them at mealtimes and evenings. The women went to enhancement programs during the day on weekdays, and they went on outings with a group on weekends. Stephanie was making new friends and having the time of her life learning to live independently. She was always excited and happy, and she called Michelle often to tell her about her new adventures. Michelle was excited for Stephanie, as well, but she missed her so much sometimes that she could feel an actual aching in her heart. She even missed her soft snores when she slept. Michelle had trouble sleeping for days after Stephanie left.

Kim and Darlene were great, but they were wrapped up in their own personal high school dramas. Michelle tried to call Sally after school, but she was never home. She stayed after to do her homework and then had to take two buses to get home. Sometimes, they were able to connect at night, and they would talk for an hour to catch up. But those calls got further and further apart as the girls started having different experiences and less in common to talk about.

In October, all the buzz was about homecoming. It would be the first dance for the sophomores, and everyone was planning on going. No one had dates, so Michelle was going with Kim and Darlene. Darlene decided to join the decorating committee for the dance and asked Michelle to join with her.

"It'll be fun," Darlene insisted. "You like to do art. Think of it as a giant art project. And we get to use poster paint."

Michelle agreed to do it, and it turned out to be a good thing. She and Darlene met a new girl. Her name was Traci Walsh, and she lived on the west side, not too far from where Stephanie had just moved. She had gone to Fremont Junior High, but she had only been there for a year since her family had moved to Eastboro from Framingham when her father got a job at Aries Corp. She had become friendly with a few kids in her junior high, but now she was looking to meet some new friends. She ended up working with Michelle and Darlene, and she liked their look immediately.

"I can really tell things about people when I look at them," Traci said. "I can tell that you two have known each other forever. And I can tell you've been through a lot. But what I can really see is that even though you already have close friends, you're still willing to make new friends to hang out with, and that's pretty cool. Am I right?" She looked at them expectantly.

Michelle and Darlene looked at each other and smiled. Then they looked back at Traci. "That's amazing," Darlene said. "Are you psychic or something?"

Traci laughed. "No, I'm not psychic. I just have a good feel for what people are going through. My mom says it's called high empathy. She says I would make a good therapist, but that's not really what I want to do. I want to someday own a store and sell really cool clothes that don't cost a lot. Like so everyone can look cool even if they don't have a lot of money. But first I'll probably have to work at some store in the mall to get experience. What do you guys want to do?"

Michelle shrugged. "I haven't really thought about it," she said. "I mean, I love art and music, but I don't really have a lot of natural talent." She pointed to the stick figure she had just painted on their banner. "See?"

Traci looked carefully at Michelle's face. She tilted her head. "Did you ever think of becoming a doctor?"

Michelle shook her head. "No, that's never even crossed my mind. Why?"

"I don't know," Traci admitted. "I guess I can just see you taking care of people. I bet you would make people feel really comfortable, and like make sure they understand what's going on and stuff."

Darlene's mouth dropped open. "That's amazing!" she told Traci. "Michelle has a special needs sister, and she is so great with her! I remember when we were really young, and her telling us all about it and explaining that Stephanie did things a certain way and why she did. At first, we were scared of Stephanie, but then, she just seemed like another kid, you know? Michelle, I think you would make a great caregiver. Like maybe a nurse."

Michelle shrugged again. "I really don't know," she said. "I'm glad I don't need to decide right now. But Traci, Darlene's always wanted to be a biologist, like a brain scientist or something."

"Yeah," Darlene said, nodding. "My dad has always told me that science is the up-and-coming field for women, and now would be a good time to break into it. I can totally picture myself in a lab with a microscope and a white coat."

Traci made a face. "I don't know," she said. "I kind of picture you working around other people, Darlene. I think in a lab, you'd feel really alone and isolated. Yeah, I can totally picture you surrounded by people. And smiling."

Darlene frowned. "That's weird. I can just see myself in the lab, or maybe working with dolphins and whales or something in the ocean. But whatever."

Traci laughed. "Well, sometimes, I am wrong about these things. Like I said, it's just a feeling. So do you guys like chocolate chip cookies? I got a craving this morning a packed a few for myself."

Michelle and Darlene turned to each other and laughed. They immediately invited Traci to join them the next day for lunch.

The four girls grew closer as the days went by. Traci enjoyed engaging in Darlene's gossip, and she always added her insight into the mix.

Darlene leaned in close to her friends one day at lunch. "Rhonda Jenkins likes Chris," she whispered.

"Rhonda Jenkins?" Michelle said quietly but with surprise.

"Yeah," Darlene confirmed. "I overheard her talking to her friends when they were fixing their makeup in the bathroom. They didn't even check to see if anyone was in the stalls. Amateur move. She says she likes him, and she's trying to get him to ask her out, but if he doesn't soon, she's gonna figure out a way to get alone with him anyway. She thinks he's wicked cute."

"Really?" Michelle asked. "Our Chris? Chris Mahoney?" Darlene nodded. "I mean, I know Sally thought he was cute but . . . Rhonda's like one of the most popular girls in tenth grade!"

Darlene shrugged. "I don't know, maybe they'd make a good couple," she said. "She seems nice enough to me. Maybe they'll live happily ever after."

Traci shook her head. "I don't think so," she said. "I get a weird vibe out of Rhonda sometimes. It just seems to me that she's not totally up front about things. I don't know what it is. But I'm guessing she wants something from Chris. And if she doesn't get it, she'll just throw him to the curb."

Kim shrugged. "So maybe that wouldn't be such a bad thing for Chris," she stated. "Maybe he needs a good kick to the curb one of these days."

Darlene gave Kim a harsh look. "What is it about you and Chris? Why are you so hostile about him? What has he ever done to you?"

"Nothing," Kim said. "He's never done anything to me. I'm just sayin', I just think he'd be better off if he just got a taste of the real world, that's all."

One week later, Darlene told them: "I overheard Roni Bishop, the Bishop girl in the eleventh grade? She was telling her friend that she heard that Carl's father has been staying with Roni's Aunt Missy, who's Carl's grandmother, one of the twins? So I don't know, I think maybe he moved out or something?"

Kim's ears had perked up. "What?" she said. She leaned in closer. "Carl's dad moved out?"

"I guess so," Darlene said softly. "Maybe they're just separated for a while or something."

Kim frowned. "I think they may have done that before," she said. "Poor Carl. I hope they can work things out. It sucks to not have your dad."

"Yeah," Darlene agreed. "And it sucks when your parents split up."

Michelle had no idea what it felt like to have your parents split up, but she knew what it felt like when a family member moved out. She felt bad for poor Carl and hoped his parents could work things out so they could all be together.

Christmas was approaching, and the girls were invited to a party at Jake Pierce's house. He was Freddy's younger brother. Jake and Freddy's parents were away in Bermuda and had trusted Freddy to look after the house while they were gone. However, Freddy took off with his junior class friends and had left Jake to his own devices. So Jake threw a party and invited everyone. And everyone came. Now Michelle knew where Freddy lived. It was nowhere near where they had followed him that day. She would have to let Sally know.

Michelle was allowed to go to the party as long as she was home by eleven thirty. Her parents were not aware that there would be no adults present, or they wouldn't have let her go. Mrs. Feinman picked her up at eight thirty and dropped Darlene, Kim, and Michelle off at the Pierce's home. When they went inside, it was still early, and the crowd had not picked up yet. Jake handed them all drinks in paper cups, and Kim and Darlene took gulps of theirs. Then they made faces.

"Gross," Darlene said. "What is this?"

Michelle sniffed hers. "I think there's Coke in there," she said. She took a sip. "Maybe rum and Coke?"

"It's good," Kim said, finishing hers off.

Michelle took a few more sips. She didn't like it much, but she was curious about what it might feel like to have a bit of a drink. But just a little bit. Darlene appeared to have made a similar choice and was now sipping slowly from her cup.

The girls started to mingle. They found some classmates and stopped to talk to them. Pretty soon, other kids arrived, and they saw more and more familiar faces. Drinks continued to appear and disappear. Michelle didn't want to drink anymore, but she held onto her cup so that no one would offer her another. Darlene did the same. Kim grabbed a second drink but drank slowly.

The front door opened, and the three posse members from McKinney High crossed the threshold. Michelle watched them scan the crowd, and Carl and Chris were handed drinks. James politely refused. He looked up and saw Michelle, then smiled and waved. She smiled and waved back. The boys started making their way around the room. Kim saw them too and followed them with her eyes. Michelle couldn't read her expression, but it was something different. She couldn't tell if it was a good or bad different.

Kim seemed a little bit tipsy, so they found a couch with room for three and had a seat. There were other kids around, and they all started to talk. Pretty soon, Chris and Carl wandered over and sat on the floor. Someone took out a joint and lit up. The smell of marijuana filled the air around them. The joint was passed from hand to hand. Kim took a drag. Then Darleen. When Darlene handed it to Michelle, she examined it and then put it to her mouth and sucked in.

She felt the burn, started to cough, and couldn't stop. She put her hand to her throat. She heard Darlene yell for someone to get a cup of water. Her eyes started to tear. She gasped for a breath, and some got through, but the coughing increased. A boy she didn't know told her to put her head between her knees and breathe slowly. She tried, and finally, the burning started to subside. She took the water from Darlene and sipped it. She felt nauseated. She wanted to lie down.

"I need to go home," she croaked to Darlene.

Darlene looked at her watch. "It's ten thirty," she said. "My mom won't be here for an hour. Where's the phone? I'll call her to come now."

"I'll show you," Jake Pierce said and led Darlene to the kitchen.

"You really wanna go?" Kim said, leaning across Michelle's lap. "I'm having such a good time. I'm not ready to go yet. Let's stay a little longer."

Michelle shook her head. "No, Kim, I have to go," she said. "I feel really sick. I think I burned my lungs."

Kim made a face. "Can someone else bring me home, then?" she asked the crowd. "I don't need to be home until midnight."

"My mom can drive you home," a girl from Michelle's English class named Nancy answered. "She'll be here at eleven thirty. I think you live near me, off of Grand Street?"

Kim smiled hazily. "Yeah, Grand Street. A grand place to live!" She laughed.

Michelle was concerned. She didn't want to leave Kim alone at the party, even with people there she knew. It just didn't feel right. But when Darlene came out of the kitchen after her call, Kim informed her of her plan.

"I'll be fine," she insisted. "My new friend Nancy will bring me home. And I'll just stay here on the couch. It's just another hour."

Darlene sighed. "Okay," she finally said. "You can stay, but I'm gonna have James keep an eye on you. He's like the only one here not drinking. Call me tomorrow to check in, okay?"

Kim put up her thumb and tried to wink, but she just closed her eyes. "Bye, you guys," she said. "I hope you didn't burn your lungs down, Michelle." She started to giggle.

Darlene walked Michelle toward the door while looking for James. She found him in the doorway to the dining room, standing under the mistletoe, lips locked with Cyndi Wells. Michelle tried not to think about Cyndi's lips and who else's lips they had touched this year. But James didn't look like he cared.

Darlene shook her head. "I'm not getting between that," she said. "Kim will be fine. It's less than an hour until she goes home. I'm not worried."

They stepped outside into the cold winter night air. Michelle could feel a new burn in her throat, but the air felt good, and she didn't cough. She hoped her clothes and hair didn't smell like pot. She wished she had access to a trough sink to rinse her hair.

When she got home, Michelle thanked Mrs. Feinman for the ride, told her mother that her stomach hurt, and went right up to bed. She slept straight through the night.

The next bit of gossip out of Darlene's mouth and into Michelle's ears rocked her entire world.

"Are you feeling better?" Darlene asked her on the phone the next afternoon.

"Yeah, much better," she told her. "I think I just inhaled way too deep. I won't do that ever again. But I'll tell you," she confided, "after the fire went out in my lungs, the rest of my body felt pretty damn good, and I had the best sleep ever, so next time, I'll just be much more careful."

"Yeah, it was pretty good," Darlene agreed. Then she paused. "I need to tell you something Michelle, and you have to promise me you'll never, ever tell anyone, especially Kim. She can't know I talked to you about this."

Michelle was intrigued but also a bit concerned by this introduction to new gossip. "I promise," she said. "What is it?"

"Last night," Darlene started, and Michelle thought she might be cupping her hand over the mouthpiece so no one else would hear, "after we left, Kim ended up hooking up with some guy at the party, and they ended up doing it in a bedroom upstairs!"

"What!?" Michelle shrieked.

"Is everything okay, Michelle?" her mother called from downstairs.

Michelle covered the mouthpiece. "Yeah, Mom, everything's fine!" she yelled back. Then she quietly addressed Darlene. "What? Who was it? How did it happen? She was only there for less than an hour!"

"I know!" Darlene said. "I have no idea. She won't even tell me who it was. And I mean really, she won't. She says it's not someone we know, but she doesn't want to talk about the details. She was crying when I talked to her."

Michelle felt queasy. "Crying? Why? Oh my God, he didn't make her do it against her will, did he? Is she okay?"

"No, no, it's nothing like that," Darlene assured her. "It's that she had always planned to lose her virginity to someone she really cares about, you know? And now she's lost that chance. And the funny thing is, I got the feeling she was holding something back. I think she actually had someone specific in mind for her first time."

"Poor Kim!" Michelle said. "Oh, that sucks. Why did she do it then? Why didn't she wait?"

"She said she didn't mean for it to happen; it just did. She'd had a couple of drinks and a few hits off that joint, and I guess she just wasn't thinking clearly." Darlene sighed. "I hope my first time is with someone I love," she said. "And I hope I'm not drunk or high when it happens. I want to be in control of what I do and when I do it."

"That's probably a good enough reason to not drink too much at a party," Michelle stated. Then a thought hit her. "Oh my God, did they use any protection? I mean, the only thing worse than doing it and regretting it would be getting pregnant, too!"

"No, Kim's on the pill," Darlene told her. "She and her mom decided she would go on it at fifteen so they wouldn't have to have any awkward conversations when the time came, or I guess if something like this happened. I mean, look at her mom. She ended up having a baby all by herself."

"Oh, Darlene, I kinda wish you hadn't told me this," Michelle said. "Now I have to pretend I don't know. Unless Kim tells me herself someday, and I can't imagine that she would. I mean, we're close, but not *that* close."

"I know," Darlene said. "I'm sorry to do that to you, but there is no way I could keep this kind of thing totally to myself. And I knew I could trust you."

"Well, thanks for trusting me, I guess," Michelle said.

When she got off the phone, Michelle threw herself across her bed. She couldn't believe that one of her friends—her elementary school friends!—had lost her virginity in tenth grade. And while drunk and high at a party! Then she remembered how she and Darlene were going to have James watch out for Kim to make sure she was okay after they left, but then they left without talking to him. And they left because of Michelle! Now she felt awful. She hoped this all wasn't her fault. She hoped Kim would be okay. She wanted to pick up the phone, call Sally, and tell her the whole thing, to see if she thought Michelle was to blame. But she couldn't. She had promised to keep the secret. And she wanted to be true to her word.

Growing up sucks, she thought.

After Christmas break, school resumed like they all had never left. But it felt like a new world. Kim had crossed the virginity bridge. Darlene and Michelle had smoked pot for the first time. Pretty soon, most of them would be turning sixteen. And all of the sudden, Chris and Rhonda were an item.

They all agreed it seemed surreal, seeing Chris walking through the halls with a swagger and a dopey smile. Seeing Chris and Rhonda holding hands on the way out of school at the end of the day. Seeing Chris and Rhonda leaning against the wall near the lockers in the morning, kissing. It was as if bad boy Chris had been replaced by boyfriend Chris, and the girls were trying to get used to it.

The boys were struggling to get used to it, too. For the first time since seventh grade, Michelle saw Carl and James standing in the hallway before school without Chris. She had to look twice. She almost didn't recognize them by themselves.

A few days later, Michelle saw James walking down the hall, and she waved. He didn't even see her. He just kept on walking, a grimace on his face. She announced this to the girls at lunch.

"I heard that James's brother, Howie, has been causing all kinds of trouble at home since he graduated," Darlene told them.

"Where'd you hear that?" Michelle asked.

"My mom," Darlene said. "Apparently, she doesn't think I can hear anything she talks about when she's on the phone. I don't know who she was talking to, but I guess Howie's been rude to his parents and trashes the house. You know, he got in a lot of trouble in high school. He's nothing like James. I think he might be a stoner."

"Really?" Michelle asked. "That's so weird. And James doesn't like to do any drugs, or even drink. It's like they're from two different worlds."

"And I heard his father's up for a manager position at Aries," Darlene went on. "He's been in the management training program, and I hear they might be grooming him for a major promotion."

"That's pretty cool," Michelle said.

"Everyone's dad works at Aries," Kim said softly. "Everyone's dad becomes a manager at Aries."

"What was that, Kim?" Darlene asked.

Kim looked up. She started stirring her cup of ice water with her straw. "Oh, nothing," Kim said offhandedly. "My dad was a human resource manager at Aries. Why does everyone work at Aries, anyway? Isn't there anywhere else to work in Eastboro?"

"There are schools and hospitals," Traci reminded her.

"Yeah," Kim said. "Hospitals for the people who work at Aries, and schools for their kids."

"I think it's because we went to DeMarco," Michelle said, "and our parents all got houses near the lake to be close to Aries. That's why my parents got our house. People who live near Sally, or near East Firehouse, don't work at Aries as much."

"What's got your panties in such a bunch today anyways, Kim?" Darlene asked. "So what if everyone works at Aries? They're a big company. They must pay well for everyone to want to work there."

Kim poked at her food with her fork, her other hand propping up her head. "I don't know," she said. "I'm just feeling sorry for myself today. Probably something to do with my dad or something."

"Well, I'm sorry if talking about dads and Aries upsets you," Darlene said. "Maybe we can talk about something else."

"Did you guys see they put out the dates for the junior and senior proms?" Traci asked them. "They do them in April here. I guess it's traditional here to do them in April for some reason instead of May. That means our junior prom will be next April. Can you imagine? Who do you guys want to go to the prom with?"

Michelle wrinkled her forehead. "I have no idea," she said. "Prom is kind of a big deal at my house. My parents went to both McKinney proms together. But I have had a total of zero crushes this year. I couldn't even guess who I would go with."

"I kind of like this one guy in my history class," Darlene said. "His name is Charlie. We have a few Charlies at McKinney. Remember Charlie from DeMarco? Michelle, what ever happened to him?"

"He moved to New Jersey with his mom and grandma," Michelle revealed. "I think that was in eighth grade."

"My crush is a junior at Murphy," Traci told them. "He's a friend of my brother. Maybe someday he'll realize I'm alive. Then I'll get up the nerve to ask him to prom."

"I guess I'll just wait for someone to ask me," Kim said. "And I'll just hope someone does."

"I bet someone does," Michelle said. "You're gorgeous, Kim. I can't even imagine how great you'll look in your prom dress. Every guy there would totally fall in love with you."

Kim started to perk up slightly. "Really? Do you think so?"

"Kim, I barely ever lie," Michelle told her. "And this is one of the times I'm not, I promise!"

Traci smiled at Kim. "Kim, you're gonna go to the prom," she told her. "And it's going to be a spectacular night for you, I guarantee it."

Darlene laughed. "I do trust Traci's gut instincts," she told Kim, "but she tried to tell me once that I'm not gonna be a biologist, so we know she can be wrong sometimes. Maybe you should have a backup plan."

Kim pondered for a minute. "A backup plan. Darlene, that's not a half-bad idea. I'll think about that."

"You have over a year," Traci reminded her. "You have plenty of time to figure out the prom."

"I wonder who Freddy Pierce is gonna go to the prom with this year," Michelle said. "Maybe I should let him know I'm open for invitations. He might not know." The other girls laughed.

Sweet Sixteen

James turned sixteen, then Kim, and Chris followed close behind. Soon, it was St. Patrick's Day, and Michelle was sixteen, too. Her birthday was on a Saturday, so she would have to wait to go to the Registry of Motor Vehicles to get her learner's permit until Monday. Kim had already gotten hers, and her mother had promised her she could have her dad's ancient Chevy Chevette once she passed her driving test in August. Michelle couldn't wait to drive. She could go visit Stephanie any time she wanted! But she would also be expected to drive her ten-year-old brothers around. It was a tradeoff she was willing to accept.

The Gormans took Michelle out for dinner on her birthday and told her she could invite one friend along. She decided to invite Sally.

They picked her up at her house on Justice Drive, only one mile away from McKinney High. "How do you really like it there?" Sally asked as they drove past the school. "Are you learning a lot? Are the other kids, like the ones not from Randall, nice? Does everyone get along?"

Michelle shrugged. "Well, it's just like any other place," she told her friend. "Some people get along, and others don't. There are cliques, but they tend to just stay to themselves. There's an occasional bully, but they don't really bother us. I think people are still a tiny bit afraid of Kim!"

Sally laughed. "That's so funny. She's only like an inch taller than you. She's not very intimidating."

"Yeah, it's a mystery," Michelle agreed. She looked carefully at Sally. "Why are you asking about how it is at McKinney?" she asked. "Are things okay at Gearhart?"

Sally shrugged. "Yeah, it's nothing specific," she said, "but sometimes I wonder now if I would have done better staying in public school. Like maybe it would have just been easier, you know? And I knew people there. It's hard to really fit in at a new place. And it's so different there."

"Different good or bad?" Michelle asked.

"I don't know, just different, I guess. It's okay, really. How are the girls doing?"

Michelle filled her in on all the latest gossip that she felt able to tell and told her about their new friend Traci.

"Maybe she could look at me and tell me who I'm gonna go to the prom with next year," Sally said.

"I don't think she can pick things like names of people she doesn't know out of the air," Michelle told her. "It's more like she can tell if someone is being truthful, or true to themselves. She's pretty good at it. She freaks Darlene out! It's hysterical!"

"Maybe I'll get a chance to meet her someday," Sally said.

The Gormans' Datsun 510 Wagon pulled into the parking lot of the restaurant, and they all piled out.

After dinner, Sally came back to Michelle's house to spend the night. "It's weird with Stephanie not being here," Sally said, putting her overnight bag down on what was now the guest bed in Michelle's room. "I bet you really miss her."

Michelle nodded. "I do," she said. "I still see her a lot, though. I'm having a birthday lunch with her tomorrow at her apartment. She's cooking for me. She's so excited. But yeah, I'm still getting used to the quiet."

"Even with the noisy twins next door?" Sally asked.

Michelle laughed. "Those guys run around so much, they usually pass out right at nine. It's kind of awesome." She paused. "Something's going on with you, Sally. You're just not yourself tonight. Did something happen that you're not telling me?"

Sally smiled at Michelle. "I thought Traci was the psychic," she quipped.

Michelle laughed. "Sally, it doesn't take a psychic to see that you haven't talked about any boys all night. And you just don't seem as excited about things like you usually do. I mean, you didn't even freak out about how good the cake was tonight. You always make a big deal about chocolate cake."

Sally nodded. Then she sighed. "Yeah, I guess I'm just not too thrilled with my Gearhart Prep experience. I figured when I went there that the kids there would be more mature, more serious about school. But they're not. They're not always very nice. And they're really not always very nice to me especially. And the classes are hard. I'm not doing very well on my grades, even though I'm trying really hard. I don't know, I had some ideas about what this year would be like, and it just hasn't turned out that way at all. Maybe next year, when I've been there longer, it will be better. I don't know. What do you think? Do you think I made a huge mistake by going there?"

Michelle thought for a minute. She really didn't want to say the wrong thing. "I don't know if you made a mistake, Sally," she said. "But you don't sound like you're very happy. And to be honest, I still miss you all the time, so if I had my way, you'd come back. But I mean, would your parents even let you come back to public school now that you've started Gearhart?"

"I just don't know," Sally admitted. "I mean, I don't want to let them down, you know? Nathan made it through four years there, and he did fine. Well, as fine as Nathan can do anywhere, I guess. I don't want them to think bad of me. I guess I'll just have to try harder and ask for more help before finals."

"Sally, you should talk to your parents," Michelle urged. "Maybe they'd surprise you. Maybe they'd have some ideas you haven't thought of."

"Maybe," Sally said. "I'm just so glad I can talk to you about this stuff. You know, I can talk to my sister about most things, but I just worry that she'd say something to my mom, trying to help me, and I really want to try to take care of this myself. But you always listen to me and try to help. I've really missed you, too, Michelle. I haven't really made any good friends at Gearhart. I wish you could go there with me."

Michelle laughed. "I doubt they would have their uniform in my size. I'd have to get a special one made in size tiny!"

They both laughed. Then they put on some old new wave music and the talk turned to boys.

It didn't take long for the heat of summer to set in. Michelle had thought about getting a job at the mall, but then her mother announced that she would be taking some college classes toward her teaching degree over the summer, and she would pay Michelle the going rate to babysit for her twin brothers. She would even give her money to buy them snacks or for entertainment. Michelle readily agreed. Her brothers knew how to entertain themselves and each other. It was a pretty easy job.

She went to Sally's house for Sally's birthday dinner in August, and then they went to a Red Sox game in Boston the next day with Sally's father. Then Sally got a part-time job at the mall, Mrs. Gorman completed her summer classes, and Michelle got the rest of the summer off from babysitting.

A week before school was to start, the phone rang at the Gormans' house. "Michelle, it's for you!" her father called out. "It's Sally!"

Michelle picked up the extension in her room, and before she even got through saying hello, Sally yelled out, "Guess what?"

"What?" Michelle asked, not daring to venture a guess.

"*I'm gonna go to McKinney this year!*" Sally shouted into the phone.

Michelle had to pull the receiver away from her ear for a second. "What?" she asked in disbelief. "What happened?"

Sally was silent for a second. "Well, it's not all the greatest news," she said, "but I lost my scholarship because my grades weren't good enough. So my parents gave me a choice again about what I wanted to do. And I told them I want McKinney! Can you believe it?"

"No, I can't!" Michelle exclaimed. "I've never been more happy to hear that someone got bad grades in my life! But are you gonna have to do sophomore year again?"

"No," Sally told her. "That's one of the great things about this. Apparently a D at Gearhart is equal to a C in the Eastboro public school district, and I only got one D. So I'll get to be a junior!"

"Oh my God, this is so amazing!" Michelle exclaimed.

"Michelle, please don't tell the other girls about my scholarship, okay? I mean, I'll probably tell them anyway, but for now, let's just keep it between you and me?"

"Of course!" Michelle promised. "I'm really good at keeping secrets. Did you get to pick your elective classes yet?"

"I filled out the forms and picked art and creative writing, but I haven't heard back yet," Sally said. "I guess I'll have to wait until the first day to find out."

"That's one week from now!" Michelle reminded her. "I really hope we're in some classes together. That would be so awesome!"

"Wicked awesome!" Sally agreed. "Promise me you'll look for me on the first day, and then you can walk with me to my house after school."

"I promise," Michelle assured her.

Sally coming to McKinney High School didn't turn out exactly the way Michelle was picturing it. Something very unexpected happened three days into the school year: James Newell asked Sally out on a date. He had seen Sally for the first time in over a year, and he had fallen head over heels in love with her. The feeling was mutual. Within one week of the first day, Sally and James had their first kiss on the top of the bridge at Twin Bridges Park. By the second week, they were holding hands in the hallways, and by the fourth week, Sally was referring to James, who she still called Jamie, as her boyfriend, and they were going to the homecoming dance as a couple. The girls from DeMarco were blown away.

"I have never seen anything like this," Kim said. "I mean, we've known James for twelve years. Would either of you ever have imagined this happening? Like even in your wildest dreams?"

"No!" both Darlene and Michelle answered at the same time.

"I mean, *James and Sally*? It's like you can't even make this shit up! And look at them! It's like they're perfect together! But like, why all of a sudden *now?*"

Traci shrugged. "Love at first sight," she said. "Or second sight in this case. It's a thing. I've never seen it happen before now, but it's a thing."

Michelle shook her head. "Sally got one of her bad boys," she said.

"It's hard to picture James as a bad boy," Traci said. "He always seems so quiet and reserved."

"He wasn't one of the more vocal bad boys," Kim told her. "That was Chris and Pete. Carl and James were more of the quiet kind of bad. Sometimes, that's even worse. It means there's something brewing under the surface. And with Carl and James, I think that's always been the case."

"Bad boys with a backstory," Darlene said. "But James is in a much better place now. I think things have really settled down for him."

"Yeah, for him and for Chris," Michelle said. "They both seem so much more mellow now. Must be the love of a good woman."

Traci shook her head. "I don't know," she said. "I mean, James and Sally seem like an awesome match. But I still don't trust Rhonda. I think she's up to no good. I think she's gonna hurt Chris badly. I just feel it."

"Do you have some sort of a thing for Chris, Traci?" Kim asked. "I mean, you've been worried about this Rhonda thing for some time now. Why do you care so much?"

Traci shrugged. "I don't know, maybe I do. I mean, I don't think I have an all-out crush on him or anything, but I just think he can do better than Rhonda. I think there's someone out there that can make him really happy. And I just don't think it's Rhonda. I don't necessarily think it's me, either. At least not in this lifetime."

Michelle lost the train of the conversation. She was caught on something Kim had just said. She had asked why Traci cared so much. Something was nagging at Michelle. She was feeling weird about Sally and James. She was happy about them being together, but something was causing her to feel an ache in her stomach. She had never had a crush on any of the bad boys. Bad boys just weren't her thing. But she realized, looking back over her school years, that if she *had* had a crush on any of the bad boys, it probably would have been James. She was feeling jealous of Sally. Not that she wanted James. No, that would never have happened, not in a million years. But it was less not James than it was not the other bad boys. That thought baffled her.

The best aspect of Sally's new relationship with James was that she was including Michelle in the entire process. She was calling her with all the details. She was asking her for her advice. She was still making plans to do things with Michelle, and she was still eating lunch with the girls on most days. So what Michelle had worked out was that her relationship with James was actually making Sally an even better person than she already was. There was nothing bad about that. As a matter of fact, that was very, very good. Michelle would try to remember that when she felt the jealousy rise.

Michelle would have her time. She would have her man. And he would be the one for her, just for her. And everyone would be happy.

One day, James approached Michelle at her locker when Sally wasn't around. "Hey, Michelle," he said, "I need a favor, and I think you can help me."

"What is it?" Michelle asked, closing her locker and spinning the dial on her lock.

James looked a bit shy. "Well, I know you're in French class with Sally, and it's your third year. If I asked you to translate some things into French for me, would you be able to do it?"

Michelle shrugged. "I guess so," she said. "If I couldn't, I could always ask the teacher for help. What kinds of things?'

James smiled. "Just little things I can say to Sally. I'm not sure what yet, but I'll come up with something. I just want to be able to, you know, surprise her every now and then. Like maybe something nice about her hair or something. Easy things. But you'd also have to teach me how to say it right. I know there are a lot of words in French that don't sound at all like they look."

Michelle nodded. "I can do that. It seems pretty romantic."

"Good," James said. "Romantic is what I'm going for. But don't tell her about it, okay? I don't want her to know how I'm learning any French. It will drive her crazy!"

Michelle laughed. "Yeah," she agreed, "it will. This is very sweet of you, James. You're a good boyfriend. You and Sally are a really good couple."

"Thanks," James said. "That means a lot coming from her best friend. And one of my oldest friends. We are a good couple. I'm crazy about her, and I can promise you, I'm gonna do the best I can to keep making her happy."

Michelle gave him a warm smile. She believed him.

After Halloween, but before Thanksgiving, Sally and James finally gave in to their sexual urges. Sally called Michelle. "Jamie just called me," she said excitedly. "He's coming to pick me up in less than an hour. We're going to a motel!"

"A motel! Sally! Oh my God! You're really gonna do it! Are you nervous?"

"I'm trembling!" Sally told her. "I'm trying to stay calm, but it's so hard. I mean, I can't believe it's gonna happen!"

"You need to call me tomorrow and tell me how it went," Michelle said. "I mean, I don't mean all the juicy details or anything, but you just need to let me know if it was amazing! Sally, things are never gonna be the same with you and James after tonight. Are you positive you're ready?"

Sally sighed. "I am so ready, Michelle. I mean, it's Jamie! He's so great. And I just want to be so close to him. And I know he wants this so much too. I can't believe we're both having our first time together. I need to go get ready, but I will talk to you tomorrow, I promise."

"Good luck, Sally," Michelle said sincerely. "I hope it's exactly like you want it to be. And be careful, okay?"

"I will," Sally promised.

When Sally hadn't called by noon, Michelle called her. Sally was still in bed and her mother took a message. She finally called back at two, before leaving to work at the mall.

"How was it?" Michelle asked anxiously.

"Michelle, I don't really even have words," Sally told her.

"Is that good?"

"Oh, Michelle, it was way beyond good. I mean, it was incredible. He was incredible. The whole thing. I can't even believe it's real, except my whole body hurts!"

"It hurt?" Michelle asked, somewhat horrified.

"Well, yeah, I had read that your first time does hurt, but it gets better. But it wasn't awful, just uncomfortable. I was worried it would be like, gross messy, but it wasn't too bad. I mean, I don't think there's any way the first time can be perfect. We barely knew what we were doing. But it was damn close to perfect. And there was a second time! And almost a third, but we ran out of condoms."

"Sally!" Michelle exclaimed. "Oh my God! I can't believe it! How are you feeling now?"

Sally sighed. "Tired, but totally in love. Jamie called me this morning to check on me. I think he's gonna tell me he loves me soon. I could feel it last night. Oh my God, I really hope all this is real. I mean, Michelle, it's so intense. I really do love him. I didn't know you could love someone so fast!"

"I'm so happy for you, Sally," Michelle told her. And she was. The way Sally talked about her relationship with James sounded like the real deal. And James was back to his old self now. He had some pep in his step when he walked down the hall. He smiled and said hi to Michelle when they crossed paths. He just seemed genuinely happy.

"Michelle, I need to go now," Sally told her. "But I'm assuming you know that this is all just between you and me. Jamie said he would tell Pete and no one else, and I told him I would tell you and no one else. We're just not that excited for the idea of everyone knowing, you know?"

"I get it," Michelle told her. "You know your secret's safe with me." Michelle was getting good at keeping things to herself.

When she got off the phone, Michelle looked at herself in her full-length mirror. She still looked like an eighth grader, no matter what she wore or how she did her hair or makeup. She hadn't even reached five feet tall. She was sixteen now, she was learning to drive, and she would graduate from high school in less than two years. She had never kissed a boy. She had never even been on a date. Now at least two of her friends had become sexually active, and Michelle had no prospects in sight. In the past, her only worry had been not getting a date for the prom. Now, she was not only worried about that, but also about the thought of dying at a ripe old age as an unkissed virgin.

Joey Baby

In mid-December, Darlene was invited to go ice-skating at the frozen Carson Lake with her crush, Charlie, and his friends. The plows had been by and had swept open an area for neighborhood residents to use. Darlene begged Michelle and Kim to come along, and much to her surprise, they both readily agreed.

"I still have to break in my new skates from last year," Kim said. "I'll probably get blisters up to my ankles, but it should be fun."

"I still fit into my skates from junior high," Michelle revealed. "My parents won't get me new ones until I grow out of them. Fat chance of that ever happening."

They all walked down to Carson Lake on a Sunday afternoon. The air was bitter cold, but the sky was blue and sunny. It was perfect ice-skating weather. Michelle had wrapped herself up in a long down jacket, mittens, a hat, and a scarf. Darlene wore much less outerwear, as she wanted to impress Charlie with her toughness and her hair and makeup.

They donned their skates and hit the ice. They quickly found Charlie and his friends and started to circle around the cleared area. After three circles, Michelle could see that Darlene's gloved hand was in the grips of Charlie's gloved hand, and she alerted Kim. They both smiled, and then gave the couple some space.

After a few more circuits, Michelle heard a familiar voice approaching behind her. "Hey there, is that Tiny Gorman?"

Michelle skidded to a stop, and Kim stopped beside her. She turned around to find two tall boys standing still on hockey skates in jeans and puffy black jackets.

"Tommy Griffith," Michelle stated as a fact. "I thought I'd seen the last of you when you started Murphy."

Tommy snickered. "Naw, you can't get rid of me that easily, Tiny. Even if you can hide behind a thimble. Hey, who's your friend?"

Michelle sighed. "Tommy, this Kim Drake. Kim, this is Tommy. He was in homeroom and core classes with me all three years at Randall."

"Oh yeah," Kim said. "You're the one who harassed Michelle all the time about her size. You always called her Tiny."

"I was only teasing her," Tommy said defensively. "It's only harassment when it's done with bad intentions."

Michelle shook her head. Her hat came loose, and she took it off to reposition. Her red hair spilled in front of her face, and she brushed it back.

The other boy with Tommy watched her with fascination, and then hit Tommy lightly on his arm with the back of his hand. "Aren't you gonna introduce me, T?"

"Oh, I'm sorry, where are my manners?" Tommy said, and then he chuckled. "This is my friend Joey Cafaro. He goes to Murphy. This is Tiny." Michelle glared at him. "Sorry, sorry," he said. "This is Michelle Gorman. And her friend, Kim."

"Nice to meet you," Joey said, sticking out his gloved hand to shake Michelle's mittened one. Then he looked at Kim. "Hi," he said. He turned back to Michelle. "I like your scarf," he told her.

Michelle looked down at her scarf. It was a homemade multicolor wool yarn scarf that her grandmother had given her last Christmas. "Thanks."

"Michelle, look, Darlene wants us to go over there," Kim said, pointing to Darlene at the side of the lake, who was waving to them. "Nice to meet you guys," she said to Tommy and Joey.

"See ya, Tiny," Tommy called out as he turned to skate away.

Joey shook his head and looked at Michelle. "He can be kind of a dufus sometimes, but he's actually not a bad guy once you get to know him. It was nice to meet you, *Michelle*." He smiled at her and turned to skate away.

Michelle was left speechless. Kim laughed out loud. "Oh, my God, Michelle," she said. "Did you see what just happened there? That was incredible. Are you bruised from being hit on so hard, or what?" She maintained a huge, amused smile.

"He was cute, right?" Michelle asked. "I mean, I wasn't just imagining that he was cute, was I?"

Kim shook her head. "No, he was wicked cute. He had gorgeous eyes. And he's built like a football player. You could see how defined he was even through his jacket and jeans. I wish I could have seen his hair. I'm guessing it's like, dirty blond and short."

"That would be nice," Michelle mumbled, and she looked across the ice at Joey skating away with Tommy. "Do you think he liked me?"

Kim laughed again. "Do I think he liked you? Michelle, as we speak, I can guarantee that he is pumping Tommy for information on how to find you again."

"But I don't think Tommy knows how to find me," Michelle protested. "Ugh, I should go chase after him and give him my number."

"Don't act so desperate," Kim said.

Michelle rolled her eyes. "I'm not acting!"

Kim laughed. "I bet that Tommy knows how to find you," Kim assured her.

"I don't know, Kim," Michelle said. "I bet if Tommy knows how to find me, I'm gonna get a call from him soon asking me how to find *you!*"

Kim laughed again, and then got serious quickly. "No, Michelle, if he does, don't give him my number, okay? I really don't want him to have it!"

Michelle smiled and nodded. Then the two friends skated over to Darlene.

When the phone rang that night, Michelle panicked. When her father told her there was a boy on the line for her, her heart started pounding.

"Don't be Tommy, don't be Tommy," she begged quietly. "Hello?"

"Hi, is this Michelle?" the voice said.

Michelle let out her breath. Tommy would have called her Tiny. It was Joey. *Yikes,* she thought. It was actually Joey!

"Yeah, this is Michelle," she said.

"Hey, Michelle, this is Joey Cafaro from the lake today? With Tommy?"

"Hi, Joey," Michelle said, hoping her voice didn't sound like a ten-year-old's.

"I hope it's okay that I called you."

"Yeah, it's good," Michelle said. "How did you get my number?"

"Tommy said your dad works at Aries," Joey said, "and he said your last name was Gorman. I just looked in the phone book under Gorman, and your address was the one closest to Aries. It was easy."

"Oh," Michelle responded, kind of wishing Joey'd had to work harder to find her. "I almost went back to find you to give it to you," Michelle said, and then immediately wanted to kick herself for revealing too much.

"Really?" Joey asked. "That's really cool. I thought maybe it would be okay to call you. I didn't want to be out of line."

"No, no, you're right in line," Michelle said. Why was she saying these things? But Joey seemed to be eating it up.

Joey laughed. It was a good laugh. "Cool," he said. "So maybe we could get together some time, like to go out?"

Michelle's heart started pounding again. She wouldn't die dateless, at least! "Yeah, that would be great!" she said. "I'd like that."

"Well, alright," Joey said. "Are you free next Saturday?"

Michelle thought about it. Then she remembered that Stephanie was coming over on Saturday to make Christmas cookies and sleep over. "Oh, actually, I'm not," she said. "I have plans with my family that day. But I am free on Friday," she offered.

"I can make Friday work," Joey said. "Maybe Friendly's and a movie?"

Friendly's *and* a movie?? "Sure, that sounds good!"

"Alright, well, why don't you pick a movie you'd like to see, and I'll call you later in the week to check in and make plans."

"Okay," Michelle agreed. "I'm looking forward to it. I'll talk to you later this week."

"Great!" Joey responded. "Talk to you later, Michelle."

"Bye."

Michelle depressed the hang-up button then released it. Then she dialed Sally's number.

"Oh my God Sally I met a boy today and he asked me out and we're going out Friday night!!!" Michelle blurted when Sally got on the line.

"What! Oh my God, Michelle! Who was he? What's his name? Does he go to McKinney? What does he look like?"

Michelle laughed. She knew she had called the right person to match her excitement. "His name is Joey. I met him skating at the lake with Kim and Darlene. He goes to Murphy. I think he's Italian. He looks like a football player! Like the ones that throw or catch the ball, not the ones that just knock the other ones over."

"Like a quarterback or a receiver?" Sally knew everything about football. "They're the best-looking players on the team! So he just asked you out?"

"No, he was with Tommy Griffith, that idiot from my homeroom at Randall that called me Tiny? And he figured out enough from him to find my number and he *called me*! My first call from a boy! A boy called me to ask me out!"

"Michelle, that's so great! What are you going to do?"

"Friendly's and a movie," Michelle said. "I shouldn't get a tuna melt, though, should I? Maybe just a salad and fries. What movie should we see? I'm supposed to pick, but I don't want to pick something he'll hate! Ahhh!"

"What about *Starman*?" Sally suggested. "It's coming out this weekend, and then you can see it and tell me if it's any good and if Jamie and I should see it. It looks pretty good in the commercials."

"I've seen those commercials," Michelle said. "It looks like it's a movie anyone could like. Yeah, I'll suggest it. I just hope it's not too crowded."

"Think about it, Michelle," Sally told her. "If it's really crowded, you'll have to sit *really close together*. It might be nice!"

The school week dragged by. There were only two weeks until winter break, and everyone was feeling the pressure. There were papers to write and exams to take. At lunch, the boys from the posse and Michelle's group of friends had started sitting at the same table. It was Sally's doing. She wanted to spend time with her friends and her boyfriend and insisted that she should be able to do both at the same time. After all, the boys had gone to elementary school with three of the girls, and the other two girls were happy to share their space with the posse. Even Rhonda joined them from time to time. Everyone was getting along well, and everyone seemed mostly content.

Friday finally arrived, and Michelle pulled Sally aside before lunch. "You have to help me," she begged. "Come over after school and help me get dressed and do my makeup. I'm too nervous. I'm gonna mess up and end up looking like a mini clown with freckles!"

Sally laughed. "I'll come over," she said. "But your freckles are adorable. Let's not cover them up. We'll just accentuate your eyes. That's what he'll be looking into anyways."

"Thank you so much, Sally!" Michelle said. "You're a lifesaver."

Sally helped Michelle with her unruly hair, and it ended up looking silky and smooth. Then she added eyeliner, eye shadow, mascara, and a touch of blush to brighten the freckles. Together, they raided Michelle's closet and found a stylish long-sleeved short dress that emphasized her chest and hid her overwhelming slimness. She put on tights and high-top black lace-up leather shoes with black laces. Michelle looked at herself in the mirror. She smiled.

"I look at least thirteen," she boasted.

Sally smiled. "You look really pretty, Michelle," she said. "Joey's gonna be overwhelmed by you."

"That's the goal," Michelle said.

Sally went home, and Joey arrived at five thirty. He came to the door and knocked. Michelle could hear her father open the door and introduce himself. She could hear muffled sounds of Joey saying something back. Her father told Joey that Michelle needed to be home at midnight and asked him to wait. Then he called for her up the stairs.

Michelle trotted down the stairs with a smile. "Hi, Joey," she said, stepping into the hall. "Let me just get my coat, and I'll be ready to go."

"Michelle, you left your glasses on the counter," her mother said, coming out of the kitchen followed by Stevie and Sam. "Hello," she said to Joey. "I'm Michelle's mother, Mrs. Gorman. You must be Joey."

She handed Michelle her glasses, and she reluctantly put them on. Her world became instantly clearer.

"Nice to meet you, Mrs. Gorman," Joey said. "Wow, you all have the best red hair." Joey's hair was indeed dirty blond.

"My older sister Stephanie, too," Michelle told him. "She looks like the Strawberry Shortcake doll. Okay, I'm ready to go. See you guys at midnight!"

Joey waved to the Gormans, and Stevie and Sam called out in their sweetest voices, "Bye, Joey!"

Michelle got into the blue pickup truck after Joey opened the door. She had to step up carefully. The Friendly's wasn't far from her house, and they were there before they had too much time to work up a conversation. They sat at a booth and looked at the menus.

"I think I'll just get a burger and fries and a Fribble," Joey said, putting his menu down. He looked up at Michelle and met her eyes. "You look so nice tonight," he told her. "I didn't really get a good sense of what you looked like out there on the ice last week. I could see your gorgeous hair and your eyes, and that was enough. But the whole package is amazing."

Michelle smiled shyly. "Thanks," she said. "I noticed your eyes, too," she said. "I had no idea what color your hair was."

The waitress came over and took their order. Michelle went for the tuna melt, after all. While they waited, they talked about their families. Joey had two younger brothers and one older sister who was in college. Michelle told Joey about Stephanie and how proud she was of all that she had accomplished. Joey sounded impressed.

"We did a service day at Murphy last year," he told her, "and a couple of us went to a group home to volunteer for the day. I had no idea what to expect. A few of the residents had Down syndrome. Each one was different and could do different things. I've heard people say that they all look alike, but it only takes like five minutes to see that's not true. We had a great time. It almost didn't seem like work."

Michelle smiled. "Yeah, Stephanie is amazing. I mean, Sally is my best friend, but Stephanie is my partner in crime, you know? And then we have the freaky twins. I don't know, I've lived with them for ten years now, and they still freak me out. It's like they have some sort of weird telepathy and secret language. I don't think one can exist without the other. It must be so weird to have an entire person who is exactly like you in every way."

"Well, that's all they know," Joey said, "so they probably think you're the freaky one!"

Michelle laughed, and Joey laughed with her.

Their food came, and they concentrated for a few minutes on eating. Then they talked about their friends and their hobbies. Michelle did not tell him about her fascination with the world of gossip. Joey did play football his first year in high school but then decided it took too much of his time, and he left the team. He still liked to work out with weights and to run, but he also liked spending time with his friends and having an occasional beer. Those things were frowned upon by the football coach. Joey liked The Beatles, and he loved classic rock in general. He, too, was the whole package.

Joey also liked adventure and trying new things. And he loved space movies. He was excited to see *Starman*; he really liked Jeff Bridges. Michelle ordered a Rocky Road cone to go, and they headed for the theater.

They waited in line for tickets but made it in before the show sold out. They found two seats near the center of the middle row and squeezed past the other patrons. In actuality, Joey squeezed. Michelle glided in with no problem. They sat down and started munching on a shared large vat of popcorn. Joey gave Michelle sips of his Coke when the salt made her thirsty. They watched the previews, and when the feature movie started, Michelle felt Joey's arm leaning against hers with more pressure. She was also getting pressure from the person in the seat on her other side.

Joey looked at her and whispered. "There's not much room. Can I put my arm around the back of your seat?"

Michelle nodded her consent. She felt his arm rest against the back of her shoulders, and she tried not to shudder. As the movie went on, Joey leaned closer toward Michelle, and Michelle leaned closer toward Joey. Before long, her head was up against his chest, and his arm behind her back. When the movie ended and the credits came on, they turned to each other, and Joey reached over and kissed her. His lips were soft, but strong, and not squishy at all. Michelle hoped she was kissing back the right way. People around them started to get out of their seats, and Joey pulled away.

"Sorry," he said. "I hope that wasn't weird. I wanted to kiss you the whole time, but I didn't want you to miss the movie."

"That was very considerate of you," Michelle told him. Then she reached back and kissed him again. They stayed until the theater was almost completely empty, then they got up and walked back to the parking lot and Joey's truck.

When they got inside, they both sat down but didn't fasten their seat belts. Joey reached across the seat and put his hand on Michelle's cheek. She leaned into it.

"You are so pretty," he told her. "You don't have to worry about wearing your glasses in front of me. I like them on you. They look classy." He leaned back toward her and kissed her some more. Then they both brought their hands up to touch each other tentatively. Then slightly more assertively. Then Joey pulled away. "I need to get you home," he said, somewhat breathlessly. "It's getting late."

They both put their seat belts on, and Joey drove out of the parking lot.

"I had a good time tonight," Michelle told him. "Thank you for dinner and the movie."

"Oh, thanks for agreeing to come out with me," Joey said. "Are you going to be around during break?"

"Yeah," she said. "We'll go over to my grandmother's house for Christmas dinner, but she just lives near East Firehouse. What about you?"

"We're going to see my mom's family on Long Island for Christmas, but we'll be back by New Years, if you wanna hang out or something."

"Yeah," Michelle answered. "I would like that."

Joey smiled. "Cool," he said. "So I'll call you between Christmas and New Years then. I mean, I'll call you before that, but I'll also call you then."

Now Michelle smiled. Joey was just as awkward as she was. She had nothing to worry about after all. She wondered if he'd ever had a girlfriend before. She would find out later. For now, he pulled up in front of her house and turned off the ignition. He got out of the truck, and Michelle let him walk around to open her door. She hopped out, and he took her in his arms and kissed her like he meant it. She meant it back. Then he walked her to the door, and they said good night.

Michelle wanted to call Sally as soon as she got to her room, but she knew she'd have gone to sleep after her good night call from James at 10:15. Even Michelle's parents were asleep when she went inside, so there was no one to ask her how her date went. She wished Stephanie were there. She would have woken her up to tell her all about it. Stephanie would have been so excited. She was fascinated about girls and boys and kissing. She would tell Michelle about the boys she would see on her weekend outings and wonder what it would be like if one of them were her boyfriend.

Michelle got ready for bed and crawled under her warm flannel sheets. It was nearly Christmas, and she felt Santa had really pulled through for her this year. But she still wanted a gift certificate to Filene's so she could buy new clothes for her dates with Joey. For now, she just said a silent thank-you to Father Christmas and turned out her lights.

She slept until 11:14, then reached for her phone before even getting out of bed. Sally was up, and she was about to call Michelle.

"I'm dying for details," Sally said excitedly.

"It was great!" Michelle told her. She told her about dinner at Friendly's and then the movie. And then the kiss at the end.

"He didn't want you to miss any of the movie!" Sally said, and she sighed. "That is so sweet. I bet you weren't expecting that."

"No, not at all. But you were right about the crowded theater. He had his arm around my back within the first two minutes. It was so cute that he thought I believed it was because there was no space! Sally, I think he really likes me."

"Of course he does," Sally agreed. "And he sounds wicked nice."

"We're gonna hang out on New Years Eve, but I don't know what to do. What are you and James doing?"

"We're going to the First Night Festival downtown," Sally said. "You should come with us! It will be fun! I'm sure Jamie would be okay with it."

The two couples attended the First Night celebration, and they all hit it off well. Michelle and Joey shared a public kiss at midnight, and Michelle felt that 1985 was already her favorite year. The only downside was Joey's declaration that, one day, he planned to join the Marines. Michelle was fine with people joining the Marines, but she wasn't a huge fan of the idea of having a long-distance relationship with a Marine. But that was way off in the future. She didn't need to entertain that worry just yet.

They fell into a nice dating routine through the next few months. They went on dates alone and with their coupled friends and hung out in their friend groups together. They got to know each other's families, and Joey went with Michelle to visit Stephanie at her apartment. Stephanie adored Joey and giggled when he complimented her on her beautiful red hair. Michelle told Joey about McKinney's April prom, and he asked her if he could be her date. She quickly accepted.

Michelle and Sally went dress shopping together. Sally already knew what she wanted, but Michelle had no idea. She tried on several dresses at several shops before settling on a beautiful Kelly-green taffeta gown that went below her knees. Exposing some leg made her appear slightly taller. But just to be sure, she also bought some black high-heeled shoes. Then they went to buy accessories. Lastly, Michelle's mother agreed to let her make an appointment with the eye doctor, and she was prescribed contact lenses she could wear to the prom.

Carl and Kim were going to the prom together. "They made a pact last year," Darlene told Michelle. "If neither of them had a date lined up for prom, they would go together. Kim just told me about it last week. I had no idea. She said it was her backup plan."

Michelle shook her head. "That's so weird," she said. "It's not like they hang out together or anything. And remember how mean she was to him when we were at DeMarco? I mean, she still calls him a moron! Do you . . ." She leaned in. "Do you think Kim *likes* Carl?"

Darlene shrugged. "I don't know," she admitted. "The pact was her idea. They were so close in elementary school until the posse got together. I mean, they used to hold hands, for God's sake. But since second grade, they've hardly spoken."

"She sits next to him when they're in class together. But they hardly say a word to each other."

Darlene contemplated for a moment. "I guess she *could* have a thing for him," she said. "That might explain why she's always so angry at Chris."

"Maybe," Michelle said. "Maybe she thinks it's all his fault that she's not close with Carl anymore. But they would be cute together. Can you even imagine? I hope they do hook up."

Darlene sighed. "It would be nice if Kim had someone to make her happy, but I'm not too sure Carl's gonna be that someone. But I'm glad she has a date. And I can't believe Traci is going with Doug O'Leary! Dougo! She didn't even know people called him that at Randall. She just knows him as her brother's friend. But she really seems to like him."

"I wonder if Traci gets little intuitive snippets about herself," Michelle pondered. "Like does she know she'll end up happily ever after with Dougo, and stuff like that."

"She's not a psychic," Darlene reminded her. "She's not always right. I'm definitely going to major in biology in college. I'm already looking into programs. It's happening."

"But she's been right about a lot of things," Michelle reminded her. "I just hope she's wrong about Rhonda. I would really hate to see Chris get hurt."

Prom plans were finalized, and the group had dinner together before the big event. They all enjoyed the dance, and then had their own afterparty at the Marriott Hotel. Everyone had gotten permission from their parents to stay the night, although Sally and James were planning on heading back to his house for a romantic sleepover before the night was through. Michelle had considered her options with Joey. There had been making out, lots of kissing and exploring by hand. There had been some experiments with other methods of pleasure, but they had yet to go all the way. Their timing never seemed right, or when it was, it just didn't feel like the right moment. Michelle knew she wanted to, and with Joey, but she would rather have it be later and wonderful than sooner and just okay. She didn't want to have any regrets.

But that didn't mean she was not attracted to Joey and drawn to him in many romantic ways. They danced at prom, pausing for kisses and close bodily contact, and once Michelle had finished one cup of champagne in the hotel room, she led Joey off to the corner of the room, sat on the floor, and they made out in plain sight, although no one was really paying attention. Especially when Kim and Carl went out for a "walk" alone together, and everyone saw Darlene slipping Charlie's car keys, not as discreetly as she thought, into Kim's purse. Soon after, Chris and a slightly inebriated Rhonda were fooling around on the armchair, Darlene and Charlie went off into the bathroom together, and last Michelle saw, Traci and Dougo were on the floor between the two full-sized beds, upright but kissing. The night was an unparalleled success.

They all talked about prom for weeks after it ended. Kim and Carl were now together, and their relationship was blooming like the roses in the schoolyard. Traci and Dougo were also an item, and even Traci's brother Bobby was okay with the pairing. Chris and Rhonda had made it through prom with their relationship intact, and Michelle, Darlene, and Traci had made it through with their virginity still intact. But now Darlene was contemplating breaking up with Charlie.

"He's just not doing it for me anymore, you know?" she told Michelle as they walked home from school. "I see the way you are with Joey, and the way Kim looks at Carl. I felt like that at first with Charlie, when it was new, but now I just don't anymore. I don't know if it's him or me, but I just don't see us together much longer."

"I'm so sorry, Darlene," Michelle said. "I know how hard you worked on getting together with him. And if it wasn't for you wanting to go ice-skating with him, I never would have met Joey. But yeah, you shouldn't be with someone if he doesn't make you feel special and happy."

"Is that how you feel about Joey?" Darlene asked.

Michelle nodded. "I do," she said. "Sometimes he looks at me like he can't believe he actually gets to be there with me. He makes me feel like I'm the only girl in the world. I don't ever want to be with anyone who can't make me feel that way. It's an amazing way to feel. And I feel lucky, too. Pete and Carolyn say people really like Joey at Murphy, and I guess there were some girls who were pissed off that he's with someone at McKinney instead of dating anyone there. But it's not like he had a girlfriend before me anyway. I'm sorry, Darlene. We were talking about you and Charlie. I didn't mean to go on like that about how happy I am."

"Michelle, it's okay," Darlene assured her. "I asked. And I'm happy for you. You were so sure no one would want to go out with you because you're small. And that's so not the case. Joey thinks you're perfect, and that's all that matters, right? It gives me hope that maybe someone who I like will think I'm perfect one day. I'm really glad you're happy with Joey."

"Thanks, Darlene. Let me know if there's anything I can do to help you if you do decide to break up. We can hang out, or go shopping at the mall or something."

Darlene smiled. "I'd like that. I'm so glad you offered me that chocolate chip cookie that day in kindergarten. I can't imagine all these past years without you, Michelle. You've been a wicked awesome friend."

Michelle was overwhelmed by Darlene's sentiment. Darlene had never expressed that type of thing to her before. She wondered if perhaps the same thing was happening to her and Darlene as happened with her and Sally when she started seeing James. Maybe being with Joey was making Michelle a better person.

The school year ended, and with it, Darlene's relationship with Charlie. Both Kim and Michelle tried to keep her busy, even inviting her along with them and their boyfriends, but she didn't really like that idea. The group of friends did their best to meet up over the summer, and Dougo, Joey, and Pete's girlfriend, Carolyn, became part of the gang. Michelle and Joey spent as much time as they could together outside of Joey working on the line at Aries for the season, and Michelle working as the neighborhood's favorite babysitter. Everyone was preparing for senior year, and the work and promise of the future it would bring.

Senior Slump

Finally, the first day of school arrived, and everyone was baffled by the absence of Chris and Traci from their morning classes. But all was revealed by lunchtime. First came Traci's tearful declaration in the cafeteria that she and her family were moving immediately to Detroit for her father's job. The girls couldn't believe this was happening. Traci was one of the gang, just as much as anyone from the DeMarco group. She fit in so well, and she rounded them out so nicely. And then just like that, she was leaving. And she hadn't even sensed it coming.

They were all still reeling from that blow when the next one hit them right in the chin: Rhonda had broken up with Chris. Today, on the first day of school. Before classes had even started. And now Traci wasn't even there to gloat about the fact that she had been right all along. Rhonda had completely and mercilessly shattered Chris's heart. He walked around for days like an empty shell of a human. And now senior year had a brand-new feel.

Everyone did the best they could to get through the first months, taking care of Chris when he needed them, working on college applications, and just getting through their daily routine. And then there was the biggest mystery of all: Carl had gotten one of the highest scores in the school on his SATs. He had also been on the honor roll for three consecutive terms. Nobody understood what was going on.

"Was he struck by lightning?" Darlene wondered. "I mean, this is Carl Bishop we're talking about, right? I didn't even know he knew which end was up let alone anything else. Carl didn't even study for the SATs. How did he score 1480?"

Kim shrugged. "I think Carl has been smart all along," she boasted about her boyfriend. "I just think no one cared and no one pushed him to do his best. It was just easier for him to follow along than to take the lead. His parents are horrible, you know? They just didn't care. Maybe it's like if you have a plant and you don't water it, it doesn't grow. But if you suddenly start to water it, it takes a bit of time, but it starts to grow again."

"So in this scenario, you're the water?" Darlene asked.

"No, *I'm* not the water. But maybe me just being around makes him want to find the water. Or maybe I'm the person with the water. Oh great, now I'm thirsty. I need some water."

Michelle laughed. "So if he's so smart," she asked, "then why isn't he making any plans for next year? I mean, he doesn't *have* to go to college if he doesn't want to, but the management at McDonald's pays you the same amount as everyone else, even if you have high SATs scores."

"I know," Kim said. "He doesn't really want to talk about it, even with me. He keeps changing the subject. I guess he'll figure something out. I mean, he is really smart and all."

Michelle had completed applications to several schools, including University of Massachusetts, Boston University, Eastboro State, and University of Rhode Island. She had decided to pursue a course of study in nursing. One of the reasons for this was the conversation with Traci two years earlier about what everyone wanted to do after they finished school. She had never thought of medicine as a career, but now it was stuck in her mind. She didn't know if Traci had put the idea there, or just nourished it with her insight. But being with Joey also reinforced her decision. Joey wanted to help people, too. He enjoyed his volunteer experiences at Murphy High, and he saw that people could make a difference, just with a smile, a touch, or a kind word. Michelle thought about Stephanie, and all of the medical problems she had as a small child. She hoped that the staff at the hospital were kind to her sister back then. She wanted to be that kind of person for someone else's sister when they were sick. She wanted to care for them and help them understand what was going on so they wouldn't be scared. So she would start with nursing school, and then see where that led.

She was accepted to her first choice, UMass, and committed to attending. After that, a sense of relief came over her, and she began to plan for senior prom. She knew this would be her special night with Joey. She was working it all out. They would meet up with their friends for dinner, then go to the dance. Then, they would get their own room at a hotel and spend a wonderful, romantic, sex-filled night together. She would tell her parents she was staying with her friends again like last year. She could see them in her mind, walking hand in hand down the hallway of the Marriott, to their own private room, sharing a secret plan, maybe even giggling about it on the way, knowing what was coming next.

Michelle made plans to go dress shopping with Sally. This year, she had a better idea of what she wanted, of what looked good on her. She would also buy new, fresh makeup. She was even considering getting on the pill. But first, they were going to celebrate Joey's birthday.

Joey was two weeks younger than Michelle. They joked sometimes about her being the older woman and robbing the cradle. Michelle planned to take Joey out to dinner to celebrate, and then go to a movie, or just park in his car, his choice. That day when she got home from school, she started to rummage through her closet to find an outfit for their date. The phone rang. Michelle picked it up.

"Hey, Michelle, it's Joey."

"Happy birthday!" Michelle said. "How's your day been going?"

"It's been great," he told her. "Everyone was really nice at school, and my mom sang to me over breakfast. And I was finally able to go down to the recruiting office and sign up."

Michelle didn't quite understand what Joey had just said. "You did what?"

"I signed up. For the Marines. You know, you have to wait until you're eighteen, and I'm eighteen now, so I signed up."

There was more. Michelle could tell. Something sounded different in Joey's voice.

"You just went down and actually signed up for the Marines on your birthday? I mean, you could have waited until graduation. You're not going to even be able to go until after graduation, right?"

Joey paused. "Well, actually, that's the thing," he started. "So I don't really have to wait. I'm eighteen now, so I can go any time. The recruiter told me that I can take my GED and I can actually go to boot camp in two weeks. So I could withdraw from school, but I would still sort of graduate. I mean, I plan to go to college at some point, hopefully through the military plan, so I'll need my diploma."

"I don't understand," Michelle said. "Why would you even do that? We're so close to the end of the year. Why can't you just wait? Why would you have to go now? I mean, I can get going after school is over, but why would you do this? Joey, if you go in two weeks, you'll miss prom! We've already made plans!"

"Michelle, you've been making plans for prom, not me. I told you a long time ago I was planning on joining the Marines. I never kept it a secret."

Michelle exhaled hard. "But you never said you were going to march right down and sign up on your birthday! Don't you want to graduate with your class?"

"That's not really that important to me," Joey said. "One thing I do regret is not being able to see you graduate. I wanted to be there for you. But my recruiter came up with this sweet deal, and he's gonna take care of all the details to make it happen. I'm excited about this, Michelle. Can't you be excited for me too?"

Michelle paused to think. *But the prom!* she thought. Then something else occurred to her. "Are we gonna break up when you go?" She didn't want to break up with Joey.

"I don't want to break up, Michelle. I just want to be a Marine! Can't we do both things at the same time? People do have long-distance relationships. I love you, Michelle. I want to make it work."

Michelle knew he was right. He had told her early on about his desire and intention to join the Marines. She was the one who pushed it aside in her mind like the time was never going to come. And she had made assumptions about prom. She had assumed they would go together, but they had never actually talked about it. She had all these grand plans, and now they would never happen. And Joey would be gone. He would be her long-distance Marine boyfriend. She wanted a short-distance, Eastboro boyfriend. Joey going to Murphy was long distance enough. Then she realized something.

"Did you just say you love me, Joey?"

"Yes, Michelle, I do. I've loved you for a long time. I don't know why we've never said it to each other. But I *do* love you. I hope you already realized that."

Michelle felt like she was going to cry, but she didn't want Joey to hear her, especially on his birthday. "I think I did realize, but it's always good to hear," she said. "I love you, too, Joey."

They finalized their plans for the evening, and Michelle got off the phone. She didn't know what to think, or what to do. For the first time in years, she didn't even want to call Sally. Sally would probably say something comforting, but it wouldn't change the fact that Joey was going away, for only God knew how long. And Michelle would not be going to prom. No comfort could take away that disappointment.

The next day at lunch, Michelle let her lunch group know what was going on. Darlene and Chris also didn't have dates, and the other friends argued that they all had to go to the prom anyway. They came up with a plan for them all to go as a group to the event and all dance together. At first, Chris held out, but eventually he caved after Darlene promised she would be there for him if Rhonda made things uncomfortable.

Sally called Michelle after school that day. "I can't believe you didn't tell me about Joey," she said. "I'm so sorry. Do you have any idea what it will be like when he goes? When will you be able to see him again?" Michelle could hear the worry in Sally's voice.

Michelle sighed. "We talked about it at his birthday dinner last night, but we didn't get very far. He doesn't know anything yet. He's meeting with the recruiter again on Monday. I mean, who tells a high school senior to drop out and take the GED? Why are they so desperate for him to sign up? They can't just say 'see you after graduation'? I want to be happy for him, and I know he's put a lot of thought into joining the Marines, but even still, it just feels like it's all happening too fast!"

"It *is* really fast," Sally agreed. "It would have been nice if he gave you some warning that he was doing this."

"He didn't want to get into it with me if I wasn't happy about it," Michelle told her. "I get that, but it's weird that he can tell me he loves me for the first time five minutes after he tells me he's kept something this important from me."

"How did his mother react?" Sally wondered.

"Not well," Michelle said. "She wanted to march him right back down to that recruiter to unenlist, but she can't do anything now. He's over eighteen, and he signed the papers. She's over the roof upset. She wouldn't even talk to him, even though it was his birthday! I think she'll come around before he leaves, but she won't be happy about it."

"Oh, Michelle," Sally said, "this is awful. I know you were all excited about prom, and all the plans you were making. And having your last summer together before college. Do you think you'll want to, you know, do it, before he leaves?"

"That's just the thing, Sally," Michelle said. "I don't know. I had my heart so set on prom night, and how wonderful it would be, and that kind of like, setting off our sex life in a way. I wasn't thinking of my first time with him, or with anyone for that matter, as being a send-off to him to go to the military! I know the prom idea is really cliche, but doing it right before he leaves seems like something you'd see in a war movie. Like rallying for our boys or something! I don't want him to go, and if we have sex, I wonder if that will make it even harder."

"Yeah, I can see that," Sally said. "And there's also the worry that if you don't, you have no idea how long it will be until you get another chance. He could be gone a long time."

Michelle swallowed a lump in her throat. "He could," she said. "I don't know if it would be better for us to end it now and just move on. But I don't want to!" The thought of breaking up with Joey finally brought tears to her eyes. She angrily wiped them away. "It's just so unfair, Sally."

"It is," Sally agreed. "I just feel I don't have all the right words for you, to make you feel better. I wish Traci were here. She'd know just what to say to make you feel better, or to figure out what to do."

"Sally, you checking up on me and letting me talk is just what I needed. Maybe I needed to cry. I hate crying, but I guess sometimes it helps."

The Last Hurrah

Michelle went with Sally and Darlene to buy prom dresses. She went through the motions and enjoyed her time with her friends, but her heart was not overly invested in the group date plan. She felt for Chris and Darlene and their plight, however, so she vowed to go through with the event, even if it was excruciating.

It turned out to be a lot of fun. Everyone actually stayed together through the night and danced in a group. Michelle was worried about having to stand on the side and watch couples dance during slow songs, but James, Carl, and Chris made sure that didn't happen. If it ever appeared someone would be left out, they danced in a group of three. Darlene and Michelle protected Chris like a mother hen, and at one point in the night, when Rhonda wandered too close with her date, and Chris looked distraught, Darlene made sure that Rhonda was looking, planted her hands on either side of Chris's face, and gave him a giant kiss right on his lips. She lingered for a few seconds to make sure no one missed the show, and then pulled away. She then nodded to Chris, and he nodded back with a stunned look on his face. But Chris immediately forgot about being distraught over Rhonda.

After the prom, they all went back to Chris's house for an afterparty/sleepover. Michelle had to admit she had enjoyed the prom with her friends but now would have been the time that she had planned to lose her virginity to Joey at the hotel. She grabbed a lukewarm berry wine cooler that had been smuggled into the house wrapped in a sleeping bag and chugged it down quickly. It tasted like fruit punch, so she had another.

Soon after, Kim went upstairs, and a few minutes later, Carl went up after her. Michelle knew what was going on. They were sneaking around to have sex, sex that should have been hers that night. So she drank another cooler out of envy. Then she started to wobble.

Sally came and sat next to her on the floor. Sally, who had the world's best boyfriend, who would never join the Marines and leave her before prom. Sally, who would never drink three wine coolers in fifteen minutes just to make her pain go away. Sally, who didn't even drink, damn her.

"I love you, Sally," she said, and she belched.

Sally laughed. "I know, Michelle," she said. "I love you too. I should tell you that more often. But right now, I think, I'm gonna have to do one of those best friend things that won't make you love me more. I think I need to tell you that you've had enough to drink. You're a little drunk already."

"Yes," Michelle agreed, "but I'm not a little drunk, I'm a *tiny* drunk!"

Sally laughed. "You're a funny tiny drunk. But you're also cut off, okay?"

Michelle leaned against Sally's arm. "Okay, Smally. Schally. I don't have to tell you your name, you already know it. I was supposed to have sex tonight. Who can I have it with now?"

"No one here," Sally told her. "We're gonna go sit with James now and just hang out. No one is having sex tonight."

"Except Kim and Carl," Michelle pointed out.

Sally rolled her eyes. "Yes, except for Kim and Carl. But they don't count. They have some special needs that we make allowances for."

"I'm special, too," Michelle protested. "My grandma said so."

"Yes, you are," Sally agreed, and she pulled Michelle to her feet. "You're a special angel. And do you know what angels need? A big glass of water. You just sit here next to James, and I'll get you one."

"Okay. Hi James. You're a great slow dancer, and you have beautiful blue eyes." Michelle slid down the wall and sat on the floor. "James. Do you want to be a Marine?"

James shook his head. "No, I'm good," he said. "I hear culinary school can be a bit like boot camp, so maybe I'll have a similar experience there."

Michelle laughed. "Do you like chocolate chip cookies, James?" she asked. "I bet you do. You should make some for Sally. She likes chocolate chip cookies a lot."

James nodded. "I have. We make them together sometimes. She made me some on my birthday both last year and this year."

"Joey likes oatmeal raisin cookies," Michelle told him. "I mean, what's that all about? Maybe that should have been my first sign that something was really off with him."

"I'm sorry, Michelle," James said, putting his hand on her shoulder. Michelle leaned over and put her head against his shoulder and closed her eyes. "It must be hard to have Joey gone. I couldn't imagine what that would be like."

Sally came back with the water. "Michelle," she said, "I brought you some snacks, too. Sit up and drink your water and eat some snacks."

"Thanks, Smally," Michelle said, and she drank her water. "This tastes funny. Did you spike it?" She drank more, then ate some chips. "Salty," she said. "I need to sit down."

"You're already sitting," James said. "Just finish your snack, then you can lie down if you're tired. We'll stay with you, I promise."

"Thanks, James," Michelle said. "You're a good egg. Don't let anyone fry you at cooking school!" She laughed, and then ate another chip. James and Sally looked at each other and grinned. Then Sally started to unroll Michelle's sleeping bag and placed it next to hers and James's, which were zipped together.

By this time, Kim and Carl had returned, so when Michelle was ready, Sally took her upstairs to the bathroom to prepare for bed. They both washed their faces, and then Sally handed Michelle her toothbrush with the toothpaste already applied.

Michelle started to brush, then she turned to Sally. "Sally, you're so awesome," she said with a mouthful of foam.

"Spit in the sink," Sally instructed, and Michelle did.

"Sally," Michelle went on, "I feel so empty now." Tears came to her eyes. "It's like I'm not my full person anymore, you know? Like I'm half a person. Or like my other half is somewhere else, does that make sense?"

"Sort of," Sally said, and then she rinsed her mouth. "You feel like with Joey gone, you're missing something. You're missing the person you are when he's with you. But you're still the same person, no matter where Joey is. You're my best friend, Michelle, and you're never alone, okay? You can miss Joey, but you still have me. You have all of us."

"Until September," Michelle said. "Then we all leave. Except Chris and Carl, and maybe Kim. But you, Darlene, James, Pete . . . and me. We'll all be gone. And no one at UMass knows Joey. Who will I talk to when I get sad, and I can't call him in the Marines? I'll have to wait until he calls me. I have to just wait for him."

"You'll talk to me," Sally assured her. "Think about all the times I've needed you all these years, and you've been there for me. It's your turn. I want to be there for you, whenever you need me. That's what best friends are really for."

"Sally," Michelle said. "I really do love you. And I'm not as buzzed as I was before. You know that, right?"

Sally smiled. "I do know. I meant it too."

"I know." Michelle rinsed out her mouth. "Thank you for taking care of me, you and James. You're a good team. I'm ready to go to bed now. Promise me you and James won't have sex right next to me tonight?"

"I promise," Sally said. "You can cuddle up with me. This is a group date. We're all in this together. C'mon, let's go down and climb into our sleeping bags."

May arrived, and the class of 1986 started to prepare for the end of the school year. Caps and gowns were distributed, and checklists were completed for graduation. Exams were taken, papers handed in, and yearbooks handed out to the seniors. The goodbyes began and summer plans were solidified.

Michelle and her friends would all be in Eastboro for the summer, and they planned to spend as much time together as they could. Not long after graduation, Kim dropped a bomb on the other girls: Carl was moving to California. He had been given an offer he couldn't refuse. He would be doing an apprenticeship with his cousin, Laine Farmer, an electrician who lived near San Francisco. And now Kim was making plans to go with him. Everyone else was headed away to college, but they would be back, for Christmas and summer. But not Kim and Carl. They would be too far away. Any contact would have to be through phone or letters. The band was starting to break up, and everyone was feeling the loss.

Then Michelle got the word from Joey. He had been planning to come home for a short leave after boot camp for a visit, but now, instead, his parents would be going out to see him and watch him graduate, and they would be spending some time together in Parris Island, South Carolina. It was a big step for Joey, since his parents had been so resistant to him joining up. He felt that if they saw him in action, they would accept his decision as the right move for him. Michelle understood, but she was still disappointed.

"So when will I see you?" she asked him when he called with the news.

"I'll most likely be coming home for Christmas," he told her. "I'll be in Texas after South Carolina. I'll be doing some technical training, and after that, I'll be going to my assigned post in Oahu. I can't believe I'll be living in Hawaii!"

Joey seemed so excited for his prospects, but Michelle couldn't hide her disappointment. "I haven't seen you since April," she said, "and now you're telling me I might see you in December, but it doesn't sound like it's for sure. Don't you want to see me?"

"Of course I do," Joey told her. "I never stop thinking about you, Michelle. And I'm always showing off our prom picture to everyone. I do want to see you, and kiss you, and all the rest. It's just that joining the Marines is a big deal, and they aren't messing around. Once you're a Marine, you belong to them. You can't just argue that you have to go see your girlfriend because she misses you. Everyone else here has a girlfriend, too. We just have to make sacrifices."

"So do the girlfriends," Michelle told him. "And I never signed up for the Marines. That was all you."

Joey sighed. "I'm sorry, Michelle," he said. "I know I let you down. But I'll make up for it, I promise."

Now Michelle sighed. "Okay," she said. "I'll trust you, but it won't be easy."

"I've gotta go. There's a line of guys waiting for the phone."

"So they've all heard our conversation?" Michelle asked.

"Well, just my side," Joey said. "You learn not to listen to other people's calls. Okay, I love you, Michelle. I'll talk to you next week."

"I love you, too, Joey. Bye." Michelle slammed down the receiver.

This was how it was going to be from now on. Short, public calls. Canceled plans. The long, long wait. And the next thing she had to look forward to was Kim and Carl's going away party. And she knew this one would hurt badly.

The party was hard, and there were tears all around. Everyone, except James and Sally, got high, and they all got very emotional. By the time they went home, everyone, except James and Sally, needed to be driven home because they were not okay to drive. They had to go back the next day to get their cars.

The rest of the summer was focused on visiting with friends and preparing for college. Michelle went shopping for room supplies and new clothes and shoes, and then went to the movies with Darlene. She packed her things and visited her grandma, and then spent the night at Sally's house. She had one last tearful goodbye with Kim and Carl the day before they left, and then cried to her mother about missing her friends. Her mother reminded her that friends were only a phone call away and that she would be making new friends. They decided they would bake chocolate chip cookies the day before they brought her to school, just in case.

The hardest goodbye was to Stephanie. Michelle drove alone to Stephanie's apartment, and they spent several hours together. They ate lunch, watched a movie, and went for a long walk. Stephanie was scared she would never see Michelle again, but Michelle assured her that this was not true. They were sisters. They would always see each other. And in this case, she would be home for Thanksgiving. Stephanie promised to bake her a pumpkin pie. After their last hug, Michelle finally said goodbye and got in the car to drive home for the last time.

She and her mother baked the cookies and packed them up. Then they went over Michelle's packing checklist one more time to make sure they hadn't missed anything. Tomorrow at school, they would set up a bank account and turn on her room phone. They would unpack the car, and then her parents would leave. Just like camp, but after a month, Michelle would still be in her dorm.

After dinner, Michelle and Darlene met for ice cream at Friendly's, and Michelle gave Darlene a bag of friend-making cookies to bring with her to college. When she got home, she made one last call to Sally then got ready for bed. As she climbed into her bed for the last time, she felt excited but also scared and sad. She figured this was normal. She turned out the lights and lay in bed for hours before sleep finally found its target.

Freshman Blues

Michelle had talked to her roommate, Mara Simpson, from Burlington, Vermont, before moving into the dorm at the end of August. They had discussed what they would be bringing to school. Michelle had a small color TV, and Mara had an old VCR. Mara also had a tiny microwave, and Michelle would be renting a mini fridge. Mara didn't smoke, and neither did Michelle. They were both not morning people. Michelle thought they would get along well.

They met on Saturday, and Mara did not look at all like Michelle imagined. She was five-foot-nine with an athletic build, and she had long curly brown hair. Not for the first time in her life, Michelle felt very small. But Mara was very friendly.

"I know everyone worries if they'll have anyone to eat dinner with on the first night," she told Michelle. "Let's just eat together tonight so we don't need to worry. If that's okay with you."

Michelle nodded and offered Mara a cookie. She took one. "That would be great," she said. "Then we have our floor meeting. We can go together."

"These are good chocolate chip cookies," Mara said, taking another one from the container.

Michelle's parents came into the room with her last milk crate filled with belongings, which signaled the time to say goodbye.

"Give Steph lots of hugs for me when you see her," Michelle told her mother as they hugged goodbye. "And don't let Sam or Steve move into my room. I am coming home for Thanksgiving."

"I know, baby," her mom said. "I won't give your room away just yet. You still belong to us for a while. I love you so much, Michelle. I'll miss you so much. Be good." She kissed the top of her head.

Mr. Gorman came up and gave her a bear hug. "I'm so proud of you, Michelle," he said. "You're gonna do great things here. Make sure to call us, okay?"

"I will," Michelle promised. "I love you guys."

Soon, the Gormans were gone, and Michelle was alone with Mara in their room. She sat on the bed that her mother had just made and contemplated what came next. Mara gave her a sympathetic look.

"You look like me, earlier today when my mother left," she said. "It's rough. But it will get better."

"This place is so big," Michelle said. "The campus is like a city in itself. I thought my high school was big."

"You'll know it like the back of your hand in no time." Mara stood in front of her quietly for a moment. "So, Michelle," she said cautiously. "You don't have any problem with, like, girls who date other girls, do you?"

"Uh," Michelle said. "I guess I never thought about it, but no, I don't really think it's any of my business who dates who. And we're in Amherst. I suspect we'll see a lot of that around here with Smith College nearby."

"Well, I'm only asking, because I have a girlfriend," Mara said. "She's a sophomore. Her name is Sandra, and she'll probably be coming over here a lot."

Michelle shrugged. "I don't have any problem with that," she said. "I mean, as long as she doesn't eat all my food or something."

Mara looked relieved. "Okay, good," she said. "You'll like Sandra. She's really cool. She's from Burlington, too. We met in high school. She's one of the reasons I decided to come to school here."

"I can't wait to meet her," Michelle said.

"She's also Black," Mara blurted out. "You don't have any problem with *that*, do you?"

"No!" Michelle said. "Mara, I can't wait to meet Sandra. I'm sure she's great!"

Mara sighed. "Okay, then, that's all. We're good." She sat on her bed. "Do you have someone? Like that you go out with?"

Now Michelle sighed. "I do have someone," she said, "but he's in the Marines, and I haven't seen him since April. So we're not really 'going out' in the traditional way. But we're still together, and I'll be seeing him over Christmas break."

"That's a long time to not see each other," Mara sympathized.

Michelle nodded. "It is. We were supposed to see each other after he finished boot camp this summer, but it didn't work out. The worst part was looking forward to it, then getting disappointed." She pulled their framed junior prom picture out of the milk crate and handed it to Mara. "This was last year. We didn't get to go senior year because he enlisted. It was a real drag."

Mara scanned the picture. "You two are a good-looking couple," she said. "And you look awesome in that dress. Well, I guess Christmas isn't that far away." She handed the frame back to Michelle, who placed it on her desk. Then they both started unpacking boxes.

Later that night, after dinner and the floor meeting, Sandra came over to see Mara's new room. She informed Michelle that she was an art major and planned to become an art teacher after she graduated.

"I just love to see people create things from their minds," she said. "I can teach them the process, but I can't give them the spark that actually makes something into art. That's what talent is for. I had a great art teacher in junior high, and she encouraged me to work harder and push myself past my doubts. I think when someone believes in you, you can do anything. And if you believe in yourself, you can do everything!"

Michelle smiled. "I love that," she said. "Can I steal that to tell my best friend Sally? She's a writer, and I think she could use that boost now that she's gonna be starting as a journalism major. It's so competitive. That's why I love nursing. Everyone needs nurses. I don't have to knock anyone else down just so I can have a place in my career, you know?"

Sandra laughed. "Yeah, I know," she said. "And yes, you can share it with your friend. Just tell her if she ever writes it into a book, she needs to acknowledge me!"

Sandra stayed to help organize and decorate their space, and then left to let Michelle and Mara continue to get to know each other.

"I really like Sandra," Michelle said. "Which I guess is good, if she's gonna be over here a lot!"

"Good!" Mara said. "She seemed to like you, too. We have registration early tomorrow. I'm gonna try to go to bed soon, but I don't know if I'll be able to sleep. Is that okay with you?"

"It sounds like you might be a good influence on me," Michelle said. "That's a good idea." She grabbed her toiletry bucket. "Let's go get ready."

Michelle and Mara ate dinner together most nights. Sometimes, Sandra would join them, and on other nights, when Mara was off with Sandra, Michelle ate with other dorm friends. She and Sally talked every weekend as they adjusted to their new rooms, roommates, and routines. As things got more settled, they mostly just called with interesting stories and news.

Michelle enjoyed her classes, not because they were easy, but because she was getting closer each day to her goal of becoming a nurse. She was meeting other nursing students and doing projects with them. She was paired with other students to do observation at different types of clinics and hospitals, and they enjoyed giving presentations to the staff. Michelle did well on midterms, and after Thanksgiving, she studied for exams and worked on wrapping up papers and projects. Christmas was coming, and she wanted everything to be perfect for her time with Joey.

The week before break, she got the next call. "Hon, I'm so sorry, but leave is canceled."

"What??" Michelle protested. "No! You can't cancel again, Joey. I've planned my break around you coming home. I've been looking forward to this for months!"

Joey sighed. "I know, babe, but listen, I don't have any say in this. I can't tell you what I'm working on, but we have access to the space we need over Christmas, and we have to take it when it's available. We're talking about the military. When they want something done, it's gonna get done. They really don't listen to people like me who want to go home for Christmas. Trust me, I wanted to come home, too. I miss you, and my family. I just have no choice."

Michelle felt tears run down her cheeks. "Joey, I've really put my life on hold for you, you know. I mean, I have my schoolwork and my friends, but aside from that, it's just me waiting for you to come home. This is getting unfair."

"I know. I understand," Joey said. "It's not always gonna be this way, I promise! I *will* get home. I think there are rules about leave. I mean, it's inhumane to make someone go so long without a break. But what I'm doing here is exciting, and I'm learning so much. I don't regret it. I only regret not seeing you."

Michelle sniffed. "Okay," she said. "I'll wait a little longer. But when you finally do come home, it had better be really worth it."

Joey laughed. "I'll make sure it's totally worth it," he promised.

Michelle got off the phone feeling sad but hopeful. She knew Joey loved her and that he would make it worth it. She just had to keep working on being patient.

She went home for Christmas, and it was wonderful to see her friends again. After they all celebrated with their families, they ended up at Michelle's house to visit. Sally remembered that Pete had promised that they would call Kim and Carl on Christmas, so they did. They all enjoyed catching up.

Michelle noticed a change come over Chris when he spoke to his cousin. He suddenly radiated a sense of calm and relief. He smiled as he listened to Carl and Kim go on about their experiences and barely said a word. As soon as they hung up the phone, she saw the grief on Chris's face. Michelle had not even thought of what Carl leaving would do to Chris. But it appeared to have done a lot. Chris had never returned to his old self (pre-Rhonda), and Carl leaving had not helped with that recovery. Michelle knew what it felt like to feel like a half a person when you missed someone. She wished she could console Chris, but they had never been as close to each other as they had been to other members of the group, so she just caught his eye, and gave him a warm smile. He smiled back. It felt like at least something.

Second semester began, and Michelle was starting to feel familiar with her surroundings. She sometimes saw people she knew around campus, and the place didn't feel so overwhelming anymore. She went with Mara to visit Sandra in her dorm and joined on-campus clubs with the two of them. Sandra was funny and compassionate, and in a lot of ways, she reminded Michelle of Sally, only with less babbling conversation. Michelle really liked Mara, and they got along well as roommates, but she came to look forward to the times when Sandra came over and they all did things together.

One time, Sandra came to visit Mara, but for some reason, Mara hadn't returned from class on time. Michelle asked her in, and they sat and talked. Sandra told Michelle about her first girlfriend, Katie Parks, and how hard it was to convince herself that it was okay to feel that way about a girl. She had waited months to tell her parents that she had a girlfriend, and while her father asked questions to try to understand and support her, her mother went silent and pretended not to know what was going on.

"So I just went about my life, and even brought Katie to dinner once," Sandra said. "My mother set a plate, and served her food, but didn't say more than four words all night, and three of them were 'pass the salt.' But my dad talked enough for both of them. So I just let it go. I come to find out later, it's not the fact that I had a girlfriend, or even that I'm a lesbian that was upsetting my mother. She really just didn't like that I was dating a white girl."

"Seriously?" Michelle asked.

"Yeah, she tells me there are plenty of Black lesbians out there and all I gotta do is look a bit harder. I just love when people just don't get attraction. You're just attracted to who you're attracted to. Anyway, I guess I'm attracted to tall pasty white girls, because, you know, Mara. How are things going with your Marine?"

Michelle sighed. "Still talking once a week most of the time," she said. "By the time I see him in June during break, it will be over a year. I have no idea if it will even be the same anymore. We've both changed, I'm sure. We've both left home and made new friends and done new things. I mean, what if the spark is gone?"

Sandra shrugged. "I guess there's only one way to find out," she said. "When he comes home, you gotta spend some time together, and talk, and do the things you enjoy."

"Yeah, I guess. But it's like you said with attraction. I would assume it will still be there, but I haven't seen him for so long, I hope it hasn't faded away."

The door opened, and Mara came in. "Hey, you guys," she said breathlessly. "I'm so sorry I'm late. I had to stay back and ask my professor a question about my paper. Thanks for keeping Sandra company, Michelle."

"It was my pleasure," she said, and it had been. She liked talking to Sandra.

Sandra started coming to the room earlier to hang out with Michelle before meeting up with Mara. They enjoyed their conversations, and they also both enjoyed playing Boggle, which Sandra brought over and left with Mara. They never met up alone without Mara, but Mara didn't seem to mind that they had become friends. And Michelle would often take Sandra's advice. She seemed wise.

After spring break, Michelle started planning for her visit with Joey. There was no way he would cancel his leave this time. He had heard what she'd said the last time. He knew she wouldn't be able to tolerate yet another disappointment.

His weekly call came on Monday afternoon.

"Hey, Michelle."

"Hey, I can't believe it's only two weeks until I see you! I have an idea about where we can go to dinner—"

"There's been a change of plans. I'm so sorry, but I'm not gonna be coming home in two weeks. I'm going to be stationed in Oahu right after my leave, and it's gonna be too hard to get across the country and back and have to relocate, and one of my buddies has a place to go there and invited me to come along, so it's just one trip." He paused. "I'm so sorry, babe. I really wanted to see you, but it's just too much traveling and paperwork for such a short trip." He paused again. "And as it turns out, I'm really exhausted and I just need to have a real vacation. I would have invited you to come meet me here, but it's kind of short notice and tight quarters." Pause. "We probably wouldn't have any privacy or time alone."

Joey kept talking because Michelle hadn't uttered a word, even during his long pauses. She had felt her heart drop to her feet, but she also heard her brain telling her *no more.*

"No, Joey. I can't do this anymore."

"What?" he said. "What are you saying? Michelle, I will come to see you, I promise, but it's just gonna be a little longer."

"No," Michelle said. "That's what you said last time. No. I can't do this again. Joey, I haven't seen you for over a year. A whole year. That's too much. I spend too much time missing you, and I'm wasting away all of my college experience waiting for you. You know I've been waiting for you, right? I mean, in more ways than just one. It's too much for you to ask me to do this anymore."

"Michelle, I'm so sorry. I don't want us to break up. I want to be able to have everything, you know? I want to be with you, but I also want to get ahead here. I want to establish my community, to be part of something bigger. Maybe it was a mistake to ask you to wait for me. Maybe it was unfair. Maybe I was being selfish to think I could have my cake and eat it, too."

"I don't think it was a mistake to ask me to wait when you left last year," Michelle told him. "I think your mistake has been not making me your priority. Not putting me first. I really needed you to be here for me, to show me how important it is for you to be here with me. I don't feel important to you anymore."

"Michelle," Joey protested, "you are important to me. You're everything to me."

Michelle paused to get her thoughts together. "I believe that you think I'm everything to you. But I'm obviously not enough for you. You need your identity to be this Marine guy. And I really don't have what it takes to support you in that anymore. Joey, I'm so sorry, but this has to end here."

There was silence on Joey's end. Michelle thought he might be trying not to cry. Or maybe trying to stop crying. Finally he spoke.

"You're right, Michelle. It needs to stop. I can't do this to you anymore. I can't let you down anymore. I'm so sorry. I never meant to hurt you, or make you feel like you weren't enough. But maybe you're right. But I think that the truth is *I'm* not enough for *you*. I haven't given you enough. You deserve so much more." He paused. "I do love you. I didn't think we'd end this conversation by saying goodbye to us."

Michelle felt tears falling onto her thighs. She didn't want to say goodbye either. "I know. I didn't pick up the phone thinking I was gonna have to say these things. Sometimes, these things just happen. I love you, too, Joey, and I hope that the Marines turns out to be such a great thing for you. Thank you for our time together. I'll never forget it."

"So this really is goodbye," Joey said. "I can't believe it. Hey, I've gotta go. I just have to go. I'm sorry. Goodbye, Michelle."

"Bye, Joey." Michelle could already hear the dial tone on the phone. She squeezed her eyes closed. She could picture Joey all the way in California, standing by the phone, staring at it, trying not to let anyone see him hurting but not being able to keep it inside. She wondered if anyone had overhead him. She wondered if he had anyone he could talk to or confide in. She doubted it. Poor Joey. He didn't have anyone like Sally.

She picked up the phone and called Sally. When she answered, Michelle broke down.

"Oh, God, Michelle," Sally said. "He canceled again, didn't he?"

"I broke up with him," Michelle wailed. "It's over. I couldn't do it anymore."

"Of course you couldn't!" Sally agreed. "You've waited too long. A whole year! I don't know anyone else who would have been as patient and understanding as you. I don't blame you for having had enough."

"It was so hard, Sally. He was totally upset. I think I made him cry!"

"Michelle, he made you cry often enough. Now it's his turn. Let him grieve for a while. I'm coming out there. I just need to let Jamie know what's going on, and then throw some stuff together. I think I can be there in less than three hours."

"No, Sally, I can't ask you to do that."

"You didn't ask me," Sally said sternly. "And I'm not taking no for an answer. So make some room over there for me to sleep, and I'm spending the weekend."

Michelle sniffed. "Thank you, Sally."

Sally arrived around eight o'clock in James's Vista Cruiser. She had stopped at a grocery store before hitting campus to pick up a gallon of ice cream. Michelle got two spoons from the common area, and together they feasted on Rocky Road while Michelle cried and told Sally all the details from her earlier call with Joey.

". . . and then he hung up, and I don't know if he was okay. What if he's not okay, Sally?"

"He's okay," Sally promised. "And it's up to him now to make sure he's okay. It's not your responsibility. And he's a big, burly Marine now! He'll be fine."

Michelle blew her nose. "I have to think about if he's gonna be okay because if I stop, I'll have to think about if I'm gonna be okay, and I'm not sure yet that I will be!"

"Oh, Michelle," Sally said. She put her spoon down and reached out to hug her friend. "You'll be okay. It will just take some time."

"But you've only ever had one boyfriend," Michelle pointed out, "and you're still together! How can you know?"

Sally nodded. "You're right," she said. "I don't have experience with a breakup, and I hope to God I never do. But I've experienced pain and loss before. Like when my Grandpa Irving died last year. And then we had to have my Grandma Fran move into that care home. And when I thought people were my friends at Gearhart, and then I found out they really weren't. And how about all those crushes I had before I started my relationship with Jamie? They never liked me back. Well, at least at the time, and that hurt. Those things might not be exactly the same thing you're going through, but I do know those things felt awful, some for longer than others, but eventually, I started to feel a little better. And then a lot better. But even now, I think about them, and sometimes I still feel sad."

Michelle nodded. "It does kind of feel like a death, but not exactly like it felt when my grandpa died. But it's that same sort of feeling of losing something you know you'll never get back, and in some ways, it's worse, because my grandpa didn't go away on purpose. And then there's that feeling that maybe, just maybe, Joey will think about our conversation, and then somehow show up at my parents' house in two weeks to be with me, but I also know that's never gonna happen. So I get my hopes up for a minute, then I get realistic again, and it hurts all over again!"

Sally had tears in her eyes as Michelle spoke. "I'm so sorry. I wish I could make it okay. What would help? Do you want to go out somewhere? Or watch a movie on TV? Or just go to sleep for the night?"

"Let's watch TV," Michelle said, "and then go to bed. Mara went home to Burlington with Sandra for the weekend so they could finish their term papers. You could sleep in her bed, but it's also okay if you want to sleep in my bed with me."

Sally dabbed at her eyes with a Kleenex. "Let's get all ready for bed, and then crawl into your bed and watch TV. And if we fall asleep, that's where I'll stay. If I can't, I'll move to Mara's bed. Are you done with the ice cream?"

Michelle looked at the half empty gallon container. Melted drips were working their way down the sides, and the ice cream that remained had gotten soft. "I think if I try to eat anymore, I might throw up," she said. Sally took that as a sign that she was done.

They lay in bed together, watching dumb sitcoms, snuggled together in their pajamas. They were quiet for a long time, and Sally thought that maybe Michelle had drifted off to sleep. But then during a commercial break, she spoke.

"I keep thinking of all the things I loved about him," she said. "Like his eyes. And his passion for things. And how he never felt uncomfortable giving compliments. Sometimes about things I didn't even expect, like my socks or something. And he has such a nice relationship with his older sister. We had that in common."

"Wasn't there anything that he did that drove you crazy?" Sally asked. "Maybe thinking about that would help."

"Sometimes he called me nicknames, like babe or hon. I never liked that. I never asked him to call me that. But I also never asked him to stop. It seemed like a bad use of the limited phone time we had, you know? But any time someone calls me little pet names, I cringe."

Sally shuddered. "I know what you mean," she said. "I can't stand it when people call me Sal. It makes me feel like some old guy in the mafia! It's like, my name is Sally. Call me Sally! I don't even like it when my family calls me Sal. But, yeah, I never say anything. Maybe I will someday." She sighed. "Jamie calls me Sally. I love that I introduced myself to him at age twelve as Sally, and that's what he calls me."

"I don't think I ever told you this, Sally," Michelle said, "but when I was a tiny little girl—I mean, I know I'm still a tiny little girl, but I mean when I was really young, my parents and grandparents called me Chelley."

"Really?" Sally asked. "That's so cute!"

"I guess," Michelle said, "but when I was old enough to express myself, I told them to stop. I wanted them to call me Michelle. It felt so much more grown up to me. It's weird, because now I wish I had never done that. I think about my Grandpa Bob, and how I would love to hear him call me Chelley just one more time. But now it's too late to change back, and I do like my name, especially because of the Beatles connection. But just like you call your boyfriend Jamie, I want to find the one person in my life that

I want to call me Chelley. For some reason, it would just feel so intimate to have just one person, just one, allowed to call me that. So if you ever hear anyone call me Chelley, Sally, you'll know it's because I told them to, because I think they're really, really special. And because we've slept together. But not one or the other. It has to be both."

"Why does it have to be both?" Sally wondered.

"Well if it was just the one, I would have had Joey call me Chelley really early on, and now it would be ruined for me. No, I have to have committed myself to be with this person, I guess like giving myself to him. I know it sounds corny, or maybe even naive to think that matters, but it really does to me."

Sally nodded. "I completely understand how you feel about that. I don't think I have ever called Jamie anything but Jamie. It's never even been honey, or sweetie, or babe or something like that. I just couldn't call him anything else now. But you have to know, Michelle, that whoever this person is, the one that you have call you Chelley, he's gonna feel like the most special person in the world. And be prepared, because when he calls you Chelley, it's gonna make you fall in love with him, and if you already love him, then it will make you love him more. So make sure you're very careful who you give permission to call you that."

"I know," Michelle agreed. "It's kind of like a secret, sacred pact. I hope there's someone out there who I find worthy. But if he doesn't seem like he earns that right, then I know he's not the guy for me. It's that easy."

"I hope it does come easy," Sally said. "The last year or so hasn't been for you, so you deserve things to be easy. But also remember, not everything is easy, even in the best of relationships. But it shouldn't always be hard either."

Michelle nodded solemnly. "I know," she told her friend. "If it ever gets too hard, I will reevaluate if it's worth it. I really don't want to waste any more of my own time trying to make something happen when it's clearly not going to. Maybe that's the plus side to all of this. Maybe I've learned a thing or two about myself and what my limits are. Maybe in the future, I'll make better, smarter decisions about my relationships, and hopefully, before it gets to the point where I can get hurt like this again."

The Deadhead and the Redhead

After Sally left, Michelle trudged through her life. Nothing had changed in actuality, since she hadn't seen Joey in so long, but there was a shift in her feelings about hope for the future. Now, she couldn't visualize her future. It was almost as if she was back in front of the mirror, junior year in high school, sizing up her appearance and feeling like a ten-year-old. Only now she was nineteen.

When she looked in the mirror now, though, she noticed something different. While she was busy worrying about Joey and her future all year, she seemed to have put on a little weight. She had noticed her jeans had been a little snug recently, but she had blamed it on the dryer shrinking them a bit. Now she noticed a little padding around her waist. And even her breasts were looking a little . . . rounder, more like that of a woman, not a budding ten-year-old. And her face . . . it looked less angular and a little softer.

She went over to Mara's side of the room and pulled her scale out from under her bed. She stepped on it, and her suspicion was confirmed. Fifteen pounds above what she weighed when she started school. She had put on the Freshman Fifteen! She had heard others talk about it, even warn each other when they took extra desserts at the cafeteria during dinner. But Michelle had always looked like a twig, so she hadn't even thought about what she ate. She did enjoy the endless food options at breakfast. And she was really enjoying what she was seeing in the mirror. She actually resembled an adult. She was still barely five feet tall, but she looked like a mature woman. She smiled at herself, her best grown-up smile. Okay, she still had some work to do on the smile, but at least now she had curves, straight white teeth, and clear skin. This was a fascinating development.

She dressed carefully for class that day. She had showered, because she hadn't for a while, and blown her hair dry and straight. She put on clothes that made her more than just comfortable but actually accentuated her new form. She swabbed and brushed on a little makeup and added some dangly earrings.

I still feel like crap, she told herself, *but going forward, people don't need to know that.*

It was Friday, one week after she had broken up with Joey on the phone. She was going to her anatomy and physiology class for the last review before the final exam. She would walk into the room with confidence. It was a good place to practice, as she had no one in class she wanted to impress. But maybe if she faked the confidence for long enough, it would be there when it mattered. *I'm strong,* she thought. *That's my thing.*

She walked into the auditorium with her head held high. She greeted other students who looked at her and smiled. When the class started and the professor asked a question, Michelle raised her hand and was called on to answer. She was correct, and the professor told her so with a smile. She smiled back.

When class ended, she got up from her seat and started out of the room until she heard a voice call after her.

"Michelle!" She turned around to see one of her classmates hurrying to catch up to her.

Sebastian, she thought. *His name is Sebastian. I think.*

He stopped in front of her and caught his breath for a moment. "Sorry," he said. "I'm a bit out of shape from holing up in my apartment studying."

Michelle tried her grown-up smile on him. "Sebastian, right?" she asked, trying to sound confident. She remembered him from a group project from the beginning of the year. He was wearing a button-down white shirt with Chinos, far more nicely dressed than any of the other students in the class. His dirty blond hair was swept back off his face and secured with gel or mousse, but an unruly strand hung loose in front of one blue eye. He pushed it back but again it fell forward.

"Yeah, but you can call me Seb if you want," he said. "Most people do, because Sebastian is a mouthful."

"Which do you prefer?" Michelle asked, remembering her recent conversation with Sally about names.

He shrugged. "Either is okay with me," he said, "but I like Sebastian better. I actually would prefer if people would call me Bastian, but it's never caught on."

"Okay, Sebastian," Michelle said. "What's up?"

"Oh, right, I just stopped you. So yeah, I was wondering if maybe you wanted to come over to my apartment tonight for dinner, and you know, to look over our anatomy and physiology notes together or something."

Michelle smiled. "Okay," she said. "One or the other. Dinner or notes? Do I bring my notebook, or my appetite?"

Sebastian laughed. "Okay, yeah. Alright. Bring your appetite. I'll put on some music, and we'll have some wine."

Michelle nodded. "Okay, deal. What time?"

She called Sally that afternoon. "Okay, so a guy in my class asked me out. And I gained fifteen pounds. Do you think those two things are related? Because I do."

"You got the Freshman Fifteen?" Sally said. "I didn't even notice when I was there. I guess I wasn't checking out your body. But it sounds like maybe someone was?"

"Yeah, I guess," Michelle said. "I've got boobs now, Sally! I'm gonna need to get bigger bras! So I wore a tighter shirt to class and went in with my head held high. I didn't know I would catch a big fish with my bait! Do you think it's too soon? It's only been a week since the breakup."

"Too soon for what?" Sally wondered. "Too soon to get engaged or move in together, but no, you can do anything you want now, Michelle. Have fun. But be careful. This is your first college date. Things move a lot faster in college."

"Yeah," Michelle said. "No curfew if I need one. I'll be careful. I'll let you know how it goes tomorrow."

Michelle arrived at Sebastian's off-campus apartment at seven. She immediately noticed the change in him when she stepped in the door. He was wearing a tie-dye Grateful Dead shirt, ripped jeans, and no shoes, and the room smelled like months and months of exposure to incense. Music was playing in the background, and Michelle immediately knew it was live Grateful Dead.

Oh my God, I'm on a date with a deadhead! she thought. *Sally is gonna die when I tell her! This is gonna be an early night after all!*

"Have a seat," Sebastian said, motioning to the futon in his living room. "I'm cooking up some stir-fry and rice. Do you want a glass of wine? I have some red opened."

"Okay," Michelle said, sitting down on the white cushion. *If I had a white couch, I wouldn't let anyone drink red wine on it,* she thought. "Can I help with anything?" she called into the kitchen.

"No, I got it, thanks," Sebastian called back. "I've already got the table set. It will just be a few minutes. Oh, and take your shoes off, okay?"

Michelle kicked her sandals to the floor. "Do you have any roommates?" she asked.

"No, it's just me," he answered, poking his head around the kitchen corner. "This is a studio. The door over there is just a closet. I actually sleep on the futon." He went back to the stove.

"Are you in pre-med or nursing?" Michelle asked.

"No, biology for now," Sebastian answered. "Maybe pre-med later. You're in nursing, right?"

"Yeah," Michelle answered, feeling like she was talking to the invisible man. "I'm gonna get my RN, and then maybe someday I'll go back for a PA or NP."

"No MD then?" Sebastian asked, coming into the room carrying a wok, which he placed on the table. He went back to the kitchen to get the rice.

"No, I don't want to be a doctor," Michelle told him. She stood and walked toward the table. "I like the idea of nursing being the base. I just have to figure out what I want to focus on, like pulmonology, oncology, neurology . . . I'm glad we do lots of clinical placements to help expose us to everything."

"I spend most of my time in the bio lab," Sebastian said, placing the pot of rice on a potholder. "Sit. I'll serve you."

Michelle sat. Sebastian scooped food onto her plate and then topped off her wine glass.

"So I don't get to see a lot of pretty girls with nice hair and makeup. Mostly, they're in lab coats and protective eyewear. You looked great when you came into class today. Your hair is wild."

Michelle smiled. "I take it wild is good?" she ventured.

"Oh, yeah, very good. It makes you look like a goddess. I'm not sure which one, but I think she's really fiery. Or maybe she's a warrior queen."

Michelle shrugged. "I'll take warrior queen," she said. "My motto would be 'she may be small, but she's mighty.'"

Sebastian laughed. "Yeah, that's perfect. Almost Shakespeare. Why did you wait until the very end of the year to finally reveal yourself?"

Michelle smirked. "I've been there all year, Bastian. It's not my fault if you didn't notice me."

Sebastian nodded. "True," he said. "That was pretty superficial of me. I apologize. I guess I just needed a little feather under my chin to pique my interest."

Michelle considered that comment. Something to pique interest. She picked up her wine and took a large sip. As they ate over the next fifteen minutes, she took several more large sips. And soon her feet were feeling lighter. Sebastian topped off her wine again. She sipped some more. Soon, they were done eating, and they went to sit on the futon. Sebastian reached behind the futon and brought back a bong.

"Do you mind?"

Michelle tried not to laugh. "No, go ahead," she said, "but only if I can have some too."

Sebastian smiled. "It would be downright rude of me not to offer." He packed the bowl and touched his lighter to the top as he took a long hit. Then he held it over to Michelle. "You know how to do this, right?"

Michelle gave him a look. "This is not my first pot party," she said. "But I do need to warn you, I always cough the first time I inhale. But don't let it freak you out."

Sebastian lit the bowl, and the bong filled with smoke. Michelle put her face to the mouthpiece and inhaled. She heard the water bubble. She held the smoke in her lungs for a brief time until the coughing started. Despite her warning, Sebastian still looked freaked out.

"You don't have asthma, do you? I wouldn't have let you do a bong hit if you had asthma."

Michelle shook her head and coughed one more time. "Way to not freak out, Sebastian," she said. "I'm fine. I can do another hit in a minute."

Sebastian shrugged. "Okay, if you're sure you can." He took another hit and then passed it to her again. This time she was fine.

She knew what would happen next. It's what happened every time she smoked pot. Enough pot. She started to feel the changes in her body, and parts started to tingle. She started having certain . . . urges. This would happen all the time with Joey. But that was safe. She never had to worry about Joey trying anything.

Why hadn't Joey ever tried anything, dammit!

She'd even get these urges when she was with her friends. She never acted on them. Luckily, she was able to restrain herself. And also, she trusted them. She didn't know if she could trust Sebastian.

But did she even have to? What would happen if they started to fool around? Did she even have to stop? She was nineteen years old! She was elderly by virgin standards! Couldn't she just go for it if she wanted? She was free as a bird now; she could do whatever she wanted. Now she wanted to kiss Sebastian. So she did.

It progressed very quickly, and it may have had something to do with her pot-induced urgency. Hands went everywhere, and then his hands went to her pants. She reached out to stop them but then stopped herself. No, she was going to do this. Why the hell not?

Her heart was pounding, and she was breathing heavily, and she was kind of scared, but she kept going. Soon she was undressed, and then he started to undress himself. He stood up and pulled her to her feet too. She self-consciously folded her arms across her bare chest as he unfolded the futon. Then he pulled her hands away and kissed her breasts, and she had no idea that it would feel so good. He directed her hands to what felt good to him, and she let him, but she couldn't look. She couldn't make herself. He went to a small table and opened a drawer and took out a tiny packet. He opened it and handed the contents to her. "Put it on me," he told her.

She had no idea what to do, but she didn't want to ask. She didn't want to divulge that this was her first time. It seemed too late at this point. She felt her way to the right place, and unrolled the condom, hoping she was doing it correctly. He helped her in the end.

Oh God, she thought, *this is it. It's happening. Things are never going to be the same.*

When it was over, she lay on the futon, not sure if what happened was what was supposed to have happened, but Sebastian was acting like it was, so Michelle just trusted him. They lay quietly for some time, listening to bootleg albums, until Sebastian jumped up.

"Oh, I've got to play you this new bootleg I just got," he said. "It's incredible. The quality is so good." He found the tape and put it in the cassette player. He hit play. The music that came on sounded, to Michelle, exactly like the music that he had just turned off a minute ago, but she nodded and smiled to be polite.

Sebastian started to put his clothes back on, so Michelle followed his lead. She wasn't feeling too buzzed anymore, but she still felt slightly high. She was ready to go home.

"I'm gonna take off in a bit," she told Sebastian.

"Okay," he said, not sounding heartbroken that she was leaving, but also not sounding overly eager for her to go. Sort of neutral. "I'll walk you to your dorm." He slipped on his Birkenstocks as Michelle fastened her sandals.

At the door of the dorm, he said, "Okay, you're home safely."

She decided not to ask him in. "Thanks for making me dinner and everything," she told him. "Sorry if I scared you with my coughing."

"That's okay, you warned me. I just don't pay attention sometimes. Thanks for coming over. I guess I'll see you for the exam on Wednesday."

"Okay, goodbye, Bastian." She gave him a brief kiss and turned away.

"Bye, Michelle."

Michelle rushed inside and to her room. As soon as she switched on the light, she grabbed the phone and dialed Sally. She got her answering machine. "Sally, it's Michelle," she said. "Call me the *second* you get this, okay? *Urgent!!!* Okay, bye."

Now she didn't know what to do. She walked around her room a bit. It was only nine thirty. Sally and James were probably out. But they were such homebodies! They should be home. Michelle wanted to get ready for bed, but she didn't want to leave her room in case Sally called. She thought about calling one of her UMass friends but decided against it. It *had* to be Sally.

At 10:10, the phone rang, and Michelle jumped. She grabbed the receiver. "Sally?"

"Yeah, it's me. What happened? Are you okay?"

"Sally, I did it."

There was a confused pause. "Did what?"

Michelle gasped. "It!" she said. "It! I did it!!!"

Sally gasped. "Oh my God, Michelle, you did it???"

"Shhh," Michelle warned. "Is James there with you?"

"No, he had to go back to his dorm. He won't be back for an hour or so. Tell me! What happened? You really didn't waste any time!"

"Why should I have?" she asked. "There was no reason to wait. I just let it happen."

"What's his name? Do you like him? Was it good?"

Michelle thought for a second. "Eh," she said. "I don't really know! I was so busy hoping I was doing it right that I didn't take any time to decide if I liked it! He seemed to, though. His name is Sebastian, and get this, he's a closet Deadhead!"

"Oh my God, Michelle. That's a riot! So I take it this was not a match made in heaven!"

"He was nice enough," Michelle admitted, "but I don't see myself getting together with him again. I mean, I guess he was a means to an end. I don't think he had any idea it was my first time, or maybe he just didn't care. But I do know one thing for sure: I really shouldn't ever smoke pot around a guy if I don't want to fool around. I become an absolute maniac!"

Sally laughed. "I remember you told me that. Why do I have the feeling that you might have taken advantage of that fact tonight?"

"Maybe," Michelle said. "I needed a bit of help to get me through it. But I did it! And I really don't even regret it at all."

"That's good," Sally said. "I hope you get to do it sometime with someone you really care about, but at least now you don't have to worry about it being your very first time. You can just concentrate on enjoying it. Did it hurt?"

Michelle thought about it. "No, not really," she said. "I forgot about that part. No, I guess I was just really lucky or something. Or maybe we just didn't do it enough. Or do it right. It didn't seem to go on for very long."

"It will," Sally told her. "Trust me. It will get better, and nicer. And you'll try new things. And you'll feel more things. And when it's someone who cares about you, he won't stop until he knows he's made you feel good."

"I hope so," Michelle said, "because it was kind of a letdown. I was expecting some big deal, and it wasn't really. And I wasn't planning on it happening, either, so I guess I didn't have a chance to let the excitement build up in my head. So now I guess I'll just wait. I waited this long, I can wait again for the right guy."

The next afternoon, Michelle called Sebastian and invited herself over for another dinner and pot party that very night.

The rest of the semester was uneventful, but there were no more dinners with Sebastian. The second time had been slightly better for Michelle, and she figured the first time probably wasn't all that bad if she had come back for more. But the music was the killer. She just couldn't stand it in the background all the time. And each song seemed to have twenty-minute instrumentals, and it was just so boring! Michelle loved classic rock and new wave, but she would have listened to heavy metal on blast for hours if it meant she could stop listening to the bootlegs. So Sebastian became just a pot-hazed memory.

Summer Stories

Michelle went home to her parents' house in Eastboro for the summer. It would be her last summer living at home. The next year, she would be doing a summerlong clinical placement. It was bittersweet, going home one last time. She would miss her brothers growing up and going to high school. She would only see Stephanie when she made a point of coming back for a visit. But she was preparing for the career she wanted, and she was excited to finally be able to get past observation and get her hands dirty . . . figuratively speaking. She would always be wearing protective gloves, of course.

She was excited to see her friends again. They had all kept in touch by phone and by letter, but as time went by, they had all become so busy with their classes and other interests that it had been hard to keep up as often. Michelle was looking forward to seeing Darlene, Sally, and the boys, but she was aware of the hole that was left when Kim and Carl had moved to California the previous year. And now they were expecting a baby.

Michelle thought back to her childhood with Kim. She had struggled so much, having to be responsible at a much younger age than most people, and now she would be a mother before her twentieth birthday. It just felt like she never had a chance to be young and reckless. Kim had told her that she was happy about the baby, and Michelle just hoped it was true. Kim and Carl deserved to be happy. They all deserved happiness.

Michelle deserved happiness. This was supposed to be her time with Joey. The first two weeks were constant reminders of the plans she had made for them before he had let her down, yet again. There would be no more letdowns now, because there was no more Joey Cafaro. At least for Michelle.

So she enjoyed time with her parents, Stephanie, and Sally most often, and Darlene, James, Chris, and Pete when she could. They would meet up at the clearing in the woods near Darlene's house and talk for hours. Their conversations these days mostly revolved around Kim and Carl, and what would happen when they had their baby. Would they move back? Would they get married? Everyone had an opinion on what they should do. Michelle watched Chris. He was hanging on every word. Chris wanted his cousin back more than anything. Michelle could see the longing. She knew what that felt like, to miss someone so much, to just want them in front of you, so you can see them, touch them, and know they're real. The phone calls were just not the same.

And Pete and Carolyn were breaking up because Carolyn was going abroad to Germany for the whole year. They didn't want to do the long-distance thing, and Michelle couldn't blame them. It was the worst. It was like having one functional lung, and the other one only worked when you were in touch with your partner. But then, the call ended, and again it was hard to breathe. The anticipation of seeing them was the drive, but then if that never happens . . . it becomes a slow torture, and the resentment builds. Michelle liked both Pete and Carolyn. Carolyn was sweet, and smart, and she hung on Pete's every word. She imagined the breakup would be hard on them both, but Carolyn was going off on an adventure, and she deserved to enjoy her time and not feel she was being held back.

Michelle wondered what it would have been like if she and Joey had broken up right when he left. Would she have pined away for ages, or would she have moved on? And what would have happened if he came home one day, and she had a new boyfriend? Would she go back to Joey? She didn't know. But that just seemed too convenient. To be off the hook while you're gone, then to just come back and pick up right where you left off. That wasn't a breakup—that was just an excuse to do whatever you wanted while you were gone. Michelle didn't like the feel of that idea. It just felt too much like a big game. Michelle Gorman didn't like those kinds of games.

This Could Have Been My Favorite Week Ever

Summer ended with a tearful goodbye to her friends and family, but Michelle was also excited to go back to school and see her UMass friends. She had been talking to Sandra over the summer, and they were planning a dinner out for Mara's birthday. Michelle enjoyed spending time with Sandra and Mara, but secretly, she wished she could figure out a way to hang out alone with Sandra. They seemed to have so much more in common. But she wasn't sure if Mara would be okay with that, so they settled for phone calls over the summer.

Mara's birthday was in late September, and after they arrived at the off-campus restaurant Elton's for dinner, Michelle told Mara and Sandra news from her Eastboro friend group.

"Remember my friends Kim and Carl, who moved to California right after high school, and then Kim got pregnant in the spring?"

"Yeah?" Mara said. "I hope you're not gonna tell us they split up. It's my birthday. I only want good news."

"No," Michelle said. "It's the opposite. They finally came clean to each other about their feelings, and now they're getting married! They're gonna do it at the courthouse soon, but then they're coming back to Mass after the baby's born to have a big wedding, and Kim said she wants me to be a bridesmaid!"

"Wow, that's so cool," Sandra said. "I wonder if they still would have decided to get married if there was no baby. I'm glad we don't have to deal with stuff like that. Not much chance of two girls having an accidental pregnancy."

"Yeah," Mara agreed. "But also not much chance of us ever getting married. I guess it's some kind of trade-off."

Michelle thought about it. "Yeah, that's so stupid," she said. "I've never really thought about it, but that's really unfair! Why shouldn't anyone be able to marry anyone they love?"

Sandra shrugged. "Well, people who are against it say that it would open the door to people wanting to marry their dog or small children and stuff like that. 'The sanctity of marriage.' These are the same people who would have also been against Mara and me getting married as recently as twenty years ago because I'm Black and she's white. I mean, who the hell cares, right?"

Michelle nodded and furrowed her brow. It really wasn't fair. She wondered if, in the old days, Kim and Carl might not have been allowed to get married due to his Puerto Rican heritage. It made her embarrassed for the white people who thought things like that.

The waiter greeted them then. "Oh, hi Michelle," he said when he saw her. It was Tony Kagan, who had lived in their freshmen dorm and was also in the nursing program with her.

"Hi, Tony," Michelle said, happy to be able to get out of the difficult conversation they had just been having. "This is my roommate, Mara, and her girlfriend, Sandra. Today is Mara's birthday."

"Happy birthday, Mara," Tony said. "Dessert for you is on the house tonight. Can I get you all some drinks to start?"

When Tony walked away with drink orders, Mara watched him leave. "I always cringe when people introduce us as girlfriends," she told Michelle. "Not that there was anything wrong with saying that, Michelle, but you just never know how people will react. Tony reacted like it was no big deal, which is cool."

Michelle shrugged. "I've just always assumed that Tony's gay," she said. "The majority of the five guys in the nursing program are. I mean, probably not all of them, and it's not a requirement or anything, but I just kind of suspect."

"I don't know," Sandra said. "He sure lit up when he saw you sitting there. I mean, he might have just been happy to see you, but I'm not getting any strong gay vibes from him."

"Yeah," Mara said. "And I haven't ever seen him at the exclusive gays-only treehouse club on campus at any point, so maybe not, Michelle." She looked at Sandra, and they both burst out laughing.

Michelle laughed at Mara and Sandra poking fun at themselves. Tony came back with their drinks and a plate of hot mozzarella sticks.

"The cook made an extra plate, and I thought I'd see if you guys wanted them. They'd probably just go into the trash otherwise."

"Thanks," Michelle said, and Tony flashed her a smile. They put in their order and went back to their dinner conversation.

After dessert, Tony came back to check on them and bring the bill. "Was it good?" he asked.

"That chocolate mousse was incredible," Michelle said. "I wish I had the recipe to pass on to my friend James. He's in culinary school, and I bet I could get him to try it out for me and his girlfriend."

Tony thought for a moment. "I bet I could get it," he told Michelle, "as long as it's just for personal use. Like don't let your friend put it on his menu someday and claim it as his own." He ripped a piece of paper off his order pad and handed it to Michelle with a pen. "Write down your number, and I'll call you and let you know if I can get it."

"Okay," Michelle said as she wrote down the number. She handed it to Tony, and he looked at the paper and smiled. "Thanks," he said. "I'll give you a call. I'll be right back with your change." He went back toward the kitchen.

Mara and Sandra looked at each other and then back at Michelle. "Definitely not gay," Mara declared. "And he just snuck your number out of you. You do realize he's not gonna call you about a chocolate mousse recipe, right?"

"What?" Michelle asked. "Oh. Oh my God. Yeah. I just gave him my number. Oh wow. Do you think now he thinks I want to go out with him? I wasn't even thinking that."

Sandra laughed. "Probably! Would you go out with him?"

Michelle thought about it. "I . . . guess," she said. "I mean, he is cute, and he is very nice, but you know, I always just assumed . . ."

"Well, it seems you assumed wrong," Mara said. "So he's cute, and he's nice, and he seems like he likes you. Sounds like some good reasons to maybe do it!"

Michelle wrinkled her nose. "Maybe," she said. "But I'm just gonna wait and see. He really just might be planning to call me with the mousse recipe."

When Tony called, it wasn't with the recipe. "I'm sorry, but I asked and the head chef said no. I'm guessing he just doesn't give that stuff out. But if you want, I can bring you some mousse after my shift on Friday. I work until ten. I mean, if you're not already busy."

It was Wednesday. Michelle hadn't made any plans yet. "Okay, yeah, that would be great!" she said. She tried to decide if she was attracted to Tony. She couldn't conjure up his image in her mind. She'd have to wait to see him in person. He would be in her anatomy and physiology II class the next day. She would check.

When she got off the phone, Mara looked up. "Date with the waiter?"

Michelle nodded.

"Ha! I knew it! Gonna call Sally?"

Michelle nodded again.

Mara stood up. "I'm going to the lounge to watch TV. Have a good chat!" She left the room.

Michelle called Sally. "Next chapter in the post-Joey Michelle dating saga," she told her. "The waiter from dinner the other night just asked me out! Seriously, Sally, it's as if I'm suddenly wearing a sign that says to 'Ask Me Out'!"

Sally laughed. "Well, last year you were wearing one that said 'Stay Away From Me, My Boyfriend's a Big, Burly Marine'! I think maybe now you just don't look so taken anymore. But that's good. I mean, it's good to practice, even if it's not someone you're super excited for. Are you excited about this guy?"

"I don't know," Michelle said. "Up until a few days ago, I honestly thought he was gay, so I never thought of him like that. I guess I'll just have to try to look at him differently now and see."

"No pot this time," Sally advised. "Let things take their own time."

"Yes, ma'am," Michelle replied.

Anatomy and physiology class was one of Michelle's favorites, but on Thursday, she found it hard to concentrate. Tony was sitting two rows over and one seat back from her, and to look at him, she had to turn her head. So she had to focus on keeping her head in one place. But the one time she slipped up and peeked, he looked toward her and smiled. She smiled back and turned away. He was cute, and he had really good wavy dark brown hair. She hadn't decided what color his eyes were yet. She'd have to get a closer look. His lips were almost pretty. They were a rosy pink, and they were just a bit plump, but not too plump to draw attention. They looked kissable. Now she thought about kissing him.

Yes, she thought. *I am definitely attracted to him.* She tried not to think about kissing him, but that ship had sailed. *I've got to feel those lips,* she thought. *I'll run my fingers through his fantastic hair, then I'll kiss those lips. I can feed him chocolate mousse off of my fingertip.... Anatomy and physiology. Focus on anatomy. I wonder what Tony's anatomy is like...*

Now she was excited for her mousse date. It didn't seem like a formal date, and she braced herself for the possibility that it was all a misunderstanding and he was really just coming by to drop off dessert. But either way, she dressed to impress. She washed and styled her hair. She put on a dab of perfume so small that someone would have to pretty much have their nose by her ear to smell it. She put on a touch of makeup and then waited. Mara was out for the night, overnight, not by accident, with Sandra.

There was a knock on her door at 10:20, and she had a moment of anticipatory panic. She jumped up and slowly walked to the door. She opened the door expecting to see Tony in his waiter uniform, but it appeared he had made a quick change. He was wearing a blue button-down shirt and neat blue jeans. His beautiful dark hair looked freshly fixed and probably gelled.

His eyes were blue, she could tell. A deep blue, like James's. Actually, aside from the brown hair, he kind of resembled James. He looked devilishly handsome as he scanned her at the door.

"Can I come in?" he asked.

Michelle realized that time had passed since she started to look him over. "Oh, yeah, sorry," she said, and she stepped aside and ushered him into her room. "You look different," she said. "Good different."

Tony smiled. "Yeah, I usually dress down a bit for class, and then there's the waiter gear. I usually don't wear that when I go out. I hardly ever get to get myself ready to go anywhere anymore."

"So you got all ready to bring me mousse?" Michelle asked. "That's a nice touch."

"Oh yeah," Tony said. He lifted a paper bag in his hand. "I brought the mousse. I only got one. I hope it's okay if we share."

"Oh, so you're staying for dessert then?" Michelle asked with a smile.

"I think I'd want to stay without the dessert," Tony said. "You look amazing tonight, Michelle. I knew you would. It's like, all of a sudden, you're a different person this year. Last year, I wouldn't have thought to approach you, but now, it's like a whole new you or something."

Michelle smiled and nodded. "It's one of two things," she told him. "I gained some weight last year from eating in the cafeteria, and I also lost about 210 pounds of absent Marine boyfriend right before finals. That must have been the change you were seeing."

"Oh," Tony said. "That makes a lot of sense. So you'd hung out the 'Unavailable' sign last year, and I guess I must have read it. It's not a jealous 210-pound absent marine ex-boyfriend, is it?"

Michelle laughed. "No, he was a nice guy, but we'd gone over a year without seeing each other, and I'd had enough. I think he's in Oahu now. No, I am unencumbered by any military personnel or anyone else at this time."

"Well, good then," Tony said. "I thought of asking you out right before summer when we were in physiology class together, but then that guy Sebastian seemed to beat me to it."

Michelle smiled. "Yeah, we went out a couple times, but he seemed to enjoy the company of Jerry Garcia live more than mine, and Jerry, although a great musician, is not my favorite all-day, all-night companion. Do you like the Dead?"

Tony shrugged. "I guess they're alright. I mean, I don't change the radio if they're on, but I also don't have any of their albums."

"Good," Michelle said. "Should I put on some music to eat mousse by?"

"What do you have?"

They rummaged through her tape collection, and Tony had a hard time narrowing it down because they had very similar tastes in music. Eventually they chose *That's All* by Genesis. Michelle realized the hour was late, so she kept the volume low, and they sat on the edge of her bed, sharing the mousse with two spoons.

"Tony," she said after they made small talk for a few minutes.

"Yeah?" he said back, looking at her.

She thought for a moment. "I don't usually act really forward, so I feel kinda strange saying this."

"You can be forward," he said. "I'm okay with that."

Michelle took a deep breath. "I had this image of us tonight . . ."

"Yeah?" Tony said, looking acutely interested.

"Yeah. It involved me taking a little scoop of chocolate mousse on my finger, like this." She dipped her finger in the mousse. "And then putting it in your mouth, like this." She put her finger in her own mouth and licked off the mousse. "Something like that. I know it's weird, but it seemed kind of, I don't know, like an intriguing thought."

Tony nodded. "It sounds like a good thought," he said softly. "Maybe one I wish I'd thought of myself. Do you want to try it?"

"I do," Michelle said, starting to feel that special tingling her body reserved just for times like this. She dipped her finger back into the dessert, lifted it to his face, and then touched it to his lip. He licked it off his lip, and then took her finger in his mouth and she let a small moan escape.

"Let me try," Tony said. He got chocolate on his finger and brought it to her lips and leaned closer. Michelle caught her breath. She opened her mouth and licked his finger, and then closed her mouth around it, and sucked it lightly. Now it was Tony's turn to moan. She removed his finger, and they looked into each other's eyes. And then they brought their lips together hard, then softer.

His lips provided the perfect pressure, the perfect amount of softness and strength, and she lost herself. They kissed like this for some time, with exploring hands, and then let themselves fall over onto her bed. They continued to kiss, tongues exploring, hands touching, and he ran his hand down her back onto her butt and squeezed and it felt so good. Then he ran it up the front of her shirt and caressed her breasts while he kissed her. She made pleased noises. She had never kissed like this with Joey before. As soon as Joey moved on to some other area of her body, the kissing would stop while he focused, but Tony seemed so good at multitasking. He moved his hand to her bra strap and unfastened it with one quick gesture. *He's done this a few times before*, she thought. Oh, he could teach her things. She wanted to learn things, things to do to him, to make him moan some more. And she wanted to moan, too.

"Tony," she whispered.

He raised his head. "Am I going too fast?"

"No, no," Michelle reassured him. "No, it's just right. It's just, I'm kinda new to all this, kind of recently, and I don't have a lot of experience. I want you to tell me, to show me what you want me to do, so I can do it right for you. Is that okay?"

Tony swallowed. "Oh my God, Michelle, I don't think you have any idea how sexy that is. You don't have any idea how sexy you are, do you? Yes, I'll tell you what to do. And I'll show you some things I can do, too, to you. This is for you, too, okay?"

"Okay," Michelle agreed breathlessly, and Tony went back to kissing her mouth and touching her body. Then, he moved away, and the next thing she knew, he was touching her in a way she had never been touched before, and she thought she might explode. This was not how things had been with Sebastian.

Oh my God, she thought. *If everything he does feels like this, I can see why people like sex so much. Ooh . . .*

After some time, and much moaning, he came up for air. "Now, let me show you what to do to me."

At first, Michelle was horrified at what he was asking, but as soon as she got the idea and the feel for it, and how it made him feel, she began to relax and enjoy it. He continued to run his hands through her hair, and touch her face, and moan her name. She didn't know that making someone else feel so good would make her feel so good. Pretty soon, he reached down and put his hands under her arms, pulled her back up to him, and kissed her. Then, he showed her how to be a cowgirl.

She felt self-conscious and exposed for about fifteen seconds, but then, out of nowhere, she felt a sort of pleasure run through her body that she'd never experienced before, and it took her over. She let out a yelp. She moved faster without even thinking until the feeling climaxed, and she felt her whole body go through spasms, and then Tony did the same.

Oh my God, she thought. *That's what they mean by climaxing. Oh God, I never knew.*

Tony stopped moving, and Michelle collapsed on top of him, breathless.

"Michelle," he said while panting. "That, that was amazing. I've never instructed anyone on how to have sex with me, and now I don't know why. Oh God, you have some amazing skills for someone who's new to this. I didn't know it could be a natural talent. I don't think I've ever seen anyone have an orgasm like that on top of me before. It was so incredible. Can we do this again? I mean, not this minute, but like again?"

Michelle laughed. "Yes," she said enthusiastically. "I'd like that. A lot. You know, that was the first time anyone's ever given me an orgasm during sex, so this is a moment I will compare them to for the rest of my life. Oh, man. I don't know if anything can top that."

"I'll try," Tony promised. "Tomorrow. Come to my room, and I'll try. I know some other things we can do, I can show you, and it will be great."

He rolled Michelle off of him and onto the bed, his arm underneath her. "I didn't think this would happen tonight. I wasn't planning it. Thank God for your chocolate mousse image. If I had known you would respond to chocolate like that, I would have brought some to you in class a long time ago."

After another half hour on the bed, Tony got ready to go home. Michelle was tempted to ask him to stay, but she would see him again the next night, and it would be good to have some time to herself in between. It was twelve thirty when they said good night, so Michelle brushed her teeth, took out her contacts, took her birth control pill, which she had started over the summer just in case, and went to bed. The sooner she slept, the sooner she could call Sally in the morning.

"Why didn't you tell me it could be soooo good? Oh God, it was amazing!" she said to her on the phone the next morning.

"Oh, Michelle," Sally said, "are you gonna do it with everyone you go out with now? Not to judge or anything, but you do know there's more to relationships than just sex, right?"

"Why?" Michelle asked. "I mean, if sex can make you feel as good as that, why would you even bother doing anything else! I'm just joking, but still, I don't know why I waited as long as I did. I'm really glad I didn't stay with Sebastian now. No, Tony knows what he's doing. I mean, really knows."

"I'm really happy for you, Michelle," Sally said. "Now you know what I've been talking about all this time with Jamie. And I did too tell you it could be great! But do you know what's even better? Doing it with someone you love, or you're falling in love with. Can you imagine it being even better?"

Michelle sighed. "Better," she said. "How do you not just die every time? I could just see myself dying of happiness!"

Sally laughed. "I swear, Michelle, sometimes you can be so weird. Are you gonna see him again?"

"Tonight," Michelle revealed. "In his room. He's gonna show me some more stuff. I feel like I'm in some totally kinky school or something! And apparently, teaching someone what you like is very sexy!"

"Do you like him?" Sally asked.

"Yeah, I do," Michelle said. "He's a nice guy. We really didn't spend much time talking, though. Maybe we'll talk more tonight. But I'm definitely attracted to him, so at least there's that."

"Maybe you can go on a date or something," Sally suggested. "Like out for dinner, or a movie or something."

"I'd be okay with that," Michelle said. "I'm not against getting to know him, it's just that, wow, he's sort of amazing, you know?"

Sally laughed. "Yeah, I know," she said. "I've got to go help Jamie with a school catering event in a few minutes, so I have to go, but update me tomorrow, okay?"

"Okay, Sally, I'll talk to you tomorrow."

Over the next few days, Michelle and Tony met up and he taught her some more new things: standing in the shower, backward on the bed, simultaneous pleasuring, and some other tricks that had no name. Michelle rewarded him by being an apt student, eager to learn new lessons.

"Maybe we should go out on a date," Michelle said on day four of their tryst as they were lying in bed after their latest encounter. "You know, to get to know each other better, and talk and stuff. To see if we're compatible away from the bedroom, you know?"

Michelle figured it was always the best idea to just state her true intentions. It had worked pretty well for her with the chocolate mousse.

"We could do that," Tony agreed. "Should we have dinner on Wednesday? I have to work tomorrow."

"Okay, that sounds great," Michelle said. "Will you still come over after work tomorrow?"

"Yeah," Tony said with a smile. "I'll bring a different kind of dessert for us to try."

For dinner on Wednesday, they went to Starlight in North Hampton. They both dressed up, Michelle in a dress and Tony in khaki pants. They ordered appetizers and talked about their classes.

"I really like anatomy," Tony said. "I find the human body so fascinating. I love learning how it works."

"How did you decide to go into nursing?" Michelle asked.

Tony smiled. "I'm glad you didn't say 'instead of pre-med.' Everyone says that. Either that, or they just assume I'm gay because I want to be a nurse instead of a doctor. Like careers have genders. But I like the practical side of medicine, being actually able to apply the treatment and be with the patient. It's really the nurse who knows what's going on with the patients, more so than the doctor. That's what I want to do, be a part of their lives, you know?"

Michelle nodded. "Yes, I totally get it," she said. "That's what I want, too. My sister had several surgeries on her heart as a child, and my mom always talked about the nurses who gave them all such good care when they were in the hospital. I want to be a nurse like that, someone who patients and families remember for their kindness."

Tony smiled. "You totally get it," he said. "That's cool."

"Where are you from?" Michelle asked after their entrees were served.

"I'm from the Brooklyn area," Tony told her. "I've lived in the city my whole life. My parents are from there too."

"Wow," Michelle said. "I can't even imagine living in New York City. I've never actually been there. Is it crazy busy there all the time? I can just imagine people walking back and forth in front of your house or apartment all day and night, and it being so noisy!"

Tony laughed. "No, not where I live in Brooklyn," he said. "It's a neighborhood with a bunch of brownstone buildings. The noisiness is usually in my house during holidays when all of my grandparents and aunts and uncles and cousins come over for dinner."

"Is your family Italian?" Michelle asked.

"No," Tony answered. "I can see why you might think so because people call me Tony. My real name is Taavi. No one ever gets it right here, so now I just go by Tony at school. I come from a really big Jewish family. My father's a rabbi, and my mother teaches preschool students."

"A rabbi!" Michelle exclaimed. "That's like a Jewish priest, right?"

"It's a religious leader and teacher," Tony explained. "Judaism is really different from Christian religions, since we study Torah and not what other people call the New Testament. The Torah tells Jewish people everything they need to know to live their lives. My father leads Torah study classes and services and studies Torah when he's at home, except when he's spending time with the family. I have four brothers and sisters, but a lot of our neighbors have lots more kids. Our family is considered kind of small, actually."

"So, my best friend is Jewish," Michelle said. "The Bachmans. But they're not as religious as all that. Sally and her mom light candles on Friday nights, and they celebrate holidays like Hannukah, but I've never heard her talk about all this other stuff. I did go to her bat mitzvah in eighth grade, though."

"She probably wasn't raised observant," Tony said. "There are lots of Jews, but some people are more serious about it than others."

"My parents never involved us in any religion growing up," Michelle said, "but my grandparents on my mom's side were Christian. I'm not sure about my dad's side. They live in Montana now and were against my parents getting married, so we don't talk to them much. But I do know that none of them were Jewish. How do your parents feel about your, uh, lifestyle? I mean, you really don't seem so religious. And what we've been doing, I mean, your father probably wouldn't be too thrilled about it, I would think."

Tony shook his head. "There are a lot of things my parents wouldn't be happy about if they knew. Like me eating this cheeseburger. I'm not supposed to eat milk and meat together. It's not kosher. And yeah, sex before marriage is very frowned upon. For some observant Jews, men and women who aren't in the same family aren't supposed to even touch each other before marriage or even be unchaperoned. But my parents and I have sort of an unspoken agreement. They don't ask me any questions, and I don't volunteer any information. It's worked so far for us since I've been in college. I don't know if it will work forever, but at least they don't give me any grief about things they're not aware of."

"So . . . if we ended up in a serious relationship," Michelle started, "you wouldn't be able to tell them about me? I mean, eventually, people might want to get married. What would happen if you decided to marry a woman who wasn't Jewish?"

Tony paused and looked in her eyes. "Michelle," he said, "that's not gonna happen. I mean, I'm gonna marry someone Jewish. I just can't imagine it if I didn't. It would probably be better for me to not get married at all rather than to marry someone who's not Jewish. I mean, I'm not anywhere near that place in my life anyway but that's just something I know."

"Oh," Michelle responded. "I mean, I'm not in that place either, but I'm under the impression that it's something you think about any time you get involved with anyone. You know, because what if you forget to break up with someone, then a few years later, you realize you love them? Then you just end it, because they're not Jewish? I mean, is that really fair?"

Tony looked down at his food. "I wouldn't let that happen. I'm sorry, we haven't spent much of our time together talking, and I guess that's been a mistake. I guess people who know me know these things about me. I just wasn't thinking. Yeah, I guess it is unfair to ask someone to get involved with me if they're thinking about the future. I apologize. Now you know, and I won't judge you if you want to step away. I mean, I'd love to spend more time with you. I really enjoy our time together, and I can see us having lots more good times together, as long as we both understand the way it is. But I'll respect whatever you want to do."

Michelle sat quietly for a while and picked at her food. This was not how she had predicted this night going. She didn't really know Tony that well, so it wouldn't be tragic if they stopped seeing each other, but she was the kind of person that felt that every date had potential to lead to something bigger. And this clearly wouldn't be the case with Tony.

"Can I think about it a bit?" she asked. "I mean, I really don't know. I've never been faced with something like this before. I'm only nineteen years old. I have years ahead of me, and I have no idea what will happen, but I know that I do want to have some say in what it is when it does."

Tony nodded. "That would be fine," he said. "Do you want me to bring you home, or do you want to come over after we leave here and, you know, do what we've been doing? There's still more that I can show you. We can still do that, if you want."

Suddenly Michelle didn't think that felt like a good idea. "I think maybe you should just take me home," she said. "No offense, but suddenly, I'm just not feeling all that amorous. I think I kind of want to be alone with my thoughts for a bit if that's okay."

"Okay," Tony agreed, although Michelle could tell he was disappointed. So was she.

When she got home, it was still early, so she called Sally and explained the situation.

"Oh, that's rough," she said. "I've met people from families like that before. They're not messing around. It's just expected that they won't marry outside their faith. It could mean that they can't see their family anymore, even their brothers and sisters. It could mean they lose a lot. I'm so sorry, Michelle."

"I should stop seeing him, shouldn't I?" Michelle asked.

"Yeah, you should," Sally agreed. "This isn't going to end well for you if you don't. You're not gonna change his mind, even if you made him love you someday. And that would just be cruel, knowing what you know now. I mean, at least he told you. It would have been nice if you knew sooner, but it's still early. I don't often tell people what they should do, but this time, you need to let him go."

Michelle sighed. "You're right, I know you are. It's just really too bad. He's really cool, and he has a body like a Greek God. I'm gonna miss that."

"Michelle," Sally said, "hang up with me, okay, and call him tonight. Just do it, don't wait, okay? Just rip off the Band-Aid. It will hurt much less. Then call me back. I'll wait."

"Okay, Sally. I'll do it. Then I'll call you right back."

Time Marches Forward

Michelle's new shine was a little bit tarnished after the Tony incident. For the rest of the semester, she went to class and did her work, but the effort to make herself appear more put together and confident was just not present. She was able to converse with Tony in classes on a civil level and even work on a class project together. Her grades were decent, and she was ready to go home when winter break arrived.

Then she heard about Chris. Poor Chris. His new girlfriend Alison had decided to go back to her old boyfriend after she had been with Chris for a blissful three months. She had broken up with her ex-boyfriend in the summer instead of trying to maintain a long-distance relationship with him, and now he was home, and he wanted her back. This just confirmed Michelle's suspicions: long-distance relationships were nearly impossible to maintain. And poor Chris had fallen victim to the game.

Everyone seemed to have plans for Christmas, but Michelle was laying low at home. She spent the day with her parents and siblings, opening gifts and listening to music, and resigning herself to the idea that it was okay to be alone. So she was shocked when Chris Mahoney called her out of the blue to see if she wanted to hang out. She and Chris had been part of the same friend group forever, but she could not remember one time in all those years when they had done something together, just the two of them. But Michelle was feeling lonely that evening, and it was a tempting thought to have the company of one of her lifelong friends.

Her time with Chris was much more enjoyable than she had expected. They had a lot to talk about. They had both been hurt in relationships, and they could relate to each other's pain. Michelle enjoyed seeing Chris Garcia, who now went by Jerry and was a Deadhead, and she agreed to partake in a few bong hits with him and Chris. But first she made a promise to herself. *I will not get horny,* she thought. *And if I do, I won't give in to my urges. I will not get high and make out with either Chris. It would be too weird. I am strong, I'm in control.*

And she was able to contain herself, even while she and Chris lay on his bed in his dorm room, staring at the ceiling, and at one point even holding hands. She had never realized how easy it was to talk to Chris, even if it might have been due to the pot. But she was laughing, and it felt good. She spent several hours not even thinking about Tony or Joey. It was nice. Chris had changed, and for the better. He was not so wrapped up in himself and being the center of the universe anymore. He asked her questions and had thoughtful responses to hers. She had known him for fourteen years, and she still felt like that night, she had made a new friend. She went home feeling good about the night, and some of her shine came back.

Second semester of sophomore year was moving along quickly. Michelle's classes were more challenging, and she had additional labs to complete outside of class time. Even though she was feeling good about herself again, and making an effort in public, she decided that she would refrain from dating, at least until after Kim and Carl's wedding. She didn't want to have to deal with the thought of inviting someone to go with her. She didn't get any offers anyway, and she figured she must be wearing her Unavailable sign once more.

Spring break arrived, and Michelle went home to her parents. She got together with Darlene, Pete, and Chris, and all the talk was about the wedding. Traci would be coming, and it would be the first time any of them had seen her since the first day of senior year. The girls were excited, and the boys were curious. It had been a long time.

The weekend before spring break ended, Darlene, Sally, and Michelle went to the bridal shop to try on bridesmaid dresses. Kim was so busy with planning the wedding from afar that she decided to trust her friends to try on and choose a dress that they liked, as long as it was one of a list of colors she liked. The girls went out to lunch first and then went to the shop. They each grabbed several dresses that they liked off the racks and headed for the fitting room.

Darlene came out wearing a pale pink sleeveless dress. It was a cute style, but everyone agreed that the lines were awkward. "Did you guys know," she said to them in a low voice, "that Mr. Drake was moved to a care facility last month?"

Sally gasped. "Oh, no," she said. "Did he get worse? I hope he can still be at the wedding."

"Well, he's not exactly worse," Darlene told them. "He's always had seizures since his accident, and now his medication just isn't helping like it used to. Mrs. Drake just can't take care of him and four kids at home anymore. They tried to have caregivers come in to help, but he was still being sent off to the emergency room in an ambulance every time he had a seizure. Mrs. Drake finally decided it was too much for everyone, so she found this place. They work with people with head injuries, so he's not with a bunch of old people. And they can go see him any time they want. I guess they have a lot of activities and stuff. Kim said that her mom thinks he's happy there. And he'll still be able to walk Kim down the aisle."

"Oh, that's a relief," Michelle said. "I know that's really important to her." She came out from the fitting room in a green short-sleeved dress.

"That color is perfect for you, Michelle," Darlene said, "but if I wear it, I'll just look like a giant pea pod. And the sleeves don't work for me."

Michelle scrunched up her nose. "Yeah, Kelly green is my best color," she said, "but it's not for everyone."

Sally pulled her curtain back and came out wearing a royal blue taffeta dress with off-the-shoulder sleeves. "This one feels good. It doesn't feel like it will fall off if we dance at the reception." She jumped up and down to demonstrate. "What do you guys think?"

Darlene and Michelle nodded at each other. "I like it," Darlene said. "And I think Kim would like it, too. Let's have them get it for all of us in our sizes and see how we look together."

While they waited, they talked about the wedding. "So I don't have a date," Darlene said.

"Me neither," Michelle said. "And I'd guess Pete and Chris are also on their own. What about Traci?"

Darlene smiled. "She's bringing her boyfriend, Paul. I can't wait to see her. I can't believe it's been almost three years! I'm so glad Kim kept her word and invited her. Do you think she still has that weird intuition thing she used to have?"

"I don't know," Michelle answered. "I don't know if that's something you outgrow. It would be nice if she were able to give us some new insight. I mean, she was right on about Chris and Rhonda, and then about me going into the medical field, and you, Darlene, not being a biologist. I mean, how did she even know that? There was no way she could know you wouldn't do well in bio class. And remember how she said that Kim would have the time of her life at junior prom? And now she's marrying Carl!"

"She never said anything about me," Sally said.

Darlene smirked. "Sally, she didn't have to. By the time you met Traci, you were already swimming in a sea of love with James. I think we all knew what would happen. It doesn't take an overdeveloped sense of empathy to figure that out."

"True," Sally agreed. "I guess I would have been more worried if she had sensed something. It might not have been good."

Michelle sighed. "Sometimes," she said, "I think it would be nice to know the future. I mean, only if things turn out well. Or maybe just have a tiny clue about what direction to go in. Like a little nudge. Maybe Traci will be able to give me one when she's here."

"That would be nice," Darlene said. "I've been seeing this guy Phil at Ithaca, and it's been fun, but we've been keeping it kind of casual. It would be good to know if Traci sensed anything from me, but if I had to guess, she'd probably say that he's not the guy I end up with. I don't think you need to be intuitive to see everything."

Everyone had the royal blue dresses on now, and they stood next to each other in front of the mirror.

"I like them," Sally said. The other two friends nodded. "And Michelle, this color looks good with every hair. I think we found our dress."

Mara's Broken Heart

When she got back to school, Mara had some news for Sally. "Sandra and I broke up over break," she said sadly.

Michelle gasped. "What happened?"

Mara shrugged. "She wanted to get an apartment together next year and live together. I didn't want to do that. I mean, I'm nineteen. She's twenty-one. She'll be graduating at the end of next year, and I'll still be in school. I just don't feel ready to be all domestic, you know? And she's totally ready for that. So when I said no, we had this big, long argument about what we're even doing together if we're not moving forward. And I guess we just decided we wanted different things. I thought we wanted most of the same things, but I guess some are just more important than others to some people." Her eyes started tearing. "She was my first girlfriend," she said. "She's the reason I realized I liked girls. I really miss her."

"I'm so sorry, Mara," Michelle said, coming closer to hug her. "I really liked the two of you together."

At the same time, Michelle could relate to what Sandra had told Mara. Why waste time? What was Mara waiting for? A certified letter?

Mara pulled away. "Sandra asked me if it would be okay if she stayed in touch with you," she said. "I told her I was okay with that, but I don't know if I really am, Michelle. Just do me a favor, okay? If you do stay in touch, just don't do it when I'm around or tell me about it. I know you're friends with her, too, but I have to live with you. I just don't want to know."

"Okay, that's fair," Michelle told her. She would have liked to have been able to tell Mara that she'd just not talk to Sandra, but Michelle knew that wasn't true. Sandra was bright and funny, and she liked her a lot. She would probably even check in with her later to see how she was doing with the breakup.

And that was what she did. She walked over to Sandra's dorm the next afternoon and knocked on the door of her single. When Sandra answered, Michelle gave her a hug.

"Mara told me about it," she said. "I wanted to come see how you're doing."

"Is she okay?" Sandra said with tears coming to her eyes.

Michelle shrugged. "I guess she's okay, but she's sad. She doesn't want to know if I see you."

They sat on Sandra's bed and talked about the breakup.

"So what are you going to do about housing next year?" Michelle asked. "Are you still gonna get an off-campus apartment?"

"I'd like to," Sandra said, "but I'll need to find a roommate. What are you gonna do?"

"I'm not entirely sure," Michelle said. "Dorm lottery is next week, and I'll try to go for a single room, but otherwise, I guess I'll talk to Mara about living together again in a double."

"Michelle," Sandra said with a sly smile, "why don't you get an apartment with me? I mean, we get along well, and you'd have your own room for privacy."

Michelle thought about it for a minute. "It would be nice to have my own place with a kitchen and a more private bathroom," she admitted, "but I'd have to talk to my parents about it. And what would Mara think?"

Sandra shrugged. "I don't know," she said. "She probably won't like it. But she made her choice by deciding not to move in with me. Now I need a roommate, and I know we're compatible, so I guess if we do it, she'll have to get used to it. I mean, we're gonna be friends anyway. She can't tell us not to. Yeah, talk to your parents, and let me know what you decide, okay? I hope you say yes. It would be fun."

Michelle spoke to her parents that night and gave them the information on the rent for the apartment and asked them to crunch the numbers. Her father called her back an hour later and informed her that it might actually be cheaper for her to live in the apartment than to stay in the dorms another year, as long as she didn't eat out every night and was careful with her phone and utility bills.

She called Sally for advice. "I think you should go for it," Sally told her. "I know you like Mara, but you really like Sandra. She would be a great roommate for you. You just have to present it to Mara in the best way possible."

"I can't imagine any way I can present it that won't piss her off," Michelle said. "I might just have to piss her off. And I'll need to tell her before the dorm lottery."

"Talk to Sandra about it," Sally suggested. "See what she thinks."

Sandra agreed with Sally. "You can tell me you want to do it now, and then we don't have to sign anything until June. I'll trust you to not back out. And then, you'll have to tell Mara later, unless she asks you about the lottery. Don't lie to her, though. She'll never forgive a lie. I learned it was better to have her mad at the truth than pissed off when she finds out you lied."

Michelle waited until the day of the lottery to talk to Mara. "Mara, I want to be upfront with you," she said, trying to sound confident. "I've agreed to move into an apartment with Sandra next year. It's just the best thing for me right now, and she and I get along really well. I don't want to hurt your feelings or anything, because I really like you, too, and I've loved living with you, but I think Sandra and I would be a good match. I mean, as roommates. You know I don't like her the other way."

Mara looked at her. "Are you done now?" she asked. Michelle nodded. "Okay. Well, then I'll say something. I'm not thrilled. But I'm not surprised. I've suspected that the two of you were becoming good friends for some time. It makes sense for you to live together. I mean, even if it was a romantic thing, it would be none of my business. Like I said, I just don't want it thrown in my face. And if we kept living together next year, I'd have to deal with knowing you were seeing each other. Maybe this is for the best. I don't know. You were probably terrified to tell me, huh?"

Michelle nodded in relief. "I didn't know how it would go," she admitted, "and we still have to live together until the end of the term. And I do really care about you, Mara. I don't want to lose you as a friend."

Mara sighed. "I care about you, too, Michelle," she said, "but I don't think we can continue to be friends next year if you're living with Sandra. At the end of the year, I'll hug you and wish you luck, but I think that's gonna be all she wrote for us. We can still say hi and everything, but I think that will be all."

Michelle nodded slowly. "I understand, Mara," she said. "Thank you for being so understanding. I hope you get a single or a good roommate next year."

Mara gave her a weak smile. "Thanks, Michelle. Let's go have dinner now and talk about something else for a while, okay?"

Kim's Wedding Extravaganza

It was finally the weekend of the wedding. Michelle completed her exams and returned to Eastboro for the long weekend.

There were going to be several activities for the wedding party, including a friend get-together at Chris's apartment on Friday, rehearsal, rehearsal dinner, and girls' night on Saturday, the wedding on Sunday, and brunch on Monday morning. Michelle booked a room in the bed-and-breakfast that was hosting the event and would stay over on Saturday and Sunday night.

On Friday, they all met at Chris's to hang out and catch up. Darlene showed up with Traci and her boyfriend Paul from Michigan, and Michelle watched the boys gawk over Traci. She had really changed. She looked older, prettier, and more settled. But when she spoke, she appeared to be the same girl whom they had said goodbye to three years earlier at lunch, and her enthusiasm was contagious. While they were waiting for Carl and Kim to arrive, Michelle excused herself for the bathroom, and Traci followed behind her.

"Michelle, I'm so sorry about Joey," she told her. "I know it's been a while, but Darlene just filled me in on the way from the airport. Are you doing okay?"

Michelle smiled. "Yeah, I'm okay," she said. "I think things are getting better."

Traci frowned and shook her head. "No you don't," she told her. "You know I can tell these things. But things are going to get better, I'm sure of it. Not right away, though. I think things are gonna be a little confusing for a bit, but then you're gonna find your happiness, and you'll never let go."

Michelle shook her head. "I hope you're right, Traci," she said. "But even if you're not, I still think I'll survive. But it would be nice if you were right."

Traci leaned in closer. "What's up with Chris?" she asked. "He looks amazing. He's so tall now, and he seems so mellow."

Michelle nodded. "Yeah, the Rhonda thing was just as bad as you thought it would be," she told her. "It took months for him to come out of it. And Carl leaving was so hard for him. It's like they took his heart with them to California. I think he's doing better, but he's had some other bumps along the way. He and I hung out over Christmas and had a good talk. I think he'll be okay."

"You hung out over Christmas?" Traci asked, looking surprised. "Just the two if you?"

Michelle nodded. "Yeah, we were the only ones in town, so he called me to hang out. It was nice. I met his roommate, and we just hung out in his room."

"Platonically?" Traci asked.

Michelle laughed. "Of course!" she said. "It was Chris Mahoney! He may have changed some, but he's still the same guy I've known since I was five."

Traci thought. "I remember in high school, I was so sure Rhonda was gonna be his undoing, and I was right. But I also had a feeling that he would end up with someone else that would be great."

"Didn't Kim suspect you had a crush on him back then?"

Traci shrugged. "Maybe? I don't know. I was sixteen. I probably had a lot of crushes until I met Dougo. Maybe if things were different now, though . . . but they're not, so I'm not gonna worry about it. C'mon, let's go back."

Michelle had finished with the bathroom, and she followed Traci back to the living room. *Traci and Chris?* she thought. *I just don't see it. But I mean, why not? If she didn't have a boyfriend maybe . . .*

Michelle ended up in the kitchen with Chris later while she held a sleeping Drake. They talked about the things that happened after they met up at Christmas. Chris did see his ex-girlfriend, for one final night, and had now moved on. He still seemed a bit sad, but she figured she, too, might still appear sad when she talked about Joey, even though she had moved on.

The rehearsal was Saturday at the bed-and-breakfast. The location was beautiful and serene, and it lent itself to feelings of love. Michelle looked around her friends and saw Chris looking at Traci. She approached him to talk, and Chris acknowledged that he thought Traci looked amazing now. She wondered if Chris was just looking, or if he was thinking about something more with their old friend. She knew Chris well enough to know he would never get involved with a girl in a relationship. But sometimes people changed, especially after rough times.

After the rehearsal, dinner was at Luigi's. Michelle quickly noticed that after Chris sat down, Traci sat right beside him, Paul on her other side. Carl sat next to his best man, and Michelle sat across the wide table from Chris, with Pete on one side and Darlene on the other. She could see Sally at the end of the table, but she couldn't chat with her through dinner. Instead she talked with Pete. She glanced over at Chris and

Traci and saw them deeply engaged in conversation while Paul was talking to James and Sally. She saw Chris smile and laugh. *Oh my God,* Michelle thought. *Paul is right there! And they are clearly flirting.*

Pete was watching, too. "It's like watching a bad sitcom," Pete said. "Traci has been talking nonstop to Chris, and he's eating it up. I wonder what they're talking about?"

Michelle shrugged. "I hope it's about how much Chris respects boundaries," she said softly, and Pete laughed.

"Fidelity is his golden rule, Michelle," he said.

Later, Michelle saw Chris eating his cake quietly, and he suddenly laughed out of nowhere. He looked up and saw Michelle smile, and he smiled back. Then Michelle turned back to talk to Pete.

"Do you think she's pretty now?" she asked.

Pete looked at her like she was both blind and insane. "Traci? Uh, yeah," he said. "I don't think there's much doubt about that. She looks like a totally different person. But she's not. But I could look at her for a while. Maybe even horizontally."

Michelle looked back at Pete with a disgusted look. "Ew, Pete," she said. "Gross. You need a date or something. Traci's my friend. Hands off, okay?"

"She lives in Michigan, remember? I don't go for long-distance relationships, especially with girls with boyfriends. And girls who are flirting with one of my best friends."

The dinner ended. The out-of-town guests left, and Kim, after kissing Drake good night, went off with Sally, Michelle, Traci, and Darlene in James's Vista Cruiser to their ladies' night, which involved going back to the B&B, having drinks and snacks, and watching movies. Darlene had wanted to take them all out to sing karaoke, a new fad that was hitting America hard, but she couldn't find a place nearby that catered to the under twenty-one crowd. They were happy enough to just stay in and spend time together.

They settled into Kim's room and decided to change into their pajamas. Then they broke open the wine coolers. Darlene put on a funny romance movie, and they all laughed and made fun of the story. Kim, Darlene, Traci, and Michelle each had another wine cooler, and Sally had a Sprite. The movie ended, and no one stood up to put on another one. They started to talk, wanting to hear every detail of what was going on in each other's lives. Kim gave them all a vivid description of what it felt like to be pregnant, and then a detailed account of giving birth. The girls all grimaced, and Kim laughed.

"Yeah, that's really what it's like!" she confirmed.

"Traci," Darlene asked, opening her third wine cooler. "Who do you think will be the next one of us to have a baby?"

Traci looked around the room once and then again. Her eyes settled on Michelle. She pointed.

"It's gonna be you, Michelle," she said. "I don't know when, and I don't know with who, but you'll be the next mom. Oh, except for Kim. I don't think Kim's quite done yet."

Kim gasped. "Me?" she said. "Oh no. I might have more in the future, but not right away. Having babies is hard work! And Drake's so little. He needs so much from me now. Maybe later."

"Whatever," Traci said, rolling her eyes. "You know who I think would make a good dad?" Everyone shook their heads. "Chris Mahoney."

Everyone looked surprised at that statement.

"Chris?" Michelle asked. "I don't know about that. I mean, he might not seem so arrogant anymore, but it's too easy to remember all those years that he was all about himself and his posse. Sure, he's changed now, and I for one like spending time with him, but I think the jury is still out on marriage and children for Chris."

Kim waivered a bit. "I don't know, Michelle," she said. "I've been watching Chris with Drake this weekend, and he's been really good with him. They're already best buddies. And when Chris makes friends, he makes them for life. I think when he finds the right girl for him, he'll fall so hard for her, and if she falls back, they'll both be set."

"Sounds like a nice little scenario," Michelle said. "Traci, you seemed to be having a good time talking to him tonight. Maybe you should get together with him. It seems like you made a good connection."

Traci looked at Michelle in horror. "Michelle, I'm here with Paul! I'm not about to go picking up some other guy right in front of my boyfriend. That's just not okay! I mean, he is pretty cute, though. I can't believe how tall he's gotten, and he has the best smile. And I love to watch him talk about Carl and Kim and Drake. He just lights up and seems so genuine. And his body . . . he's definitely much more man-like than he was last time I saw him. His ass is pretty sweet. It would be kind of cool to grab it—"

"Traci!" Kim exclaimed. "This is Chris you're talking about! He's sort of my cousin now. And I've known him since I was five! His ass *is* pretty good, though. But enough already!"

Traci made a face and tilted her head. "I don't know, I'm just sayin'." She suddenly turned to Michelle. "Check him out tomorrow. Then let me know what you think. Don't think of him as the Chris you knew in high school. Think of him as some guy you're sitting at a table with at a wedding, and you're seeing him for the very first time. Then let me know what you think."

Michelle shrugged. "I guess there's no harm in looking."

The next morning was crazy. The girls got up and had breakfast in the dining room and then had to take showers one by one in the shared bathroom. After showers, professionals arrived at the B&B to complete hair and makeup on the whole wedding party, including Mrs. Drake. Once hair and makeup were finished, they were all served sandwiches from a platter and given sparkling apple cider to drink. Then, they put on their dresses. Darlene helped Kim into her fragile, lacy, white wedding gown and helped her secure her veil in her hair. Her train snagged on a nail in the door frame and tore. Kim struggled not to cry. Mrs. Drake had been standing by with a needle with sturdy white thread and saved the day. Sally couldn't find one of her bridesmaid gift earrings, and everyone had to get down on the floor to search, but eventually it was found. Someone had stepped on it and bent the post, but this was quickly fixed with a pair of pliers found in the B&B toolbox.

The wedding planner came in with the schedule for the day. The wedding party would be getting their photos taken before the ceremony, girls first, then boys, and more would be taken later, since the groom could not see the bride before she presented at the ceremony. After photos, the wedding party would be given snacks until they were ready for the procession. Then they would all take the places they had been assigned at the rehearsal, and the wedding would commence. The recessional ended their responsibility, and once photos were completed, they were free to enjoy the reception. It seemed like a lot, but the planner assured them it would all go very quickly.

The girls went outside for pictures. The photographer posed them in many different ways and then allowed them to partake in some fun poses. Then the girls milled around the lawn as the photographer took shots of Kim and her parents and siblings and each bridesmaid individually.

Suddenly, a limo pulled up in the parking lot, and Michelle could see that it was filled with the groomsmen and the Grams. She watched as it pulled in. She could see Chris sitting in the seat closest to the window, looking around the lawn. Then he looked at her. Their eyes locked for a moment, and they both smiled. The boys got out of the limo and went inside. Michelle went to get her picture taken with Kim, who then went in a side door to the bridal preparation room so she wouldn't see Carl. The girls started toward the back door to wait for the boys to have their photos. As they walked in the door, the groomsmen were coming out, and Michelle looked up and almost ran right into Chris. Again, they smiled. He was looking at her strangely, and she wondered if she was showing too much cleavage or something.

Soon, it was time to walk down the aisle. When it was Michelle's turn, she walked down slowly next to Pete. "You look really pretty, Michelle," Pete said quietly as they walked. "That dress goes really great with your hair."

Michelle was shocked. Her high school guy friends never said things like that. But guys at college did. They said things about her hair all the time. Sexy things. Was Pete looking at her through different eyes? Michelle stood up a bit straighter and smiled a little bit brighter. She took her place at the altar and looked over at the groomsmen. They were all so handsome in their tuxes. These were her guys, her childhood friends, and she was so proud of them today. They were all beautiful.

Then she remembered what Traci had said to her the previous night. Would Chris be even more handsome if she looked at him through different eyes? She tried. She imagined him on the cover of *GQ* magazine. She imagined him walking toward her as a stranger on the street. She imagined him as her waiter in a restaurant. And lastly, and unintentionally, she imagined him lying naked across her bed. And then she felt that feeling. That one she felt when she found someone attractive. The one she had felt for Joey, and for Tony. But this wasn't Joey or Tony. This was Chris Mahoney. *Chris Mahoney! My friend! Leader of the Bad Boy Posse. He used to chase me around the playground in third grade!*

The ceremony started, and the officiant started to speak. Michelle paid attention and tried not to turn her head and look at Chris again. She continued to try. And try. She turned and looked at him. And he turned to look at her. He smiled. She smiled back. She looked away. She turned back and he was still looking. Then he turned away. And then the glass wall had been shattered, and suddenly, she forgot where she was and why she had come there in the first place.

PART THREE
HOW WE
MAKE IT HAPPEN

Carl's Wedding

When Michelle smiled back, Chris felt something new that he hadn't felt before. It was kind of a confused familiarity. It made him want to keep smiling at her. She maintained his eye contact for several seconds, but then she turned away. She turned away. Why did she turn away?

He hadn't noticed how the royal blue of the bridesmaid dress had made her skin glow until now. Her hair was shining in the sun. She was wrinkling her freckled nose. She looked back at him caught him looking. He turned away and instantly regretted it. His eyes passed Traci. She was looking at him with a smile on her face, but he didn't make eye contact. He looked at Gram instead. She smiled. He smiled back, then looked down at his shoes. It occurred to him that he should watch the actual ceremony. He focused on the back of Kim and Carl's heads. He hadn't missed too much. The officiant had just started talking about love and commitment.

He felt like he was fourteen again. Why had he not noticed that Michelle had gotten hot? Was it such a slow process that it was imperceptible to the eye? She was always cute, like a puppy or a kitten were cute. She was like a cute little sister. But hot? Well, like Pete had said last night, all that flaming red hair, and the way it spilled down her back . . .

Pay attention to your best friend's wedding! his inner voice told him. *This is why you're here. You can look just one more time, but that's it!*

So he did. She was watching the ceremony. She was smiling. *Maybe she just smiles a lot,* he thought.

He pulled his eyes away and focused his ears on the words. The officiant was saying something about making sacrifices for love. Carl and Kim would know all about that.

They would go to the ends of the universe for each other. Their love had no bounds. *I should be officiating this wedding,* Chris thought.

They finally came to the vows. The bride and groom faced each other. They repeated the words, looking into each other's eyes. They were holding each other's hands. Tears dripped from Kim's cheeks, and she let them go. Even without seeing Carl's face right then, Chris knew his cousin's eyes were misty, which made Chris's eyes well a bit. He wondered if Michelle's sparkling green eyes were misty. He turned his head slightly. She was dabbing her eyes with a Kleenex, and he wondered where she had stowed that away in her smooth, form fitting dress.

Now Carl and Kim were saying "I do." Chris snapped to attention. He had to do something soon.

The officiant asked for the rings. Chris stepped forward and produced the rings from his tux pocket, one for Carl, one for Kim. Suddenly, Drake started to cry, and Kim instinctively started to reach for her breast and then stopped herself. In the front row, Aunt Missy produced a bottle out of nowhere and stuck it in the baby's mouth. The crying stopped. Kim looked up at Carl, and they both laughed. Then, on cue, they slipped the rings on each other's fingers. They were directed to kiss and then were declared married. For the second time.

"May I introduce to you all," the officiant said, "to Mr. and Mrs. Carl and Kim Bishop!"

The music started back up, and Kim and Carl turned back to the aisle. Then Kim diverted to the front row, scooped their son into her arms, and together the family of three walked the length of the aisle.

Reception Is Good Here

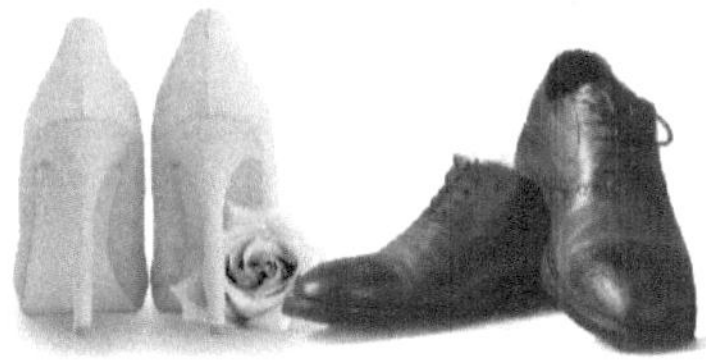

Everyone milled around the lawn eating appetizers off of trays and sipping wine dispensed by roaming waiters to those who looked over twenty-one. The caterers scurried around, moving chairs from the ceremony around large, round tables for the meal. Place cards were set out on a square table, and everyone located their table numbers. Chris saw Michelle head to the table the wedding party had been assigned to, put down her purse and flowers, then walk away. Chris discretely made his way over to the table and stuck his place card on the plate next to hers.

A DJ set up in the yard and started to play light music that served as background to all the conversations. Chris mingled with his relatives and caught up with the lives of his cousins. Pretty soon, guests made their way to their tables. Michelle sat down first, and Chris watched her glance at the place card he had left next to her seat. He saw her smile. He smiled to himself, then walked up to the table. He pulled back the chair and sat.

"Hey, Michelle," he said.

"Hi Chris," she said.

"The ceremony was really nice."

"It was."

They were silent for a while. Chris suddenly wished that he wasn't finding himself sexually attracted to one of his lifelong best friends; it made it hard to come up with things to say to her. He was about to tell her she looked beautiful when several of their friends reached the table and sat down.

Michelle cleared her throat and looked around the table. Of course Carl had settled right next to Chris, and Kim beside him. Traci sat down on the other side of Michelle, then going around it was Paul, James, Sally, Pete, and Darlene next to Kim.

Chris had deliberately chosen to sit next to Michelle. She had turned around and seen him go over to stow his place card on the plate. He had seen her put her things down only seconds before, and he sat next to her. On purpose.

The first smile in the parking lot was really nothing. Just two friends seeing each other at a mutual friend's wedding, no big deal. The second smile was suspiciously deliberate, and it made her curious. But the third smile during the ceremony left nothing to guesswork. They had made eye contact across the aisle, smiled, and held it. Then she had looked away. But when she looked back, he was still looking. Then he looked away. There was no doubt about it—they were checking each other out. Her limbs had started to tingle at the time, and even now, she could feel the pins and needles. And when they both sat down at the table, they had both suddenly gotten shy and couldn't think of what to say. It usually came so naturally to them.

She had been thinking about him the night before, after Traci had said what she had said about seeing Chris through different eyes. Michelle had lay in bed, trying to bring up his image in her mind, trying to see what she had missed, why she hadn't seen the changes in him. But that was her, in the privacy of her room. No one else knew her thoughts. Yesterday was normal. But today, things were different for her. But they were also different for Chris. And she wondered why.

She talked to Traci for a while, and then Traci turned to talk to Paul. Michelle turned back to Chris. He wasn't talking to anyone. He was staring at his plate in thought. He looked up at her. She looked at him, and electricity flashed through her body. She smiled. He smiled back.

"So what did you guys do last night?" Chris asked. "Wild party with livestock?"

Michelle laughed. "Yeah, right," she said. "We were all staying here, so we just hung out, had some drinks and some snacks, watched some movies, and talked about boys, just like we've always done. What about you guys?"

"Oh, you know, strip clubs, lap dances, Jell-O shots, the whole deal."

Michelle smirked. "You did not," she said. "You went to your place, drank beer, and played video games."

Chris nodded. "Yeah, pretty much. And you forgot talked about girls. Man, we still have a lot of growing up to do, don't we?"

"That's okay," Michelle said. "I'm in no real hurry."

Chris nodded slowly. "Me neither," he admitted. He cleared his throat and looked at her. "You look really beautiful today. I've been wanting to tell you—"

The DJ interrupted his train of thought. "Would everyone now please direct your attention to the best man, Chris Mahoney, for his toast to the bride and groom!"

Everyone applauded, and Chris reluctantly stood up. He was handed a microphone at the end of an extended cord. He looked at Michelle, shrugged, and then picked up his notes. Then he put them back down.

Chris Improvises His Toast

All eyes were on him as he started from scratch. "I had a story prepared to tell you today about Carl and Kim," he started, "but then I saw something earlier that made me change my mind. Instead, I want to tell you—off the top of my head, so my thoughts might be kind of rough—about the time during our senior year in high school when our group of friends, all of whom are here today, went to the mall to go Christmas shopping together. We split up into pairs to shop for each other, and as usual, I paired up with Carl. Carl was worrying over what to get for Kim, since it was the first time he was buying her a gift as her boyfriend. He picks up this stuffed giraffe off the shelf in the Hallmark store. I'm thinking, 'Okay, amateur move.' I was sure she'd like the giraffe and all, but I told him, 'Dude, you've got to get her some sort of jewelry, too.'

"Now what most of you don't know is that one of our good friends pretty much used his entire life savings to buy a totally gorgeous promise gift, a necklace, for his girlfriend not that long before." He looked across the table and smiled. "Yes, I'm talking about you, James and Sally."

He could see Sally fingering the necklace she wore around her neck, and James smiling lovingly at her.

"So the bar had been set kind of high for fancy romantic gifts in our friend group. Carl wanted to get something nice for Kim, but he didn't want to scare her away so quickly with expensive, fancy, romantic gifts. He didn't want her to think that he was thinking about things like promises and the future, not just yet. He knew that would come later, but their relationship was still pretty new. So off we went to the jewelry store. Then Carl sees this earring and necklace set, with rhinestones and pearls, and immediately tells me that's what he's getting for Kim. He thought it would look really pretty on her. It was a very sweet moment, actually. You could just tell when he was thinking about Kim, he was just picturing her getting this gift and being happy, and he was smiling.

"Well, it turns out his gift did look really pretty on Kim, and Kim loved it. As a matter of fact, during the ceremony today, I looked at Kim, and I noticed that she's wearing the very same pair of earrings and necklace that Carl gave her that Christmas, while making some pretty serious promises about loving Carl for the rest of her life."

He could see Kim reach a hand up to her earlobe. Carl was beaming at her.

"Carl, from this day on, I'm letting you do all my jewelry shopping for me, because you sure know the way to win the heart of a beautiful woman. And by the way, not only does Kim still have that stuffed giraffe with her in California, but I hear that Drake now has a matching giraffe, too."

He heard a few guests say "aww," and Kim nodded at him.

Chris raised his champagne glass and looked back at his notes for the last part of the toast. "So tonight, I want to make a toast to the groom, my cousin, my oldest friend, my brother, and yes, my soul mate, Carl Bishop, and his bride, my friend, my cousin, and my true confidante, Kim Bishop. You are a beautiful and talented couple, you are fantastic parents to baby Drake, and you are the best friends any guy could ever hope for. May you have years and years of love and happiness together, and may we all be able to share in all the joy you create in your lives, your marriage, and your family. May we all be as lucky to find the type of happiness you two have found with each other. To Carl and Kim."

There were some cheers and then clinks of glass and guests echoing, "To Carl and Kim!"

Carl and Kim reached over and grabbed Chris's hands and thanked him for his words. He sat down and Darlene stood up as she was introduced by the DJ.

"I'll never be able to follow that," she mumbled as the microphone was handed to her. Everyone at the table laughed.

Darlene made a touching toast and received a warm reception. Chris toasted with Carl, and then Michelle on his other side, and sipped his champagne. Michelle leaned in close to his ear.

"Your speech was better than hers," she whispered, her warm breath colliding with his skin, causing shock waves to his brain and his other body parts. He turned to look at her. Her lips were still near his ear, and she pulled away before his nose made contact with her mouth.

He smiled. "Thanks," he said, feeling deprived of that near-accidental contact. She smiled back. "You're welcome."

Chris could see that Michelle's champagne glass was empty. His was still half full. He took a sip and put it back on the table. He had intended to hit the champagne heavily after his toast, but now he just didn't feel in the mood to get wasted. He wanted to know what was going on during every moment, to be in control of himself for the night, since he knew he could not control anything outside of himself. As it was, he was having feelings he couldn't recognize. He knew that if, for any reason, he ended up in a close, intimate space with a certain redheaded siren before the end of the night, he wanted to experience it all with every one of his senses, none of them being the least bit impaired.

After salads and entrees were served and devoured, the DJ announced the traditional wedding dances. Carl and Kim danced the first dance together, and then Kim danced with her father while Carl danced with Mrs. Drake beside them. Then Carl danced with Aunt Missy while Chris danced with Gram Cissy. Chris's Grandpa Clyde danced with Kim's Grandma Susan. Then the wedding party was asked to come out to the floor. Chris danced with Darlene, and then Sally, and then Michelle. When he finally got to Michelle, he put one hand on her waist and one on her shoulder and felt his palms start to sweat. She placed her hands on him and looked into his eyes, and he looked back, and they danced, gazes still locked, with their friends dancing around them, not seeing them at all.

Chris could feel his heart beating hard, and he could see Michelle's chest rising and falling. The song ended and they still held on. Neither of them made a move to let go. This dance had confirmed it. They had seen it in each other's eyes. Now they both knew for sure: there was something new going on between them. Now they had to figure out what would happen next.

They dropped their arms to their sides and quickly left the dance floor. Back at the table, they stole looks at each other, and moments passed without a single word exchanged.

Michelle finally spoke: "I think it's pretty clear to both of us what's happening here, right?"

Chris sucked in his breath, relieved that she had said it first. "I think so, yeah," he confessed.

Michelle gave him a desperate look. "So what do we do now?"

Chris shrugged. "I don't know yet. But I do know I can't leave the wedding. I'm the best man. And I've barely been able to pay attention all day as it is. I've been so preoccupied with . . . well, whatever's going on between us. I want to go with you, somewhere, and we could, you know, figure it out together. But I have to stay until the bitter end."

"Right," Michelle said, nodding. "And we can't let anyone figure out what's going on here," she added. "I mean, I don't know what this is. And I don't want anyone else trying to figure it out before I do."

"I agree," Chris said. "Let's keep quiet." He looked at his champagne glass. "And Michelle, I don't want to assume that anything's gonna happen, or if it does, if it's going to be today or some other time, but let's not get drunk, okay? That's not what I'm imagining. I'm imagining something where we're both very, very present."

"How long have you been . . . imagining this, Chris?" Michelle asked curiously.

"Um, since this morning, in the limo," Chris admitted, "when I saw you through the window."

Michelle closed her eyes for several seconds. "Oh my God," she said. "Now I'm imagining something too. What's happening here, Chris? Twenty-four hours ago, I didn't feel this. But now, oh my God, it's all I feel. How long is this party supposed to last?"

Chris shuddered at what she just said. "I don't know. I've been looking forward to this wedding for weeks, and now all I can think about is sending Carl and Kim off to their honeymoon suite and everyone else home. And you're right. Twenty-four hours ago, I never would have imagined even thinking about what you would look like lying next to me naked in my bed tonight, but now, well . . . This is totally insane."

"Yes, insane," Michelle agreed. "Crazy. Wild. Out of control."

"Are you talking dirty to me, Michelle?" Chris asked softly.

"No, but I'm thinking dirty about you, Chris." She kept wanting to say his name out loud. "In my fantasy, your hands start near the bottom of my back, and then they start to move lower on my hips . . ."

"You're killing me, Michelle."

"I think I'm already dead, Chris."

Darlene came back to the table and plopped down on the chair next to Michelle. "I love that song," she told them, although neither one of them had any idea what song she was talking about. "I can't resist dancing when it comes on. Aren't you guys gonna come dance? Everyone else is out there."

"Yeah," Michelle told her. "I just came to get Chris to come dance with us." She stood up and reached out her hand. "C'mon, Chris." She smiled slyly at him.

Chris reached out for her hand and let her pull him to his feet. They held on a few seconds longer than necessary, but Darlene's attention had already been drawn away by a full champagne glass on the table. She took a large gulp.

"This is just like the prom again!" she exclaimed. "C'mon, prom buddies!"

Chris and Michelle followed Darlene out to the floor, which was a portable square of parquet on the grass. Sally, James, Pete, Traci, and Paul were all dancing close to the bride and groom, and the three of them joined in. The DJ played all of their favorite dance songs, and the friends danced. At one point, Chris saw Gram and Aunt Missy dancing together, each one grasping the stem of a champagne glass. There were children dancing and running around, and everyone was having a good time. Chris started to relax and enjoy himself. He made sure that he was dancing as close to Michelle as he could, and they continued to lock eyes. They often found reasons to make what appeared to be incidental body contact. They were all crowded by Bishops, Farmers, Lesters, Drakes, and other relatives and friends. They danced circle dances, the bunny hop, and the hokey pokey. Michelle was laughing with her friends and watching her made Chris smile.

When everyone started to feel tired from exertion, the DJ brought the intensity level down a few notches and played a slow song. Traci tapped on Chris's shoulder and asked him to dance. He didn't know what to do. He glanced at Michelle, and she nodded discreetly. Then she asked Paul to dance. They danced near each other, and near Carl and Kim, who were kissing in the middle of the floor. Chris and Michelle glanced at each other over their partners' shoulders. Then as if by a miracle, Paul asked Michelle if she minded if he danced with Traci, and he left to cut in. Chris ended up toe to toe with Michelle.

At first, they stood stone still. Then Michelle reached her arms up and around Chris's shoulders, and he held her tiny waist. And they danced.

"I get to touch you," Chris said quietly, "in front of everyone, and no one knows that I'm enjoying it much more than I should."

"Can you move your hands around just a little?" Michelle asked. "Just a tiny bit, so I can feel it, but no one can see it."

Chris moved his hands and felt the warmth of her skin below the taffeta of her dress. "Michelle," he said, risking moving his head near her ear. "We were lying on my bed together, in December, in my room, with no one else there, and we did nothing. Why did we do nothing back then?"

"It wasn't nothing," Michelle told him. "It was something. It was just something else, not this. But there would be no this if there wasn't that, you know?"

"I want to kiss you so bad."

"Not here, though."

"I know. I just wanted you to know what I want to do. Do you want to kiss me, too?"

"I so want to kiss you. I want to kiss your mouth, and your ear, and your neck . . ."

"Keep going."

"I *will* keep going, I promise."

The song ended and a fast-paced one started up. The sun was setting, and the pond was reflecting its brilliance. Chris longed to take Michelle's hand and lead her down to the water, and hold her in her arms, and . . .

Gram Cissy approached them. "They're going to cut the cake after this song. It's chocolate and buttercream with strawberries. It's your grandpa's favorite. It should be fantastic. Why don't you go find your seat?"

"Thanks, Gram," he said. "Are you having fun?"

Gram laughed. "I've had three glasses of champagne, and your grandpa took me out to dance slow. What do you think, Christopher?" She danced away, and Chris smiled.

"C'mon," he said to Michelle, "let's go sit."

They sat down at their marked places, and a few minutes later, Carl came by with Drake. The baby was sound asleep on his shoulder. "Chris, can you take him while we cut the cake?" He gently transferred the baby to Chris's possession. Drake opened his eyes, made a noise of protest, then curled up and went back to sleep. Carl walked away to join Kim by the cake table.

"You look so good with a baby," Michelle told him, thinking about what Traci had said about him being a good dad someday. "So you're Drake's godfather, huh?"

"Yeah," Chris said. "They asked me to be his godfather right after Alison and I broke up. I think they were trying to cheer me up, but I'm gonna take it seriously, you know? This little guy deserves to have the best of everything." He paused. "Someday, I'm gonna have kids that will be best friends with Carl's kids. Maybe not Drake. Maybe Drake is meant to be close with Laine's new baby. But someday, maybe, it will happen. And then we'll all go to Disney World."

Michelle smiled. "That sounds nice," she said. "I could see that for you two. I hope that happens."

Chris smiled at her warmly. "I may be holding a cute little baby right now," he said softly, "but that doesn't stop me from wanting to ravage your hot little body when this is over. You know that's gonna happen, right?"

Michelle bit her lower lip. "If I understand what you're saying to me, you're saying that when we're alone later, you're gonna remove all of my fancy clothes, including what I might or might not be wearing under this dress, and make mad, passionate love to me?"

"Oh, God, Michelle," Chris said. "I've never done anything like this before. This is like hours and hours of foreplay. When I finally get you alone, it's gonna be so amazing."

Michelle nodded. "So, so good."

"So it's taking forever for them to get to the cake cutting. It's like one of the last things they do at a wedding, right?"

"And the bouquet."

"That's not much."

"No, we can do this."

"When was your last time, Michelle?"

"November. What about you?"

"January. So we can wait, like, another hour."

"An hour? You think this will take a whole hour?"

"I just don't know! I hope not."

The cake ceremony began at last. Carl and Kim joined hands, held the knife together, and made the first cut. As this was going on, the rest of the wedding party took their seats to wait for cake. Carl gently placed a bite of cake into Kim's mouth, and she returned the favor, and then they kissed. Chris shifted Drake on his lap and remembered why they were there in the first place. And he smiled for his friends.

Cake was served, and cake was eaten. The cake was delicious. Kim came by and got Drake from Chris. And suddenly, Chris realized they needed a plan for the night. Michelle was staying at the B&B along with the rest of their friends. He couldn't just pretend to be driving her home. He waited until their table mates wandered away from the table.

"I'm supposed to go home after this," he told Michelle. "I didn't rent a room here for the night. I have my car. Somehow my car and I are supposed to leave here after the reception. And I don't have a change of clothes for tomorrow. And I need to be back here again by ten tomorrow morning for the brunch, in a change of clothes. People would suspect something if I showed up in my wrinkled tux."

"You'll come up to my room," Michelle conspired. "You'll stay as long as you need. As long as we need. Then, after everyone's asleep, we go to your car, and we drive to your apartment. And we dump your tux. Or, I will gently and deliberately help you out of your tux. And then, well, then we use *your* bed. Then you shower and get dressed. Then we come back here. And then at some point, you sneak out of my room, and you go downstairs. And then you're just there early for brunch. You were just so excited about the waffle bar! And if for some reason someone catches you coming out of my room, we can say something about how we're friends and no one would really suspect anything. They would have no idea. Why would anyone even think that you might be coming out of my room after . . . well, after you know . . . after the mad, passionate making love stuff that's gonna happen, between me, Michelle Gorman, and you, Chris Mahoney."

Chris smiled at her. "You are so fucking adorable," he told her. "I love listening to you coming up with stealth plans for us to get it on. How did I not know you were so clever and devious? Okay, we have a plan. Should we synchronize our watches?"

Michelle laughed. "I don't wear a watch." She held up her wrist.

Chris noticed people were starting to approach Carl and Kim to say goodbye. "People are leaving," he said with relief.

"Goodbye, people," Michele said, with a small, dismissive wave.

"I probably need to say goodbye to people, too. They are technically still my family and everything. I'm gonna go over to Gram. Don't go anywhere. I mean, you can leave your chair, obviously, but don't like, run screaming from the B&B, okay? I'm coming back for you."

Michelle shook her head. "I'm not going anywhere."

Chris approached the group with Gram, including Aunt Missy, Carl, Kim, and the sleeping Drake, as well as other close relatives. For the next thirty minutes, they bade farewell to aunts, uncles, cousins, and friends. The crowd thinned. Darlene yawned and decided to head up to her room for the night. Then James and Sally, and Traci and Paul, and Pete started to follow. Pretty soon, only a few guests remained. Scott lingered, talking to Carl and Kim. The Grams started to yawn. Mr. and Mrs. Mahoney, as well as Mr. and Mrs. Drake, and their younger kids got ready to head out. Everyone hugged and kissed goodbye. The wedding was finally ending.

Finally...

*

Chris found Michelle. "I'm gonna say good night to Kim and Carl, and then go park my car around the corner. Then I'll come back. You should go upstairs and come back down to sneak me in in about fifteen minutes. Everyone should be gone by then. Does that work?"

"That works," Michelle said. She smiled. "I can't wait, Chris." She leaned closer to him. "There's this tiny little area in the middle of your chest that I've always wanted to see, and I can't believe I get to see it soon."

He grinned at her. "For me, it's your upper left shin," he said. He brushed his hand against her bare arm and walked toward the bride and groom.

Chris got in his car like he had a purpose, and he did. He found a safe place to park, took off his jacket, and left it in the car. Then he doubled back to the B&B. Everyone appeared to be gone except the catering crew, but he could still hear people talking. When he got closer, he could see Carl and Scott, sitting on a bench near the water, having a heart-to-heart conversation. Chris was happy for his cousin, who had been craving time with his brother, but now he had to figure out how to get by him unseen. He had no excuse to use if he got caught. Finally, he saw Michelle poke her head out the back door. He signaled to her to meet him around the front. She disappeared back into the building, and Chris ran around to meet her by the door. She let him in, and she led the way up the stairs. The risk of getting caught and the thrill of what was coming next were causing his heart to thump. She opened her door, and he dashed inside.

Then they were alone. They turned to face each other, both breathing hard. Chris bent down toward Michelle. Their lips touched, and their hands were soon on each other's bodies. The hours of talk were finally coming to fruition. Chris pulled away from her.

"Let's go slow," he whispered. "We have all night. Let's make this last."

Michelle put her hand on his cheek. "I can do slow."

She stood on her tiptoes and reached up for his mouth. Her lips were soft, but her kisses were aggressive. Chris reached behind her back and ran his hands through her hair, and ever so gently grabbed a bunch of it in his fist, just to hold. She held her hands against his chest for a moment, and then clasped his shirt. She felt for his buttons as they continued to kiss and started to undo them, one by one. Soon, she slid his open shirt off his shoulders and onto the floor and ran her hands over his bare chest. Then he moved her hair aside and unzipped her dress. It slid to the floor on top of his shirt. His belt came off next, and then his pants. She slowly removed his briefs, and he, her fancy wedding underwear. She wasn't wearing a bra.

Their hands stayed in motion. Her lips moved around his face, and his body, as she had promised earlier. They kept all of their promises. He caressed and kissed her breasts and told her they were the most beautiful breasts he'd ever seen, and they were. He felt he had to have her, and soon, or he would surely die. They slowly moved to the bed, and he eased her onto the mattress. She reached for his head and pulled him closer. He explored her body with his hands and his mouth. She moaned with pleasure, and he joined her, as they both tried to keep quiet but couldn't keep it all in. Finally, he had reached a point where he couldn't wait any longer. He was gentle because he was so afraid of hurting her small body. He flipped over to his back and encouraged her to take the lead. She straddled his body and anchored her hands behind his neck. They moved together slowly, taking their time, relishing their sensations. He rested his hands on her hips and felt her movement, encouraging it to go on, and on. She closed her eyes, then opened them and looked into his eyes.

"Chris," she said. "You get on top now,"

They turned over and switched positions. "Let me know if I'm hurting you at all," Chris said softly.

"Why would you hurt me?" Michelle inquired.

"I'm like, twice your size," he said. "I don't want to smother you."

"I love the idea of you being on top of me, feeling the weight of you on my body, looking up and seeing you above me." She moaned as he started to move above her. "Just like that," she whispered.

They went on moving slowly, until Chris felt he couldn't go on any longer. He moved faster, and they both closed their eyes. Chris shut his eyelids tight. He began to see white light, and it got brighter and brighter. *Oh my God, I'm going to die,* he thought. *But it's so worth it.* This thought went on for about thirty seconds, and then the light started to fade. He opened his eyes, panting.

"Oh my fucking God," he said aloud. Now he no longer felt like he was going to die. Now he felt like he was going to live forever.

They lay silent together, both lost in their thoughts about what had just happened. Then Chris spoke softly. "That was undeniably the best, most intense sex I have ever had in my life," he said truthfully. "Please, tell me it was the same for you, even if you have to lie to me."

Michelle shook her head. "I don't have to lie, Chris," she said. "That was amazing. I don't think I can feel my legs right now. I'm totally numb. I think the secret was the anticipation."

Chris smiled. "The five hours of verbal foreplay and knowing you would be here at the end of it. It was so worth the wait."

They lay on the bed for some time, just touching and learning each other's bumps and curves, kissing elbows and shoulders. They whispered their thoughts into each other's ears and nibbled on each other's earlobes. After a certain amount of time, they got their second wind, began the process again from the start, and relived the pleasure of their earlier intimacy, despite the lack of hours of anticipation this time around.

Now Chris was getting drowsy and wanted to get some sleep. Michelle slipped on a white T-shirt and a pair of UMass boxer shorts, and headed for the shared B&B bathroom to take out her contact lenses. When she got there, Kim was already there, brushing her teeth.

Michelle pushed aside the awkwardness she felt with seeing her friend at this juncture in both of their evenings. She smiled at Kim. "How are you doing after all of the excitement?"

Kim spit out her toothpaste and rinsed her mouth. "Michelle, it was so much fun," she admitted. "I thought it was gonna be too much, but it wasn't at all. Having Drake there was amazing. And when I saw Carl at the end of the aisle, and I was with my mom and dad, it was just perfect."

Michelle smiled. "It was a perfect wedding, Kim. Perfect wedding night, too?"

Kim grinned. "This is gonna sound corny, Michelle, but every night is always amazing with Carl. But still, yes. Perfect wedding night." She touched her breast with her palm. "But to be honest, it's been a bit uncomfortable, not being able to nurse Drake every time. I look forward to having our routine back."

Michelle washed her hands and opened her contact case. She squirted contact fluid in the two small sections. "I'm so happy for you guys, Kim," she stated as she maneuvered her right contact out of her eye.

"Thanks." Kim dabbed makeup remover on her eyelids. "And I'm happy for whoever else was getting it on in one of the rooms on our floor tonight. I have no idea who it was, but I guess it must have been Sally and James or Traci and Paul, but they sure sounded like they were having a good time."

Michelle's mouth dropped open. "You could hear someone having sex in another room?" she asked, feeling horrified.

"Yeah, I'm surprised you couldn't. It went on for a while. Carl and I were giggling! I was hoping they would call out each other's names so we would know who it was, but they didn't!"

Michelle laughed, mostly because she was relieved that Kim and Carl hadn't figured out her secret, but it passed for amusement to Kim. "Yeah, I was reading with my headphones on, so I didn't hear a thing," she lied.

"Maybe they'll go again," Kim said hopefully. "I know I sound like a pervert saying that, but I'm just happy for my friends, you know, benefitting from my wedding! Okay, I'm going back to my husband now. If you hear anything coming from our room, you can be pretty sure it's us, getting it on." Kim giggled. "Good to know that champagne makes me giggle! Good night. I'll see you at brunch tomorrow."

"Good night." Michelle finished putting her contacts away, washed her face and brushed her teeth, and returned to the room. When she walked in, a naked, sleepy Chris rolled over, looked at her, and smiled. Michelle could hardly believe that he was really there, in her bed, and what happened between them had actually happened.

"We were overheard," she told him.

Chris's smile dropped away. "Really? By who?"

"Kim and Carl, of all people. But Kim said she didn't know who it was, so that's a relief. But she thought it was great!" Michelle laughed.

Chris smiled. "Get into bed and cuddle with me," he instructed her. Michelle took off her clothes and climbed in.

"I never thought I'd hear Chris Mahoney utter the word *cuddle*," Michelle teased.

Chris sighed as he wrapped his arms around her. "I like to cuddle. I'm not ashamed."

"Chris," Michelle started, "we're friends, right?"

"Of course," he replied, nuzzling her ear with his cheek. "We're very, very close friends now."

"But this, tonight," she said, "this was a one-night stand, wasn't it?"

Chris thought about it. "I haven't really thought about what this is yet," he admitted. "I just know it's amazing, and I don't want the night to end."

Michelle turned to face him. "I go back to Amherst tomorrow, and I start summer classes on Tuesday. I won't be here for the summer like I have been. And I'm going to have my clinical placements, so my time is really limited."

"I'm taking classes summer term, too," Chris said. "And I'll be working three days a week on the lawn crew this year."

Michelle sighed. "We're both really busy," she said. "It seems that we both don't really have time for anything else in our lives right now."

There was a short silence. Then Chris spoke. "So, okay, this was a one-night stand, and we're friends. But maybe we're friends that can have more than one one-night stand. I mean, we'll see each other again. We always see each other. Maybe, if we're unattached when we see each other, we sneak off together, and like, fuck, like friends sometimes do."

Michelle laughed. "Now you've got me wondering about all your other friends, Chris. I don't know. I guess that might work. I just don't want us to ever stop being friends. I don't want anything to happen to us to change that."

"We won't let anything happen," Chris said sincerely.

"But what if one of us starts dating someone else?" Michelle wondered.

"Well, then, the rule for that is that we're just friends. Hands off. But still friends."

Michelle turned onto her back and looked at the ceiling. "I hope that works," she said. "Have you ever had a one-night stand before, Chris?"

"Just once, years ago" he told her, "but it's one of my biggest regrets, sexual or otherwise. I've also had one two-day stand, but everything else has been during relationships. What about you?"

"One two-night stand, and he was my first. And one one-week stand, and that's it. Just two guys, ever. Until you." She held up three fingers to show him.

"Really?" Chris said, lying on his side and propping his head up on his arm. "Just two guys? What about Joey?"

Michelle shook her head. "Joey and I never had sex, at least not in the traditional way," she admitted. "I wanted to, but it never happened. I had this big grand plan for senior prom, but as we all know, he ruined that, and then I never saw him again."

"Michelle, that sucks," Chris told her. "No wonder it was so hard to wait for him, and he never came home. So you stayed a virgin all through your freshman year for that guy?"

Michelle nodded. "Yeah, now you know why I was so angry and frustrated all the time. It wasn't fair of him to make me wait. But, to be honest, it wasn't even a week after I finally ended it with Joey that I actually lost my virginity, and it was to a deadhead!"

Chris's mouth popped open. "No!" he exclaimed. "You did it with a guy like Jerry? That's unreal, Michelle. I couldn't even imagine that."

"He wasn't really like Jerry," Michelle said. "He was always dressed nicely for class and was very well spoken. But he invited me for dinner at his place one night, and pretty soon broke out the bootlegs and the bong. And I just said what the hell and went for it. It was okay. I mean, the earth didn't shake or anything, but strangely enough, I ended up calling him the next night and inviting myself back over! That was my two-night stand. The one-week stand probably could have lasted much longer, but it didn't because of some circumstances I won't get into right now. What about you?"

"Well, my two-day stand was also when I lost my virginity. It was to a friend of my cousin's, and I was fourteen. I was way too young. My one-night stand was at a party, but it's not something I'm proud of. I mean, we were both into it at the time, but it just wasn't the right thing to do." He paused. "I'm amazed you have had so little sex. You are a sexual powerhouse. You've got some major skills going on. I don't know how you did it, but I almost blacked out there for a minute the first time."

Michelle laughed and shrugged. "I don't know, I guess I must be a natural talent or something. Or maybe it wasn't me, it was the two of us together. But it was amazing for me, too."

"This one-night stand isn't over yet," Chris assured her. "Let's get some sleep, and then we'll go over to my place like you said, okay?"

He reached over to kiss her, and it turned into a prolonged kissing session extending to the use of hands on bodies. Finally, they rolled back to their pillows and closed their eyes, but neither one slept. Too many private thoughts were racing through their minds.

They woke up at five, proving they must have somehow dozed off at some point. Chris put on his fancy tuxedo pants and shirt, and Michelle pulled jeans up over her boxers. Michelle left the room first, making sure the coast was clear. Then Chris followed her down the stairs, and they escaped out the front door. Michelle eased the door shut. They ran quietly down the block and jumped into Chris's car. They looked at each other and laughed.

"We made it!" Chris exclaimed.

"We're free!" Michelle shouted, since no one else could hear her.

Chris started the car and pulled out of the space. It was a ten-minute drive to his apartment. When they got inside, Chris removed his tux. "I'm so glad to be done with the monkey suit," he said. "I'm glad the brunch is casual." He unbuttoned Michelle's jeans. "No one else is here, so let's go take a shower, and then we can break in my new bed."

They quickly rinsed off and soaped up in the shower and came out still wet. They hustled back to Chris's room and fell onto the bed. No longer needing to explore every inch of each other's bodies, they focused this time on the parts that felt the best. Michelle liked to kiss, and she did it with great skill. This was new to Chris, who was not used to kissing throughout intercourse, but found it to be exciting and enticing. And incredibly sexy.

They fell back asleep until eight and panicked when they woke to find that their plan had failed. They had overslept. But they came up with a new plan. Now, if they were seen, they would say that Michelle had come out to Chris's car because he brought something for her. Chris found an old zip-up sweatshirt of Amanda's that had been left behind the previous year and now lived in his dresser drawer. The story was that Michelle had left it in his dorm room on Christmas night, and she had remembered that morning to call him to ask him to bring it by.

They made it halfway up the inside steps of the B&B toward Michelle's room when Darlene came bounding down from the second floor. She assumed that Chris and Michelle had been heading in opposite directions.

"Hey, Chris," she said. "You made it in time for brunch! Are you going up to get Kim and Carl? I saw them in the hall earlier. See you in a bit. Michelle, you should have knocked on my door so we could have gone down together. Let's go. Man, you were quiet getting ready this morning. I didn't hear you at all!"

She grabbed Michelle by the arm, and they headed for the dining room. Chris shrugged and headed up the stairs. He knocked on the bridal suite door.

Carl opened the door. "Hey, man," he said, grinning at him. "You got here early. We're just about ready. Kim is dying to get Drake from Gram. I bet she's already here with him. C'mon, Kim, Chris is here to go to brunch with us."

Kim appeared in the doorway, clasping an earring onto her ear. "Okay," she said, stepping out into the hallway. "Let's go find our baby and eat. Mama's starving!"

Chris laughed. He realized all of the planning he had done with Michelle had been for nothing. No one would have suspected a thing if they had seen them together. They were high school friends. It was no big deal. They were overthinking it. He started down the stairs after his cousins. But then he stopped when he suddenly realized that he and Michelle had to be just friends again in the presence of their friend group. There would be no more touching, or kissing, or holding hands. And he didn't know when he would see her again, or what it would be like. This made him sadder than he would have ever imagined, and he wondered how it made her feel. He didn't know if he had the time or the nerve to ask her. He continued to the dining room to join his friends.

After brunch, everyone planned to check out and go home. Carl and Kim would still be in Eastboro until the next day, but everyone else had places to be after the long holiday weekend. Sally and James would be in Providence, shopping for an apartment together. Pete would be heading back to Boston to prepare for his summer internship. Darlene was going home to pack for her trip to Europe. And Michelle would be going back to Amherst to start classes in the morning.

Chris didn't know how he was going to say goodbye to Michelle until he realized that he had never handed her the alibi jacket. He waited for her to say goodbye to everyone who was left and start walking to her car. Then he called after her and followed behind. She turned around and she smiled.

"You forgot this," he announced, handing Amanda's jacket to her. "I wouldn't want you to leave without, you know, giving it back to you."

Michelle reached out and gently touched his arm briefly, then took the jacket. "Chris," she said in a hushed tone, "I hardly even know what to say to you. That's not like me."

"No, me neither," he said. "It's weird, huh?" Michelle nodded. "This may sound even weirder, but thank you."

"You're thanking me?" She laughed. "Well, that's new. You don't need to thank me."

"But I do," he said softly. "You made yesterday so good for me. The whole day. From the moment I saw you through the limo window, all the way until this morning. It was exciting, and fun, and it was the first time I looked forward to anything so much in a long time. You took a chance and hung out with me on Christmas night, something we'd never done before, and that was amazing. Now when I think about it, like you said, it had to happen exactly like it did back then for yesterday to happen. I'm gonna miss you, Michelle."

Michelle looked at the ground for a moment and then back up at Chris.

"Well, then, you're welcome, Chris," she said sincerely. "And I'm gonna tell you a little secret now." She leaned in closer to him. "I agree with what you said last night," she whispered. "I don't think that this is our last one-night stand."

They smiled at each other. Then Michelle got in the car, and she drove away.

Summer School

"Hello?"

"Hi, Chris?"

"Oh, hi Michelle. How are you doing?

"Good. How's your summer going?"

"Pretty good. I can't believe it's already August. I'll be getting my student teaching assignment soon."

"That's so cool. I'll be getting my Fall clinical assignment soon too. I can't believe we'll both be juniors."

"Me neither. How's it going living with Sandra?"

"It's been great! The apartment is so roomy after being in the dorm for two years, and we get along so well. So listen, the reason I'm calling is I'm home for the weekend right now, and my mom just told me she wants me to do something with that sweat jacket. You know, the one from the wedding? She's tired of seeing it lying around. And I think maybe *you* should hold onto it, you know, and maybe if you ever see Amanda someday, you could give it back to her. She probably wonders where it went. Or, you could just keep it at your place in case anyone ever needs to use it."

"Yeah, I guess that makes sense."

"Yeah. So I was thinking maybe I could drop it by your place, tonight, like around nine? You know, as long as your girlfriend doesn't mind. . . ."

"Michelle, I don't have a girlfriend. I'm not seeing anyone. I haven't been seeing anyone since the wedding. No one. At all. And I would love for you to come over and bring me the jacket. You don't have to wait until nine, though. I'm free right now, and for the rest of the night. Oh, and into tomorrow morning. Late tomorrow morning."

Fall Seminar/Junior Year

"Hello?"

"Hi, Michelle."

"Chris! Hi! How are you? I haven't heard from you in a while."

"I know, I've been so busy. You know, making lesson plans and stuff. You actually have to do all that stuff at home after school. And now I'm also taking some graduate level courses. It's a lot of work. Oh, and I got placed at Murphy High! Can you believe it?"

"Oh my God, that's amazing! Do you have any kids you know in classes?"

"Pete's sister, Hannah. And there's a Rob Cafaro. I'm assuming . . ."

"Yeah, it's his youngest brother. Wow. He's a nice kid. I just hope, for his mom's sake, he has no aspirations to join the military like his brother."

"Yeah, I know. It's okay at Murphy. It's so different from McKinney, though. It takes some getting used to. Where did you end up getting clinicals?"

"Oncology treatment clinic. I love it so far. I get to help people while they're going through their chemo treatments. It's tough to see them go through it, but they are so grateful to the nurses. It's like a little family on treatment days."

"That's so awesome. I'm glad you got something you like. You're gonna be such a great nurse, Michelle. So listen, there's a seminar that my roommate Grant is going to about new developments in early childhood education at Hampshire College next week, and I thought it sounded pretty good, so I signed up too. It's all day Friday, and I figured I'd find a place to stay the night instead of coming right home, since it will be late, and you know, there would be a lot of traffic. Grant's not going to stay over, so I'm kinda on my own. I thought maybe if you didn't have any other plans, like a date or something . . ."

"No, no date. Not on Friday. Not on any other night either, actually. You know, it might be hard to find a motel room if there's a seminar going on in town. I have some extra room. Uh, I mean in my room. At my apartment. Why don't you just come stay with me?"

"Oh, okay. Wow. That would be great! Yeah, maybe we could do some catching up. Maybe get a bottle of wine, and you know, hang out. And I was thinking . . ."

"Yeah?"

"It's getting pretty cold now, and I know it gets much colder out there this time of year. I know you said that sweat jacket was too big on you, but I thought I'd bring it back, you know, just in case. I know you don't like being chilly."

"That's so thoughtful of you, Chris. Yeah, that would be great."

Sally and James Get Engaged

"Hello?"

"Hi, Chris."

"I was just gonna call you, Michelle. That's so weird!"

"I'm guessing you got the invitation."

"To the engagement party? Yeah. In today's mail. I can't believe that James and Sally are finally engaged. I mean, we've always known it was coming, but now it's finally happening. I'm guessing you've heard all the details about the proposal."

"Are you kidding me? Sally called me from a pay phone in the restaurant lobby five minutes later! I can't believe James used the diamond from her promise necklace for her engagement ring. That has to be the most romantic thing I've ever heard!"

"Well, you know James, always raising the bar for the rest of us. So you're coming to the party, I assume."

"Of course. Sally's my best friend. And you'll be there?"

"I wouldn't miss it."

"Are you, well, coming alone?"

"Yes, I'm coming alone. I know it's been a while since we've, uh, seen each other. It's been so hectic over here, with everyone graduating and moving out. Grant and I had to find a new apartment, and we'll be moving in before the end of June. We've still got a year of graduate courses to complete, and now we're also looking for teaching positions for the Fall. Oh, by the way, congratulations on your new job! I'm so happy that you were able to find something in oncology. I know how much you like working with those patients."

"Well, it's not the treatment room, but the clinic is good too. I love my new coworkers. I think I'm really gonna like it."

"That's so great! Michelle?"

"Yeah, Chris?"

"I'm excited to see you at the party. Are you . . . are you going to bring the jacket? My new apartment has more space, if you need me to keep it for you for a while. It looks like it's gonna be a long, hot summer."

"I'll bring it to your new place myself to hang it up. I'd love to see your new room. I'm really looking forward to seeing how you fixed it up."

"I'm looking forward to you seeing my room, too, Michelle."

Dress Shopping with Sally

"Are you bringing a date to our wedding?" Sally said from the other side of the curtain.

"Uh, I don't think so," Michelle called back as she reached behind her to do the back-of-the-dress-zipper dance. "I'm not seeing anyone. I don't really want to bring anyone just to have a date, you know?" She stepped out into the open fitting room space and stood in front of the three-way mirror fixture.

Sally scrunched her nose. "I don't like the eggplant color on you," she said, "but that dress in another color wouldn't be bad."

"Wouldn't be bad?" Michelle asked. "Don't you think the bridesmaids deserve better than not bad?"

Sally laughed. "This is why you're my maid of honor, Michelle."

Michelle smirked. "I thought it was because your sister Andie is pregnant and due too close to your wedding date to do it. But I'll take the compliment anyway."

"Baby number three," Sally rolled her eyes. "I just wish she had kept her hands off of Derrek for a few more months so she could have been in the wedding party. But Michelle, having you is probably gonna be even more fun." She sighed. "But I worry about you sometimes. It's like you don't even care that you're not meeting anyone. I hope your job isn't keeping you from being able to get out and socialize."

"No, it's not," Michelle promised. "But you don't need to worry about me. I'm fine."

"Yeah, that's the problem, you're too fine," Sally said. "Do you have some kind of secret love affair going on that you haven't told me about?"

Michelle was in the middle of taking a sip of water that had been provided by the bridal shop attendant. She started to cough.

"Are you okay?" Sally asked, coming to her side.

Michelle cleared her throat a few times, and she nodded to reassure her friend. "I'm okay," she said. "I just had some water go down the wrong pipe. Uh, secret love affair? Why would you think that?"

Sally shrugged. "I don't know. But from what you've told me—" She lowered her voice discreetly. "—you haven't had sex since sophomore year, and that's a long time."

"Sally," Michelle said, "that's not actually one hundred percent true."

Sally was looking at another of the dresses she had brought back, but now she looked up at Michelle. "What??" she asked. Then she whispered, "You've had sex you haven't told me about?"

"Well, yeah," Michelle answered awkwardly. "I mean, I tell you most everything, but not completely everything."

"Who?" Sally asked. "Is it just one person, or more than one?"

"Sally!" Michelle protested. "That's kind of rude. That's private!"

Sally looked down. "I know, I'm sorry. I just can't believe you've been keeping that kind of information from me. I've never kept anything from you. I'm just surprised, that's all."

Michelle shook her head. "Sally, now I'm wondering if part of preparing for Jewish marriage is lessons on inducing guilt! You're already very good at it." She sighed. "Okay, it's one person. But we're not dating. It's just a series of one-night stands over the past two and a half years. Kind of like an affair of convenience. It's worked out well for us so far."

"Oh my God, Michelle. You really are having a sort of affair. He's not married, is he?"

Michelle gasped. "No of course not!" she protested. "Sally! You know I would *never* do that! No, it's just that both of us are really busy all the time, and we don't have time for more than what we're doing now."

"Do you love this guy?" Sally asked.

"Love?" Michelle asked. "I-I don't know. I mean, I'm fond of him, and the sex is, well, for lack of a better phrase, earth-shatteringly fantastic, but love isn't something we've discussed at all."

The attendant came into the fitting room area and handed Sally several additional white gowns for her to try on. "How are we doing in here?" she asked, glancing at the dress that Michelle still had on from ten minutes earlier.

"Fine," Sally said, and she handed Michelle the same dress in Kelly green. Michelle stepped back into the curtained area.

"Michelle," Sally said when the attendant left, "I'm really glad you have someone at least, but it worries me a little. I mean, you're not gonna bring this guy to my wedding, but you're also not gonna bring anyone else. It seems like he might be holding you back from meeting someone else."

Michelle unzipped her dress and it slid to the floor. She had a sudden flashback to her first night with Chris at Carl and Kim's wedding. She imagined what dress would slide to the floor this time. She knew she had to lie to Sally to keep her off her trail. She wasn't ready to give up her secret.

"No, he's not holding me back," she said, immediately knowing that this was, indeed, a lie. Chris was totally holding her back. One day, he might call her, and want to have one of their infamous one-night stands. It wouldn't work if she was seeing someone else. She would have to say no. And then their fragile arrangement would shatter, forever. She didn't want it to shatter. She wasn't ready for that. "Don't worry, Sally, I've got everything under control," she went on as she zipped up the green dress. "It's best for me not to have an emotional attachment right now. I'm just not ready for something serious. So a sex-only thing is ideal. Really, things are good, you don't need to worry." She stepped out of the curtained area.

Sally looked at Michelle in the green dress. "Oh, yeah, Michelle," she gasped. "That's the dress. You look so beautiful in that color. I don't even care how it looks on Kim, Darlene, and Erin. That's the dress for my bridal party."

Michelle gave her a big smile, and then Sally took a few pictures. Then she went into the fitting room herself to try on some bridal gowns. She was duly distracted from the details of Michelle's love life, and that's the way Michelle wanted it.

Reading the Signs

"I'm sorry that the wedding's so close to the end of your term," James told Chris over lunch at Saydie's Diner a month before the wedding. He was in town working on wedding details with Sally's parents and had called Chris to catch up. "It was the only weekend we could get the old barn, and Sally really wanted the old barn."

"No, I get it," Chris assured him. "It's a big deal. It's just one weekend of my life, but it's the biggest weekend of yours. I'll figure it out."

"I'm psyched that Carl and Kim are coming with the kids. We finally get to meet Elena. And Drake is almost three. That's nuts."

"Yeah, I'll never forget when Carl told me they were actually trying for a second baby so close after their wedding," Chris said. "I thought they were out of their minds. But Kim wanted so badly to have her kids close in age, like her brothers and sisters were. I guess she really felt she missed out on that as a kid."

"Yeah, eighteen months apart," James said. "That's a lot of diapers to change. No, I think my parents did it right. Three years, at least, between kids. That's what Sally and I are planning on doing."

"Man, shut up," Chris said, holding up his hand. "You're freaking me out. Another one bites the dust. And you're even talking about your kids! I still have to think about finishing grad school."

"Don't you want kids someday?"

"Yeah, of course," Chris replied. "But I still feel so young and immature most of the time, you know? I sometimes feel like I'm still seventeen. It's like everyone around me is starting to grow up."

James laughed. "Well, it was bound to happen eventually. Time goes by. But you have to have a partner in crime if you want to go the wife-and-kids route."

"Yeah," Chris said quietly. "The wife-and-kids route. You can't do it alone."

"Any prospects? I haven't heard you talk about anyone new for a long time."

Chris shook his head. "Not really," he said. "But I'm not really out looking for someone, either. It's not like I'm all alone all the time. I mean, I still have some company from time to time, you know, just not anything that would lead to a wife and kids right now. It's better that way. I can't really even imagine those things yet."

"Well, it's probably not the right time then," James said. "When it's right, you'll know it. Do you still like working at Randall?"

Chris smiled. "I do," he said. "It took a couple of months for it to seem real, you know, but it helps to have Angela Fox and Dante Jackson still there, and the office staff is great. Sean, I mean Principal Jeffries, still shakes his head sometimes when he sees me. I think I broke his spirit all those years ago. I think I might be responsible for at least half of his gray hairs. But he'll be retiring soon, and I'm betting Dante will be the new principal."

"Mr. Jackson was pretty cool," James said. "It's awesome that you're good friends now."

"Yeah, he really helped me out of a bind in high school," Chris agreed. "I don't know what things will be like next year when I'm done with grad school. It's gonna feel like a vacation, just working and not having to go to classes and write papers anymore. I'll have so much more time to myself."

James nodded. "Yeah, I get it. Well, maybe that will be when the time is right to meet someone. But when you leave school, there'll be fewer people to meet. It's a trade-off. Maybe I can introduce you to some of the staff at the Marriott. There are some great hostesses and waitresses, and a lot of them are just finishing school. Some of them will be at the wedding."

Chris froze. The wedding. Michelle would be at the wedding. The best day of his life to that point had been the day he spent with Michelle at Carl and Kim's wedding, and he was hoping for something similar at James and Sally's. Well, they would never be able to re-create that first time exactly. It had been the perfect day. A hall of fame day. They had created many other days and nights since then, and every one of them was incredible. He had never known another body like hers. He had never craved the touch of any woman more than hers. He could not take any risks that James and Sally's wedding night was not going to be another magical night for Chris Mahoney and Michelle Gorman.

"Thanks, man, but I think I'm gonna hold off on anyone new right now, you know, just until things settle down a bit with school and everything. Plus I just kinda want to be able to concentrate on our old friends. We just don't get to see each other so often anymore with everyone working and hanging out with other friends. I mean, Carl and Kim will be there. And my godson."

James nodded. "Yeah, I guess you're right. I could always introduce you to someone later. And I bet Sally would be able to find someone perfect for you at some point. She's good at that stuff."

"Carl's already gonna start his second year of his electrical engineering program at USF in the Fall," Chris said, adeptly changing the subject. "They're gonna let him start taking graduate classes already. He told me he's really excited about it. He's really good at it, and he thinks the work projects are fun. I wish I'd ever felt that way about school."

"That guy is really living the good life now, isn't he?" James said. "He got his electrical license, a wife, two kids, a house, and a community he loves. After senior year in high school, I would never have imagined he would have come this far, and in less than five years. It's quite a story."

"It is," Chris agreed with pride for his cousin's accomplishments. "And Kim getting a job at Head Forward as a group facilitator right after graduating from USF was pretty sweet, too. They let her work flexible hours and, sometimes, she can even bring the kids to work. They love her there. I can see her running that place someday."

"It's like the two of them have some sort of guardian angel looking out for them."

Chris nodded. "Yeah, two of them. Named Missy Bishop and Laine Farmer."

Michelle could not stop thinking about her conversation with Sally. She tried to put it all in perspective. She had not dated anyone else for the almost three years that she and Chris had been engaging in whatever it was they were engaging in. He had also not seen anyone else. They kept making excuses to get together, and each time they did, it was magical. They knew every inch of each other's bodies now. They knew how to make each other moan and sometimes even yelp. Then they would talk. Sometimes they talked all night, or sometimes just until they fell asleep in each other's arms. These times were easy for them. They were friends. Very, very good friends who fucked, as Chris had put it so delicately their first time together.

But there was never talk of the future. It was always about the moment they were in. There was no mention of love. She knew she loved him in a way, at least as a friend. But she wasn't sure if she loved him as more than that. *Then why am I holding myself back for him?* she asked herself. *Don't I deserve to have love in my life? Isn't that the ultimate goal? Isn't that why I ended it with Joey?*

But she was scared. It was her biggest fear all over again. Being alone. And if she allowed herself to start to feel love for Chris, there was the risk of him not loving her back. It was a big risk. If she loved him, and he didn't love her, then they would have to stop what they were doing. No more serial one-night stands. No more world-rocking sex. No more all-night conversations and falling asleep in each other's arms. And, possibly, she could lose Chris as her friend. That part was unfathomable.

The wedding was coming up soon. They would find an excuse to spend the night together, like they always did. They would flirt all day, working themselves up into a sexual lather, and then finally find relief later in the evening when they were alone. Even thinking about it now gave Michelle the shivers. She thought about finding a reason to see him sooner, but there was just too much going on with work, and he was wrapping up school on top of working full-time as a teacher. There might be more excuses this summer, when he graduated and was off work for the summer. But for now, she would just have to wait for the wedding. One more month. She could last that long. She had lasted longer stretches of time between their trysts.

Chris kept worrying that their fragile house of cards would eventually blow down in the winds of change. Time was passing. Michelle had graduated from college and was working in a job she excelled at. He was getting close to graduating with his master's degree, and he was also employed in the work he had aspired to. Miraculously, they had both reached the goals they had established for themselves back in high school. Professionally, things were right on track. Romantically, he was satisfied with his relationship with Michelle, at least sexually satisfied, although he wished he could satisfy his needs more frequently. Michelle. She was an amazing woman. She was smart, sexy, funny, sensitive, pretty—everything a woman should be. He thought about her when they weren't together, and he couldn't even imagine being with someone else, even just on a date. He had his rule, and he was committed to it. One woman, no cheating. But was that even right? Could you cheat on someone you weren't even in a committed relationship with? Did his rule even apply to their . . . relationship?

He couldn't help but feel that it was his rule that kept her available to him. It had been almost three years now. He hadn't been with anyone else, and neither had she. He knew it was not a coincidence. It wasn't that they didn't both have opportunities; they were both choosing to be alone so they could be together. Or . . . were there other reasons they were doing this?

They were both keeping themselves from relationships that could lead to more, to everything. Love, family, security. So he worried that he was holding her back. They had both just turned twenty-three years old that month. Their second set of friends was about to get married. One set even had kids. Michelle had to be thinking about the future. And he wanted her to be happy. What he didn't know was if he could be the one to offer her that happiness, or if he would have to consider letting her go so she could find it with someone else.

That idea led to a wave of nausea. He didn't want to let her go. Letting go, saying goodbye. These were the worst and hardest things he ever had to do in his life, even when it was the right thing to do. He had worked so hard to keep this thing casual, at least when they talked about it. But it would still be a painful goodbye if they ended it. Oh, he did not want to say goodbye to Michelle. He would have to just wait for the wedding, to see what happened, to be aware of the cues, to feel it out. For now he would ignore the nausea. Maybe he had just eaten some bad fish.

Wedding at the Barn

It would be a dry wedding, except for one glass of champagne for toasts for the people who chose to partake. No one in James's family drank due to family addiction issues, and Howie, James's brother and best man, was a recovering addict. Sally and James had made a choice in high school to abstain from drugs and alcohol, as they didn't want to take any chances that James had inherited the propensity toward alcoholism from his paternal grandfather. Sally's parents respected their choice and arranged to have a wedding bar filled with mixers and sodas for mock cocktails.

The wedding was taking place at an old barn in the country. It looked rustic from the outside, with chickens roaming the grounds freely, goats in a fenced area, and even a pair of donkeys, but inside, the barn was elegant and fancy. The wooden beams and lofts were authentic, and the decor was romantic. There were strings of white tea lights hanging from the walls tastefully. There was a giant sliding barn door that could remain open in the nice weather for an indoor-outdoor hybrid event and could be closed in the rain or cold for comfort. The wedding party gazed around in awe of the space when they arrived for the rehearsal on Friday evening.

"I can see why Sally was willing to compromise on an April wedding to get this place," Darlene said, looking up at the underside of the barn roof at the ancient rafters.

"It doesn't seem like much of a compromise," Michelle said, dodging a frantic chicken running straight at her legs. "The weather is beautiful, and the barn door faces west. There should be a beautiful sunset during the reception."

Traci spun around in the vastness, her long peasant skirt circling high around her knees "This place just makes me want to dance!" she said. "I'm gonna dance all night tomorrow!" She looked at Michelle and gave her a sly smile.

Michelle snuck a glance at Chris, and they both grinned. They couldn't wait for the dining and dancing and what would inevitably come after.

Later, they sat across from each other at the rehearsal dinner, which took place in the Bachmans' screened-in porch and backyard. Everyone made small talk as they ate. But all Chris could focus on was Michelle's dress. She was wearing a long black cotton tank-style dress with spaghetti straps. And she clearly wasn't wearing a bra. Michelle could get away with going braless and still look tasteful due to her petite size, and most people would pay no heed. But Chris wasn't most people. He was blatantly aware that under that dress, her breasts were unencumbered. He had to touch them. He had to touch her. He had to have her. There was no waiting until after the wedding reception. The distraction was overwhelming him, and he knew if he stood up, his arousal would be apparent to everyone around him. So he devised a quick plan.

"Michelle," he said, as they sat with their friends at a picnic table in the yard. "You're gonna see your parents while you're here, right?"

"Yeah," she said, looking at him with curiosity to see where this was going. "I'm staying over at their house Sunday night and leaving on Monday. Why?"

"Oh, last time I saw your mom over at Eastboro State," he lied, "she asked me if I still had any of my undergrad teaching textbooks that I wasn't using, and I said I would see if I could find any for her. So I have a few in my car to give her, and I thought maybe we could just put them in your car to give to her. Otherwise, I'll just forget, and I'll be driving around with them in my back seat for months before I remember to drop them off. Would you mind?"

"No, not at all," Michelle said. "Do you want to do the transfer right now while we're thinking about it?"

Chris put down his fork and wiped his mouth with his napkin. "Oh, okay, good idea. Let's go do that."

They both stood and excused themselves and casually headed to the house. As soon as they got inside and away from prying ears, Michelle stopped, "There are no textbooks," she said confidently. "Am I right?"

Chris smiled. "You are absolutely right," he said softly.

Michelle exhaled. "Oh thank God." She grabbed him around the neck and pressed her mouth against his. They both moaned immediately with the familiar pleasure.

"I couldn't stop thinking about you in that dress with no bra," Chris said, reaching down to touch her, "and I just needed to touch those fabulous breasts of yours. I just can't wait for tomorrow night. You've spent a ton of time in this house. Where can we go right now?"

Michelle thought fast. Then she perked up. "The basement. It's part furnished, and no one will hear us down there, even if they come inside." She opened the cellar door, and they quietly moved down the stairs. When they got to the bottom, they surveyed the area. Both sets of eyes landed on an armless swivel desk chair, and they went to it by silent assent. They stood looking at each other, then Chris reached out to caress her breasts again over her dress. Her head tilted back, and she enjoyed his caress through the fabric. Then he lifted her dress and touched her skin. She shivered. She lifted his shirt, and they kissed skin to skin. Michelle felt her body tingle against the warmth of his, and she let her mind drift to where they were going next. Her panties came off and his pants were pulled down and he sat on the chair. She climbed on and straddled his body, wrapping her legs around his back as far as she could, and they moved. The chair swiveled slightly with a creak.

"No one can hear us," Michelle reminded him with a whisper.

Chris covered her face with kisses, and then touched his tongue to her erect nipples.

"Chris," she said, and he knew there was no reply required. They reveled in their closeness until there was no more space between them, and they called out softly into each other's ears.

When they were done, they stayed locked together and slumped over on the chair, holding each other like life preservers.

"That was uniquely wonderful," Chris croaked. "I've never done it on a swivel chair before."

"That was a first for me, too," Michelle admitted, still catching her breath. "I want to stay like this all day. But they'll wonder where we went. Textbooks may be heavy, but not *that* heavy. Besides, last time it was your best friend's wedding. This time it's my best friend. I'd better stay focused."

"I know," Chris said. "This whole ruse was all done with the purpose of helping us stay focused on our friends. I couldn't wait until tomorrow night. But now I can, and I promise, it will still be as great as always, even without the wait."

"I know it will," Michelle agreed with a grin. "I did something sneaky, Chris. Sally reserved a block of rooms together in the hotel for tomorrow night, and I 'accidentally' may have asked the desk clerk to put me on a completely different floor on the other side of the hotel than everyone else, so—"

Chris kissed her hard on the mouth. "You are an absolute genius," he whispered in her ear. "So no one sees us sneaking in, and the bride and groom don't overhear us getting it on during their wedding night."

Michelle smiled. *Maybe one of these days we can get a room together,* she thought, *and we won't need to sneak around anymore.* Then she caught herself. *Where the hell did that thought come from?*

They got up, redressed, and headed upstairs. They stopped quickly in the bathroom and then returned outside.

Carl looked up at Chris as he sat back down. "Everything went okay with the textbook exchange?" he asked him.

Chris smiled warmly at his cousin. It was always hard to believe that Carl was actually there with him when he was in town. It was like his groomsman gift from Sally and James.

"Yeah," he said. "It's pretty cool that Mrs. Gorman is wrapping up getting her teaching degree after all this time."

"Yeah," Carl agreed. "The Gormans are good people. It's nice that you can help them out. Michelle's been in our lives forever. I'm really glad she's still part of our little posse."

Chris nodded and went back to his now cold entree. Carl was being sentimental in his old age. Maybe fatherhood had made him a bit softer. But he was right. Michelle was, indeed, pretty special.

The wedding day was unseasonably warm. One hour prior to the ceremony, the outdoor temperature was a balmy seventy-eight degrees with a light wind and wispy clouds whose sole purpose was to paint the sky into a more beautiful landscape for James and Sally.

The bridesmaids were in green, and the maid of honor shone with her dress against her long red hair and green eyes. Kim and Darlene also looked beautiful, along with James's sister Erin, rounding out the bride's side. Howie, the best man, was the picture of health and happiness. He was five years clean and sober and had completed his undergraduate coursework. He would be attending USF law school in the fall. James's groomsmen were Pete, Chris, Carl, and Sally's brother, Nathan, who was doing his residency in pediatric medicine at Cedar Sinai Hospital in Los Angeles and raising a toddler along with his wife. Sally's niece Josie was the flower girl, and Kim and Carl's son Drake carried the wedding rings tied onto a tiny silk pillow.

The ceremony took place outside the barn. It was mainly Jewish by tradition. They had hired a rabbi that catered to private, mixed marriages. When the vows were exchanged, and the rings securely fastened, the bride and the groom stomped on a glass to symbolize that once glass is broken it can never be reassembled, such as it is when vows are made, they cannot be taken apart. After the crunch of what was really a light bulb wrapped in a napkin was heard under Sally and James's feet, the couple was married, and everyone applauded. The bridesmaids were all in tears, dabbing their eyes with delicate monogrammed handkerchiefs that had served as bridesmaid gifts. The love story of Sally and James had reached legend status, although happily ever after was still awaiting them in their lifetime together.

Chris and Michelle had already started the prelude to their night together, with looks and discrete touches and whispered words and promises. Half of the fun was the secret nature of their affair and the feeling that it was just the two of them in their little universe. *Then why was I thinking about going public yesterday so we wouldn't have to sneak around?* Michelle thought.

The reception was lovely, the food was good, the music was entertaining, and the company they were in was their closest friends in the world. The night was a success. A couple of times through the night, Michelle caught Traci's eye, and Traci gave her knowing smiles. Michelle smiled back but had no idea what that was all about. But at least Traci wasn't flirting with Chris this time, but neither was she with a date. She and Paul had broken up over a year earlier, and Traci seemed content enough to be at the wedding on her own, dancing and chatting with her McKinney friends.

When the night wound down, the guests were shuttled back to the hotel in shifts by a van service. Michelle stayed until the very end, and then lined up along with some other guests to wait for the van. Chris, along with Carl, Kim, and their children Drake and Elena, came up to the line behind her. Michelle yawned.

"I can't believe the kids are still up," she said to Kim.

"My kids?" Kim smirked. "My kids never sleep. It's like they're driven by an invisible motor all the time, especially Elena. She wants to be part of everything. They were having too much fun dancing with Sally and James's nieces and nephews. But they will be tucked in and in dreamland very soon. Are you heading for bed?"

"Yes, I *am* going right to bed," Michelle said honestly.

Chris coughed. Michelle suppressed a smile. The van pulled up. As it filled up, there wasn't enough room for all of them.

"You go ahead, Michelle," Carl said. "We'll wait for the next one. That will give us a little more time to hang out with Chris."

"Thanks, Carl," Michelle said. "Good night, you guys. Good night, Chris." She gave him a smile.

"See you later, Michelle," Chris said back. He had her room number and her extra key.

Michelle got back to the hotel and lingered in the lobby. There was a woman playing standards on the piano. She stood and listened to her for a few minutes, then placed a dollar in her tip glass. She hoped that Chris would arrive while she waited, but it was looking like his van was lagging behind. She decided to go upstairs to wait in her room. She pressed the elevator button, and when it opened, she stepped inside. She pushed the button for the fifth floor, and the door started to close.

Suddenly, she heard a voice yell, "Hold the door!" and an arm shot through the small opening. The door slid back open, and Chris stepped into the elevator. Michelle felt all her senses heighten. "Why, hello, Miss Gorman," he said stoically. "Going up?"

Michelle looked at him with no visible expression, and replied, "Oh, hello Mr. Tyler. No, I'm going . . . down."

Chris gave her a huge smile and then they laughed. Then, as the door closed again, he grabbed her gently and kissed her.

Their first sex after long events was always exhilarating, albeit sometimes desperate and rushed. After, they lay in bed, as usual, staring at the ceiling, both of them thinking about squirt gun paint patterns. Chris ran his fingers through Michelle's hair and kissed her neck by her ear. She felt like a contented cat.

"I missed you, Chris," she told him softly. "It was too long this time."

"Hmm," Chris replied, giving her earlobe a nibble. "It's always too long."

Michelle considered her new thoughts about Chris. She wondered about something. "Christopher Jerome Mahoney," she said with authority.

Chris raised one hand. "Present."

"Do you know my middle name, Chris?"

Chris smiled. "I do," he told her, lying back on his pillow. "When we were in sixth grade, Mrs. Dixon was teaching us about mnemonics and memory devices. She asked if anyone could give an example. You raised your hand and said something like, 'You can use them to remember names, like my mother's friend who always forgets names. I told her to always remember that I was named after two Beatles songs. Michelle and Rita.' Your parents were really young, and they were huge Beatles fans when you were born. I'm surprised your brothers aren't named Rocky Racoon and Billy Shears! So yeah, mnemonics work."

"Oh my God, I can't believe you remember all that," Michelle said. She was feeling a strange stirring in her gut, and it was compelling her to speak. She stayed on her back, still looking at the ceiling. "Remember that night at your dorm? When we were looking at the ceiling, and we thought that they sprayed on the paint with squirt guns?"

Chris laughed. "I think that I just proved to you that I pretty much remember just about everything about you."

Michelle turned to face him. "Everything?"

Chris nodded and spoke softly. "Everything." He paused. "Chelley."

Michelle suddenly felt lightheaded. He had called her Chelley. He had remembered when she had told him about that during their night in the dorm, too.

"Chris," she said, "has it been long enough for you, you know, since . . . last time? Would you be able to like . . ."

Chris smiled and reached out for her. "Why don't you find out for yourself," he whispered, and he kissed her hard. He was ready.

She felt like she was on fire, and while she burned, so did he. There was symbiosis. He caressed her to the point she almost begged him to get on top of her, and when she was about to climax, she prompted him by saying, "Chris."

And right on cue, he said it. "Oh, Chelley," and she nearly lost her mind. She felt the intensity run down her arms and legs and she cried out, not caring who could hear her, and he cried out too, and he thrust harder and she thought her body might have split in two because she was feeling double the pleasure until it was too much, but she still couldn't get enough, so she kept going until he stopped her so he could breathe and he kissed her neck and she still shuddered and her back stayed arched until she finally collapsed in exhaustion. Then she felt like she'd been given a sedative, like she had once when she had work done on her braces, and she felt sleepy, and satisfied, and completely, and totally, made love to.

Chris panted for several seconds. "What the hell was that?" he asked. "Where did you get that? Michelle, for the second time, I almost blacked out making love to you. How do you do that? How can I make that happen every time? Oh, my God." He collapsed back onto the pillow. "Oh my fucking God."

Michelle lay back with a pleased expression on her face. She didn't answer Chris's questions. She knew what had happened. She knew why her body led her in those directions. Chris had called her Chelley. It was like a magic word, with sexual qualities.

She remembered her conversation with Sally back in college, when she told her about her desire to have someone, just one man, call her Chelley. She tried to remember everything they said that night. She said they had to be involved in a sexual relationship. And she said she had to find him very, very special. And Sally had said that when this person called her Chelley, she would fall in love with him. And if she already loved him, it would make her love him with an intensity she never knew existed. Intensity. Like the white-hot power of one thousand suns. Like what had just happened with her and Chris when he called her Chelley, which she had not been expecting. And he'd felt it too.

I think I might love Chris Mahoney, she thought.

She looked at him, and he looked back. And then she said, "Oh my fucking God!"

Manufacturing Trysts

There were no more weddings, no more seminars, no more excuses they could use to see each other that summer. Chris had to get back to her. He couldn't wait several months again. He couldn't go all summer without her touch, her hair, her skin, her voice. Her laugh. Her. Chelley.

He didn't know what, but something had changed. It was something powerful, something bigger than him. It was like nothing he had ever felt, not for Rhonda, not for Alison. It was beyond his experience with anyone, ever. It made him forget things, like his own limitations, and sometimes even his own name. She was doing something to him that made him feel . . . incredible. And it scared the shit out of him.

This was little, tiny Michelle Gorman, the small girl with the braces and the glasses and the freckles and the unruly red hair. The girl who clung to Darlene for dear life in elementary school so she wouldn't be left behind. The girl who became awkward when faced with most social situations in junior high and often avoided them all together. She was always there, always part of the background, but Chris Mahoney was always part of the foreground. Sometimes, he *was* the foreground. But now, he felt like he was standing on a higher level beside her, a place he had never been before, and she knew the way, but he was still lost.

But the way she blew his mind could not be ignored. *This must be the way sex is supposed to feel, but never has,* he thought. Was she just that good? Or was there more to it than that? There was no place in the encyclopedia where he could look this stuff up, and he didn't dare ask his friends. They might think he was insane. He wasn't sure if this was a normal way to feel. *Maybe there's something wrong with me,* he thought.

He sat down on the couch to watch TV with Grant. Now that summer had arrived, and they had completed their master's degrees, they had time to do frivolous things, like watch TV, or shower and eat every day. It was like living in the lap of luxury. Chris saw a postcard on the coffee table and picked it up. He realized it was Grant's mail, but he had glanced at it quickly before putting it back. It was a reminder of Grant's five-year class reunion at Pawtucket High School. Five-year reunion? The Randall Middle School math teacher added it up in his head. Yes, it *had* been five years now. Did McKinney have a five-year reunion?

Chris went back to his room and picked up his phone extension. He dialed the Newells' phone number. Sally picked up.

"Sally, do we have a five-year reunion at McKinney?"

"Of course we do," she replied as if he should instinctively know these things. "James and I had thought about going, basically just to show everyone that the junior prom's cutest couple actually did end up getting married. Didn't you get the mailer?"

"No," Chris said. "I never get anything from anyone. I don't think they even have my current address. It's probably sitting in a pile on a table at my mom's house, waiting for me to come pick it up. When is it? I didn't miss it, did I?"

"No, it's the third weekend in June," Sally said. "I wouldn't even think you'd be interested in going to something like that, let alone be worried you might have missed it."

"I could say the same thing for you two party animals," Chris replied. "But I don't know. I just might want to go, especially since I have more time now. Is anyone else from our group going? I mean, no offense, but if it's just you and James, I already see you guys all the time anyway."

Sally laughed. "Well of course Kim and Carl can't make it, but I think Darlene was thinking about going. I need to check with Michelle and see if she's interested in coming. It would be fun if we all went."

"Yeah, you should call her and see," Chris said, trying to sound like he was lowkey, but feeling his heart speed up at the prospect of being able to manufacture another tryst with Michelle, and so soon after the last one.

"Yeah, I'll call both of them and check and let you know," Sally said. "I'll let them know you might be coming. Maybe that will entice them a bit."

Chris laughed. "Or maybe scare them away," he quipped.

When he got off the phone, he sat on his bed with his thoughts. He had to see her. He even felt like just getting into his car and driving to her apartment in Amherst and ringing her bell, but that seemed to be outside of their unofficial rules. Was it, though? Or had there just never been an occasion? No, he finally decided, because that might set a precedent and be too confusing for both of them. He would just wait to see if she was coming to the reunion, an event he never would have even dreamed of going to before this moment, but that now he was willing to pay exorbitant amounts of money to go to if needed, if it meant he'd get another chance to be with Chelley. He had to see Chelley.

Michelle answered the phone.

"Hey, Michelle, it's Sally."

"Hey, Sally, how's it going in newlywed land? Still in the honeymoon period?"

Sally laughed. "Always!" she said. "We're still waiting on the photo proofs from the wedding, but they said they'll take a while. But people are starting to send us copies of the pictures they took, so we'll have to get together and look at them soon."

"I'd love that," Michelle told her. A welcome distraction.

"Hey, I'm actually calling to see if you're gonna go to the McKinney five-year reunion in June," Sally said. "We were thinking of going, pretty much just to show off that we actually got married." She laughed. "But it might be fun if other people from our group go, too."

Michelle thought about it. She wasn't planning on going, since there was really no one she needed to see except her own group anyway, but if there was any chance that Chris was going. . . .

"Have you talked to anyone else about it yet?" She had been thinking about putting in some overtime at work on the weekends by covering for staff at the treatment clinic, which was really the work she liked the best.

"Strangely enough," Sally said, "it was Chris that made me think of it. He called me to ask if we were having a reunion, because he didn't get a mailer. And then he asked me if anyone else was going. Kind of like you just did! I told him I'd call you and Darlene. I just left a message for Darlene."

"Oh, really?" Michelle asked. "So Chris instigated this? It doesn't really seem like a reunion would be his kind of thing."

"Yeah," Sally said. "I said the same thing. But he said he has more time on his hands now with being done with school and would think about going if other people in the group were going. What do you think? Do you want to help me entice Mr. Mahoney into coming to the reunion by going yourself?"

Yes, yes, I do want the man I'm falling in love with to be there, and to be the one who arranged it so we would both be there at the same time, she thought.

"I might be able to work that out," she answered vaguely. "I was thinking about doing some overtime that weekend, but it's not set in stone yet, so I can think about it."

"Oh, come on, Michelle," Sally begged. "Just say yes. Just come. It will be near my two-month anniversary. Do it for me, as an anniversary gift."

Michelle pretended to sigh. She loved to be sought after like this. "Well, okay, I guess I can work out a different weekend to work. It's not like they'll discover a cure for cancer any time in the next few weeks. There will be other shifts to cover."

When she got off the phone, Michelle fist-pumped the air and said, "Yes!" Sally had just done Chris's bidding for him, to get them at the same place at the same time, so they could be together, and everyone was none the wiser. It was brilliant.

Oh, but she longed for the day when she could openly and honestly tell her best friend the best of all the news she could possibly tell her: that she was finally open to falling in love again.

The First Date

One week before the reunion, Chris called Michelle.

"Hey, Chelley," he said, his heart pounding from hearing her voice.

"Chris! Hi!"

"How's your summer going so far?" he asked, biding his time.

"It's been getting pretty warm," Michelle told him, "but there's always a breeze, so it's not too bad. The air-conditioning at the clinic is so cold, I actually have to dress for winter at work!"

Chris laughed. "We don't have any air-conditioning over here, so Grant and I just walk around in boxer shorts. And it's just gonna get hotter as the summer goes on." He paused. "Listen, Chelley, I just RSVP'd for the McKinney fifth reunion, and I wanted to see if you were going."

Liar, Michelle thought. *You know very well that I'm going.*

"Oh, you're going?" Michelle played along innocently. "Yeah, I'll be there. I was going to call my parents and let them know I'm gonna be home for the night—"

"You know," Chris interrupted, "it might be a late night. I know your parents go to bed early. Maybe it would be better if you just stayed at my place, you know, so you don't disturb your family."

"Hmm." Michelle pretended to think about it. "Well, that does kind of make sense," she agreed. "Yeah, okay, I will. Because my parents go to bed early. Thanks for the offer." She loved these coy little exchanges.

"Great," Chris said. "You know, maybe it would be even better if you came up on Friday night instead of waiting for Saturday. That way, you won't be all tired from driving at the reunion."

Two nights together! Michelle knew if she came up Friday night, they would *both* be tired on the day of the reunion, but she played along. "Okay, yeah. I like that idea. I'll come on Friday night. It's just more practical."

"Yeah," Chris agreed. "It's all about being practical. And maybe on Friday night, we can have dinner together. I can cook something up, or maybe we can go out somewhere."

Is he asking me on an actual date? Michelle thought. Her brain felt addled.

"Okay, that sounds good. I'll be there Friday night, and we'll have a meal together. That should be nice. And practical." She grinned to no one but herself. "I'll just bring my things to work and leave from there."

"I'm really looking forward to it," Chris said. "You know, the reunion." Then he paused. "And seeing you, Chelley."

Michelle shuddered. Yes, Chris was acting differently. But a good differently. When Michelle got off the phone, she counted the days until Friday. Six days. Six long, hot, work-filled days.

When Chris got off the phone, he was confident Michelle knew that he was talking about a date. They had never been on a date with one another. The closest they had to a date was sharing pillow talk and breakfast the morning after sex. But Chris had to spend time with her, time away from bed, or swivel chairs, or whatever they had near them, to see what was going on. He needed to know if there was more. He needed to know if he felt anything else for Michelle aside from attraction and familiarity. And in order to do that, he needed to take her on a date. Just like normal people did.

But what should they do on their date? He could cook for her. He had a few items on his personal menu. That meant asking Grant to make himself scarce for the night, and the kitchen was quite close to the bedroom. No, it would be better if he took her out. But where? And what if they were seen by someone they knew? Well, that was easy enough. They were high school friends, catching up over dinner the night before a reunion. That was easily believable. But maybe still, they should go somewhere outside of Eastboro so they didn't have to worry.

The worry was reserved for what the date would reveal, and Chris suspected what that would be. He suspected that time alone with Chelley would be wonderful. He would enjoy her company, and they would share engaging conversation and be truly interested in each other's opinions while still feeling themselves drawn together by sexual attraction. Chris knew what this meant. He wasn't naive or stupid. He was falling for her. He probably already had fallen. In love. He couldn't stop thinking about her, and not just about joining their bodies together in the throes of passion—he had to stop that train of thought and take some breaths.

What if I do love her? The word *love* gave him the shivers. *What do I do then? Do I give in to the feeling, or do I resist? Can I do this again? If we love each other, can I totally give myself to her? I would never be able to stand it if I did and then we had to say goodbye.*

He did his best to push those thoughts away, too. He would have a nice dinner with Michelle, enjoy the time they had to talk, and then the time that they had become accustomed to. He looked forward to both scenarios.

On Friday, Michelle arrived at Chris's apartment at six thirty. They gave each other a kiss in greeting, but then both stood awkwardly not knowing what to do next. Chris was thinking it might be best for them to go to his bedroom first so they wouldn't be distracted throughout dinner, but that might also lead to a post-sex high that affected the way they acted when they were out together. He was nervous. With Michelle Gorman. It felt strange.

"So I was thinking about the Honolulu Restaurant in Westboro?" Chris suggested.

"Oh!" Michelle said, perking up instantly. "I love that place! My Grandpa Bob used to bring us there all the time when I was a kid. They had great spareribs and sweet and sour shrimp. I wonder if they're still as good as they were back then."

Chris smiled. He liked to see Michelle get excited about things. She would wrinkle her cute little nose. "Only one way to find out," he said.

Michelle changed out of her work scrubs and into a black sleeveless mini dress and pulled her hair up into a ballerina bun. She had transformed herself in minutes flat as Chris waited on the couch. When she came out of the bedroom, ready to go, he stood.

"You look really, really good." He had to get her away from the bedroom fast.

"Thanks," she said with a smile. She grabbed her purse from the table. "Let's go."

Chris grabbed his wallet and keys, and they were on their way.

They were seated in a circular booth that could probably fit eight people. They weren't too sure how far to slide in, so they stayed close to the end and sat next to each other. Chris thought a table for two would have been more conducive to easy conversing, but he kept that thought to himself.

They reviewed the menus. "I think it's the same exact menu as before," Michelle said. "All my old favorites are still here. Beef and Pea Pods, Shrimp and Lobster Sauce, pu pu platter. Maybe we can get a pu pu for two!" She giggled. She had such a cute giggle.

"All of those sound fantastic," Chris said honestly. "And maybe some chicken fried rice."

They ordered their food and made small talk until the appetizers arrived. Then they warmed their beef skewers over the tiny Sterno fire and started to eat.

"Oh my God I'm having flashbacks to my childhood," Michelle said. "I had forgotten how good the food was here."

Chris swallowed his bite of beef and smiled. "It is good," he said. "Aunt Missy and Uncle Cecil used to take me and Carl here when we were about six, probably, because Uncle Cecil died not long after that. I think they had some sort of arrangement with Carl's parents that they got to see him once a week or something, because if they didn't arrange it formally, they'd probably never see him. I remember his first cousins were always jealous of Carl, because he got tons of time with their grandparents, but I don't think the cousins realized at the time that it was because they were trying to compensate for him pretty much being ignored at home."

Michelle paused her fork on the way to her mouth. "It's unreal to me to think of that little boy at school, who was always with Kim at recess, going home and just being ignored. It's like a miracle that he made it through school and graduated and is doing so well now, don't you think?"

"Chelley, can I confide something to you?" Chris asked cautiously.

He wanted to share things with Michelle, to make them less ominous, to have her understand. Michelle nodded. He gathered his thoughts.

"Around high school graduation," he started, "Aunt Missy called me to ask me to help convince Carl to take the apprenticeship in California. It hadn't been offered to him yet, but it would be soon, and it turns out the whole thing was a scheme between Aunt Missy and Laine Farmer to get Carl away from Eastboro and into a place where he could be better supported. They want to give him a chance to learn new things and expand his knowledge. Then she told me something that blew my mind."

He stopped, drank some water, and leaned in closer to Michelle. He could smell her perfume. He refocused.

"When Carl was six, he was tested at DeMarco."

"Tested?" Michelle asked. "Like for what? Learning disabilities?"

Chris shook his head. "The opposite. His first-grade teacher noticed that Carl was actually way ahead of the other kids in his class. He was already adding rows of numbers, doing double-digit multiplication, and reading at a seventh-grade level. The teacher wasn't sure what to do with him, so she talked to the school counselor, who arranged to have a psychologist come in and do a battery of tests. They got Rosa and Jack to agree to it because they told them it would help them work with him better at school, and I guess they probably figured that meant they could do less for him at home or something. So they gave him these tests, and then they found out that Carl has an IQ that's in the high genius range."

Michelle gasped. "Are you kidding me?" she asked. "Carl? The same Carl that never knew the answers to the teachers' questions in class? When I think of Carl in grade school, I just remember him saying 'I don't know' all the time. And the whole time, he *did* know?"

Chris nodded. "It's pretty mind-blowing, I know," he continued. "Aunt Missy gave me more details a couple of years ago. She said the teacher and the school counselor set up a meeting with Carl's parents to talk about what to do next. Jack and Rosa didn't believe them about the genius stuff. They barely even wanted to discuss it. So the teacher told them that the school was recommending transferring Carl to the Johnson Learning Center's Gifted and Talented Program."

Michelle squinted toward Chris. "Johnson Learning Center? That's where my sister Stephanie went to school! She was in their program for kids with learning difficulties. Have you ever met Stephanie, Chris?"

Chris shook his head. "I've heard you talk about her, of course," he said. "But by the time I ever went to your house, she had already moved out. Yeah, so back then, they had special schools for people on either end of the learning spectrum, like Stephanie and Carl. They kept them separate from the average students and put them together in other locations with specially trained teachers. I learned in college that a lot of genius kids end up with behavioral issues if their ability isn't discovered and nurtured early enough, because they're just too under-stimulated. They either tune out, or they act out. Carl did kind of both, but back then, it was mostly tune out. They're starting to mainstream these kids back into the neighborhood schools now, because they've figured out they need to be around all sorts of other kids, and the teachers are being better trained, but back then, they basically had a 'not my problem' attitude in the public schools and sent the kids away."

Michelle shook her head. "But Carl never left DeMarco," she recalled. "Why didn't he go to JLC?"

"Because of Rosa and Jack, of course," he told her. "They were in denial. They couldn't possibly have a genius kid, especially Carl. They thought he was lazy and dumb. And they probably didn't want to have to deal with getting him there every day. It seemed like everything was a hassle to them. The counselor pretty much begged them to think about it. But they refused because they're basically trash people. So DeMarco did the best they could. The teachers tried to work with Carl over the years, but the classes were too big, and I'm guessing at some points, he learned past what they were able to teach him. And then, well, you know. There was the Bad Boy Posse and getting in trouble. Probably my fault. But I had no idea! I mean, Carl was my sidekick. He never showed any signs of any kind of gift. Well, until about tenth grade, when something seemed to click for him, and he started doing better in school and got on the honor roll."

Michelle nodded. "That was around the time when you started dating Rhonda, and Kim started paying more attention to Carl. They made that prom pact. So he had less of a bad boy influence going on, and maybe more hormones influencing him, and next thing you know, our Carl's on the honor roll."

"That's pretty much it," Chris agreed. "But, Chelley, here's the kicker. No one ever told Carl that he tested off the scales on his IQ. And the other tests he took, too, but all anyone ever cares about is the IQ. I think by now he's figured out that he has some unusual talents, but neither he nor Kim know why. I've never told anyone until tonight, because Aunt Missy asked me not to, and she was directed not to by Rosa and Jack."

"But why?" Michelle asked. "Why on Earth would they keep something like that from him? What purpose did it even serve?"

"I've asked myself that same question many times over the years," Chris admitted. "And all I can think of is selfish purposes. They didn't want him to know because they couldn't handle the fact that the son they thought was dumb as dirt all those years was actually worlds smarter than they were. And if they did admit it, they'd have to do something about it. So instead they did what they always did for Carl. Nothing."

Michelle looked horrified. "It's like our whole childhood was a lie," she said. "I mean, Carl is still Carl and everything, but he's got this other dimension to him that none of us realized. I have to admit, I'm glad his parents didn't send him to JLC, even if it was for the wrong reasons. Can you imagine what our lives would have been like without Carl at Randall and McKinney? He would have had a whole other group of friends, and his life would have turned out so differently. Ours, too. I know you would still have seen him since he's your cousin, but the rest of us, especially Kim ..." Michelle shuddered.

"I know," Chris agreed. "It's a scary thought. But like you said, Carl is Carl. No matter what. And if his life had been any different going along, things probably wouldn't have ended up the same."

"Chris," Michelle said seriously. "Carl deserves to know. When does the moratorium run out on this vow of secrecy? I mean, he's a grown man with a family now. Doesn't he have the right to know something like this about himself? It's like not telling him he was adopted, or that he was born with only one kidney or something. And maybe he'll need to know in case there's something similar with any of his own kids. I don't think it's his family's secret to keep anymore."

Chris nodded. "I agree. I think he should have been told before he went to California, but I respected Aunt Missy's wishes to keep quiet. Plus, I was still in a bad place back then after the breakup with Rhonda and with Carl leaving. We were only eighteen. But now we're older. I just want to have a chance to talk to Aunt Missy first. I think that's only fair since she's the one who confided in me in the first place, and we can work out the details on how we tell him and how we can support him once he knows."

Michelle gave him a sincere smile. "Chris, what a hard thing to have to keep to yourself. I'm really flattered that you chose to share the secret with me. I don't have any cousins that I'm as close to as you are to Carl, but you know I would take a bullet for my sister in a second. I totally understand what it feels like to want to protect someone the way you want to protect him. And it sounds like letting him go five years ago was the best way to do it at the time. Now maybe the best way is to tell him the truth."

Chris looked at her warmly. "Chelley, this is the reason I felt comfortable talking to you about this. And you really helped me to make up my mind. Thanks." He reached his hand across the table and put it over hers. He kept it there for several seconds, and then took it away.

The main courses came, and they dug in. The food was delicious. They talked about their work.

"I like my job and I really like my patients. I get to see the same patients pretty often. They get to ring a bell when they come in after their last chemo treatment in the treatment center. Everyone gets so excited."

"I enjoy teaching the eighth graders the best. They have such attitudes. I try to figure out on the first day of class who will be the first one to mouth off to me or say something rude or disrespectful in each of my classes. I usually deal with it without sending them to the principal. I take them out to the hall to have a talk instead. They hate the talk. It usually works. I keep waiting for Sean, I mean Mr. Jeffries, to call me into the office because I haven't met my detention quota."

They talked about their roommates.

"Sandra likes to make these big fancy dinners for herself that she plans to eat for days, but then she just leaves the leftovers in the fridge for like a week until they rot, and I end up having to throw away the smelly, moldy food. Then she comes home and gets mad at me because I threw away her dinner and doesn't believe it went bad. Otherwise, she's lovely."

"I've lived with Grant for over five years now, and he's pretty easy to get along with. Except he likes to eat his meals on the couch while he's watching TV, and he's really messy. Sometimes I find dried up bits of meatballs or tiny shriveled pieces of broccoli on or under the cushions. Don't get me started on the popcorn and grapes."

They talked about their families.

"Stephanie is going on a trip to Disney World with a few of the other residents in her program next month. It will be her first time on an airplane. They have one staff member going with them. And the twins are excited about applying to college next year. It's possible that they'll end up going to different schools. Steve wants to study film, and Sam is more interested in English and foreign languages. Maybe they can find a place that does both. Or maybe it would be good for them to be apart for a while to get to know themselves as individuals."

"Can you believe Melanie finished her first year at BU? She loved it. She even has a new boyfriend. And Scarlet's gonna apply for college next year, too. It's weird that she and your brothers never really became friends. I guess they just ran in different circles. Both of our parents are gonna have empty nests in a year. Weird."

They finished their food. The waiter took away their leftovers and brought them back in little white boxes with metal handles. The check came with two fortune cookies. Chris reached for the check immediately. Michele glared at him.

"Chris, I can pay half," she insisted.

Chris shook his head. "No," he responded. "I'm the one who asked you to dinner. My treat."

Michelle smiled. "So this is a date then?"

"I guess it is," Chris replied and quickly reached for his fortune cookie. He broke it open and read it aloud. "'Fortune favors one who prepares in advance.' In bed."

Michelle laughed and broke hers in two. "'Confucius says, he who laughs last, did not understand the joke.' Oh, that's not fair. In bed? I'm not sure that works. I'm not gonna eat my cookie in protest."

Now Chris laughed and handed her half of his cookie. She ate it.

They drove back to Chris's apartment mostly in silence, both of them feeling the jitters about what was coming next. This would be the first time they had sex together after an actual date. It almost felt like it was their first time. In a way, it was.

When they went into Chris's bedroom, they moved very slowly, casing each other like prey. Finally, Michelle reached down and pulled her dress up over her head. She had purposely not worn a bra with her dress. She knew what Chris liked. He stepped forward and ran his hands up and down her body as slow as he could, knowing that once he kissed her, all restraint would be lost. But her lips beckoned, and he stooped over to touch his lips to hers, and it was as if the genie had come out of the bottle for both of them. Their hands grasped at each other's bodies, and their lips touched flesh on each other's necks and chests and kissed and bit lightly. The rest of their clothes were discarded, and they were on the bed, rolling around, wrapping limbs around limbs, and making pleased noises. As if by silent agreement, they both suddenly stopped and made eye contact. The intensity increased as they stared, and then they both laughed and got back into action.

Unknowingly, they shared the same private thoughts as they made love: something major had changed, something between them had shifted. They weren't just making love in name; they were literally making love.

When it was over, they lay in bed side by side, caressing each other with their fingertips. They were both silent, each waiting to see if the other would speak. Michelle broke first.

"Remember that time," she started, "the very first time, at Kim and Carl's wedding? Remember we had that dance, and we both looked at each other, and both of us just knew, in that moment, that there was something going on with us?"

Chris nodded. "How could I ever forget that moment?" he said softly. "It was the very moment that I knew my friend was gonna become my lover, and it was intense. I knew we were both thinking the same thing. It was like a turning point." He kissed her forehead.

"Yes, exactly," Michelle agreed. "And I think we might be at one of those turning points again now. I feel it, and I'm pretty damn sure you feel it too."

Chris's heart started to pound. "I do feel it," he admitted. "I feel it a lot."

"I think I've felt it for a while now," Michelle admitted. "Since right before Sally and James's wedding. I didn't admit it to myself then, not until the night of the wedding, but in retrospect, it was there before. Chris, I've been doing exactly what I've told myself I would never do again. I'm holding myself back for someone who's not with me, who has not been able to be with me. But I couldn't stop myself if I wanted to. I don't want to be with anyone else. I only want to be with you. Not just for sex. I think it's been a while since it was just for sex. I want to be with Chris Mahoney, the man. I want to be Chris Mahoney's woman."

His heart was still pounding, but now it felt like it had skipped a beat. He maintained his Farmer sensitivities and sat quietly for several seconds.

"I want that, too, Chelley," he said. "I think about holding you sometimes, for hours, just to know you're there, and when you're not there, I miss you. I don't like missing you and not knowing when I'll see you again. Tonight . . . I needed to see what it was like for us together when we went out. Was it more than just friendship? And Chelley, it is. I know it is. I want you in my life. I want to call you at times when I just want to tell you something. I want to tell people that I have this amazing woman in my life. I want it all. But at the same time, I'm also totally terrified."

Michelle sat up. "Why?" she asked. "I just told you I want it, too. I don't want you to be scared, Chris. I want us to be happy. I want to make you happy."

Chris smiled. "I know. And I want to make you happy, too. I have to take this really slow, Chelley. I have to make sure we do this right, okay? Can we spend tonight and tomorrow together, and go to the reunion, and talk about it again after, and figure out what we need to do? I'm so sorry, I wish I could just say that it's easy, that we can just fall into this magical fairy tale, but just like you learned from your past relationships, I've learned from mine. And if I let you in, all the way in, and then we have to say goodbye, it would kill me, okay? Absolutely kill me."

Michelle stared at his face. "Chris . . ." She wanted to promise him that they would never have to say goodbye, that she would never do anything to hurt him, or make him sad, but she stopped herself. "Okay," she said. "Let's go to sleep now, and we'll see what happens tomorrow. But Chris, I don't think I can go home with this unresolved. We'll have to talk about it again and make some decisions. After tonight, things change for us. There's no turning back on this. Things will be different, one way or another."

They got ready for bed and turned out the light. They kissed good night, then they went silent. Michelle could not even think of sleeping. All she could think is that it might end. That after tomorrow, there might be no more Chris and Michelle, that she had just spent three years investing all of her emotional currency into a failing company. *No, please,* she begged the universe. *Not Chris. Please not Chris.*

She didn't want to start over. She didn't want to be with someone else. She would be alone forever if she had to. No, she didn't want to be alone ever again. She only wanted to be with Chris.

On the other side of the bed, Chris was wide awake, too. Michelle was one foot to his left, but it felt like she was thousands of miles away. He wanted to reach out to her, to touch her, to hold her, but he lay frozen in place. Chris wanted to give her everything she wanted. He wanted to tell her that he would quit his job, move to Amherst, and devote his entire life to making her happy. But it almost felt like there was a physical barrier between him and romantic happiness. He didn't know how to knock it away.

She's the closest thing I've ever seen to perfection, he thought. *Am I allowed to have someone who's perfect? What if she's not actually perfect? What if she leaves me someday? What if Joey suddenly turns up back at her door? What if she comes to her senses and realizes it's me she's with and she can do so much better?*

He didn't want to wake her by turning over, or getting up, so he just stayed still. Eventually he fell into a restless sleep, and in the morning, he didn't remember any of his dreams.

The Reunion

Michelle got up first and made breakfast and a full pot of coffee. They sat at the table and ate together quietly.

"Is there anything you want to do today?" Chris asked.

Michelle nodded. "I'd like to go see my sister while I'm here. Do you want to go with me and maybe we can take her out somewhere?"

"Sure," Chris agreed. "What does she like to do?"

Michelle shrugged. "Eat, see movies, go to the park, go to the mall . . ."

"It might be fun to get lunch and see a movie," Chris said. "I'll run down to the street and get the newspaper from the machine so we can see what's showing."

Michelle called Stephanie, and they arranged to pick her up at noon for lunch and an early show. They decided to see *Sister Act*, a movie they would all probably enjoy. They both took showers separately and got ready to go. The reunion started at seven, so they would have plenty of time after they dropped Stephanie back home before dinner.

Chris was impressed with Stephanie's apartment, and with how much she actually resembled Michelle. It was mostly their smiles and their hair. Stephanie was happy to meet him and very curious about who he was and what he liked to do. She asked him question after question about various subjects, and he patiently answered everything.

"Are you Chelle's boyfriend?" she asked over lunch.

Chris froze. He didn't know how to reply. He looked at Michelle.

"Sort of, Steph," she said. "We've been friends for years, and recently we've been much closer and been spending a lot of time together, but we don't really have a name for it yet."

"Oh," Stephanie said. She paused. "I don't know what you mean by that, Chelle. Why isn't he just your boyfriend?"

Michelle smiled at her sister. "Steph, you're being nosy. I don't have to tell you *everything,* do I?" She poked her sister in the ribs.

Stephanie giggled. "Yes," she said. "You have to tell me everything! I tell you everything!"

Now Michelle laughed. "That's only because you can't keep a secret," she said. "But you know who can?"

"Who?" Stephanie asked.

Michelle gave her a sly grin. "Me!" she exclaimed.

Chris laughed. He was enjoying watching the sisters interact. It was a part of Michelle he had never seen before. Every time he had seen any of her family, it had been in the context of their friend group gathering, and never just the two of them together. He wondered what it would be like to hang out with her parents and brothers at her house, to bring her to dinner at his parents' house, or with his Gram and Grandpa. They would all love her, and he would watch them laugh and tell funny stories about his childhood. They would show her his baby photo album. It was so idyllic in his mind. Maybe, just maybe . . .

He brought his attention back to his food and took a bite of his burger. He rejoined the conversation and enjoyed his time with the Gorman sisters.

They went to the movie, and they all enjoyed it. Stephanie liked Whoopi Goldberg, and after the movie, she said her name with glee. "Whoopi Whoopi Whoopi! I bet she has brothers that tease her about her name!"

Michelle turned back to look at Stephanie in the back seat. "Do you think that's the name her parents actually gave her when she was born," she asked, "or do you think she picked it herself?"

"You can pick your own name?" Stephanie asked. "Like we used to call you Chelley when you were a tiny baby, and then you made us stop and call you Michelle?"

"That's different," Michelle told her, glancing at Chris. "Michelle is my real name. I wanted everyone to call me the name Mom and Dad gave me. But yes, you get to have a choice of what you want people to call you. Steph, what name would you pick for yourself if you could?"

Stephanie thought about it. "I think I'd want to be called Whoopi!" she declared. "What about Chris?"

Chris smiled. "I think I would like to be called Sting," he said, and Michelle laughed.

They dropped Stephanie off at home and returned to Chris's apartment. They plopped down on the couch and slumped down. They were both tired from the lack of restful sleep the night before. Chris turned to look at Michelle.

"I loved watching you with your sister," he told her. "You two are obviously best friends. My sisters are pretty close, too. I guess there's just something about sisters."

"Stephanie was my first friend," Michelle said. "I remember being distraught when we didn't go to school together. It was hard for me to make new friends in kindergarten without her. But then I found Darlene and bribed her with a cookie to be my friend, and the rest is history."

Chris smiled. "I think I've heard you girls joking about cookie bribes before." He paused. "So tell me about Chelley. It was your nickname when you were a baby?"

Michelle thought for a moment about what she wanted to reveal to Chris. Then she figured it didn't really matter. After today, they would either be together, or not. It made no difference either way.

"Yeah, they called me Chelley until I was three or four," she said. "Then, I started to assert my opinions quite vocally, and made sure everyone knew that my name was Michelle, not Chelley. Then I wouldn't talk to anyone who called me Chelley. It was very effective. Pretty soon, no one called me Chelley, but I still let Stephanie call me Chelle. It's really just short for Michelle. But there was a time, later on, when I kind of regretted my decision. One thing I regretted was making my grandparents stop, and another was that I realized that a nickname can be a very special thing. It was a term of endearment. Like when Sally calls James Jamie. So I decided that, someday, someone would call me Chelley again. And when they did, it would be because they were special, and because I wanted them to be endeared to me. After I broke up with Joey, I told Sally about it, because I was worried I'd never meet anyone I'd want to call me Chelley. She told me that I would know when I met the right person, because when he called me Chelley, it would make me love him, and if I already loved him, it would make me love him more."

Chris considered this. "So at the wedding, when I called you Chelley the first time," he said quietly, "you didn't stop me. As a matter of fact, we made love, and it was some of the best sex I ever had. And you never asked me to stop calling you Chelley after that."

Michelle nodded. "Yes," she said softly. "I was totally shocked when you said it. I couldn't believe that you did it without me even asking you to. When you called me Chelley that night, I thought it might make me love you, but as it turned out, I already did."

Tears developed in the corners of her eyes.

"Chelley," Chris said. "So that's your magic secret, huh? How you rocked my world and almost put me in a coma. All I had to do was call you Chelley."

Michelle shook her head. "No, it wasn't just being called Chelley," she explained. "It's that you, Chris Mahoney, were the one that called me Chelley. It's just you, Chris."

Chris felt his heart melt. He took her gently in his arms and kissed her. Then he kept his arms around her.

"Chelley," he said and stood. He took her by the hand and helped her stand. Then he led her to the bedroom. They stood in the doorway, kissing deeply and intensely for a long time before they moved to the bed. They slowly undressed, caressing each other's bodies. Then they fell to the mattress and met each other's most desperate needs.

They didn't have long until they had to get ready to leave for the reunion. Their friends were expecting them there. But they stayed in bed for just a little while, in each other's arms, both knowing that making love didn't just solve everything. They still needed to talk. They needed to make a decision before the night was over.

They arrived at the reunion shortly after seven. They checked in at the registration table and got their ID tags with their yearbook portraits printed on them. They both hadn't changed enough from graduation for people not to recognize them. They could see Sally, James, and Darlene mingling with some of their old classmates across the room, and Michelle and Chris quickly assumed their friends-only roles.

Sally rushed over and hugged them both. "You guys carpooled?" she asked. "That was smart. Rob Novak, our junior class president, is here. He was blown away that it took us five years to get married!" She laughed. "No one here seems too surprised that we did it! Chris, I did see that there was a name tag out there for Rhonda, but she's not here yet. Maybe she won't show up. I didn't know if you saw."

"Yeah," Chris said, "I did notice. But it's okay. I mean, it's been five years now, and I'm here with my good friends. She can't do anything to me now."

Michelle gave him a small smile. Rhonda. The girl who broke Chris. Who made it so hard for him to trust in love. Michelle still wanted to punch her in the face for what she did to Chris in high school, but she would wait, because it was possible that by the end of the night, it would be Chris that she wanted to hit.

They greeted James and Darlene, and they updated each other on how work was going and what they had been doing for fun. Darleen was working at a group home with adults with mental illnesses. She was up for a supervisor position at a different residence, which might mean she would need to move a few towns over. But she was enjoying her work and glad she was able to work around people. James was head chef at the Providence Marriott and was hoping that at some point the manager position would open. He wanted management experience so someday he could open his own restaurant. Sally would be starting to work on her master's in fine arts in writing in the Fall, and she had finally started to write her novel.

"It's coming along nicely so far," she said. "It's fiction, but I've borrowed a lot of stuff from my own life to create the story. I mean, it all comes right from my brain, so it's bound to reflect a lot of my thoughts and experiences. My biggest worry is that someday my mother will read it and think it's autobiographical, and it will freak her out. And there are lots of sex scenes!" She laughed. "Someday, James and I will have kids, and they're not going to be allowed to read my work until they're at least eighteen!"

Everyone laughed. Michelle couldn't wait to read Sally's book. "Let me know if you need someone to be a test reader for you," she offered. "I would love to be one of the first readers. I hope you based a character on me!"

Sally smiled. "You'll have to wait to see," she teased.

They found other alumni who they had known from DeMarco or Randall and caught up. Everyone seemed to be settling into new jobs or planning to go on in school. A few had gotten married and even fewer had kids. It appeared that Kim and Carl were miles ahead of the rest of the pack, not unusual for Carl. The biggest surprise was that one of the minor bad boys the posse had been friendly with at Randall had hooked up just one time with one of the brainy girls that Sally had been friendly with at Lincoln Elementary, at a graduation party, and ended up with a baby. No one could believe it, but there they were, both with other partners, showing off pictures of the four-year-old child they shared. Sometimes life happened when you least expected it.

The announcement was made that dinner would be served, and then Rhonda walked into the gym. She was holding hands with a tall, dark-haired man, and she appeared to be about five months pregnant. Chris watched her walk in and followed her progress with his eyes. She went right to the table where her friends were sitting, and everyone got up to hug each other. Chris glanced at Michelle and saw that she was watching Rhonda, too, but he couldn't read her expression. Rhonda's eyes scanned the room and made contact with Chris. She smiled. He smiled back. Then they both looked away, and that was that. Chris would not approach her. He would not ask to be introduced to Rhonda's husband. He would not inquire about her baby, or her due date. There would be no pleasantries. The time for pleasantries had long since passed.

They ate dinner and continued catching up. Michelle found herself tuning out of the conversation a few times, thinking about what was coming next and what it would be like if everyone at their table knew what was going on with her and Chris behind the scenes. Sally poked her in the arm.

"Michelle, you seem kind of distracted tonight," she said with a concerned expression. "Is everything okay?"

Michelle forced a reassuring smile. "Oh, yeah," she said. "I just have a lot going on this week, and I'm kind of thinking ahead."

Sally leaned in closer. "Are you still seeing the serial one-night stand guy?"

Michelle thought about how to answer that. "It's kind of precarious," she said. "We've still been getting together, but we're starting to talk about whether we want to take it any further. It's kind of complicated. But I can assure you, whatever ends up happening, you'll be the first to know."

Sally nodded. "I hope it works out for you," she said. "He's taken up a lot of time in your life. And also, I would love to be able to meet this mystery man."

Michelle smiled. "Yeah, that would be great. I think it's safe to say that you would probably really like him."

After class announcements and dessert and coffee, the reunion ended. There were promises of everyone seeing each other at the ten-year reunion, but Michelle doubted she would go. They said goodbye to their friends, and she and Chris headed for the car.

They were quiet in the car, but they held hands like a lifeline as Chris drove.

Chris parked, and they walked the two flights up to his apartment. Then they were back slouched on the couch.

They looked at each other. "The thing is," Michelle said, "I love you, Chris."

Chris was slightly taken aback. He was not expecting her to come right out and say it. He was expecting to have to ask the question.

"Michelle," he started, deliberately not using the nickname that he knew influenced her. "I . . . I have really, really strong feelings for you, too, but I'm just not ready to be in love. I probably already am on some level, but I somehow can't let myself feel it on the surface. It would be like stepping in front of a speeding train and hoping they can hit the brakes fast enough to not hit me. You just don't do that."

Michelle nodded. "So it's possible you love me right now," she said, "but you can't let it out or tell me. You can't tell me when or if it's going to happen for you."

"Chelley," Chris said, "I want to love you. I want to open myself up to you, to just let myself go, but I'm too afraid. Haven't you ever felt like this, like if something hurt you before, you're just too scared that it will happen again, and you just don't think you'll come out intact this time?"

"Of course I have," Michelle replied. "You know that. You know what happened with Joey. I waited for him. I waited a long time. And I ended up getting hurt. It's just like you're saying. I don't want to wait again. I don't want to put my life on hold while someone else decides if they want to be with me, no matter how much I love them. It's like living half a life, Chris, and not the half that feels meaningful."

"Michelle, maybe if I could have just a little time—"

"Why, Chris? What's gonna change if you have time? How will you know when you've had enough time? It's already been three years. What if it's never enough? Then we have to have another talk like this?"

Chris was quiet for a moment. "I don't know," he admitted. "But it kind of sounds like we're on opposite ends here, and I don't want that. Why did we have to go and get feelings for each other? Things were going so well all this time—"

"Were they, though?" Michelle asked. "I mean, don't you think this was a progression over time? I don't think we just caught feelings like you catch a cold. They built up. It was bound to happen. Chris, at Carl and Kim's wedding, we set something in motion that was bigger than both of us. It couldn't go on forever like it was. I think we both knew, it had to either go forward at some point, or it had to end. And I guess this is that point."

Chris grimaced. "Chelley, I don't know if I'm ready to go forward," he admitted, "but I also don't want it to end. What do we do?"

Tears had started down Michelle's face. "I think we both know what we have to do. We have to stop this. If you can't go forward, you need to let me go. And I can't give you the time you need, so I need to let you go. This is not what I want, believe me, but I think it's the only fair thing to do, for both of us."

Chris had a lump in his throat the size of his fist. Yes, he needed time to figure things out. But he understood everything she was saying to him and agreed. But letting her go would mean saying goodbye, and in his mind, that was a million times worse than any other option.

"Okay," he said, choking back tears. "You're right. We need to stop this. We can't go on like this, and I'm not ready to go forward. So . . . we say goodbye."

A sob escaped from Michelle's gut. "This is what I was afraid of from the first day," she told him. "That something like this would happen, and we wouldn't be able to part as friends. I mean, how could we? I won't be able to. How can I talk to you as a friend knowing I love you as so much more? Chris, if we say goodbye today, it's really gonna have to be goodbye."

Chris's tears were flowing freely now, and he didn't care. "Chelley."

"No, Chris," she said, putting up her palm. "Not anymore, okay?" She stood and walked alone into the bedroom. She came out carrying her bag. "I have to go now."

"Michelle," he said, the name now feeling uncomfortable on his lips. "It's late. Just stay the night. I can sleep on the couch."

"No," she said. "I need to be at home now."

"Can you at least call me to let me know you made it safely?" Chris asked.

Michelle shook her head. "No," she said. "I'm not going to do that. There are going to be plenty of times I come home late, and you won't know if I made it safely. This is just going to be the first one. Goodbye, Chris." She gave him a kiss on the cheek, went to the door, and let herself out.

Chris remained on the couch, staring at the back of the door. He had no idea how long he sat there. Eventually, he got up, brushed his teeth, peeled off his clothes, and crawled into his bed. He had just endured another goodbye. And this one was the worst by far. This time, he'd had to say goodbye to Michelle Gorman. Chelley.

Michelle drove back to Amherst in the pelting rain. It felt appropriate as she cried giant tears for the entire hour-long drive home. When she got there, she wanted to call Sally. She didn't care if she woke her. But she decided not to call. How could she tell her best friend that she had just broken up with Chris Mahoney? Sally and Chris were friends, and she needed them to stay friends. Chris would need his friends now, and she didn't want Sally to shut Chris out. So instead, she knocked softly on Sandra's door and let herself in. Sandra sat up in bed and asked what was wrong. And Michelle proceeded to sob out the entire story.

Telling Ourselves We're Okay

The next day was Sunday, and Chris let himself stay in bed until he had no choice but to get up and use the bathroom. Then he went out to lay down on the couch. He didn't have the energy to make coffee. His body hurt. He wondered if he had somehow caught the flu. Grant came out of his room, already showered and dressed.

"Hey, man, are you okay?" he asked. "You look like shit. Where's Michelle?"

"She left last night," Chris told him.

"Oh, no," Grant said. "Did you guys have a fight?"

Chris looked at him blankly. "I guess you could call it that," he said. "We decided not to see each other anymore."

Grant sat down on the end of the couch. "Oh, man, that sucks," he said sympathetically. "I thought things were moving along for the two of you. What's it been, three years?"

"Sort of," Chris said. "But we really just had our first real date this weekend. It's so weird. Yeah, I think I might be getting sick. I might have a fever."

Grant patted his feet. "Yeah, you got something alright, C.J.," he said, standing up. "And it's gonna feel like shit for quite a while, but I don't think you need to go see a doctor. I'll make you some coffee."

"Thanks," Chris moaned and let his head fall on the throw pillow. Coffee might help him to at least feel human and give him the strength he needed to lift his head for prolonged periods of time. Once he got to that point, he needed to make a plan to get through the day.

Chelley, he thought. *Oh God, how am I gonna get through this? I can't do this. I'm not strong enough.*

Grant brought him a mug of hot coffee with milk. He swallowed it down, but it felt like bricks in his throat. "I'm going to Valerie's in a few minutes," Grant said. "Is there anything you need before I go? Do you need to talk or anything?"

"No, that's okay, thanks," Chris said. "Once I get motivated, I'll give Carl a call. But I don't know what to say yet. I never told him I was even seeing Michelle. I'm not sure if I'm ready for any of my high school friends to know. I just don't want anyone to feel they have to choose sides, you know? I don't know, maybe Michelle needs them more than I do. But I need Carl."

"Yeah, you do," Grant said. "He helped you after Alison. He's a good guy. Give him a call. You'll know what to say. Well, I'm gonna head out then, but I'll check on you later. If I decide to stay at Val's, I'll give you a call, okay?"

Chris forced a smile. "Thanks, man. I appreciate it. Say hi to Val for me."

After Grant left, Chris stayed on the couch. He turned on the TV and flipped channels, but he couldn't find anything he wanted to watch. He turned off the TV and stared at the ceiling. Time was standing still. He felt nauseated. He thought about calling his mom and asking her to come over because he was sick and needed her to make him soup and toast. He was feeling desperate. He reached for the phone and dialed Carl's number.

"You sound awful, bro," Carl said after they greeted each other. "Are you sick?"

"Sort of," Chris said. "I just, God it's hard to even say, but this girl and I . . . we just ended it last night and I'm not sure what to do."

"Chris, you never even told me you were seeing anyone. Who was it?"

Chris made an instant decision. "That doesn't really matter," he said, "because it's done now. I'm not gonna see her again. I can't believe it, I'm not gonna see her again." He sucked in his breath.

Carl paused. "Man, it sounds like it was pretty serious."

"It was getting that way," Chris admitted. "It didn't start that way, but that's the way it ended. We started to get serious, and you know me. I couldn't handle it. I needed more time to figure it out, but she couldn't wait. I don't blame her. Man, what we had was powerful. Like mind-blowing sex, and she's so beautiful, and smart. What the hell is wrong with me, Carl? How could I let the perfect woman go?"

"Chris, I am so, so sorry," Carl said, and Chris could tell he was. "I was really hoping the next woman in your life would be the one. And it sounds like she could have been. There's nothing wrong with you, man, but God, that's got to hurt."

From his tone, Chris thought that Carl was feeling this almost as much as he did. He was so grateful to have Carl, someone always there to help him through his pain.

"I can't do this anymore," Chris said. "I'm done. From now on, it's just casual for me. Relationships just set me back. I just let myself get too close. I have two choices right now. Either I get in my car today and drive to her place and tell her I was wrong and I want to make this happen, or I just have casual sex with strangers for the rest of my life."

"Maybe there's a third choice," Carl suggested. "Maybe you can just do nothing for now and give it some time, so you can see how you feel later. Do you really have to decide the rest of your life today?"

Chris thought about it. "No. I think that's what we did last night."

Carl sighed. "Chris, can you come out here and stay with us for a while? You know we have a room for you here. Kim would love it if you came, and you could spend some quality time with your godson. You've only ever seen him at weddings. And you're off work for the summer. I can take a few days off. We can go to a Giants game in San Francisco or something."

Chris considered this. "Yeah," he said. "I'm gonna do that. I can't see any reason not to. I'd love to spend time with you guys. Let me make some calls and see if I can get tickets. Can I just come whenever?"

"Yeah," Carl assured him. "Whenever works for us. Even if you can fly out tonight. You're always welcome here."

In Amherst, Michelle was trying to plan her day. She hadn't slept well after getting home late and keeping Sandra up until the wee hours of the morning with her sorrow. She knew she needed to distract herself in some way. She wanted to call Sally, but then Sally would tell James, and James would want to call Chris, and she didn't want to start the whole ball rolling yet. Instead, she put romantic movies in the VCR and cried as she watched lovers in love on the screen. Then she watched comedies and laughed through her tears. She was about to call the treatment center to see if they needed any coverage that night when the phone rang, and Sally was on the line.

"Hey, just calling to make sure you made it home safely last night."

"Yes, I got home safe and sound," Michelle assured her.

"Good," Sally said. "I'm a bit worried about Chris, though."

Michelle's stomach tightened, and she felt she might vomit. She swallowed. "What do you mean?"

"Well, he called Jamie a little while ago and told him that he's heading out to California tomorrow morning to go see Carl for a while. Just out of the blue. Jamie said he sounded awful, like something was really wrong, but he said he was fine. I don't know. I mean, he said he was fine seeing Rhonda at the reunion last night, but maybe he wasn't as fine as he let on. How was he when he drove you back to your car last night?"

"Uh," Michelle started. "Uh, he seemed okay, I guess. But I wasn't really paying too close attention."

"You were still thinking about your one-night stand guy, weren't you?" Sally asked.

"Yes, I was," Michelle said honestly. "I was pretty preoccupied thinking about him last night. I hope Chris is okay, though." She nearly prayed that Chris was okay.

"Oh, I think he will be," Sally said. "I mean, if he's going to Carl's, even if something's wrong, he'll be okay. They'll take good care of him."

"Yeah," Michelle agreed. "I'm glad he's going to Carl's. It's a smart thing for him to do." Michelle wondered how long it would be before Carl and Kim found out about their relationship.

When she got off the phone, Michelle let herself cry for a good long time. Then she called the weekend supervisor at the treatment center and made arrangements to work shifts for the next four weekends.

Chris stayed with the Bishops in Seska, California, for ten days. He would have stayed longer, but he didn't want to wear out his welcome. He went with Carl, Drake, Laine, and Benjamin to a Giants game in San Francisco, and afterward they spent some time roaming around the wharf. He was there for the Fourth of July. Laine had a barbecue in his backyard, and then they all went to watch the fireworks from the high school parking lot. Chris couldn't help but remember the Fourth of July celebrations at the Eastboro airport, and he pictured a younger Michelle dancing around to the rock music in the tight crowd in her shorts and tank top. He tried to clear these images from his mind. He played action figure games inside and ball games outside with Drake and roughhoused with little Elena. She was a ball of excess energy, and Kim was grateful any time he could tire her out before bedtime.

When it was time to go home, Chris said goodbye to Kim, Laine, Beth, and the kids at Carl's house, and then Carl drove him to the San Francisco Airport.

As they neared the exit to the airport, Carl checked in with Chris. "Dude, are you gonna be okay when you get back?"

Chris nodded. "Yeah, I think so," he said. "It really helped to be away for a while. I'm really grateful that you offered for me to come here. And it's not too long before school starts up again. And you know there's no room for moping when you're teaching. Especially those rowdy Randall delinquents."

Carl laughed. "Well, they're all still probably trying to beat out the legend of that bad boy posse you used to run there ten years ago. You know, Chris, we didn't really talk too much about this girl you were seeing. You know you can tell me anything, right?"

"I do know that," Chris confirmed. "I will talk about her at some point. I'm just not ready yet. I just need some time and distance from the relationship. Then I'll tell you everything. I promise."

Carl nodded and pulled the car up to the departure area. They both got out of the car, and Carl lifted Chris's luggage out of the trunk and placed it on the sidewalk. The two cousins shared an embrace.

"I'm really gonna miss you, my brother," Carl said. "It's like we're always saying goodbye to each other."

Chris tried not to wince at the word. "I know," he said. "Goodbyes are the worst. I love you, man. I'll call you when I get in."

"I love you, too, Chris. Safe travels. Give the Grams hugs for me."

With a final wave, Chris entered the airport to check in for his flight.

Michelle was working her ass off. She worked her regular hours at the clinic, and then she worked one or two ten-hour shifts per weekend. She loved the treatment center. She loved being able to sit in front of the patients, to have her hands on them as she worked, and to be able to talk to them, to catch up. She could be herself with the patients. She laughed with them, and sometimes held their hands while they cried. She didn't think about herself and her problems while she was working. It was a relief. But it wasn't a pace she could keep up forever. She could maybe last the rest of the summer. Then she would need to take a break. But to stop meant to think, so even after she scheduled time off at the end of August, she put it out of her mind and concentrated on the tasks at hand.

She talked to her UMass friends and her other Amherst friends, and sometimes she would join them for lunch or dinner. She attended a wedding in North Hampton and a baby shower in South Deerfield. She smiled and laughed with the bride and mom-to-be and pretended that everything was okay. July moved into August, and the days grew hotter. She went to Sally and James's house for Sally's birthday party. James made a fancy, delicious cake. Darlene and Pete were there, along with a few of Sally and James's other friends from school and work. Michelle still hadn't told Sally about Chris, and it appeared no one else had either. Chris was not at the party.

"He said he had a conflict," Sally told Michelle when she asked. "He's gonna come out to see us next weekend. I wonder if maybe he had a date? That would be good. Chris has been alone for a long time. He deserves some happiness in his life."

When she saw the look on Michelle's face, Sally pulled back. "Oh, Michelle, I'm so sorry," she said. "I know it's been a long time for you, too. You deserve happiness. I hope one-night stand guy is giving you some. I mean, some happiness!" Sally laughed at her blunder.

Michelle smiled at Sally. "Very funny," she said. "I haven't seen him for a while. That's how it is for us. But it's all okay, Sally. I'm doing okay. I'll meet someone who's right for me, someday."

Sally gave her a sympathetic look. "I'm sorry," she said. "It sounded like maybe things might have been getting more serious with one-night stand guy around our reunion. You know, if you told me his name, I could call him that instead of one-night stand guy."

Michelle shook her head. "It doesn't really matter," she told Sally. "If nothing comes of it, you don't need to know his name anyway."

James joined them and handed Sally a cup of lemonade. "Talking about boys again?"

Sally smiled. "Always," she said, grabbing onto James's arm affectionately.

"You know, Michelle," James said, "I actually know a guy in Amherst that I went to school with. Really nice guy. His name is Steve."

Sally perked up. "Oh, Steve!" she said. "He makes the best baklava! He's a super nice guy. I didn't know he was still in Amherst."

James nodded. "Yeah, he went back after he got his MBA. He's head chef now over at a place called Rotini's."

"Oh, yeah," Michelle said. "I've never been there before, but it's near my work. Italian pasta place. Obviously."

"Maybe the two of you could meet up some time," James suggested. "I wasn't thinking of a fix up, but I do think he's single, and so are you, so maybe you could just meet. The worst that could happen is you make a new friend, or get an in at a good Italian restaurant."

Michelle shrugged. "Yeah, I guess so," she said. "I mean, I don't really want a fix up, but I am always willing to make a new friend."

After the party, Michelle drove home and got into bed. She reviewed the evening. She'd had fun with her friends, but things were off. It was the first event where one of them had declined to come. Chris had stepped back to let her celebrate her best friend's birthday. This would be the first time of many. Eventually their friends would notice the trend. She realized now that she had subconsciously wished that Chris had been there, and her disappointment that he wasn't was palpable. They really just couldn't be friends anymore. It was official. And now her friends were scheming to fix her up with other men.

She had no doubt in her mind that Sally and James had contrived this whole idea of meeting his friend Steve in Amherst, who just happened to be single. And she had agreed to it. She had no reason not to. So now she would get a call. About a date. With a man that wasn't Chris. And she would go. But for now, she just sobbed tears of despair until she eventually fell asleep.

Chris spent the last six weeks of summer doing hard labor on the university hospital lawn crew. It only took one call to his cousin to set it up. He had worked there in the summers since he was seventeen and had been planning to take this one off, but now the work was a welcome distraction.

He had been invited to Sally's birthday party, and almost accepted out of habit, until he remembered that she would be there. Chelley. He couldn't see her. He couldn't pretend to just be her friend in the company of all their other friends. So instead, he gave Sally an excuse and spent the day at his parents' house. His sisters were home for the summer and bored, so they all hung out and watched TV together. When they got hungry, he decided to take them out for dinner, a siblings-only night out.

"Why are you being so nice to us?" Scarlet asked in the car. "Are you dying or something? Wait, is it *me* who's dying?"

"Don't be an idiot," Melanie told her younger sister. "It's Saturday night, and Chris is hanging out at home with his family. It's obvious that it's him who's dying."

The girls giggled. "Okay, enough, you two," Chris said, rolling his eyes. "No one's dying. I just wanted to spend some time with my parents and sisters for once. Is that a crime?"

The girls looked at each other. "It's got something to do with a girl," Melanie said. "Either you've got a girl and she's not around, or you like a girl, and she doesn't like you."

"Or maybe," Scarlet ventured, "a girl dumped you."

Chris shot them a stern look.

"That's it, isn't it?" Melanie said. "Someone broke up with you. You're pining away. That's why you went to California. Who is she? Do you want us to go kick her ass for you? We will, you know."

Chris laughed. "No, I don't want you to kick anyone's ass," he said, "but I appreciate the offer. No, I didn't get dumped, but yes, I just got out of a relationship with a girl. A woman."

"You weren't having an affair with Mrs. Fox from Randall, were you?" Scarlet asked.

Now Chris laughed harder. "Angela Fox? Scarlet, she's like, sixty and married. But we are friends. So no, it wasn't her. It's no one. It's over. You don't need to worry about it. I'm gonna be okay. I just need some time to recover."

"Recover?" Melanie asked. "So she really did break your heart. I'm so sorry, Chris, I didn't mean to make fun of you like that. Broken hearts are the worst. I know. Remember when Juan broke up with me senior year? It took me forever to get over that. But then I met Marcus at BU, and he's so much better. Maybe that will happen for you, too."

Chris smiled at his sister. He didn't tell her that Alison was better than Rhonda, and Michelle was better than any woman he'd ever met. Or probably ever would meet.

"Thanks for the encouragement, Mel," he said. He pulled the car into Luigi's. "Let's go have some good food and only talk about happy things, okay?"

Two weeks into August, Michelle got the call she was expecting.

"Hi, Michelle, my name is Steve Karras. I'm a friend of your friend James Newell?"

"Oh, yeah," Michelle responded. "I told James it was okay to have you call. How are you?"

"I'm doing well," Steve said. "I hear you've been in Amherst for some time. I'm surprised James and Sally didn't try to introduce us a long time ago."

"Were you at their wedding?" Michelle asked. "I was the little redhead in the green dress up front with Sally."

"No, I had a family wedding the same weekend," Steve told her. "I hated to miss the fairy tale wedding of the century though."

Michelle laughed. "Yeah, take it from someone who's been there through the whole relationship. You can't write romances like theirs."

"Maybe we can get together some time and chat," Steve said. "I can tell you all about my adventures with James and Sally in culinary school, and you can fill me in on the high school years."

"That would be fun," Michelle replied. It might be fun, but it ached to even say that. "I'm really busy the next couple of weeks at work doing overtime, but things clear up for me toward the end of the summer."

"Yeah, now is our busy time at the restaurant, too," Steve said. "Maybe we can get together for lunch on a Saturday afternoon near Labor Day. I can call you back as it gets closer, and we can set up a day and time."

"Okay, that sounds good," Michelle agreed, trying to commit herself to moving forward, but still hoping that Steve, who sounded great, might somehow meet his soulmate in the next two weeks and call to cancel. Or maybe the entire world would just come to an end. A girl could hope. She had no way of knowing how close to the truth she actually was.

Someone's World Just Comes to an End

Chris almost didn't answer the phone when it woke him up at seven thirty on Saturday morning, but he realized it could be something urgent. He hated when he was right about these things. It was Gram Cissy.

"Christopher, I'm calling with some very upsetting news," she said soberly. "Missy got woken up by the Sheriff's department at her door late last night. Somehow, she was listed as the emergency contact for Rosa Bishop. Chris, they found Carl's mother dead last night, apparently of a heroin overdose."

Chris shook his head to try to rouse himself. "What?" he said. "Heroin overdose?" He sat up straight. "Oh, my God, Carl!"

"Missy called Carl as soon as the sheriff left," Gram informed him. "She told him everything she knows, but it's not much. Rosa was living in a group home for felons in recovery. I don't know what her felony was, or how she ended up there. Or how she got the drugs for that matter. Hopefully, someone will talk to Carl and give him more details. And we need to find Scott."

"I need to call Carl," Chris said, pivoting off of the side of the bed and standing up. "I need to talk to him."

"Chris, it's four thirty in the morning there," Gram reminded him. "Why don't you wait a few hours."

"If I know Carl at all, he's not sleeping right now," Chris said. "But I don't know about Kim and the kids. I'll wait. But I'll come by your house later, okay?"

"Of course, Chris. Missy's here already. I've also spoken to your folks. They'll be by later this morning with the girls, as well as some of Missy's other children and grandchildren. Please, though, talk to Carl. I'm sure he needs you very badly right now."

"Of course, Gram," Chris assured her. "I'll do whatever I can. Has anyone been in touch with Jack? Are they even still married?"

Gram sighed. "As far as I know, neither one of them has ever filed for divorce, but Missy hasn't heard from him in months. She doesn't even know where to start looking. I don't think he's living in Eastboro anymore, and he's definitely no longer employed at Aries. Maybe Scotty will know when we find him. I'll keep you up to date."

"I can call James later and see if he can ask his dad if he knows where Scott is. I don't know if he still works for J.D., but if he's still at Aries, we should be able to track him down by Monday."

"Thank you, Chris," Gram said. "I hate to think he might find out about his mother from someone outside the family. That just wouldn't be right."

Chris paused. "Is . . . is someone gonna do something? Like a funeral or something?"

"I just don't know yet, Chris," Gram said. "She was Catholic. I'm not sure what will be expected. I don't know if she had any family left in Puerto Rico who would want to be consulted. We'll talk to Scott and Carl about what they want. We'll do whatever they want."

Chris nodded. "Yeah, that makes sense. Okay, Gram, I'll see you later. Thanks for letting me know. I love you."

"I love you, too, Chris. Take care of your cousin."

"I will."

Chris hung up the phone and stood up, but his next thought blew him back off his feet and he had to sit down. *I need to call Michelle. I need Chelley.*

He paced himself. He made a pot of coffee and drank his first cup. It was a day that would need to be measured in pots, not cups, he could tell.

"Have a cup of coffee." "Let me fix you some more coffee." "What do you like in your coffee?" "Do you still take cream and two sugars in your coffee?" It was the busy talk of loss. It was what you said and did when someone died. You made coffee. You brought casseroles. But at the moment, he could do nothing for Carl. He didn't even know what Carl would need him to do. Probably he would listen. Or maybe, if Carl had nothing to say, he would get him to talk. Chris got in the shower. He stood under the hot water for a long time, doing nothing.

Rosa Bishop was dead. She would have been somewhere around forty-six or forty-seven. A drug overdose. Heroin. He couldn't wrap his head around that. Rosa, his cousin Jack's wife, the mother of his lifetime best friend. There had never been a time in his life when Chris didn't know Rosa. Rosa, who had changed his diapers. Rosa, who took him and Carl to the Children's Science Museum in elementary school, before things got so bad. Rosa, the maker of thousands of peanut butter and jelly sandwiches for Carl's school lunch. Rosa, the mother who had abandoned her sixteen-year-old son when he needed her the most. The sixteen-year-old son who was now almost twenty-three and married with two children of his own, who was thriving in California. Carl, who had made a life for himself, despite the odds. The lost boy who had been found. The man who no longer needed his mother. But now she was back, forcing one final farewell.

Chris realized he had been standing idly in the shower for several minutes. He turned his attention back to his hygiene. He washed his hair and his body. He toweled off, put on his briefs, and went back to the sink to shave. When he was done, he looked at his bedside clock. Eight forty-five.

He got dressed, then plodded into the kitchen to find some breakfast. He took the carton of milk from the fridge and sniffed the contents. It hadn't turned yet. Grant must have gone shopping recently. He grabbed his box of Frosted Mini Wheats and poured himself a bowl full. He refilled his mug with black coffee, sat down, and poured the milk, first into the bowl, then into the mug. Then he ate slowly.

I have to hear Chelley's voice, he thought.

He cleared his dishes and stowed the milk. He walked to the living room and sat down on the couch to put on his shoes.

Then he thought about Jack Bishop. His cousin, and Carl's father. He married Rosa when they were in their twenties. Maybe they had been already expecting Scott, he didn't know. But he never saw them together happily, and Jack always had a beer in his hand. Jack always said the wrong thing, whether it was a derogatory remark about one of his sons, or something racist or sexist about his wife's Puerto Rican relatives and friends. He was unfaithful to his wife. He never aspired to anything beyond working at the receiving dock at Aries Corps. And he was gone for good from Carl's life right after his seventeenth birthday. This man, who Chris's parents had appointed as his godfather when he was born, because he had been Chris's mother's best friend in school, just like Carl had been Chris's, with one gigantic difference. Chris and Carl took responsibility for their lives. They both wanted to do something important, and they both were capable of loving the people in their lives and learning how to navigate difficult times.

All except for one.

She must be up by now, he thought. *What if she's not home? What if she met someone? It's been over two months.*

Quick clock check. Nine thirty. He would wait. He would figure out something else. He wouldn't call her. He told her he wouldn't.

He picked up the phone and pushed the buttons.

"Hello?"

Pause. "Chelley."

Pause. "Chris. Oh. Hi."

"Chelley, I had to talk to you."

"I don't really think this is a good idea. We talked about this. And it's not a good time. I have plans. I'm getting ready to go out in a little while."

"Chelley, I . . ." Chris didn't know which words to use.

"Chris?" Michelle said. "Somethings wrong. What's wrong?"

"Chelley, Carl's mother . . . Rosa . . . she died last night. Of a drug overdose. Chelley. Carl's mom. I'm not sure what to do. I haven't called him yet. I don't know how he's gonna be. I mean, I can't even imagine. I can't believe she's really gone. She's been gone for a long time, but now she's really gone."

"Oh, Chris," Michelle said. "Oh my God, I'm so sorry. Oh, poor Carl. Oh, he's already been through so much. He just doesn't need this. Are you going to Gram's house? You need to be with your family."

"Yeah, I'm gonna go after I call Carl," Chris told her. "I had to wait until I knew they'd all be up for the day with the time difference. Chelley, I'm so sorry to just drop this on you. Gram called me, and all I could think of was that I needed to hear your voice. I-I'm sorry. I don't need you to do anything, I just needed to talk to you."

He could hear Michelle sigh over the line. "Chris, it's okay," she said. "I'm glad you called to let me know. I need to know what happens, if Carl's gonna come back. If there's gonna be a service or something. I've got to talk to Kim and see what I can do. And Chris?" There were a few moments of silence. "I'll drive in tomorrow night. I can be there at five. I'll stay at my mom's."

"Chelley . . ."

"Chris, don't ask me to stay with you," Michelle begged. "Don't do it. I'll be there, but I'll be there on my own terms, okay?"

Chris felt relief that she would be there. "Okay, your terms. Fair enough. Thank you, Chelley."

"See you tomorrow, Chris."

"Bye, Chelley."

Chris hung up and swore at himself for being so weak. He couldn't do it. He couldn't face something like this without her. This wasn't what he wanted, or what she wanted, but he knew what he needed. And it seemed she needed it, too.

It was time to call Carl.

He dialed the number and waited. After two rings, Kim picked up. "Chris," she said softly. "I'm so glad you called."

"How is he doing?" he asked, although he suspected he already knew. He could hear toddler chatter in the background.

"Sorry, Chris," Kim said. "Drake and Elena are so wired already this morning. They know something's up. I'm giving them some breakfast right now. How is he? I don't know yet. He's not giving away too much about his emotions. He's being Carl Bishop, which is what I'd expect. But I have no idea what's going on in that genius mind of his. He could be sad, angry, relieved . . . I just don't know."

"How are you holding up?"

"I talked to Darlene already," she responded, "so that helped a bit. I keep having to remind myself that my kids just lost their potential for another grandmother. I've spent so many years so angry at her for what she did to Carl, it's hard to let that go just because she decided to up and die, you know? But I'm still aching for Carl. She was his mommy once. A long time ago, but she was. You know, the PB and J's." She paused. "And it brings up all that stuff about Jack, too. And just when he's about to start a new semester in school. He doesn't need this right now. You're gonna go be with the Grams, right? They've got to be all worked up by now. Poor Missy, having the cops just show up like that in the middle of the night."

"I'll head over as soon as I'm done talking to Carl," he assured her. "Is he nearby?"

"He's upstairs. Let me just strap Elena into her highchair, and I'll yell up the stairs. Hold on."

Chris could hear the busy noises at the Bishop house, and he wished he was back there and part of the mayhem. He heard Kim call out, and the click of an extension being picked up.

"Hey, Chris," Carl said.

"I'm hanging up, Chris," Kim said. "Thanks for checking in with us. Bye."

"Bye, Kim." Her extension clicked off. "Carl, man, I'm so sorry. Gram called me at seven thirty and told me to wait until a decent hour to call you."

"I was up," Carl said. "I didn't sleep at all. Elena was being fussy, so at least that gave me something to do all night."

"You okay, man?" Chris asked.

Carl sighed. "Yeah, well, I don't know what I am yet," he said, "but I know that I'm pissed at her for dropping back into my life all the sudden without asking, you know? It makes no sense, but it's just how I feel. I was doing fine without thinking about her for a long time. Now I have no choice. She's taking away my choices. Again."

"Yeah, I didn't really think of it like that, but I can totally see it," Chris said. "It's like it's really selfish of her to do this. I guess that kind of defines her last eight or so years. Selfish. This is her last selfish act."

"Yeah, exactly," Carl said. Then he was quiet. Chris waited. "So I need to fly out there, don't I?" he asked. He knew Chris would be straightforward with him.

"Yeah, I think you do," Chris replied. "The Grams expect you and Scott to make some decisions about what to do next, since you guys are her closest relatives. I'm so sorry, man. I wish I could do it for you, but I can't."

"No, I get it," Carl said. "I just need to talk to Kim and figure out how we're gonna do this. I don't know if we want to haul two little kids across the country again, but I also don't want to leave Kim here alone with them. Elena's been really challenging lately. We could ask Beth for help, but she's dealing with a toddler over there, too. I just have to think about it. Are you going over to my Gram's?"

"No, they're all over at my Gram's house, since there's more space, I guess. Or maybe Aunt Missy's just not up for hosting. I'm gonna call James before I go over there to see if he can have J.D. track down Scott. So let me worry about that."

"Thanks, man," Carl said. "I don't think I can handle having to track him down right now. I wish he would just call me when he moves or changes his number to let me know." He paused. "I suppose no one knows how to track down Jack, either, and I'm okay with that. He doesn't deserve the courtesy of us looking for him."

"I'm cool with that," Chris agreed. "I'll do whatever you ask me to do. If you need anything, call over to my Gram's later. If I don't hear from you, I'll call you tonight."

"Okay, Chris. Thanks. For everything."

After he hung up, Chris immediately called James and Sally's number. James agreed to call his father and work on finding Scott and to call Pete to tell him the news. Pretty soon everyone who needed to know would know. Chris headed to his Gram's house.

Gram's House

Chris went into Gram Cissy's house, and the first thing he did was hug his mother. She held on to him tightly and rubbed his back. "I know, Chris. I know. We're all feeling it." She released him, and Chris wiped stray tears off his face with his hand. He tried to imagine his eighth-grade math students witnessing him crying. He would lose control of the classroom for an entire school year, maybe more.

He hugged the Grams and filled everyone in on his call with Carl and Kim. He let them know Carl would somehow be coming soon, and that James was taking care of locating Scott. He spent some time talking to Carl's aunts, uncles, and cousins, and then he went to the kitchen to help his Gram prepare snacks for everyone.

Chris sat down next to his dad at the kitchen table once everyone else had left the room. "How's Mom holding up?"

Mr. Mahoney shook his head. "Sometimes it's hard to tell with those Bishop girls," he said. "She's okay, but Rosa's death is bringing up a lot of memories of Jack, and how close they used to be back in school. It wasn't long after Jack met Rosa that he changed. I don't know if the changes were already in motion when he met her and it just pushed him over the edge, or if the marriage was the catalyst. Whichever it was, though, your mother was really hurt by him pretty much just dropping her out of his life like she was nothing. They really were as close as you and Carl are, at least as much as they could be being different genders. Sometimes, they were even teased about being kissing cousins, which of course they weren't. This was all before I met your mom, so everything I'm telling you is what she's told me."

"Dad," Chris asked carefully, "why didn't anyone ever tell me that Jack was my godfather? Why did I have to find out from Carl when I was nineteen?"

Mr. Mahoney sighed. "I'm sorry about that, Chris, but we weren't deliberately keeping it from you. I objected to your mother wanting him as your godfather because I wasn't very fond of Jack, right from the very first time I met him. And by the time you came along, Rosa was pregnant with Carl, and things were already pretty contemptuous between them as a married couple. But your mother was feeling very sentimental about Jack, and she had just given birth, so I gave in. But it was clear very early on that he wouldn't be able to contribute anything meaningful to your upbringing, so I quietly asked him to just butt out of your life. He pretty much did. I don't know if he ever said anything to your mom about that, but he stayed your godfather in name only."

He sighed. "But I wish we would have been able to be more of a part of Carl's life in his early years. I would have loved to be his godfather, for what that's worth. You did everything you could to help that boy, and I think you made much more of a difference than anyone else could have. Without you, I think Carl would have probably dropped out of school at an early age, and maybe even gotten into drugs or run away. Or both. But now, he's got a career, a family, and so much to look forward to. You did that, Chris. You let him know he was part of something bigger than himself, even though you might have led him down the wrong path for a short time. But even then, you guided him, gave him a purpose, looked out for him. You're the closest thing to a godfather that Carl ever had. I know you're only six months older than him, but when it comes down to it, you instilled the values that you learned in him, and he respects you."

Chris was tearing up again. His father laughed. "Let me guess," he said. "Farmer sensitivities?"

Chris nodded. "Damn them." He wiped his damp eyes. "Dad," he said. "Thanks for telling me all of this. Maybe I should have asked earlier, I don't know. But you have to know that if I added any value to Carl's life, he added double that to mine. There were times, back in high school and college, and even recently, when I didn't know if I would be okay. And I was scared to talk about it with you and Mom, not because I didn't think you would help me, but just because I'd somehow worked it out in my head that I couldn't ever be wrong, or let anyone down, that I was always in control of everything. I guess looking at it now through a teacher's eye, I can see it was probably some kind of perfectionism, but it's what drove me.

"But Carl, he's what got me through. His courage, and his drive, and his passion. I owe him so much. There's still so much I want to say to him, to let him know and to thank him, but right now, it's not about me. It's about Carl and getting him through this loss. Dad, they don't write about things like this in the textbooks you read in college. I need to help Carl, and I just hope I know what to do, or that I'm strong enough."

Mr. Mahoney put his arm around Chris's shoulder.

"I'm so sorry we weren't able to help you when you were having such a hard time. If you ever feel that way again, please let us know and we'll be there for you, whatever you need. You definitely don't have to be perfect for us. And sometimes, everyone feels like they've lost control of something. But you have to remember, you're pretty much the strongest man I know. I say man because I've met the Bishop women!"

They both laughed, knowing this was true.

"But Chris," his father went on, "you'll do the right things for Carl. You'll know what to say and how to help. You know him so well. And hey, if you mess up in any way, just tell him you messed up, and try again. He'll appreciate that."

Chris nodded. "I guess sometimes just telling someone you screwed up and trying again is just as effective as doing something to try to control the problem or the outcome. I'll have to remember that."

His father looked at him carefully. "Chris, I'm not sure what's going on with you now, and you're always welcome to talk to me, but just remember, that advice applies in many different areas, not just with your cousin." He stood. "Let's go check on your mom and Grams, okay?"

Chris nodded. "Thanks, Dad."

Mr. Mahoney smiled. "You're welcome. You know, you're never too old to have a heart-to-heart talk with your old man."

When Chris got home, he called Carl to check in. He and Kim were flying out of San Francisco the next morning, but with layovers and connections, they wouldn't be in until late. When he got off the phone, he noticed there was a blinking light on his answering machine. He pushed play.

"Chris, are you screening your calls? It's Michelle. Chelley. I'm coming tonight. I hope you'll be there at seven. I changed my plans after we spoke and I . . . wanted to come tonight. I hope you'll be there. Oh, I already said that. Okay, I'm leaving now. I'll be a little over an hour. Okay. See you soon. I hope. Bye."

Chris looked at the clock. It was six fifty. Holy shit, she would be there any minute. He rushed around the apartment, putting away dirty dishes and throwing away trash. He stacked the mail on the table into one neat pile. He checked the bathroom, just to make sure the seat was down and everything was flushed. He shoved all of Grant's belongings into his room and shut the door. Then he went into his own room, pulled his comforter up in an attempt to make his bed, and—there was a knock. He froze. Then he made himself walk slowly to the door and opened it.

They were on each other before either of them could get out a word of greeting. Her lips were on his, her hands digging at his shirt. His hands went to her waist and pulled her close. He kissed below her ear.

"Stay with me tonight, Chelley," he whispered.

"Okay," she breathed back as she pushed the door closed with her foot. They made their way to the bedroom. They fell on the smoothed comforter and grasped at each other's bodies greedily. "I've missed this," she said as she unfastened his jeans.

"I've missed you so much," he said as he pulled her shirt up over her head.

"I want you to make love to me and hold me all night," she gasped, rolling onto her back.

"I can do that for you," Chris said hungrily as he pulled her jeans off her ankles. "I can do that."

The first time they made love was fast and desperate. The second was slow and deliberate. Then they slept. When they awoke, they held each other, making invisible lines on each other's skin with the tips of their fingers. Finally, they made love again, then lay awake, holding on to each other tight, staring at the ceiling, lost in thought.

"This was a huge mistake," Michelle stated unconvincingly.

"Yes," Chris agreed as he reached back toward her face and nibbled on her earlobe, not sure which mistake she was talking about. "I make a lot of mistakes," he confessed. "Some I'm more willing to live with than others."

Michelle reveled in the attention lavished on her, then pulled away. "What's happening tomorrow?"

Chris turned toward her on his side and propped his head on his hand. "Carl and Kim are flying in. They get to Boston at eight at night, and they're taking an airport shuttle to Aunt Missy's house. Beth's mom is gonna stay with the kids. She knows them really well, so they feel comfortable with that, but Beth can help if she needs it. They're only staying until Tuesday. J.D. Newell gave me Scott's number and I called him. I had to tell him that his mother was dead. I've never had to do something like that before. He's so much like Carl. It was like he was pissed at his mother for inconveniencing him with her death. I don't blame either of them, honestly. You're still staying until Monday, right? We can all get together on Monday. James and Sally are coming up tomorrow and staying at her parents' house overnight, and Darlene and Pete are trying to arrange to be here, too. It would be great if you could stay, Chelley."

"Chris, when you call me Chelley, I would do anything for you, you know that," Michelle said with her eyes closed. Then she opened them and looked at him. "I'll stay, but I told my mother I would be spending the night there, and I'm gonna do that. I think it's probably the best choice. I do want to see everyone. I haven't seen them since James and Sally's wedding, and I want to be with them now."

"It wouldn't be right if you weren't there," Chris agreed. "I wouldn't want to be with them all without you. These times, these moments I'm with you, Chelley, I feel so alive. I only feel like this with you. I haven't felt so alive since I was sixteen, and even then, it wasn't the same. I've felt so alone, Chelley, but not with you."

"Chris—" Michelle started.

"No, Chelley, don't cut me off. Please. I was there after the reunion. I remember everything. Every word. But now, I don't feel that way anymore. I was hurting and scared this morning, and my first thought was to call you. I don't know what that means, but it means something important."

"I don't know, Chris," Michelle said, propping herself up on her pillows. "It might mean something, but do you think about me when you're happy or excited, too? I don't want to be the one that has to be there to pick you up when you're down, but nothing else."

"Chelley," Chris said, looking in her eyes, "I'm only happy or excited when I'm with you, so you're already there."

Michelle was rendered speechless. She sat on the bed, her mouth agape, trying to find words. She shook her head. "I'm not sure what you're saying to me here. What are you saying?"

"I'm saying that I screwed up. That I want to try again. We have a connection," he told her. "I feel things for you, not just when we're physically together in bed. I think about you, even when there's nothing there to remind me of you. I want to call Carl and talk to him about you and tell him your name. Chelley, this is really hard for me to say, but I'm gonna say it anyway. I don't know a lot about love. My only experiences with love turned out very badly, as you know. And I know yours weren't storybook endings either. But now I'm pretty damn sure that the feelings I have for you, that they're, well, love. I know I might be messing things up by saying all this, especially with the way things were after the reunion, but I think it might be worth it to talk about it again, to see if, maybe, now, we can be together. Like really together."

Michelle stared at him with no expression while she contemplated what he had just said. She remembered every one of their encounters. She remembered the joy, the happiness, and ultimately the pain when they decided they couldn't be together. Then, she remembered how she canceled her lunch date today so she could be at his side, in his bed, to hold him, to comfort him, and his words right now were so . . .

She grabbed him behind the neck, pulled his head to hers, and kissed him hard. Then she let go. "I love you, too," she told him. "I want to be with you. Let's be together, okay? Let's not *not* be together anymore. That just sucks way too much."

"Holy crap, really?" Chris replied, not believing this could really be happening. He had missed her so much. He cleared his throat. "I mean, yeah. Let's do that. Good." He nodded, to give proof this was good. Then he smiled.

"Don't give me that smile, Mr. Mahoney," Michelle teased. "I know what that smile means. No more sex for you tonight. You've officially worn me out. But you can start doing the holding-me-all-night part."

Chris nodded, lay down, and extended his arm. Michelle curled up against his body. He wrapped his arm around her and nuzzled her neck. "This work?" he asked.

Michelle nodded. "And you have my permission to tell Carl anything you want about us," she told him. "Including who I am. But use tact, okay? The guy just lost his mother."

Chris had forgotten about Carl and his mother for just a few moments. It all came rushing back. "I promise," he told her. "Scouts honor. You don't have to convince me to be there for my cousin. I can assure you, that just comes naturally to me."

Michelle rolled even closer to him. "So we're together now, then."

Chris nodded. "We're together now. Really together."

"So I can love you publicly now."

Chris smiled as his heart thumped. "You can love me wherever and whenever you want," he said. "Just don't ever stop loving me, okay?"

Michelle lay quietly for several seconds. "A woman reserves the right to change her mind," she told him. "I might not be as worn out as I originally thought."

Chris rolled on top of her. "I was hoping you were gonna say something like that, Chelley." He reached down to kiss her and to love her to her heart's content.

When they woke up on Sunday morning, they lay in bed a few minutes smiling at each other as they remembered the night before. Then they got up, and Chris gave Michelle one of his T-shirts to wear. On Michelle, it looked more like a dress. She felt like an elf sleeping with an ogre. She giggled.

"What's so funny?" Chris asked her, putting his hands on either side of her waist.

"Oh, I was just thinking, if I had a belt to put around me, this shirt could be a whole outfit!"

Chris smiled and kissed her. "So what do I say to you?" he asked. "I'm gonna have to get used to expressing how I feel to you, but I want to say something right now to let you know how I feel."

"We could make up a gibberish word," Michelle suggested. "Like . . . blotchnik."

Chris laughed. "I don't think so," he said. "I still have my former bad boy reputation that I need to maintain, at least in my own mind. How about . . . oh, here's one I heard Beth say about Carl and Kim once. Smitten, as in 'I'm smitten with you'?"

Michelle pondered. "Smitten like a kitten. It's kind of cute. Okay. Smitten. I'm good with that."

"I was thinking more like sultry and smoldering, but I guess kittens will do, too. Chelley Gorman," Chris said, pulling her closer. "I am smitten with you. So, so smitten." He nuzzled her neck with his lips.

"I'm smitten with you, too, Chris," Michelle replied. "Now let's get some breakfast, and then go see your Gram."

"I have a better idea," Chris said. "Let's make love first, then go to my Gram's, and let her make us breakfast. Actually, it's probably already made in anticipation of people coming."

Michelle grinned. "And I thought Carl was the genius cousin." She pulled the giant T-shirt back off.

Sunday Breakfast Gram

Chris and Michelle arrived together, but no one gave a second thought to an old high school friend driving another to his grandmother's house. They were getting used to people seeing only what they expected to see. Mr. and Mrs. Mahoney were already there with Melanie and Scarlet, and Aunt Missy was on the phone in the kitchen. Michelle sat on the couch, and Gram Cissy pulled Chris into the guest bedroom.

"How are you doing?" she asked him as she closed the door. "It's been pretty strange over here. Scott's coming over later, and I have no idea how that will go."

"I'm okay, Gram," Chris told her. "It's still hard to wrap my head around everything. I'll feel better when Carl gets here. And then all of our friends will be here tomorrow. That's what we all really need."

Gram looked at him inquisitively. "You look different today," she told him. "Peaceful, even with everything going on. More grounded than yesterday. More confident. It's been a long time since I've seen you look like this. You even seem taller. What's going on, Chris? Are you seeing someone new? You are, aren't you? You were with a girl last night after you left here. It's written all over your face. Might as well be in Sharpie on your forehead."

Chris almost laughed but caught himself. This was not a laughing occasion. He gave Gram a smile instead. "Yes, Gram, I am seeing someone. I didn't realize I was advertising it."

"Who is she?" Gram probed. "How did you meet her?"

"Gram, I met her in kindergarten," Chris revealed. "She's sitting on the couch with my mom right now as we speak."

"Michelle?" Gram's hand flew to her mouth when she realized she had spoken loudly. "Michelle?" she repeated more quietly. "How did this happen? Are you saying that the girl who gave you your confidence back was there all along, but you're just figuring it out now?"

Chris gestured for Gram to sit on the bed, and he sat next to her. "It's complicated, Gram," he told her. "There's been something with me and Michelle ever since Carl's wedding, on and off for the past three years, but we just haven't been able to pull it together, with her living in Amherst, and me here, and just everything else going on in our lives. We actually decided to call it all off after our five-year reunion in June, but that just didn't take. I-I think we're together for good now, as of last night, and we're gonna make it work."

Gram reached out and hugged him. "Chris," she said, "I'm so happy for you! It's hard to be happy right now, but you've gone long enough struggling to find happiness. It's your time. Michelle is such a lovely girl. She's been part of your group for years, and you share friends. Those are important things. I wish the two of you the best of luck, and I hope it works out." She took his hand and squeezed it. "You've kept this to yourself for a long time, it seems, and I hate to ask you this, but maybe it's a good idea to keep that up a few more days? This *is* your time, but unfortunately, it's not the best timing. We all have to concentrate on Carl and Scott, but you know that."

Chris nodded. "You remember what I said about Carl practically being my identical twin, Gram." He assured her using a reference he knew she understood. "I will always be there for him. He's my first priority. And Michelle knows that, too. She's here to support me so I can support Carl. And she'll be here for Kim."

"Of course she is," Gram said. "When this all blows over, I'll have you both over for dinner so I can catch up with her."

Chris smiled. "I'd like that," he said. "Hey, you remember that Michelle has younger brothers who are identical twins, right?"

Gram chuckled. "Oh, that's right," she said. "We met them at the yearly Eastboro Twin Club get-together a few years back with their mother. The boys with the bright red hair and freckles. Stevie and Sam. But just so you know, Christopher, identical twins do not run in families, even if both of you have them in yours. We're basically freaks of nature. At least that's what our brothers used to call us. Just wanted to reassure you, in case you need to know someday."

Chris couldn't help but laugh. "Okay, you're getting just a few steps ahead of us now, Gram," he said, "but that's good to know."

Gram looked off into the distance. "Do you remember," she started, "when you were a little boy, and we were trying to explain twins to you and Carl, but you couldn't pronounce identical, so you called us 'dental twins'?"

Chris smiled. "That sounds vaguely familiar," he said. "And knowing me, I probably insisted that I was the one who was saying it right, and everyone else had it wrong."

Gram smiled. "Actually," she said, "everyone thought it was just adorable, so no one ever tried to correct you! Come on, let's get you back out there to your girl."

They went back into the living room and found Michelle engaged in a discussion with Chris's mom about the state of healthcare in Massachusetts. His dad was watching TV, and his sisters were playing gin at the dining room table. Grandpa Clyde was reading his newest *Reader's Digest* on his recliner and sipping coffee from a mug that declared "World's Best Grandpa." Chris was willing to bet that he had several of those in the cabinet in the kitchen, one of them having come from him.

Aunt Missy came back in from the kitchen. "Hello, Chris," she said. "I was just talking to Scotty," she told the room. "He's renting a room in a shared house over by East Firehouse. He's the floor supervisor in his area at Aries now, and he's happy there. He's going to come by my house later tonight after Carl and Kim get in. Chris, you missed that I talked to the coroner's office earlier this morning. They're finished with Rosa and can release her to a funeral home once we get the name of a place from the boys. Then we can decide what to do next."

She looked over at the couch.

"Oh, hello, Michelle. I didn't see you there at first. Thanks for coming." She looked carefully at Michelle and then back at Chris. "You two are together now, aren't you?" she intuited. "Like romantically?"

Mr. and Mrs. Mahoney and their daughters all looked up at Missy, then at Michelle, as if synchronized.

"Missy!" Gram Cissy called out.

"What?" Missy replied. "I'm not wrong, am I? Cissy must have inadvertently sent me a twin telepathy, only now I am gathering from the way she's looking at me that I've just blown some kind of secret. Sorry, you two."

"Is this true?" Mrs. Mahoney asked, glancing at Chris and then back at Michelle.

Michelle gave her a soft smile and nodded. "It's true," she said. "We're together, and it's not a secret. It's just that it didn't seem like a good time to make that type of announcement, if you know what I mean."

"Be that as it may," Mrs. Mahoney replied, "I'm very pleased to hear this. Congratulations, you two." She reached out to hug Michelle. "I never could have imagined that the tiny little girl with the little orange pigtails and the plaid jumper dress on the first day of kindergarten would end up with my son, almost twenty years later!"

"Mom, you and me both," Chris said, moving to the couch and sitting down next to Michelle. "We still have some things to figure out."

He reached out and put his arm around Michelle's shoulder. He had never done this before in public. It felt right, especially when she turned to him and smiled.

"We live over an hour apart," he went on, "which isn't really a long-distance relationship, but it's also not the most convenient. And we both really like our jobs. So we might only be able to be together on weekends and holidays, at least for now."

Michelle shrugged. "It's not a bad drive," she said. "I wish there was a good halfway point. Sally and James found a great town halfway between Providence and Eastboro that works well for their work and being close to their families, but there's really nothing that great between Eastboro and Amherst, except a long daily commute for both of us."

Chris looked at her. "You've actually thought about this?"

"Of course I have," Michelle replied. "I'm a girl. We think about these sorts of things. I mean, not for right this very minute, but for the possible future, you know?"

The phone rang, and Grandpa Clyde picked up the extension on the lamp table beside him and put it to his ear. He held the receiver out to Missy.

"It's for you, Melissa."

Missy spoke into the phone and listened for a few minutes, making agreeing sounds. Then she gave the caller Gram's address and signed off.

"That was a woman named Tania Sanchez," she told her family. "She said that Carl would know her as Tia Tania?" Chris nodded. "She said she has some information for us about Rosa and would like to come by tomorrow morning when Carl and Scott are here, so she can give everyone the details. Ten o'clock, she's coming."

"The tias were Rosa's friends," Chris explained. "They would come over for gossip and drinks. I think some of them may have known each other from Puerto Rico. I don't think anyone was actually related to her, but they liked to see themselves as Carl and Scott's aunts. Carl couldn't stand it when they came over. He never knew what they were talking about in Puerto Rican Spanish, and when they did speak to him in English, they would sometimes say nasty things. He would come over our house a lot when they were there, until he and Kim got together. Then he'd go to her house instead."

"They sound lovely," Gram Cissy said, rolling her eyes. "But maybe this Tania can shed some light on what happened over the last few years and how Rosa ended up where she did. She's all we have for now. We'll see what she has to say."

James and Sally arrived shortly after two, looking more relaxed and content than both Chris and Michelle had ever seen them. Marriage appeared to suit them very well. Gram gave everyone drinks and snacks, and then they all sat down to catch up.

After they finished their food, Michelle got up to bring her dish to the kitchen. Chris held up his plate. "Chelley, would you mind taking mine, too, while you're going in there?"

There was a loud clank as Sally's empty plate slipped from her hand and hit the table.

"You okay, Sally?" James asked, taking the plate from her and putting it on top of his.

Sally regained her composure. "Yes, I'm fine," she said. "It just slipped." She stood. "I'm gonna go help Michelle in the kitchen. Jamie, let me take our plates."

She snatched the plates out of James's hands. Then she and Michelle looked locked eyes for a few seconds and turned to go to the kitchen.

"What was that about?" James asked Chris.

"I have no earthly idea," Chris admitted. "Some sort of best friend code?"

Sally quickly put her plate on the counter and turned back to Michelle. She pulled her over to the kitchen table and they sat down.

"Michelle," she said, leaning in close to her best friend. "Chris just called you Chelley. Why did Chris call you Chelley, Michelle? Why? Why?"

Michelle smiled. "Oh, he did, didn't he? I didn't even catch that. I was wondering why you were acting so strange." She took a deep breath to prepare for the big reveal. "Sally, Chris calls me Chelley because I want him to."

"Oh my God, Michelle! You and Chris are . . . seeing each other? You and *Chris?* That's like, not something I can even fathom in my brain. Michelle and Chris. No. This is going to take some getting used to. How . . . when did this happen?"

"Sally, you're gonna be mad at me when I tell you," Michelle said.

"It was our wedding, wasn't it?" Sally probed. "You hooked up with Chris at our wedding."

Michelle nodded. "Yes, we did hook up at your wedding. And your rehearsal dinner. But that wasn't the first time."

Sally looked at her best friend with wide eyes. "My rehearsal dinner? At my parents' house?? Oh my God, Michelle. How long has this been going on?"

Michelle braced herself. "It started at Kim and Carl's wedding."

"No!" Sally exclaimed, banging her hands on the table. "Michelle, that was more than three years ago! How is that even possible?" She gasped. "Oh my God, Michelle, Chris was your serial one-night stand man!"

Michelle sighed. "Yes," she admitted. "The first time was pretty much a one-time thing. But then we started to have other one-night things. Then we started looking for excuses to be at the same places at the same time. But then, after the reunion in June, we decided to call it off."

"So that's why you were so distracted, and Chris took off for California!" Sally realized. "And why you came to the reunion in the same car! Why did you end it? What happened?"

"What happened is that we started to have, like, major feelings for each other. And he couldn't handle it. It wasn't just me. It was both of us. We both felt it. But he just wasn't ready to feel that way. I was ready. But I didn't want to keep waiting to see if he would get ready. I didn't need another year of celibacy and waiting, like with Joey. So we had a big talk, and we decided that we couldn't do it anymore."

"So, it's over then?" Sally said sadly.

"It was," Michelle said, grinning, "until last night. He called me yesterday morning. He was upset about Carl's mom, and he needed me. He wanted me there. I agreed to come tonight, but then I couldn't wait. I had to see him. So I came out last night. We went straight to bed. But then, without me even having to say anything about it, he told me that he wants to be with me. For real. He's ready to admit he loves me now. He wants it all."

"Oh, Michelle, that's so huge."

"It is," Michelle admitted. "And now his family knows. Sally, it's kind of scary. This is Chris Mahoney. I've known him forever. I know so much about him. He was always there, you know? But it was never in that way. I never, ever, thought of him in a romantic or sexual way. I actually just kind of tolerated him for a lot of years. He could be kind of too much at times, with his overconfidence and his bad boy posse. But he's changed, so much. He's not the same person we knew in junior high, or even high school. What happened to him after he and Rhonda broke up, it changed him. And then the fiasco with Alison. He struggled for so long. But he's come out of it now. He seems like he's figuring it all out. And he wants me to be there with him. And I really want to be."

Sally looked as if she might cry. "Michelle," she said softly. "I'm so happy for you. You deserve to be with someone who makes you number one in their life. It's not like things were so easy for you once Joey left for the Marines, and it's been a long road for you. And you've changed, too. You're like, a responsible adult. You have a real job, and you help people. You deserve all the happiness. I hope Chris makes you happy."

Michelle smiled. "He does," she admitted. "He makes me feel so alive. He makes me feel things I never felt, and I like it. He's smitten with me."

Sally laughed. "Smitten! He told you that?" Michelle nodded. "Well, smitten is a very good start. And he calls you Chelley. Does Carl know?"

"Not yet," Michelle admitted. "We both decided from the beginning not to say anything to anyone. I hated to keep things from you, and Chris didn't like keeping it from Carl, but things were so precarious, you know? And now with Carl's mom . . . but everyone else here knows now, well, except James, so Chris is gonna have to say something to Carl before someone else does. And Darlene and Pete will be here later, too. It's so weird. It's gonna be strange for me, with everyone from DeMarco knowing about us. Kind of surreal."

"Yeah, it is," Sally said. "But it's a good surreal, right?"

"I hope so," Michelle said, and she sighed. "I just worry he's suddenly gonna realize what he said to me last night and freak out. I mean, we're twenty-three now, we're not sixteen. I hope that means when we say things, when we make promises, we really mean it. I don't want to give my whole self to him, and then have him go and change his mind."

"I'm not gonna change my mind, Chelley."

Michelle looked at the doorway. Chris was standing there, looking at her so sincerely that all of her fears fell away. "How long have you been standing there?"

"Just long enough to hear you worry about me changing my mind," he responded, walking toward her. He reached out for her hand.

"Chelley," he said, "I won't change my mind. I said what I said, and it's all true. I am absolutely and totally smitten with you. I'm with you now completely, I promise. As long as you don't come to your senses and run screaming away from me, we're both in this now."

He pulled her to her feet and secured his arms around her. He whispered in her ear, "When I say *smitten*, I really mean the other thing, Chelley, you know that, right?"

He pulled her closer and kissed her tenderly, forgetting Sally was there.

James came into the kitchen to see where everyone had disappeared to and happened upon this scene. He stepped back reflexively when he saw two of his best friends engaged in an intimate kiss. He stared in absolute shock.

"Chris!" he exclaimed. "Oh my God, what the *fuck*?"

Sally laughed.

The last of the DeMarco gang to check in were Darlene and Pete. They arrived at Gram Cissy's together around four but were definitely not there as a couple. James and Sally stuck around for another hour to catch up with all the news and happenings, and then went back to Sally's parents' house for dinner with her family.

Michelle was feeling fatigued with all of the weird secret relationship revelations, so as soon as the Newells left, she sat next to Chris on the couch and turned to their friends.

"Pete, Darlene," she started. "I'm gonna get straight to the point, so hold on to your socks." She put out her hand and Chris took it. "Chris and I are a couple now."

Darlene and Pete looked at each other, then back at Michelle and Chris. "Where, in the *Twilight Zone*?" Darlene quipped. "C'mon you guys, this is not a good time to be kidding around about things like this."

"We're not kidding around," Chris assured her. He squeezed Michelle's hand. "We're together, Darlene. And we're very excited about it."

Darlene looked back at Pete. He shrugged. "I didn't know anything about this," he told her. "But I mean, they did go to the prom together."

Darlene rolled her eyes. "We all went to the prom together!" she said. "There were seven of us! You guys, how did this even happen? Chris, you're in Eastboro and Michelle is in Amherst. How are you making this work?"

"Badly at first," Michelle admitted. "But we'll work that stuff out eventually."

"It's been a hard road for us," Chris said, "but we're figuring it out now."

Darlene shook her head. "I mean, I'm happy for you two, but I'm just so shocked! I never thought about the two of you . . . I mean, it never even crossed my mind. Like if one of you told me you had a crush on the other one in high school, maybe . . ."

"No crushes in high school," Michelle told her. "We've been over this. This is totally a relationship founded in adulthood. Whatever that means."

"I'm psyched for you guys," Pete said. "You look great together. I mean, once the shock wears off, I think we'll all be good with this. It's just so . . ."

"Surreal?" Michelle offered.

Pete nodded. "Yeah, that's a good word. I can't believe there's another couple coming out of our little Randall Junior High gang. James and Sally, Kim and Carl, and now Chris and Michelle. Ack, I'm gonna have to get used to that. Chris and Michelle. That just leaves me and Darlene, and don't hold your breath about that happening. No offense, Darlene, but I've definitely got other specific plans for my future."

"No, I'm okay with that," Darlene agreed. "I like you, Pete, but, uh, yeah, just not like that." She looked back at Chris and Michelle. "I'm sorry for not giving you the most enthusiastic response right away. I'm just a bit overwhelmed. I mean, you two have known about this the whole time, but we're just hearing it now for the first time. It's kind of . . . unexpected. But I really am very happy for you. But like Pete said, I'm just gonna have to get my head around the concept for a while."

"That's okay," Michelle assured her. "I do too. It's new for this to be public information, and we're all gonna have to get used to it."

"Wait," Darlene said, turning to face Pete. "What other specific plans for your future?"

Pete smiled. "You caught that, huh? Well, it turns out Carolyn and I have gotten back together."

Michelle gasped. "Oh my God, how did that happen?"

"Well, as you know," Pete said, "we broke up when she left for Germany. And we both had other relationships for the rest of college and after. We didn't see each other or talk at all during that time. Then we ran into each other at Murphy at our fifth reunion in May, and neither of us was involved with anyone. I swear, we said hello, and it's like we had never been apart a day. We were back together by the end of the night.

I think this is it for me, you guys. I could see us getting engaged in the next few months, if I even wait that long. I really don't see any reason to wait."

"Wow, Pete," Chris said. "Congratulations! Does James know?"

Pete laughed. "James got a call the night of the reunion. It's kind of our thing to tell each other stuff first, kinda like you and Carl."

Michelle glanced at Chris, and then back at Pete. "Pete, I've always liked Carolyn. I'm glad she's back in your life. And our lives. Congratulations!"

Darlene and Pete stayed for a dinner of leftovers and chocolate cake. Pete was picked up by Carolyn, and Darlene left on her own, both with the promise of everyone getting together the next afternoon. It was getting late, and Chris started to yawn. He had gotten up early the day before and was up very late with Michelle the previous night. He was not going to be able to stay awake until Carl and Kim arrived at Aunt Missy's house.

"So you're going to your parents' house?" he asked Michelle.

"Yes, they're expecting me," she replied.

"And there's no way I can convince you to come home with me?" he asked. He refrained from saying Chelley because he knew that was unfair.

"No," Michelle replied, "but why don't you come home with me?"

Chris laughed. "Are you serious?" he asked. "Come stay with you, in your old room at your parents' house?"

Michelle shrugged. "Chris, we're twenty-three years old. I think it's okay for me to bring my boyfriend home to my parents' house."

"Your boyfriend," Chris said softly. Then he nodded. "You're right. I'll do it," he agreed. "It means I get to be with you, even if I'll be squirming around your dad. But it's worth every squirm. Thank you, Chelley."

Michelle felt an affectionate *whoosh* go through her body. "Thank you, Chris, for getting it."

Gram Cissy was packing things up to go spend the night at Aunt Missy's house, to keep her company until Carl and Kim arrived. She said good night.

"So Chris, try to be here before ten tomorrow, so you can talk to Carl before this Tania woman shows up." She gave him a hug. "Sleep well, sweetheart, and hug your girl tight tonight. Tomorrow might be a little rough."

They drove past Twin Bridges Park, and on a whim, Chris pulled over on Wichita Street and parked. "Let's go walk around a bit," he suggested. "I could use a little air."

They got out and slowly cruised the walkway, holding hands. "I can't believe I'm walking with a boy around Twin Bridges Park," Michelle said, smiling. "In high school, everyone thought it was such a romantic place to go after a date. James and Sally had their first kiss on that bridge." She pointed to the taller of the two bridges. "People get married here, too, when the rhododendrons are blooming in the spring. It's beautiful during the day and at night."

"So are you," Chris said, with a corny smile. "That's Farmer humor. Better get used to it."

He turned to her and leaned down for a kiss. They were standing in the light of an old-fashioned streetlamp, and their bodies cast lopsided shadows along the sidewalk. They came apart, and Chris directed them toward the tall bridge.

"Let's try it out," he told Michelle. "I've never been here with a girl before, either. It will be the first time for both of us."

When they got to the Gormans' house, Chris and Michelle had a talk with Michelle's parents and explained what was going on.

"Michelle," her father told her. "It's true, you are twenty-three and you can do whatever you want in your life, and it's okay this time, but please, next time, give us a bit of advance notice, okay? You still have young brothers living here, and it's a good idea to give them a heads up."

He turned to Chris. "I'm so sorry for your loss," he told him. "Please let Carl know he's in our thoughts, and let us know if there's going to be a service or something."

"Thanks, Mr. Gorman," Chris replied. "I appreciate it."

Mrs. Gorman reached for Michelle's hand. "We're really happy for you two," she said. "You look like a very sweet couple. I'm glad you're both here."

Michelle smiled. "Thanks, Mom," she said. "That means a lot." She yawned. "It's been a long couple of days. I'm ready to go to bed. Thanks again for letting us stay here tonight. Good night."

She hugged her parents, and Mrs. Gorman gave Chris a hug.

Michelle and Chris headed upstairs to Michelle's childhood bedroom. It was a small room containing two twin beds, and it was easy enough for them to push the beds together to make space for them to sleep side by side. Michelle gave Chris a new toothbrush, and together they prepared for bed. Before they climbed under the covers, Michelle put her arms around Chris's neck.

"Earlier tonight," she said softly, "you told me that when you said you were smitten with me, you really meant the other thing. Chris, tell me the other thing now."

Chris looked in her eyes and felt his soul melt. He smiled. "I love you, Chelley," he said. And for the first time in his life, he understood just how much he meant those words.

Michelle smiled back. She blinked slowly, then returned his gaze. "I love you, too, Chris."

They removed the clothes they were wearing to bed and climbed under the sheets. They very quietly made love with the knowledge that they were in love with each other for the first time, making sure the beds didn't creak against the floorboards or bang up against the wall. There was a quiet intensity to their joining, and they lay silent and contemplative after it was over.

"Well, that was less frantic than usual," Michelle stated.

"Yeah," Chris agreed. "It's always been like we didn't know when or if it would ever happen again, and we had to do everything all at once. Now that I know that it will happen again soon, I don't feel so rushed."

Michelle nodded. "Yeah," she said. "Normally, you exhaust me! But now I just feel sleepy. I could just fall asleep." She cuddled up against the side of Chris's naked body, feeling the warmth of his skin like a hot water bottle against her side. "We'll see Carl and Kim tomorrow. And that Tia lady's coming over. We're finally gonna know what happened to Rosa."

Chris sighed. "I know," he said. "I just hope that whatever she has to say, it brings Carl some closure and doesn't open up a whole new world of hurt."

What Tia Tania Reveals

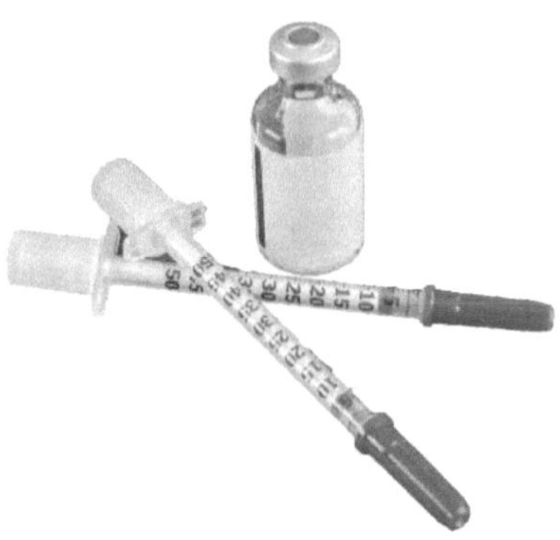

Chris and Michelle arrived at Gram Cissy's house at nine. They ate breakfast, and then waited for Carl and Kim to arrive. When they got there, they all embraced, and everyone expressed their condolences. Scott arrived and greeted everyone before taking a seat on the loveseat. Chris asked to have a moment alone with his Aunt Missy. Once in the guest room, Chris checked in on her well-being, and then he got to the point.

"Aunt Missy, I just wanted to let you know as a courtesy," he said, "that I'm going to have a talk with Carl while he's here. I'm gonna tell him about the testing he had in school, about his gifts. It's time for him to know."

Aunt Missy sighed and nodded. "You're right," she said. "It is. I don't like having secrets from Carl. His mother is gone, and for all intents and purposes, so is his father. There's nothing holding us to it anymore. Do you want to do it, or would you rather have me?"

"I think it should be me," Chris told her. "I think it would be better coming from me. Let me take the heat for not telling him as soon as I knew, and then he'll have time to get used to the idea before he talks to you. And I also need to tell him about Michelle. He'll be happy for us, but he won't be too happy about me keeping it a secret. I'm just not gonna keep anything from him anymore, ever. I'm done."

Aunt Missy patted him on the knee. "Christopher, you were just doing as I asked you to do. You haven't done anything except keep your word to me. It was all for the better as it turns out. Things always have a way of working out, don't they?"

Chris looked carefully at Aunt Missy. For the first time, she looked old to him. The lines on her face looked deeper. She looked tired and worn out. Chris would have to take a closer look at his Gram when they went back out there to see if she was looking identically aged.

He spoke softly. "You didn't do anything wrong either, okay? You did whatever was in your power to protect your family, and that's never wrong. None of what happened was your fault."

Aunt Missy smiled. "You grew up to be a good man, Chris Mahoney. I always knew you would. Thank you."

They went back into the living room and sat down to join the conversation. Kim showed them pictures of Drake and Elena and spoke of their accomplishments since they had visited in the spring. Then they spoke about Tia Tania.

"She was the worst of the bunch," Carl told them. "Aside from my mother, I guess. She could be mean. And she sometimes said things to me that weren't appropriate. I wouldn't get close enough to any of them for them to touch me ever, because I never knew what they'd do. They were always drinking something. I learned to get out of the house when they were there, just to avoid them. I've never even given them another thought since I last saw them when I was sixteen, until last night. I don't even know what to say to her when she gets here."

"I'm not too fond of them either," Scott said. "They weren't as bad when I was younger, but they got worse. When I was a kid, they would dote on me, give me gifts. Then one time, one of them gave me some of her drink. I was probably eight at the time. After that, Mom kept a closer eye on them, but only so much. It got worse the more they drank. When Dad would find them there when he got home from work, he would get mad, and yell at Mom, and then he'd take off again."

"I remember that," Carl said. "And as time went on, Mom started going out more, probably to their houses to get away from Dad. If Tania starts in on anything with us when she gets here, I'm kicking her right back out the door. I don't care what kind of information she has."

Scott nodded. "I'm with you on that, brother."

The doorbell rang, and Gram Cissy went to get the door. Kim was sitting to Carl's left, and Chris to his right, his personal bodyguards. Scott sat on the loveseat next to his Gram. Grandpa Clyde was in his recliner. Mr. and Mrs. Mahoney and Michelle left the room.

Cissy came into the room with a shrunken, gray-haired, overweight Puerto Rican woman in a pink sleeveless terrycloth dress. She gave a weak smile as she came into the room, but no one returned it.

"Scotty, Carlos, you're big men now," she said. "But I'd recognize you anywhere." Cissy directed her to a chair, and she groaned as she lowered herself down. "I am so sorry about your mom. I know you haven't seen her in years, but I know a loss is a loss. So I'm sorry."

She took a deep, wheezy breath, then coughed.

"And also, I want to say, before I say anything else, I am so, so very sorry for my behavior toward both of you when you were younger. I was not a good person at that time, and I have no excuse. I have spent a lot of time regretting what I have done, and I know my regret isn't your problem, but I want you to know it anyways. I have made very positive changes in my life since then, and done some hard work, and I want to let you know that if there's ever anything I can do to make it up to you—"

"There's nothing you can do," Carl interrupted. "It's the past. We've moved on. Just focus on what you need to focus on for yourself and don't worry about us." Kim reached out and took his hand. "This is my wife, Kim. You remember Kim from back then, and my cousin Chris, and the Grams, and my Uncle Clyde." Everyone nodded at each other. "Now you have some things to tell us? We're ready to hear it."

Tania nodded. "Okay," she said, "fair enough." She took another breath. "Your mama was in prison for drugs. Heroin. She was caught and arrested for possession with intent to distribute, and she pled guilty. She was given three years in the poky."

Scott grunted. "She was dealing heroin?" he said with disgust.

"She was delivering heroin to the dealer," Tania explained. "But she was also involved in some of the dealing." She sighed. "I'll give you a little background before I tell you what happened. Your mom got involved with a bad man, years ago."

"Tio Paco?" Carl guessed.

Tania snorted. "He told you to call him Tio? He was just as much your tio as Lassie was a cat. But yes, Paco."

Carl shook his head. "I always wondered what that guy's deal was. He gave me my first beer when I was twelve. I thought maybe he was married to one of the other tias. No wonder my father got so weird about him when I mentioned him."

Tania shook her head. "No, Paco was a friend of a friend. He sold drugs. He used to supply us with pot. We'd all smoke from the pipe, and chill out, have a few drinks, have fun. It was innocent fun back then. We were unhappy with our lives, and it was our little escape. But when we started getting bored of the high, Paco was there, and he offered us a little bit of coke to try. So we tried it. And we liked it! So we kept trying it. It made us feel so superior, so invincible. We would sit at Maria's house on the floor in front of her mirror-topped coffee table and snort lines.

"This went on for some time, but after a while, some of the girls stopped, and it was just me, Rosa, and Maria, and then we started doing it even when we weren't all together. Rosa had it the worst. Rosa was snorting coke too much, and pretty soon, Paco was gonna cut her off because she didn't have enough money for what she needed.

She was of no use to him without money. But she begged him to keep supplying her with drugs, and she would find the money to pay. And he latched right on to that.

"Next thing you know, your mom is doing work for Paco. She was delivering drugs, and sometimes he had her selling drugs on her own. He had her doing all sorts of things she never would have done before. When that wasn't enough, he started demanding personal favors. He would keep her at his place all weekend or longer sometimes, just doing what he wanted, when he wanted. Pretty soon, she was so far in, there was no way out, but she wasn't even looking for one. In the meantime, Maria and I saw what was happening to Rosa, and we couldn't do anything to help her. But we knew we could help ourselves, so we went to a place, and asked for help, and we got it. But for Rosa, things kept getting worse. Paco kept wanting her to do more and more for him.

"Pretty soon, he was trying to pimp her out for more income. Rosa resisted him at first, but it was no use. It wasn't long before Paco introduced the heroin. I think it was to quiet her down, to make her more compliant. Which it did. Rosa was hooked. She was begging Paco to let her onto the streets so she could get more dope. It was pathetic. I couldn't see her anymore. It was too bad. I was surprised she lived long enough to get arrested. But she did, a few times. And the last time, she went to prison, which we all thought was actually the best thing that could happen to her."

"When was this?" Kim asked.

"In 1989," Tania told her. "She went to prison and went through a terrible withdrawal. But she was clean. Then she got an offer. Six months into her sentence, she was offered a spot at a program for women who came to prison with addiction. There was a house on the prison campus where they kept twelve women who were there by choice, and if they were able to participate in the program for a year, they would receive early release to a group home in the city and stay there until they were eligible to be released by a special court. It was a wonderful deal, and since she was already detoxed, Rosa jumped at the opportunity. And she did great. She did the program, did all the steps. She made amends, wrote letters, went to meetings, and found her higher power. She mentored younger inmates. She befriended the staff. She did extra chores. She was a model resident. That was when she and I got back in touch. I was so proud of her, and I told her when she got out, I would go to meetings with her, whatever she needed. So after the year was up, she moved into the group home."

"Did she ever say anything about finding me and Scott, making amends to us, when she was going through all this?" Carl asked.

Tania nodded. "She talked about it all the time," she said. "She didn't think anyone would help her find you by then. She knew where Jack's mom lived, of course. But the house she had lived in with you was abandoned, and she didn't know where you both were. When she moved to the group home, I drove over there with her to see before a meeting. Everything was gone and there was a foreclosure notice on the door. Her plan was to get more stable in the community, and then reach out to Missy and see if she could convince her to have her boys come and see her, or at least call her, so she could start apologizing and making amends."

"I never got a call from her," Aunt Missy said.

"I know," Tania said softly. "Before Rosa had a chance to track down the boys, Paco tracked her down. He waited for her outside the house when she came out to do yard work. He had been watching the house and knew her routine. She saw him and went back into the house. She called me. I came right over, and we talked to the staff. They said there was nothing they could do, because he wasn't trying to come inside, and he wasn't threatening her, so she wouldn't be able to get a restraining order. She just had to keep her distance. She was able to, for some time, but then this past week, I guess he must have broken her down.

"I don't know exactly what happened, but from what I can put together, he must have somehow found her outside a meeting and offered her drugs. I think she probably tried to refuse, but eventually took what he offered, either to get away from him, or to think about it for a while, I don't know. Rosa had a serious addiction. I don't know what she was thinking. But what I do know is that when they found her, she had a needle in her arm and had overdosed. It was too late when they found her that night. I think Rosa forgot about something very important. You build up a tolerance to drugs over time, and you have to use more and more. But when you stop, like your mom did for about two years, you can't go back to what you used to use. It can kill you. And I think that's what did it."

"So," Scott said, leaning forward and putting his elbows on his knees, "what you're saying is you think it was an accidental overdose? You think she just took more than she could handle? You don't think she was trying to off herself?"

Aunt Missy put her hand on his back.

Tania shook her head. "No. Rosa didn't believe in suicide. She was raised Catholic and was sure that she would have a much worse fate if she ended her own life. And she was doing so well. She was going to try to find her boys, to make amends. She had too much to live for." She stopped talking and waited.

"What . . . what would she want us to do?" Carl asked. "Would she want to be buried? Would she want a funeral?"

"I don't really know," Tania said, "She was so young. We never spoke about things like that. But I think she would have been fine with whatever the two of you decided to do."

"I think we should have her cremated and throw her ashes in Carson Lake," Scott said. "I mean, why not? She used to take us swimming there. We should find out if it's legal."

"Are you serious?" Carl asked. "Carson Lake? Would you want to swim in ashes? This isn't India, Scott. I don't think they'll let us do that. But I do like the idea of releasing her ashes somewhere rather than burying her in the ground."

"I'll look into how to do that," Aunt Missy said. "But I have to ask you something, Tania. Why? Why was Rosa always so unhappy? What did we ever do to her to make her so angry? We tried so hard, Cecil and I, in the early days, but she just rejected us outright, and we had to fight to see our grandchildren. And she and Jack, they were never happy. Why did they stay together?"

"Mrs. Bishop," Tania said, "I can tell you all of this, but it might be very painful to hear."

"You can talk in front of all of us," Carl said. "We're all adults here. We have the right to know, and if you're the one who knows, we need you to tell us. Please, Tania."

"Okay," Tania agreed. "I can tell you what I know. So as you may know already, Jack and Rosa met in San Juan. Jack was there with a friend for a two-week break, and he met Rosa at a club. She was a twenty-one-year-old local, and she was very beautiful. They got together one night, and she sought him out the next night. They started an affair. She wanted to go back to the mainland with him when he left, but he didn't want that. San Juan was Rosa's reality, but not Jack's. This was just a vacation fling to him. But Rosa, she was the seventh child in a family of eight kids, and they were living in poverty. Her father, Pedro, was a very hard worker, and she adored him, but he was already old when she was born, and he couldn't do the kind of work he did as a young man. So resources were scarce. Rosa's childhood was tough, and I don't think her older brothers left her alone, if you know what I mean. She wouldn't talk about it, but it was always there. She would have done anything to get out.

"So after Jack left to go home, Rosa was thrilled to find out she was pregnant. She thought this would be her ticket to a better life. She knew how to track Jack down, because she had gone through his wallet and knew where he lived. So she contacted him, and told him she was expecting his child, and that he needed to bring her there to take care of them. Well, Jack wasn't at all interested, and he told her so. But Rosa was going to get her way. She was stubborn. She threatened him. If he didn't do the right thing, she would let her brothers know where to find him, and they would not be as kind as she was. So finally, Jack backed down, and he arranged for Rosa to come to Eastboro. Rosa wanted to get married, for the baby's sake, so they did. But Jack was not very happy about it.

"And soon, Rosa found out about the real Jack. She thought he drank a lot in San Juan because he was on vacation, but it turned out that Jack just drank a lot. And when he drank, he would either become very amorous, or very angry, and she never knew which it would be. He didn't actually hit her, or physically force her to do anything, but he would shout at her, and make threats, or belittle her, and it scared her.

Sometimes he would take off for days and leave her alone with little Scotty, and she would be frightened, but also relieved that he wasn't there.

"Rosa realized she needed to do something to make some money, just in case for some reason Jack cut her off, so when Scott was just three months old, she got her job as a housekeeper at the Breakaway Motel. And that's where she met me and Maria. We all became friends. Mrs. Bishop, you were taking care of the baby so she could work, and she was so grateful for that. Sometimes, we would even take her out for a coffee after work so she could get a break. But next thing we knew, Rosa was pregnant again, with Carlos. She didn't know what to do, so she just kept working, and then one day after work, she went to the hospital and had the baby.

"She was so proud of her beautiful boys and talked about them all the time. But now she couldn't work anymore and was staying home with the kids. Her extra money ran out. She feared that Jack would leave, and then one day, he threatened that he would. She didn't know how she would survive. By this time, her father had died, and she had no home to go back to in San Juan with two children. So she told Jack that she would never give him a divorce. It was against her religion, and she would fight him at every step if he tried to leave or cut her off. At that point, he told her he would stay married to her, but he would do whatever the hell he wanted, whenever he wanted. So that's what happened. And it went on like this for several years, and just thank Jesus she didn't get pregnant again. But things got really bad for Rosa when Carlos started school and they found out about his special gifts."

Chris felt his blood run cold. He saw Gram Missy shift in her seat to say something, but it was Carl who spoke. "What the hell are you talking about?" he demanded.

Aunt Missy leaned forward. "Carl, I swear, we were going to talk to you about this now, this weekend . . ."

"No, Gram, stop," Carl said. "Let Tania talk. What special gifts are you talking about?"

Tania looked around the room in confusion, and then back at Carl. "I'm so sorry, Carlos. I didn't know that no one told you."

"Rosa didn't let us," Aunt Missy pleaded.

"Tell me what?" Carl insisted. "Tell me!"

Both Chris and Kim reached out and put their hands on his knees, as if to restrain him.

"Carl, when you went to school," Tania started, "you could do things that other kids your age couldn't do. You could already read and write, and you understood numbers. You were putting puzzles together as a baby when other babies were just chewing on the pieces. You started taking things apart to see how they worked, and then put them back together. You were five! Rosa knew there was something special about you, but she didn't know what to do about it. In first grade, the teacher came to your mother and father and told them they wanted to test you at school. Your mom agreed because she wanted to know what was going on. When the test results were back, they met with your parents to discuss them. What they found out was that you had a high genius IQ. You were leaps and bounds above the other children in your grade. Probably two or three grades above you, too. They wanted to send you to a special school, where they could teach you more and better prepare you for your future."

"Wait," Carl said. "So they did tests on me and found out I'm an actual fucking genius? When I was six? I'm twenty-three years old right now, and people have known this since I was six, and no one ever thought to tell me? What the fuck?"

He stood and started pacing the room. Kim looked like a deer in headlights.

"But I never went to a special school," Carl went on. "Why? Why didn't they send me to the place where they could teach me better?"

Tania exhaled. "Your father didn't believe them," she said. "He didn't believe that your mother could have produced an actual genius, and he told her so. I think what he was thinking was that he himself wouldn't have been able to produce a genius child. He even insinuated that you might not be his, but I mean, look at you, Carl. You are definitely a Bishop. And your mom swore you were. But your father, he said no special school."

"He always told us it was her idea to keep him in regular school," Aunt Missy said. "He blamed her, said she couldn't handle having a genius for a son. He lied to us."

"Gram, I can't believe you knew about this and never said anything," Carl said angrily.

"We were going to tell you this weekend," Aunt Missy pleaded.

"We?" Carl asked. "Who else has known about this? Is it everyone but me? Kim, did you know?"

"No, I swear to you, Carl, I didn't know either. I'm just finding out," Kim said. "But it explains so much."

"Carl, it was just me and Cissy back then," Aunt Missy said, "until later—"

"I knew about it, Carl," Chris said, "but not until we graduated from high school. And your Gram's telling the truth. Your parents made her keep it quiet. She was just respecting their wishes. She only told me because she wanted me to talk to you about going to California. I didn't want you to go, so she had to tell me why it was so important to get you to Laine's. She knew being with Laine would be the best thing for you, and she was right, you have to admit. But Aunt Missy and I planned for me to tell you while you were here this time, now that your mom's gone. It's not her secret to keep anymore."

Carl sat down and put his elbows on his knees and lowered his head to his hands. "Scott?" he asked.

Scott shook his head. "I had no idea," he said. "I always knew that there was something odd about you, but I didn't know it was that you were an actual fucking genius."

"Tania, you said that my gifts made things worse for my mother," Carl recalled. "Why?"

"She felt like she wasn't the right mother for you," Tania said. "She felt she couldn't properly take care of you. She couldn't help you learn. She believed your father that she was stupid, and if you were a genius, you would surpass what she knew in no time flat. You would know the truth about her, and you would judge her. She couldn't stand the idea of you looking down on her."

"Scott," Carl said, tears starting to fall from his eyes. "You promised me it wasn't my fault. Before I left for California, you said that. But it was clearly my fault! She probably started using drugs because of me. She couldn't deal with me. You said it wasn't my fault!" He hung his head down and started to sob. Kim reached over and put her arms around him.

"Carl, baby, it's not your fault," she said softly. "You were a child! She was a full-grown adult! It was her job to take care of you, not the other way around. Think about it. While all this was going on, you and I were swinging on the swings in the playground at DeMarco and holding hands in the hallway. There's no way this is your fault."

"She's right, Carl," Aunt Missy said. "You didn't—"

"I don't want to hear anything from you right now," Carl snapped at his Gram.

"Carl—"

"And I'm not too thrilled with you either, Chris. Just give me some space, okay?"

He got up and walked to the guest room, and Kim followed him and closed the door.

Aunt Missy started to cry softly, and Gram Cissy went to her, put her arms around her, and talked to her in soothing tones.

Tania looked at Chris. "I'm so sorry," she said. "I didn't know it was a secret. I was just trying to help, so the boys could be at peace."

Chris nodded. "No, it's okay," he assured her. "Thank you. You did the right thing. It's our fault. We should have told him a long time ago. We need to fix this."

Tania started to stand. "I should go," she said. "This is a family matter now."

"Can I get your phone number?" Chris asked, standing up. "Just in case Carl has some questions later. And maybe we can let you know if we're having a service or something?"

He looked at Scott, and Scott nodded. Chris got a piece of paper and a pen and handed them to Tania. She wrote her number, and then Grandpa Clyde walked her to the door.

Chris looked at Scott. "Are you okay, man?"

Scott nodded. "Yeah, I guess," he said. "I just can't believe it. I mean, if what Tania said is true, that means that all the shit that Jack told us about Rosa over the years were lies. I mean, she's not an innocent party in all this, but I mean, maybe if she'd had a chance to find us, maybe we would have given her a second chance. I don't know. Now I'll never know." He looked down at his shoes.

There was silence, and then Aunt Missy came back over to Scott and embraced him. Chris looked at his Gram. She nodded. Chris got up to go find Michelle.

Michelle was in the kitchen with Mr. and Mrs. Mahoney.

"How much could you hear?" Chris asked them.

"We heard the shouting and the crying," Mrs. Mahoney said. "Then Michelle listened at the door and heard about the secret. She told us what she heard. Chris, Jack is a despicable person. How did I not see this growing up? How could I have been such a bad judge of character?"

Tears rolled down her face. Chris motioned her to stand and went over and gave her a hug. "Mom, it's okay," he told her. "It sounds like he had a lot of people fooled. Aunt Missy is a wreck. Maybe you could go to her. She can relate."

Mrs. Mahoney nodded. "Okay, that's a good idea," she said. "Kenny, can you come with me?" Mr. Mahoney nodded and followed her into the living room.

Michelle stood up. Chris went to her and put his arms around her. She held him tight. "That feels better," he said softly.

"Chris, I heard what he said to you," Michelle said. "He was just upset, angry. He's obviously a smart guy. He knows who's on his side. He'll come around."

Chris leaned down and buried his face in her hair. "He's my best friend. I am never, ever going to keep anything from him again. No more lies, no secrets." He let go of Michelle. "But I guess to be fair, he doesn't have to know that I confided in you."

"No, I agree," Michelle said. "But you need to tell him about us soon, before someone else does."

Chris nodded. "Yes. As soon as I can. I want him to know."

"I feel so bad for Gram Missy," she said. "She loves him so much. She just wanted to protect him."

The kitchen door opened, and Kim came in. "How is he?" Chris asked.

Kim bobbed her head from side to side. "He's exhausted and confused. And angry. But the anger will be the first to be resolved. He's in there now talking to Missy. He'll want to talk to you next. Are you guys doing okay?"

They both nodded. "Kim," Michelle said, "before we do anything else, we have to tell you something."

"We?" Kim said. "What is it?"

Michelle and Chris looked at each other, and Chris nodded.

"This may not be the very best time to tell you this," Michelle said, "but in the interest of not keeping secrets, Chris and I have been keeping a big one from everyone."

"Oh my God," Kim said. "Oh my God, just tell me."

"Kim, Chris and I are in a relationship. We're in love, and we have been for some time."

"No!!!!" Kim exclaimed. "Get out of here! No you aren't. You are? No!"

Chris laughed. "Yes, Kim!" he told her. "It's true! I love her. She loves me. It's the real thing." He put out his arm, and Michelle came to him. He kissed her ear. "I have to tell Carl, but to be honest, you two are the last to find out. We told everyone else yesterday."

"Yesterday!" Kim said. "Why? Why did you wait?"

"Long story," Michelle said. "But I will let you know the whole thing, I promise. I'll tell you while Chris is talking to Carl. But Kim, the one thing you need to know is that we've been together in some respect for a really long time. Like a really long time."

Kim looked at her suspiciously. "Like how long?" she asked. "Not in high school?"

"No, not that long. But almost. Kim, we hooked up at your wedding."

"My wedding? No! How? Where? Oh my God! It was you in the B&B that night, wasn't it!!"

Chris was impressed. "How did you work that out that fast?"

"It just makes sense now! Michelle, you came into the bathroom to take out your contacts. You said you were reading with your headphones on. But you never did that! You can't concentrate on reading and listening to music at the same time. Oh my God, I'm so stupid! Oh, but I'm so happy, too!" She threw her arms around Michelle's neck. "Oh, the pieces are all coming together now. Just the looks you gave each other, carpooling together . . . Oh God! I still don't get it. Why did you keep it a secret?"

Chris sighed. "Because we were kidding ourselves for three years that we weren't in love. That it was just an attraction. I mean, it was an attraction, for sure." He squeezed Michelle closer to him. "But we didn't know it was love until a few months ago. We broke up for a while, but now we're back together. Now we know, and we want our friends and family to know."

"Oh, okay," Kim said. "I get it now. That's why you came out to see us in June. That's what you were dealing with. Carl's gonna be so excited for you! Once he stops being angry."

Mrs. Mahoney came into the kitchen. "Aunt Missy is done with Carl now, Chris. He's ready to see you, if that's okay."

"Of course," Chris said. He kissed Michelle and started toward the door. His mother approached the girls, and he heard her say to Kim, "Oh, good Kim, they told you!"

Chris knocked on the guest room door, and Carl called, "Come in."

Chris turned the knob and stepped inside. Carl was sitting on the end of the bed. He motioned for Chris to sit on the desk chair.

"Carl," Chris started, "I'm so sorry—"

"No, let me," Carl said. "I get to go first. Chris, I talked to Gram, and she told me the whole thing about why she arranged for me to go to California to be with Laine. And that you knew about it. The whole thing blows me away, man. I mean, I'm really hurt that people didn't think they could just be direct with me, but then I think about what Tania just said about how messed up things were with my parents. Gram had to tread carefully. She did the right thing. Actually, the thing that blows me away the most, is that you encouraged me to go.

"I can't even imagine what that took for you. I don't know if I could have done the same thing if it had been me. I would have begged you to stay. Gram said it was hard for you, but you knew what was best for me because you loved me. I just thought people wanted me to go at first because they didn't think I could do anything on my own. They were right, actually. But I've been so fortunate in my life, Chris. I have four guardian angels, Gram, Kim, Laine, and you. That's four more than most people get. I had to get mad, you know that. Anyone would. But the four of you, I could never stay mad at. I love you guys so much. Just no more secrets, okay?"

Chris nodded. "Okay," he said, "no more secrets. After the one I'm about to tell you right now."

Carl nodded. "Is it that you and Michelle have been having a secret affair for over three years?"

Chris's head jerked back. "What?" he asked, stunned. "How could you possibly know that? Did Aunt Missy tell you?"

Carl shook his head. "No, man, I worked it out myself. Weren't you there earlier when Tania was talking? Chris, I'm a certified fucking genius! I know things! Did you already forget?"

Chris laughed. "Yes, Michelle and I are together. We're very happy now. But I need to know, how did you work it out?"

"Okay, man. Here it is. So after Kim and I, uh, consummated our marriage, we were hungry, so we were snacking in bed, when all the sudden we heard a couple getting it on in the other room. Kim thought it was hysterical. We kind of listened a bit to see who it was, and if maybe one of them would say the other one's name, but that didn't happen. But just at the point where it was coming to its, uh, natural conclusion, I heard some guy with your voice say 'oh my fucking God,' and I immediately knew it was you. It could only be you. But I didn't know who you were with until the next morning, when I saw the rooms everyone was in. I didn't tell Kim, you know, because I just wasn't sure how she would feel, because of your history and all, but I watched you. I saw the little looks between you and Michelle at brunch, and how you ran to her car to give her that jacket that was clearly not hers and to say goodbye. I was happy for you, and I was waiting for you to tell me about it, but you never did, so I thought that it was either just a one-night stand or you regretted it and were embarrassed."

Chris nodded. "At that moment, one-night stand. With one of my best friends. Confusing, but with totally no regrets. I just wasn't ready to talk about it yet."

"Yeah, that's okay," Carl said. "I've only ever had sex with one woman in my life. I don't know all there is to know about being a single adult. I forgave you. But then, I kept an eye on you when we came back for James and Sally's wedding. Then I got the clue I needed at the rehearsal dinner. You brought Michelle to your 'car' to get 'textbooks' for her 'mom.'" Carl made multiple air quotes. "C'mon, Chris, I knew you always sold your textbooks back. It was just too random. I don't know if you remember, but I asked you how it went when you got back. I was glad the two of you were still getting it on. But then after the reunion, you called and told me you had broken up with someone, and you sounded awful. I figured it had to be her. That's why I invited you out to California. I figured if you just lost Michelle, you wouldn't be okay alone for a while, and it was pretty clear that you weren't. I just wish you could have come to me earlier, Chris. Maybe I could have helped you more."

"You did help me," Chris told him. "You're always helping me. Just being able to talk to you helped. You're the first person I called that day. I needed to talk to you. Then when I was there, you gave me the space to try to heal. That's what I needed. Michelle and I finally just found our way back to each other, literally two nights ago, but the time we spent apart was like torture. God, it just always seems like someone's asking me to keep things from you, Carl, but not anymore. From now on, I'll just tell them no. No more secrets. And my apologies for ever keeping them."

"Accepted," Carl said and stuck out his hand. Then he pulled Chris to him for an embrace. "And along those lines, I have to tell you a little secret." He leaned in closer. "Kim's pregnant again."

"Oh my fucking God, Carl."

What Comes Next

Michelle had taken the week before Labor Day off. It was her planned vacation. She stayed in Eastboro with Chris. Eastboro schools didn't open until the following Tuesday, and he didn't have to present his lesson plans until Friday.

After getting together with their friends as planned on Monday afternoon, they went out shopping to get Michelle some underwear and clothes to get her through the week. They walked through the Main Street Mall hand in hand and bought cookies to share from The Cookie Place. Michelle showed Chris where she bought her prom dresses and shoes, and they remembered their time together at senior prom. They walked through the Hallmark store, and Michelle admired a stuffed koala bear on a shelf. Chris, remembering Carl's good choice with the giraffe at the same store years before, snuck it away when she wasn't looking, and bought it for her. He gave it to her when they left the store, and Michelle held it tightly in her arms as they walked back to Chris's car.

On Tuesday, they had dinner at Gram Cissy's house with Carl, who had extended his visit to help make final arrangements for his mother, while Kim went back home to be with their kids. Scott came by, along with Chris's parents and Scarlet. Melanie had already returned to BU.

After dinner, Aunt Missy and Gram insisted that Michelle must see the Bishop-Farmer wedding album, and then baby pictures of Chris. Michelle enjoyed the pictures and articles about the wedding that she had heard so much about since she was small. Chris smiled as the Grams told Michelle the stories that he had heard over and over again his whole life. Then Michelle opened the cover of Chris's baby album and gasped.

"Where did you get this photo?" she asked Gram Cissy.

Gram glanced at the picture Michelle was pointing to. "Oh, I took that at the hospital when Chris was born. That baby was right next to Chris in the nursery, and we thought she was so adorable, with that hair and that beautiful skin. Everyone was raving about her and taking snapshots. I just put it in here with the rest of the pack of pictures because it was so cute."

"Uh," Michelle said, looking at Chris. "Chris, you do know who that baby is, right? Take a closer look."

Chris leaned in and squinted at the photo. "It's the baby from Gram's photo book," he said. "I've been looking at it all my life, and . . . holy crap that little redheaded Troll doll is you, Michelle, isn't it?"

Everyone leaned in to look. They all looked skeptical. "What?" Michelle exclaimed. "Don't you think I know me when I see me? That's me! My father took almost the exact same picture, and it's in my parents' photo album. It makes sense! Chris was born on March 15th, and I was born on March 17th, and I'm assuming he was born at Eastboro Memorial, and so was I!" She looked closer at the picture. "So this little hand over here, on the right? Is that Chris?"

Gram looked, and then compared it to other pictures on the page. "Yes, I actually think that *is* Christopher's hand!"

Michelle started looking closer at the other pictures of Chris. "So that's me, right there," she said pointing. "You can see my foot. And in this one, you can see part of my face and a bit of my hair. Oh my God, Chris, this was our very first date!"

Chris looked at Michelle and grinned. She was so excited, she was bouncing on the balls of her feet. "This is amazing," he agreed. "These were taken five years before we thought we actually met. I can't believe after twenty-three years, we've finally identified the mystery baby, and she's my girlfriend!"

Michelle threw her arms around him. "This is a sign that we made the right choice, isn't it? We were meant to be together from the very start, there's no denying it now."

Chris held her tight and closed his eyes, not caring who was watching. "No," he said softly, "there's absolutely no denying it now."

The rest of the week flew by, as they assisted Carl with his tasks, visited with family, and went on nightly dates to dinner or the movies, both alone and with Sally and James. On Sunday night, they made love by candlelight in Chris's bedroom. Michelle would have to leave the next day to go back to Amherst for work on Tuesday morning, and they wanted a night to remember until they could be together again. After, Chris hovered over Michelle, kissing her face and her neck, and her mouth, wanting to memorize every taste, every texture. He looked into her eyes, and he knew at that moment that he never wanted to say goodbye to her again, even for a little while.

"I can quit my job. I'm sure I can find an opening somewhere in or near Amherst. I can teach any grade, math or science. There's got to be something there for me."

"No, Chris," she said. "You love working at Randall. They need you there. It's the place that made you want to become a teacher in the first place. No, I'll find a job in Eastboro. My family's here, it's close to Stephanie, and I'll be with you. That's all I want."

"But Michelle," Chris protested. "You love your job. I can't ask you to leave it."

"You're not asking me," she told him. "The truth is, Chris, I love my work, but I don't love my job. I love working in the treatment center, but they don't have a position for me. I worked myself ragged this summer to put in shifts to do the work I love. I can change my job. I can always find a nursing job. Nurses are in demand. Teaching jobs are scarce. Let me do this, Chris. I want to come to you."

Chris looked into her eyes, and never felt love so strong. It would have overwhelmed and terrified him two weeks earlier, but now, it motivated and drove him.

"Chelley," he said. "I was thinking about something Pete said about him and Carolyn last week. He said he saw no reason to wait once he knew he wanted to be with her. He made so much sense. Chelley, I don't want to make love to my girlfriend anymore." He paused. "I want to make love to my wife."

Michelle's eyes grew wide, and she opened her mouth to speak. Chris put his index finger to her lips.

"Chelley," he said, "will you marry me?"

Michelle's mouth dropped open and she gaped at him. Then tears ran down her face, and she put her arms around his neck and looked into his eyes. "Yes," was all she said.

He looked at her and didn't know what to do next. He thought maybe kissing her would be the right thing, so that's what he did. He didn't know what to say, so he just kept kissing her. Finally he pulled away, somewhat frantically.

"Chelley," he said. "I didn't plan this. I didn't know I was going to propose to you tonight. I don't have a ring. We need a ring."

Michelle laughed. "They have rings at jewelry stores," she told him. "Or you can use a twist tie like Carl did, I don't care! I just want to marry you. Nothing else matters, Chris. I just want us to get married."

"I don't see any reason for us to have a long engagement," Chris said. "But I do want a real wedding."

"Me, too," Michelle agreed.

"So let's just get married as soon as we can plan it. Let's do it soon. Oh my God, Chelley, I love you so much," He held her tight and rolled over on his back, pulling her on top of him and reaching for the back of her head.

Fifteen minutes later, they came up for air. "What time is it?" Michelle asked.

Chris looked at his bedside clock. "It's seven thirty in Seska, ten thirty here. Let's make the calls. You call Sally first."

The next morning, they were both awake and alert early. They lay in bed, looking at each other once they had both opened their eyes.

"It wasn't a dream, was it?" Michelle asked.

"No, it was a dream," Chris said, "but it was real."

"So we're getting married," she said, feeling the strange words on her tongue. "I'm going to be Michelle Mahoney."

"You don't have to change your name," Chris told her. "A lot of women aren't these days. Although I like the way it sounds. Chelley Mahoney. Michelle Rita Gorman Mahoney. Mrs. Mahoney. Oh God, that's my mother's name!"

Michelle laughed. "No, I want to change my name. I want us to have the same name. Mr. and Mrs. Mahoney. I like that."

"Speaking of Mr. and Mrs. Mahoney," Chris said, "I think we should get up and go see our parents before you leave. We have some things to talk to them about."

"Well, this is a surprise," Mrs. Gorman said when they all settled in to visit in the living room. "We weren't expecting to see you again before you headed back to Amherst, Michelle. I'm so glad you decided to stop by."

"Mom, Dad," Michelle started. She couldn't think of what else to say, so she deferred. "Chris has something to say." She looked at him pleadingly. He smiled.

"Mr. and Mrs. Gorman," he started. "I love Michelle very much, and I think you know we're very happy together. So last night, I asked Michelle to marry me, and she said yes."

Mrs. Gorman gasped and put her hand to her mouth. Mr. Gorman smiled. "Congratulations, you two. That's wonderful news! We thought maybe something like this was coming, especially when you showed up unannounced."

"Oh my," Mrs. Gorman said. "I thought maybe this was going to happen, but you never know how you'll react until you hear the news. I'm so happy for you both!"

Steve and Sam came through from the kitchen with their hands full of snack food. "What's going on?" Steve asked. "Family meeting we weren't invited to?"

Michelle grinned at her brothers. "Chris and I are engaged!" she said.

"Oh, great! Congrats," Sam said. "Can we drink champagne at the wedding?"

The twins sat down and simultaneously opened the wrappers to their granola bars.

"Have you picked a date?" Mrs. Gorman asked.

"Not yet," Michelle told her. "But we don't see any reason to wait a long time. It's already been three years. We're ready."

"What about winter break?" Mrs. Gorman suggested. "That way, Chris is off of work anyway, and that gives us three months to prepare."

Chris and Michelle looked at each other and nodded. "That would actually be great," Michelle said. "Kim's pregnant again, and she and Carl probably wouldn't be able to travel much later than that. Can we pull it together that fast?"

"We'll get the Grams on board," Chris told her. "They can make anything happen in record time."

"Can we be the flower girls?" Steve asked.

"I don't think so," Michelle said, giving him a look. "You're a bit too old and gangly."

"But you will be groomsmen," Chris assured them. "This is gonna be a Bishop-Farmer wedding. Everyone gets to do something."

"I'm gonna have Stephanie be my maid of honor, and Sally be my matron of honor," Michelle announced. "Then, of course, Darlene will be a bridesmaid, but I don't know if Kim will be up for it, being pregnant and all. And Sandra. Sandra's earned her place. And, of course, Melanie and Scarlet."

"Scarlet's cute," Sam said. "Can I walk down the aisle with her?"

"I think we might be able to arrange that," Chris said. "You might even get to dance with her at the reception. I'd like Drake to be in the wedding, too. Maybe he can be the ringbearer."

"Elena would be the cutest flower girl," Michelle suggested.

Mrs. Gorman beamed. "My little Chelley's getting married," she said. "And Steph will be so excited. You have to take her with you when you pick dresses."

"Of course," Michelle replied. "Stephanie will be part of this from the start." She turned to her father. "And I'm assuming you'll walk me down the aisle," she said affectionately.

Mr. Gorman smiled. "I would be honored," he told her. "I always imagined this day would come, but it's hard to believe it's here. For us, it seems like it's happening so fast, but for the two of you, it's been a long time. Gloria and I got married at nineteen and had our first child at twenty. I guess twenty-three seems a reasonable age."

Michelle got up to hug both of her parents then motioned Chris to do the same. Then she looked at the twins.

Sam held up his hand. "We're good, thanks," he announced.

They left soon for the Mahoneys. As soon as they walked in the door, Mrs. Mahoney said, "You've come here without calling. You have something to tell us, don't you? I have four brothers and sisters and nine hundred cousins. I know what an unannounced visit means."

Chris and Michelle laughed. "Yes!" Michelle said. She was going to say it this time. "We're engaged! We got engaged last night!"

"Oh, I was hoping that's what it was!" Mrs. Mahoney threw her arms around Michelle and then Chris. "Congratulations! Kenny! Scarlet! Come here! Chris and Michelle are here!"

They all sat down and talked about the early stages of planning their wedding. "I know Gram'll want to be involved," Chris said. "I remember Carl's wedding."

Mrs. Mahoney smiled. "I think my mother's expecting this news. She's been waiting for it since the day she found out about you two. You'll have to go by there before you leave today, Michelle. My dad will be so pleased, too. It's so nice to have something to look forward to now, after all this unpleasantness with Rosa this past week."

She motioned to her husband, and they excused themselves and left the room.

"Scarlet," Michelle said, "I would love it if you'd be one of my bridesmaids. I'm going to ask Melanie, too."

Scarlet smiled. "That would be so much fun!" she said. "Do I get to go to the bachelorette party?"

Michelle shrugged. "It depends on what Sally and Stephanie plan, I guess."

Scarlet nodded. "Are the twins in the wedding, too?"

"My twins?" Michelle asked, thinking of Sam's earlier request. "Yes, they'll be groomsmen."

"Do you think you could work it out so I can walk down the aisle with Steve?" Scarlet asked. "He's cute."

"What about Sam?" Chris asked. "He looks exactly like Steve. Would that work?"

Scarlet shook her head. "No, I'd prefer Steve," she said. "He's cuter."

Chris and Michelle looked at each other with confused expressions. "We'll see what we can do," Michelle told her. *Yikes,* she thought.

Mr. and Mrs. Mahoney came back. "Chris," Mr. Mahoney said, "I have something I want to give you. This belonged to my mother, and now I want you to have it. To do with whatever you choose." He handed Chris a small white cardboard box.

Chris lifted the top, and then quickly put it back down. "Dad," he said, "are you sure?"

Mr. Mahoney nodded. "She would want you to have it. And I noticed it might be something you need."

Chris stood up and hugged his dad. "Thank you so much, Dad," he said. "This means a lot."

He stepped in front of Michelle, and then got down on his knee.

"Michelle," he said, "I know I asked you this question last night, but I didn't do it quite right." He opened the box and held it out to her. "Michelle Gorman, Chelley, will you marry me?"

Michelle looked in the box. Inside, on top of a padded layer of jewelry cotton, sat a small silver band with a large diamond in the center, with a tiny ruby and diamond chip set on either side. Michelle put her hands to her face.

"Oh, Chris," she said softly. "It's so beautiful! Yes, of course I'll marry you!"

Chris took the ring between his thumb and index finger. "My grandmother was a very small woman," he told Michelle. "The ring might actually fit you. If not, I'm sure we could bring it to a jewelry store and get it adjusted easily."

Michelle held up her left hand, and Chris started to slide the ring onto her fourth finger slowly. It slid down the length of her finger and rested at its base. "It fits perfectly," Michelle announced.

Chris leaned toward her and put his arms around her. "It's another sign," he said. He kissed her and held her again. He held up her hand and looked at the ring, and then showed his parents and Scarlet. "It's perfect," he said.

The last stop was Gram's. When she opened the door, Chris handed her a piece of paper with the Gormans' phone number written on it. "What's this?" she asked.

Chris smiled at her. "Call them," he instructed her. He held up Michelle's left hand to show her. "You've got some planning to do!"

Gram made a happy surprised noise and threw her arms up in the air.

"Oh, Chris! Michelle! Congratulations! Clyde! The kids are engaged! Did you tell Carl? Of course you did! Oh, come in, let me make you both a sandwich! Let's talk!" She stopped. "Wait, let me call Missy real quick!"

The phone rang just then.

"That'll be Missy calling," Gram said. She picked up the phone. "Yes, they're here now," she said. "Yes, they're engaged! It's so exciting! Of course you can help!"

Grandpa Clyde came over and shook Chris's hand. "Congratulations, boy, you found a good one. Will there be champagne at this wedding? Cissy likes it when there's champagne." He hugged Michelle, then went back to his chair and picked up his *Reader's Digest*.

After they were done with their rounds, they returned to Chris's apartment. They sat on the couch and relaxed. Then Chris got serious.

"Chelley," he said, "we need to talk about something before you leave. Something I never told you because you didn't really need to know. But I don't want there to be any secrets between us at all, so I have to tell you before we get married."

"Okay," Michelle said, looking at him curiously. "Is it bad?"

Chris looked up to his left and thought. "Not bad," he said, looking back at her. "But maybe a bit uncomfortable. Everyone else involved knows, and we've all moved on, but I think if you're gonna be my wife, you have the right to know."

"Okay then, tell me." Michelle squirmed a bit in her seat.

Chris sighed and took a breath. "Okay, here goes. I told you a long time ago that I had a one-night stand that I regretted after. I think I told you about it the first night we were together, right?"

"Yeah, we were talking about our previous experiences. I remember, you had a one-night stand and a two-night stand," Michelle said.

"Right, so I told you that it happened, but I didn't tell you why I regretted it."

Michelle cringed. "Oh my God, Chris, you don't have a kid out there somewhere, do you?"

"No, no, nothing like that," Chris assured her. "I promise. What I regretted was how it happened." He paused. "And who it happened with."

"Tell me," Michelle insisted.

"It was at a party," he said. "I was pretty intoxicated. I was high. I wasn't planning on anything happening, but I saw her, and she was high, too. We didn't even say anything to each other. We just started kissing. And one thing led to another . . ."

"How old were you?"

"We were both fifteen, almost sixteen," Chris said. "And it didn't mean anything at all. For either of us. We never, ever, had anything happen again. It was consensual, Chelley, and we both regretted it, but we couldn't take it back once it happened. It led to some pretty major issues later, though. There were some hard times, and some hard feelings."

"Your one-night stand was with Kim, wasn't it?" Michelle asked. Chris looked at her, and then nodded. "I was at the party, remember, Chris? I started choking after taking a drag on a joint, and Darlene had to call her mom to come get us. Kim didn't want to leave, and she asked someone from one of her classes to bring her home later. We were gonna have James look out for Kim after we left, but he was making out with Cyndi Wells under the mistletoe, so we just left. Darlene called me the next morning and told me that Kim told her she lost her virginity to some guy at the party, and she was crying, but she refused to say who it was. I blamed myself, because Kim was distraught, and we had just left her there. That's why I've always remembered that night so clearly. God, Chris, it was you. Oh God. You said everyone knows. So Carl knows."

"Kim told him at junior prom," Chris said. "He was upset. He confronted me. I apologized and told him it meant nothing to me and I didn't want it to get in the way of him being with Kim. He forgave me, even though we both agreed that I really didn't do anything wrong. But everything changed after that. Nothing was ever the same with Carl and me. I mean, we're as close as brothers, closer even, but he changed after that night, and so did I. It took two years for me and Kim to finally talk it out, but we're totally at peace with it now, and we're good friends. We're family. I forget most of the time that it even happened, but it did. And you have the right to know."

"That explains Kim being upset when she came back to the room after going off with Carl at prom," Michelle said. "It explains a lot, actually." She sat silently for several seconds, averting eye contact, thinking. "I'm still gonna marry you," she told him. "This doesn't change anything. I promise. But oh my God, Chris, I'm gonna have to take a little time to absorb this information. Just like a few hours or something. Oh God, can I tell Kim I know? Is that okay?"

"No secrets, Chelley," Chris told her. "You can do whatever makes you feel comfortable. She'd probably be relieved that you know. We've all moved on. There are no victims here, just personal regrets. But from now on, no regrets."

Michelle nodded. "No regrets," she agreed. "Now everything is out there. And I still love you, Chris. That's not gonna change."

"I love you too, Chelley," Chris said. "Is there anything I need to know about your past?"

Michelle shook her head. "No, there really isn't," she said. "My life's pretty much an open book." She sighed. "The more I think about it, the more I'm glad it was you with Kim that night. I just kept imagining it was someone horrible, and that's why she was so upset. But that's not it. She was upset because she already loved Carl, and she thought she had messed everything up by having sex with his best friend. Chris, if she was with you, I know you were kind and gentle with her. And you kept her secret. I guess there's a lot to be said about that." She nodded. "Yeah . . . I'm going to marry the hell out of you, Chris Mahoney. Absolutely no regrets."

Chris smiled and took her hand. "Michelle almost-Mahoney, you are a remarkable woman. I am one lucky guy."

The Future Starts Now

Soon it was time for Michelle to get ready to leave. "Chelley," Chris said, putting his arms around her waist and pulling her close. "I don't want you to go. I'll come out there on Friday. Please give them your notice. I have savings from all my summers on the lawn crew. We can live on my salary and savings until you get a job here. Just don't stay away."

Michelle put her head back so he could kiss her neck. "Only one good thing came out of us breaking up this summer, and it's that I worked a ton of overtime. I have some savings, too. I'll give my notice tomorrow. And I'll let Sandra know it's time for me to go. Our lease is up at the end of October. I can pay rent until then, but I don't have to stay."

Chris pulled back. "So in two weeks, you'll be with me forever."

"Yes," she whispered back.

"We'll find our own place," he said.

"Yes," she said.

"So I probably need to tell Grant," he said.

"Yes!" Grant called out from behind his closed bedroom door. "I'm happy for you guys and all, but you know these walls aren't soundproof, right?"

Sally and James came over two weeks later to help unload Michelle's belongings from the U-Haul. First they came upstairs to get some cold drinks, as it was an unseasonably warm September day. Sally and James were uncharacteristically quiet. They looked tired and emotionally drained.

Michelle was concerned that they might have had a fight. She was going to wait to see if they talked on their own, but her concern overcame her. "What's going on, you guys?" she asked. "Sally, something's wrong. Tell me."

They all sat down at the table. "We were planning on coming here today and giving you guys some great news," Sally started. "Three weeks ago, I took a home pregnancy test and it was positive. We were so excited, but we waited to say anything when everyone was here for Carl because it was so early, and I wanted to get it confirmed by a doctor first. Well, we went to the doctor yesterday, and we were expecting to hear the due date and maybe even hear the heartbeat, but it turns out that there was no sign of any pregnancy. They even tried the ultrasound. The doctor thinks that I spontaneously aborted, and this morning, I got my period. There's no baby."

Tears started down Sally's cheeks. James scooted his chair up closer to hers and put his arms around her. She rested her head on his chest.

"Oh, Sally," Michelle said sadly. "I'm so, so sorry. I know how much you want kids. This must be devastating for you both."

Sally nodded. "I was so excited that Kim and I would have babies at the same time," she said. "Now that's not gonna happen. The doctor said there's no reason for us to think we'll have any trouble getting pregnant again, but it's just so hard to think about going through this again. I mean, we will. We'll keep doing it until it works, but it's so weird. I already wanted *this* baby, the one that will never be. I miss it."

James stroked her back. "I know, Sally," he said. "I was excited too. It's so hard."

"Do you need to skip the moving thing?" Chris offered. "I mean, Michelle and I can handle it if you need to go home and chill out."

Sally shook her head. "No," she said. "I need to be with you guys today. Jamie agrees. I'm not gonna lift anything, but I need to be with Michelle. Is that okay?"

Michelle nodded. "Of course," she said. "That's what best friends are for."

They sat together at the table talking softly for some time. Then Chris spoke. "Why don't James and I go start bringing things up, and you two just hang out here, okay? I think we can get it all pretty quickly. Michelle, I'll let you know if we need another set of hands for anything."

Sally and Michelle nodded gratefully. Once the men left, Michelle felt her tears rise. "Sally, what can I do to help?"

Sally looked at her hopefully. "I wanted to talk to you about that," she said. "I've been thinking about it. You could get pregnant with me. I mean, not right away. Like after you get married. We can have our babies together, and go through it together."

Michelle was speechless. Finally, she tried some words. "I don't know. I mean, Chris and I want to have kids, but I don't know when we'll want to start trying. But wow, that's an amazing thought, us having our babies at the same time, going through pregnancy, breastfeeding, raising tiny people. It's an exciting thought." She paused.

"Sally, I can't promise you I can do this, but I'll talk to Chris. Not right away, though. I mean, we're planning a wedding now. That's our priority. But I don't want you to stop trying in the meantime."

"Michelle, I need a break," Sally told her. "This might be the first positive test we've had, but this is not the first month we've tried. I won't stop having sex with my husband, but not with any intention for now. I'm thinking we'll start trying again in the new year. That seems reasonable. New year, new intentions."

"That should be the title of your novel," Michelle quipped.

Sally laughed. "Michelle," she said affectionately, "this is why you're my best friend. Only you could make me laugh while I'm in the middle of a miscarriage. I love you so much."

"I love you, too, Sally," Michelle said. She started planning how she would broach the topic of having babies with Chris.

The wedding was two months away. Chris and Michelle were living together in Eastboro in his apartment, and they were making plans for the future.

"The lease is up on this place in January," Chris said. "Grant's going to look for a place with Valerie, and we can either stay here and have you be the second on the lease, or we can try to find a smaller, cheaper one-bedroom apartment."

"What if we started looking into buying a house instead?" Michelle asked. "Maybe a small house, not too far from the lake. Near our families and near Randall. Maybe a big enough yard for a garden and a swing set."

Chris thought about it. "We could probably call Kim's mom. She's a great realtor and she could tell us if it was something we could do realistically." Chris paused. "A swing set? That's an interesting thought. How many swings are we talking about here?"

Michelle smiled. She loved it when Chris spoke in metaphors, like the sweat jacket. "I'm thinking, I don't know, maybe two or three swings?"

Chris shrugged. "Some houses have swing sets with four swings, like your house had. I'm thinking three or four swings would be okay, but it sounds like we're both okay with three swings. It's a good place to start."

"So Chris," Michelle said cautiously. "What would you say if I told you I wanted to start thinking about, you know, working on getting our first swing, like, early next year? Because I would kind of be interested in looking into that."

Chris froze. "You haven't already bought a swing and just not told me yet, have you?"

Michelle laughed. "No, Chris, I'm not pregnant. I promise. But after Sally had her miscarriage, she and I talked about it, and we thought since we both want, well, swings, that maybe we could think about trying to do it at the same time. I mean, I don't think it's that unusual for best friends to want to do that. We'd go through it together, and so would you and James. Just imagine what that would be like, experiencing that sort of thing with our friends."

"You have to say the word first, Chelley," Chris said playfully.

"What?" She laughed. "Okay, I'll say it. Baby. Babies! Now you say it."

Chris put his arms around her waist, and she put hers around his.

"Baby," he said. "Yes, Chelley, I would like to have a baby with you. A baby would be amazing. You and I make a family, but a baby, or several babies, would make us a posse. Let's start trying in the New Year. I'll call Mrs. Drake to see if we can afford a place to put up that swing set." He pulled her in close. "And in the meantime, maybe we can stay here and rent month to month."

Michelle felt butterflies dancing in her stomach. This was her life. Her real life was starting, the life she had chosen. Chris was choosing to be there with her. And they were going to be a posse.

A month before the wedding, RSVPs started to arrive in the mail. The Farmers and the Bishops from Seska had bought their plane tickets. Hotel rooms were being booked. Michelle's dress was being altered. And the bridesmaids had found their dresses—a compromise between Stephanie and Sally, who both looked beautiful in blue. The bridal party met at the store, and everyone was fitted. Stephanie was so overjoyed to be included that Michelle felt that the whole event was already a success, even before the ceremony occurred.

Chris and Michelle registered for gifts, and three weeks before the wedding, the bridal party threw Michelle a shower at Gram Cissy's house. They hired James to make the cake and food for the party. Michelle opened her gifts, and her attendants stuck the ribbon bows to her back. Sandra took notes on what she said after each gift was revealed.

"These are the things that Michelle will say to Chris on their wedding night," Sandra said after all the gifts had been opened. She read her list. "'Oh my God, I've always wanted one just like this!' 'I had one sort of like this in high school, but this one is much bigger.' 'I'm not one hundred percent sure this will fit, but we'll give it a try,' 'Oh, wow, it's so soft!' 'Oh, thank you so much, I didn't think anyone would ever be able to find it, but you did!'"

Michelle was laughing so hard she almost dropped her cup of punch. Darlene made Michelle stand up and spin around. When she was done, Darlene told everyone, "The number of ribbons left stuck to Michelle's back will be the number of babies she and Chris will have." She counted. "Seven," she said. "Oh, wait, another one fell off. Six. Six babies. Michelle, do you want them all at once, or one at a time?"

Michelle laughed. "One at a time," she said. "And maybe just three. And I checked on it. Identical twins don't run in families. Fraternal twins do, but neither family has any of those, so I don't think we have to worry about multiples."

The cake was served. Once everyone was done, they went around the room and gave Michelle advice for her marriage.

"Tell your husband you love him, every morning and every night, even when he pisses you off," Gram Cissy told her.

"Always remind him of your birthday and your anniversary in advance," Aunt Missy said. "If you don't, and he doesn't remember, it's a set up, and it just ruins your day. If you make sure he remembers, you both have a good time."

"Always tell your husband what's upsetting you," her future mother-in-law advised. "Don't make him guess. He will never guess right, even if he really wants to."

"Touch him all the time," her own mother suggested. "Just a little touch, on his arm, on his face, on his chest. Remind him that touch is important by touching him. Even in public."

Sally went last. "Treasure him," she said. "Let him know how important he is to you, and how special he makes you feel, every day. And when anything big happens, call your best friend. She wants to know!"

Michelle was tearful once everyone had spoken. She was so grateful for her community, her family and friends. She couldn't believe that in just a few weeks, she would be married to Chris Mahoney. And everyone here was celebrating her and her happiness. She had been to several weddings, but she had never quite understood. Now she did. She would never take her marriage for granted. She would take the opportunity of her wedding to celebrate her love with Chris and their guests, but she would somehow continue to celebrate in some way every day thereafter.

The shower ended, and Chris arrived to help haul off all the gifts. He was amazed at the pile of presents before him. "Wow," he said. "We are gonna need a bigger place. These are only shower gifts. We might need to get a truck for the haul we're gonna get on our wedding day from the Bishops and Farmers."

Michelle threw herself into his arms. "I'm so glad you're here," she whispered to him as he closed his arms around her. "We are so lucky, Chris. We are so loved. We have to remember this forever."

Chris laughed. "It's our wedding," he told her. "We'll remember it forever. That's also why we have a photographer!"

The week before the wedding, Michelle got a welcome call. When she hung up, she had to talk to someone. She thought about it. Chris was at school. She couldn't call unless it was an emergency. Her friends were all at work. Then she thought of her mother. She quickly punched her number into the phone.

"Mom!' she said. "I got the job! At the treatment center! It's my dream job. Aaaah!"

"Michelle, that's great!" Mrs. Gorman said. "Oh my goodness, it's all coming together for you now, isn't it?"

Michelle gasped. "Don't say that!" she said. "That's what they say in movies right before everything goes wrong!"

Mrs. Gorman laughed. "Michelle, we aren't magical," she reminded her. "We can't make everything go wrong with our words!"

"Okay, Mom, well just tell that to my panic attack, alright? But yes, it's so exciting! One more week until I'm married, and then I go to Cancun, and then I get to be married even when I get back from Cancun!"

"Yes, that's how it works, Michelle," her mother agreed. "You and Chris will be here tomorrow night for dinner with Chris's Gram and Grandpa so we can wrap up the final details, and then it's almost time for the wedding. When are you picking up your dress?"

"Wednesday."

"When is Chris getting his tux?"

"Thursday."

"When do the best man, ring bearer, and flower girl arrive?"

"Thursday also."

"And when do you start work?"

"I have no idea," Michelle admitted. "Human resources said the manager will call me this week. I hope they call me before Thursday, or else they may have a long time before they hear back from me."

The manager called that afternoon, and Michelle let her know that after Saturday she would officially become Michelle Mahoney, and she wouldn't be available for three weeks because she was getting married. They told her they would have her start orientation in three weeks and congratulated her on her pending nuptials.

By the time Chris came home from school that day, Michelle had it all arranged. She would start her job the second week of January after they got back from Cancun. And at the same time, they would start "shopping for swing sets." She and Chris celebrated with dinner out and a practice session for their honeymoon.

The Scheme of the Schemer

Chris and Michelle couldn't leave during their own rehearsal dinner for clandestine sex. Nor did they want to. Their relationship was public now. Their joining would be condoned. No more sneaking around. The night before their wedding went quickly, and soon it was time for their celebrations with their friends.

Sally and Stephanie planned the girls' night out together, and they included Scarlet and Melanie, who were still under twenty-one. They found a Chinese restaurant that rented a room with a karaoke machine. The older guests could purchase drinks from the bar, and the younger ones, and Sally, could still have nonalcoholic beverages. They ordered platters of appetizers for the group.

Darlene was excited about singing with her friends. She pored over the list of songs, choosing the ones she knew the words to, and the ones she thought Michelle would enjoy. She was the first up to sing, and she made Kim, Traci, Sandra, Carolyn, and Sally join her. They sang "Going to the Chapel." Darlene followed with a solo of "White Wedding," and then she dedicated the song "You're Having my Baby" to Kim. Everyone laughed.

Stephanie sang a couple of songs, and then Scarlet and Melanie sang some popular duets. Traci declined the microphone, saying she needed a few more drinks to get up her nerve. "My Guy" came on, but Michelle would only sing if Sally and Stephanie sang with her, and then she bowed out, laughing. Sandra sang "My Girl," and all of Michelle's friends joined her.

Michelle glanced over and saw Traci across the room, holding a cocktail. Traci looked at her and gave her a conspiratorial grin. Michelle had had it. She needed to know why Traci always looked like they were sharing a secret when she saw her. She walked over to her, gently took her arm, and led her to a table to sit.

"Traci," she said, "you've been doing that since Sally's wedding. You smile at me like there's something I'm supposed to know, but I don't know what it is! Please, let me in on the secret."

Traci grinned at her. "You really don't know, do you?"

Michelle shook her head. "No, I really don't."

"Okay, then," Traci said, nodding. "I'll fill you in. I've known for a very long time that you and Chris were meant to be together."

"You did?" Michelle asked. "Like, your intuition?"

Traci nodded. "I mean, way back in high school, I didn't know. I just thought that both of you weren't with the right people, but you would be some day. I knew when you found the right people, you would both be happy for the rest of your lives. I just didn't know at the time that it would be with each other."

"When did you know?" Michelle asked.

"It was that night at Chris's apartment, before Kim and Carl's wedding, when Darlene brought me and Paul there from the airport. You and I were talking at one point and you mentioned getting together with Chris during Christmas break. I know nothing happened, but that intrigued me even more than if something had happened."

"Why?"

"Because if there were no feelings, no latent attraction," Traci explained, "I think the two of you would have hooked up that night casually. It would have been no big deal. You would have moved on after like nothing had happened. But you didn't. So I watched you. I watched Chris go sit with you in the kitchen when you were holding baby Drake. I watched you talk to Chris while he was checking me out during the rehearsal at the B&B. I watched both of your body language. I watched you during the rehearsal dinner. I saw you talking to Pete and glancing at me and Chris. And then I made my decision."

"What decision was that?" Michelle asked.

"I decided to do whatever I could to help make the two of you look at each other in a different way."

"Traci," Michelle said skeptically, "you were flirting with Chris all through that dinner! We all saw it."

"Yeah, I was," Traci admitted. "Pretty crappy of me, right? With my boyfriend sitting right next to me. What a jerk, huh?" She giggled. "Well, there was something I remembered about Chris. I knew he had very strong feelings about never being unfaithful, or being involved with someone who was being unfaithful. So I flirted with him because he was checking me out, and I knew it would freak him out. And then, later that night, I started telling him all sorts of stuff about you. All true stuff. Like how beautiful you had turned out, and how great you were. He said he hadn't noticed how hot you had gotten, so I kept talking about it. Then he started looking. I could tell. And then the next day, he started looking even more. I was watching, during the pictures and during the ceremony. I could see what was going on with the two of you."

Michelle contemplated. "The night before the wedding," she finally said, "we were all in Kim's room, and you started talking about Chris probably being a good dad. You said he'd turned out pretty hot. I thought you were actually considering going after him, and I thought that seemed weird. But then, you told me to look at him again. To try to look at him with different eyes, like I was meeting him for the first time. And the next day, during the ceremony, I did just that."

"And he saw you doing it, too, and it intrigued him. Because he already had the thoughts in his head from the day before, what he and I had been talking about, and it was on his mind. And then there you were, checking him out."

"Holy crap, Traci, what are you, some kind of magical wizard?"

Traci laughed. "No," she said. "Well, maybe. But I just made you two look at each other. I couldn't make you see anything that wasn't really there. That was all you. Everything from that point on was you. Then I just watched." She giggled. "And heard. That night."

Michelle felt her cheeks grow warm. "Oh, my God," she said. "We were trying to be so discreet, but it sounds like everyone heard us! That's so embarrassing!"

"It was wonderful," Traci told her. "Knowing that the two of you had connected. That's what I was hoping for. Watching you sneak peeks at each other at brunch the next day, and Chris running up to your car with some lame excuse to say goodbye when you left. And no one else even seemed to catch on! I'm just sorry it took so long for the two of you to realize you were in love. I knew the whole thing would be confusing at first, but I thought it would happen faster. I underestimated the effects of your baggage from your past relationships. Plus, I was kind of caught up in my own drama with Paul at the time, so I was distracted. But none of that matters anymore. You're together now, and you're happy. And it's gonna last. The two of you have so much love, and you'll have so much to give your family."

Michelle smiled at the thought of their family. The swing set. The posse. She reached over and hugged Traci. "Traci," she said softly, "thank you so much for setting our love story in motion."

"Can I tell you a little secret?" Traci asked. "I think that your love story is even more amazing than James and Sally's. Or Carl and Kim's. Because even though their love is beautiful, and enviable, you had to go through so much more to get to each other. You've been meant for each other since the day you were born, but it took you years to come to that conclusion, and so much time and struggle. It was like an epic journey, where you had to fight monsters, cross chasms, and learn lessons. And in the end, you were victorious. Your love conquered all. Now that has all the components of an epic love story if I've ever heard one. And thank you for letting me have even the smallest part in it."

Michelle could feel tears rising, and she'd be damned if she let them ruin her eye makeup.

"Let's go pick a song," she said to Traci. "I think my alcohol level is high enough for me to feel brave. Come, sing with me."

They got out of their chairs, and Michelle grabbed Traci's hand and led her to the list. They picked "In My Life," by The Beatles, and when it came on, all of her friends sang it together.

Bowling and Beers

Chris and his friends were not strip club types of people, but they all, except for James, did enjoy a few beers every now and then. However, since their party included Sam and Steve, they decided to go bowling.

"This is where Kim and I had our first real date," Carl told Chris.

Chris smiled. "Good choice, then."

The snack bar sold beer, and the over-twenty-one members of the party sipped from plastic cups between their turns. Sam and Steve snuck sips from the cups while the owners were taking their turns, but no one made any attempts to stop them. As always, James was the designated driver, so the group let loose.

When Pete and Grant started getting drunk and throwing gutter balls, it was time to end the night. Chris didn't want his groomsmen stumbling down the aisle on his wedding day. James dropped him and Carl off at Gram Cissy's house, and they all planned to meet up the next day at Gram's to prepare for the wedding. Carl retired to his room with Kim and the kids. Seeing that Kim had returned, Chris picked up the phone and called the hotel. Seconds later, Michelle was on the line.

"I just wanted to say good night," he told her. "Did you have fun tonight?"

"I did," Michelle said. "I'll tell you all about it later. But it was great. Did you have fun?"

"I'm not the best bowler," Chris admitted, "but it was a good time. It would have been more fun if you were there."

Michelle sighed. "Same here. I wish you were here with me now."

"Me too," Chris said. "But after tomorrow . . ."

"We'll always be together," Michelle finished for him. "I can't wait."

"What are you wearing right now?" Chris asked.

"Hold on a second," Michelle said. There was a pause. "Okay, to answer your question, I am now wearing nothing but a smile. And I'm on my bed. It will be our bed tomorrow night. What about you?"

"Hold on," Chris said. He pulled off his jeans and his shirt and crawled naked into his bed. "I'm in bed naked and thinking of what I want you to do. But I'm at Gram's, so we have to be quiet."

"Okay," Michelle whispered, giggling. "I'm running my hands over your chest, and now I'm kissing your neck. Can you feel it?"

Chris shuddered. "Oh, yeah," he said softly. "And I'm flipping you on your back and kissing your gorgeous breasts, and running my hands down your body . . ."

"Oh, yeah," Michelle muttered. "Now you're kissing my belly button, I can feel it. Don't stop there, keep going . . ."

Chris told her what he was going to do next, and she moaned her consent. This exchange went on for several minutes, until they both were lying relaxed on their backs, three miles away from each other, in different beds.

"Why didn't we ever do that before?" Chris asked. "Between seeing each other?"

"Because we never thought of it," Michelle said. "We're idiots. No time like the present, though, to try something new."

They stayed on the phone for several more minutes, and then agreed they needed to try to get some sleep. Tomorrow was going to be a very big day for them both.

I Want to be Mahoney

The morning of the wedding finally arrived. Michelle woke to knocking on her hotel room door, and after she shook the cobwebs from the previous night loose in her brain, she got up to open the door. It was Sally and Stephanie, who had shared a room for the night, and were now making sure that Michelle was awake and on track for her big day. These women took their bridal team roles seriously.

"We've booked the three of us a spa mani-pedi in the salon downstairs, and they'll supply us with delicious breakfast foods while we soak our toes," Sally said. "And then the makeup and hair lady will come and fix us all up after. We'll get dressed here, and then a limo comes and takes us to the chapel to start taking pictures. After the ceremony, you and Chris get a private ride from the chapel to the hotel for the reception. And Michelle?"

"Yeah?" she said, covering a yawn with her hand.

"Pay attention to every moment, okay?" Sally told her. "It's gonna go so fast. Just revel in it. Don't rush anything. Let everyone else take care of things. Steph and I will make sure everything goes perfectly on our side, and Carl knows what to do for the groomsmen. So have fun, okay?"

Michelle smiled. "I will have fun," she promised. "But first I need to submerge my exhausted self in shower water. I'll be quick."

Soon, the three women were sitting in massaging spa chairs with their feet soaking in soapy water. They all sipped on virgin mimosas, otherwise known as orange juice in a large glass. Stephanie was enjoying feeling sophisticated and worldly. She had recently been on a movie date with a man from a different supported apartment program, whom she had met at an outing, and had received her first kiss at the door at the end of the night. She had been giddy ever since and was talking about scheduling a follow-up date. She had wisely decided not to invite him to the wedding, since she would be so busy taking care of Michelle.

When the spa treatment was done, Michelle received a French manicure, as brides often do. After all three of them had their polish applied, they went back to the room to meet the other bridal party members. They ate sandwiches from room service between hair and makeup. Michelle played her *Rubber Soul* and *Revolver* CDs, her two favorite Beatles albums. She and her mom sang along with every song. Once the group was all dolled up, it was time to dress the bride.

At Chris's parents' house, Chris and Carl were having a quiet morning. They had showered, but not yet dressed in their tuxes, as they were awaiting the arrival of the rest of the groomsmen. Chris was making some last-minute adjustments to his vows and reading them back to Carl.

"I can't believe you two decided to write your own vows," Carl said. "I've never known anyone who's done that before. Aren't you nervous to do it in front of all the people?"

Chris smiled. "Dude, I'm a middle school teacher," he said. "If a group of twenty-five eighth graders doesn't faze me, then I don't think a room full of Bishops and Farmers could do a thing to me. Plus, I only wrote the first half. Michelle and I wrote the second half together. Just tell me if my vows sound okay."

Carl nodded. "They sound great," he said sincerely. "I still can't believe you're marrying Michelle Gorman. It feels like it happened so fast. I mean, you guys went public, and then like, three months later you're getting married. I know it wasn't just three months for you, but to everyone else, it's like you crammed all this great stuff into such a short time. Well, I can say, though, that you seem happier than I've ever seen you in our whole lives, so I know you made the right choice."

Chris smiled. "Is this all from the top of your head, or are you rehearsing your best man speech? Because that's some good stuff in there."

Carl snickered. "Naw, I'm just warming up," he said. "I'm gonna have the whole Farmer family weeping their sensitive little eyes out, you'll see."

"Chris!" Mr. Mahoney called up the stairs. "The guys are here."

Chris and Carl went downstairs and greeted James, Pete, Grant, Sam, Steve, and Mr. Gorman in the den. Pete and Grant appeared to be nursing slight hangovers from the previous night but swore they would feel better after they had some food. They ate lunch, then the tuxes were distributed to each of them, and they put them on. Gram Cissy had arranged for a limo for the groomsmen, fathers, and grandfathers of the groom, and now they waited.

Chris missed Michelle. He thought it would have been fun for them to do all of this together. If he had it to do over, he would plan for them to skip the traditional separation of bride and groom on their wedding day. He'd had some say in planning their day, but this part had been non-negotiable with the Grams. He felt that on the day they committed to be together for the rest of their lives, they should have been allowed to wake up together in the same bed, maybe even make love before getting up, and revel in the excitement of their celebration all day long. He reminded himself that after today, they would never need to be separated again, and that's what he wanted. No more goodbyes.

Soon, everyone was on their way to the wedding chapel, and Michelle was in the bridal room with her friends and her mother, waiting for her cue. She had already posed for several pictures by the altar, with friends and family, and even groomsmen, but not yet with her groom. She was physically craving his presence. She knew it wouldn't be much longer, but it was hard to wait, to be social, and talk to people when all she wanted was his arms around her. She felt so cliche, but if she was, that was okay. She was the bride. It was her day.

Finally the time had come. Everyone else had gone already, and they were ready for her to start her trek down the aisle. Suddenly, she felt self-conscious and shy. Her father held her right arm and stood up tall and proud. Michelle took this as her cue. She would be strong. That was her thing. She lifted her chin slightly and gave the world a taste of her ginger attitude. She and her father started their walk. She saw Chris. And he saw her. And then she *was* strong. And then they made eye contact, and her knees went weak. But she made it. And her father kissed her cheek. And she took Chris's hand. And everyone else disappeared, except Michelle and Chris. And then a voice, talking about them, and them being together, forever. *Yeah,* she thought. *That's good. That's exactly what I want.*

Chris became lost in Michelle's green eyes and forgot that he was standing in front of his friends and family. He held her hands tight and would not let go. He would never let go. Well, maybe to eat, use the bathroom, and he couldn't really bring her to school . . .

It was time for their vows. Chris went first. He brought out a folded piece of paper, mostly as a prop, and held her other hand.

"Michelle," he started. "My Michelle. I don't know if I can say it any better than Paul McCartney did, but I'll try my best. Michelle. My Chelley, you are the most beautiful, the strongest, the smartest, and the most wonderful of all creations on this planet, and the fact that I somehow found you amid billions of other humans just astounds me. That I get to be lucky enough to be able to wake up every day with you by my side, to hear you speak, to watch you listen, to know your smile. I am the luckiest man in the world, and I will never forget that. I am absolutely and totally smitten with you. I promise you, I vow to you, that you will never, ever be alone again.

"Michelle Rita Gorman, my Chelley, I promise that I will love you, cherish you, adore and admire you, support you, encourage you, trust in you, take care of you and let you take care of me, and be your partner and friend for the rest of our lives."

Michelle had forgotten about her eye makeup, and now it was doomed with her tears. It was her turn to make vows to Chris.

"Chris," she started, "you have brought a love and a friendship into my life that I never thought I could ever feel. You make me happy, you make me strong, and you make me want to be a better person. You believe in my dreams, and I believe in yours, and now our dreams belong to each other. We found each other in plain sight many years after we first laid eyes on each other, and our timing couldn't have been more perfect. I am one smitten kitten. Chris, I promise you today, that we will never, ever say goodbye to each other again.

"Christopher Jerome Mahoney, I promise that I will love you, cherish you, adore and admire you, support you, encourage you, trust in you, take care of you and let you take care of me, and be your partner and friend for the rest of our lives."

Now tears streaked both of their cheeks. "Damn those Farmers," Chris whispered, and Michelle laughed.

The officiant continued to speak, and then asked for the rings. Drake, who was well versed in the tasks of ring bearing, presented his tiny pillow to his father, and Carl handed them to the bride and groom. Michelle and Chris repeated the proper words and slipped the rings on each other's fingers. They were then told to kiss as a married couple.

They looked into each other's shiny wet eyes and smiled, and then slowly moved toward each other and their lips met. Every kiss was still like the first, but this one brought massive applause. They were married. They were introduced as Mr. and Mrs. Mahoney, and then they started to recede up the aisle to the Beatles song "Here, There, and Everywhere."

There was much hugging and kissing, as well as ado and picture-taking as soon as the ceremony ended. Finally, Chris and Michelle were able to escape to their private limo to head to the reception. It was a ten-minute ride, but they asked the driver to take it slow and to possibly park somewhere for a few minutes of alone time. As soon as the car pulled away, they put their hands on each other's cheeks.

"We did it," Michelle said.

"We did," Chris agreed.

"And everyone knows it."

"They do."

"You're my husband now."

"And you're my wife."

"You said some amazing things about me."

"And you said some amazing things about me."

"Shut up and kiss me," Michelle said, pulling him toward her.

They made out in the back of the limo like horny teenagers going to the prom, and by the time they arrived at the hotel, they were ready to face all the people.

Michelle had not realized how much being a bride involved hostessing. She and Chris were expected to travel from table to table to greet their guests. She knew, in theory, that there were a lot of Bishops and Farmers, but to see them all in one room was overwhelming. And Chris not only knew all of their names; he also knew all of their personal trivia and the names of their children and grandchildren. This was Chris's Farmer charisma, a side of him she had always heard stories about but had never seen. They all seemed to adore him. She could understand. She did too. Her favorite part of the reception was when people rang the "kiss bells" on their tables, and she and Chris had to stop what they were doing and kiss. She wondered if this was something she could do in the future at home to end fights or disagreements, if they ever had any.

There was a meal, then the traditional dances. Then it was time for the best man and the maid and matron of honor to give their toasts. Stephanie went first because she was so eager.

"Hello," she started out, holding up her glass of sparkling cider. "Chelle is my sister, and my best friend. She told me Chris was only sort of her boyfriend, but now they're married, so I think they changed their minds. She let me help pick out the dresses, and she looks like a supermodel! Chris looks kind of like a Ken doll. If they have babies, I'll be their aunt, and I'm going to be a great aunt and I'll give them cookies and ice cream. I hope they all have red hair. I hope Chelle and Chris are really happy. I like it best when Chelle is happy, because then she's a lot more fun. So I need to tell Chris to keep making her be happy, okay Chris? Okay, everyone can drink their drinks now. Thank you."

Everyone applauded and toasted the couple. Michelle got up to give Stephanie a big hug as the microphone was handed to Sally.

"Hello, I'm Sally, the matron of honor, and I can't say anything better than what Steph just said. Chris makes Michelle happy. And Michelle makes Chris happy. Both of these humans deserve every second of happiness they have. I met Michelle in art class in seventh grade. She immediately accepted me as her friend and brought me into her friend group. Every single member of that group is here today. We have all grown together over the years, and we knew everything there was to know about each other. Or so we thought. No one, and I mean no one, including Michelle or Chris, would ever have expected us to be gathered together someday to celebrate these two getting married. As a matter of fact, some of us are still getting used to the idea, but it's an idea we can totally get behind. These are two of the kindest, most loyal, dependable people you could ever meet, and when these two make a promise, you know that promise will be kept. You know if they get behind you, and support you, that you are fully and totally supported. Michelle, you are my best friend, and Chris, you are my real, grown-up friend, and I love you both so very much. To Chris and Michelle, may happiness be yours today, and for all the days of your life. L'chaim."

Sally wiped tears out of her eyes as she embraced the new Mr. and Mrs. Mahoney. Then she passed the microphone off to Carl.

"Hi, I'm Carl Bishop. I'm the best man and cousin and best friend of the groom, and a lifelong friend of the bride. I am so happy to finally have the chance to talk about this guy, and what he means to me. As some of you might know, Chris and I have basically been together since the day I was born, exactly six months to the day he was. He took it upon himself from a very young age to protect me and make sure I was always okay. I'm talking about since the age of five, and he's still doing it now. He made sure that I was safe, and fed, and never left out of anything that he was involved in. He made sure no one ever messed with me. I am who I am today because Chris Mahoney gave a damn about me. And that's just who Chris Mahoney is. He's a guy who gives a damn about what happens. That's what makes him such an awesome teacher, and such an amazing friend. Imagine someone who always has your back, even when you're wrong. Someone who believes in you that strongly.

"And then there's Michelle, the little redheaded spark plug from our childhood, with her strong opinions and her fierce loyalty. And basically, just her fierceness. Her protectiveness. Her kindness, and her humor. These two, together, while I never would have predicted it, now I can never imagine it any other way. These two will do things together that will be amazing. I can't wait to see what happens next. Their love story may be in its early chapters, but I know all the plot twists and turns will be exciting and captivating, and the ending will always be happy.

"So on behalf of my wife, Kim, and our children, Elena and Drake, who is Chris's godson, I raise my glass to Chris and Michelle. My true brother and my wonderful friend. May you have decades of happiness with each other, and may you always be surrounded by the love and support of your family and friends."

Michelle glanced at the Farmer tables and saw them all dabbing their eyes with formal handkerchiefs. She smiled as she dabbed at her own. She and Chris embraced Carl, and then moved down the line to hug the rest of their wedding party.

Just as Sally had said, the celebration passed quickly, and it was almost time for it to end. But the night was still young. Michelle couldn't wait to get her husband out of his wedding suit and into his birthday suit. She knew he felt the same. True to form, they had been building up the anticipation all day with looks and touches. They even had private signals and signs. Now they were saying good night to their guests, but they were secretly planning their next move.

And soon enough they were in the bridal suite, and their wedding clothes were sliding to the floor. Their lips were frantically moving over each other's bodies and their hands were in motion.

"We have all night," Chris whispered. "Let's take it slow."

"I can do slow," Michelle answered, as she took his hand and led him to the bed.

PART FOUR

AND THEY ALL LIVED HAPPILY EVER AFTER

What Chelley Forgot

After the honeymoon, Michelle went off the pill. She heard it would take some time to get the hormones out of her system to get ready to get pregnant. She and Chris decided not to actively try to get pregnant yet, but they also didn't do anything to stop it if it happened on its own. They were newlyweds. They felt like every day was still their honeymoon, and they took advantage of that feeling.

Michelle started her new job at the oncology treatment center, and she knew right away that she would love it there. She even recognized one of the rounding doctors, who had previously taught at her nursing school. Everyone was welcoming, and they could all tell that Michelle was the right person for the job.

In March, Mrs. Drake assisted them with making an offer on a three-bedroom, one-and-a-half-bath house on the east side of the lake, less than one mile from each of their parents' homes. The offer was accepted. The house had a small, neat front yard, but a big backyard with plenty of room for a garden and a large play structure with a swing set. They planned to purchase a grill and picnic table and one day build a deck. The closing date was set for mid-April.

Michelle also started keeping track of her ovulation, and they made their first attempt to conceive. She was disappointed when her period arrived as scheduled, but she also knew she was young, and she had time. It could take months. She was prepared to keep trying.

In May, Michelle, Chris, Scott, and the Grams flew into San Francisco and took a shuttle to Seska to meet their newest family member, Kim and Carl's infant daughter, Amelia Jade Bishop. Amelia was the name of Jerome Farmer's wife, and the Grams' mother, and Kim thought she was disgracefully underrepresented in the Bishop-Farmer naming process. Jade was just a name they liked.

They also took the time while everyone was there to have a celebration of life for Rosa Bishop. Kim had found a big field of wildflowers on the outskirts of town, and they all gathered around while Carl and Scott opened the urn of cremains and scattered her ashes in the wind. Scott said a few words about forgiveness and second chances. Then they all went out for lunch. The Grams and Scott left for the airport that afternoon, and Chris and Michelle stayed behind for two extra days.

On the day before they left to go home to Eastboro, Sally called the Bishops' house and asked to speak to Michelle.

"Kim's gonna be pissed," she said, "but I had to talk to you first. I'm pregnant, Michelle! And it's confirmed! I'm due January twenty-third. The doctor said everything looks good, and there's no reason for me to be worried any more than anyone else!"

"Sally! That's fantastic!" Michelle said. "Congratulations! I'm so happy for you! I'm guessing you've told your mom?"

"Yes, and Andie, but then you next. Michelle, I'm so excited! I hope you get pregnant soon, and we can go through the morning sickness together!"

"Yeah," Michelle said sarcastically. "That will be great. We're gonna try again after we get back. I hope it doesn't take too long."

"It won't," Sally assured her. "But Traci was wrong. She said you'd be the next one to have a baby after Kim, but it's me! But maybe she was just slightly off."

They finished talking, and Michelle passed the phone to Kim so she could hear the news. Then Michelle went to tell Chris. He put his arms around her.

"It will happen soon for us," he promised her. "I have a good feeling about it. We won't stop until it happens."

The next day brought a new goodbye for Carl and Chris.

"I don't think there will be any more weddings coming up until Pete and Carolyn set a date," Carl said. "And no more unexpected deaths, please. For a long, long time. If Jack drops dead, don't make me come home, okay?"

Chris agreed. "Just come to visit, just to see us sometime," he said. "No big deal, right, dragging three little kids all the way across the country? But if we have kids, you'll have to come."

Carl nodded. "I'll find a way. Maybe just me, Drake, and Elena. You've got a deal." He embraced Chris. "I love you, bro. I'm so glad you and the wife made it out here to see us. It means everything. Take good care of the Grams."

"I love you, too, man," Chris said. Chris hugged Kim while Michelle hugged Carl, and they all said goodbye. Then Laine and Beth drove them to the airport.

When they arrived back home, they left their bags at the bottom of the stairs. Then they slouched down on the couch to relax for a few minutes. Michelle took out her calendar to look at her work schedule for the next week.

"Holy shit, Chris," she said softly. "What's the date today? Is it the twenty-third?"

"Yeah, all day," Chris said. "Why? Did you miss something while we were gone?"

"Yeah," Michelle said, turning to look at him. "My period. It's three days late. Oh my God, Chris. My period is never late. I swear, I've been on a twenty-eight-day cycle since I was thirteen. How did I not realize I was late?"

Chris stared at her. "Chelley, are you sure?"

She nodded. "See? Here on my calendar, I always mark the first day of my period every month so I can keep track. Right here?" She pointed to a day. "That was thirty-one days ago."

Chris thought quickly. "But periods can be late sometimes, right?" he said, not wanting to let his mind settle on the fact that Michelle might actually be late and what that would mean for them.

Michelle shook her head. "Maybe for some people, but not for me. God, I wasn't paying attention! I was too preoccupied with our trip. Chris, we need to go to CVS right now and buy a pregnancy test."

"Right now?"

Michelle stood. "Yes, right now," she demanded. "You can test on the first day you're late. You can have false negatives, but if it's positive, it's positive. Put your shoes back on. Let's go."

They left, then came back, and Michelle peed on the stick. She held it in her hand and stared at it, willing the blue line to appear and not wanting to put it on the sink and wait. Chris stood with her, his heart pounding.

As soon as the pee crossed the test area, the blue line appeared.

Michelle shrieked, then looked up at Chris, and he looked at her. Then, they both burst out laughing.

"Oh my God," Michelle finally said. "That was way too easy! We did it in two months, and we weren't even trying this past month. Chris! We're gonna have a baby!"

Chris threw his arms around her and squeezed. "Chelley, I can't believe it. We did it! Holy shit, you're pregnant. I made you pregnant! On purpose!"

They held each other for a long time in silence, then let go and looked into each other's eyes, which were wet with tears.

"What do we do now?" Michelle asked. "What do you do after you pee on the stick and it's positive?"

Chris shrugged. "I don't know! You're the nurse! I guess we plan to call the doctor tomorrow and make you an appointment to make sure. Then we . . . make dinner?"

"Then I call Sally," Michelle said. "But just Sally."

"Then I call Carl," Chris added. "But just Carl."

"And we tell them not to tell anyone yet. Because it's too early. We need to wait."

"Right," Chris said, sitting down on the closed toilet. "Even though that just leaves Pete and Darlene, so that's kind of weird. And at some point, we leave the bathroom. We can't stay in the bathroom all night."

Michelle laughed. Chris loved Chelley's laugh. It was so genuine and real. Everything about Chelley was. And a baby. A baby would be so real. Something of his love for Chelley that he could hold in his arms. Something that only the two of them shared. The only person in the world who he would love as much as Chelley, maybe even more in some ways. Chris felt the empty spaces inside of him start to fill up. There would always be spaces to fill, but now they felt more solid, more secure. He and his wife—his beautiful, amazing wife—were going to have a baby. He couldn't ask for anything more than that.

Eight weeks later, they took the afternoon off for Michelle's routine ultrasound. They were excited to see their baby on the screen, but there was some slight concern for Michelle's growth. They might not have calculated the due date accurately, or it might just be that she was so petite. The doctor just wanted to take a closer look. Michelle was nervous, thinking that there could be something wrong with the baby.

Before the exam, Michelle had to drink thirty-two ounces of water in an hour. "Sally said they press the ultrasound wand on your bladder until you cry," she told Chris after she swallowed another mouthful. "They're some sort of sadists."

Chris laughed. He knew that millions of women went through the procedure every day, and it most likely wasn't as bad as Michelle was letting on. But he drank water with her, and kept up her pace, to show support.

"You'll be fine," he told her. "And it will be worth it. We'll finally get to see Peanut." A peanut had been the approximate size of the fetus the previous week, according to the baby books. It had also become the baby's nickname.

Michelle smiled. She couldn't wait.

After the tech looked at several views of Michelle's abdomen, she let her use the restroom, then come back for more views. Michelle looked at Chris with relief until she heard the tech say, "Oh, my."

Michelle and Chris looked at each other. "What is it?" Michelle asked with dread.

The tech smiled. "I'm gonna go get the on-call doctor to take a look, but I do have a question for you. Do twins run in your family?"

Michelle and Chris were both silent, then burst out laughing together.

"Uh, yeah," Michelle answered. "Chris's grandmother is an identical twin, and so are my little brothers, but we were under the impression that identical twins don't run in families."

"I've heard that, too," the tech said. "But who knows. Let me get the doctor to take a look. I'm not one hundred percent sure of what I'm looking at here, and she can tell you more." She left the room.

Michelle and Chris looked at each other. "Twins?" Chris said, shaking his head.

Michelle shook her head. "It can't be," she replied. "It must be something else. And if it is twins, it's got to be fraternal twins. There's no way."

The doctor entered the room, introduced herself, and squeezed more gel onto Michelle's abdomen. "Oh, yeah," she said as she moved the wand around. "There are two babies in you. I see two distinct sets of limbs, and I can see two tiny hearts beating. And two cute little noses, see?" She pointed to something on the screen that looked nothing like a nose. "Do you want to know their genders? It's a bit early, but I might be able to see something—"

"No!" Michelle and Chris called out together. Michelle went on.

"Can you tell if they're fraternal or identical just by looking?" she asked. "I'm just asking because it's got to be fraternal. I mean, there's no way they can be identical. I mean, the odds have to be astronomical!"

The doctor continued to explore. "Okay, I'm looking at the placenta now for baby A," she told them. "And I'm looking for a second placenta for baby B. I don't see a second placenta. The two babies are sharing a placenta. I think it's pretty safe to say that the two of you are expecting identical twins. I don't know much about the odds, but I do know a lot about science. It is what it is. Everything looks really good in the ultrasound so far. You seem to have a healthy set of identical twins. Would you like to hear the heartbeats?"

Chris and Michelle nodded enthusiastically. Soon, they were able to hear one heartbeat, and then the other. Chris grabbed Michelle's hand, and they both laughed. Michelle had tears in her eyes. The doctor smiled.

"It's pretty amazing, huh? I'll leave some information on expecting twins for you up front at reception, and we'll calculate your due date. Sometimes, with twins, they come a bit early, and sometimes the pregnancy can be considered somewhat high risk. I'll have your doctor give you a call after she gets the report." She took off her gloves and threw them in the trash. "Congratulations, you two." She opened the door and stepped out of the room.

The tech handed Michelle a towel. "You're all set," she said. "I got all the pictures I need. Go ahead and clean yourself off and you can get up and head out. I'll leave the information for you to pick up on the way out. You two take care. Congratulations." She left the room.

Michelle sat up, and she and Chris looked at each other and stared.

"Oh my fucking God, Chelley," Chris finally said with an exasperated grin. "We're having dental twins!"

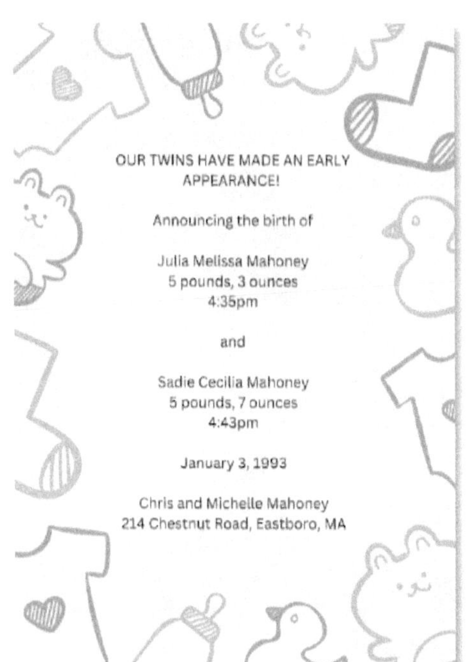

OUR TWINS HAVE MADE AN EARLY
APPEARANCE!

Announcing the birth of

Julia Melissa Mahoney
5 pounds, 3 ounces
4:35pm

and

Sadie Cecilia Mahoney
5 pounds, 7 ounces
4:43pm

January 3, 1993

Chris and Michelle Mahoney
214 Chestnut Road, Eastboro, MA

Our family has grown by
two feet!

Introducing for the first time ever

Jessica Marie Newell
Born January 17, 1993
7 pounds, 3 ounces, 18.5 inches

To proud parents
James and Sally Newell
1652 South Kenyon Street, Uxbridge, MA

Acknowledgments

I wrote a lot of this book on the phone. Sometimes on the bus, sometimes in the car, and sometimes during breaks at work. Thank you to all of the people who understood when I bumped into them on the sidewalk.

Thank you to my brother, Jonathan. You have worked almost as hard as I have trying to get the word out about McKinney High. And at the same time, you were still alpha reading my new books. I'm glad I can provide you with ongoing reading materials!

To Clint Chico. Please read my books forever, and keep writing yours just as long. I hope we are always able to read each other's work. Thank you for everything you have done for me!

Thank you, Missy, for your red hair and glasses back in the best decade ever, and thank you for our renewed friendship! Thank you, Tanya, for your undying support.

I know I dedicated this book to my daughter, but I have to mention her again. Even though you haven't read any of my books, you listened to me read this one out loud, at least half of it, while lounging at the Cape on hot summer nights. So thank you for continuing to indulge me as I live my dream.

Thank you, Nicole Frail, for fixing up my work to make it pretty, and Jai Design for keeping the beautiful graphics coming.

And last of all, thank you, Al.

Debby Meltzer Quick is a full-time social worker in Portland, Oregon. She has been writing for fun since age twelve. Growing up in Massachusetts, she became a huge fan of Boston sports, especially the Red Sox and the Patriots, and she aspired to be a sports reporter. She is an avid reader of fiction. She lives with her husband, daughter, two cats, and one rabbit. She plans to release four more books in the series, *McKinney High Class of 1986*, and she is now working on a new series that takes place in the world of Eastboro, Massachusetts.

Don't miss the next installment

in the

McKinney High Class of 1986

series:

The Stories That Must Be Told

Coming in the Fall of 2024

Please enjoy the following excerpt

FRIENDS FOR LIFE

Barbara Feinman picked up a magazine from the waiting room table and flipped through it, looking at pictures of skinny women in maternity clothes. She made a face. These women hadn't spent a minute pregnant in their whole brief lives. They should hire real pregnant models, with swollen feet and puffy faces. That would be an ad campaign Barbara could get behind. She checked the clock. Ten after ten. The obstetrician must be running late. That was the risk at these appointments. An unexpected delivery. She sighed and shifted in her chair to get more comfortable. She might be there a while.

The door to the doctor's office opened, and a young, very pregnant woman walked in. She signed in at the front desk, took off her coat, and then sat down in a seat facing Barbara. She looked at Barbara and smiled, and then picked up a magazine.

She looked like a child. A beautiful child. She had long, straight, thick dark hair held back with a wide bright green fabric headband. Her skin was clear and rosy. She was wearing a long-sleeved dress that ended just above her knees and was covered with a bright floral pattern. And go-go boots. She wore false eyelashes and thick blue eye shadow. Barbara stared. This child looked like a pregnant brunette Nancy Sinatra.

The girl looked up and caught Barbara staring. She smiled again. "Hi."

Barbara smiled back. "Hi," she said. "When is your baby due?"

"March first," was her answer. "It's a leap year this year, so if she comes one day early, she'll only have a birthday every four years." She laughed. "How about you?"

Barbara's hand shot to her belly. "May fifteenth," she said. "So you don't have much longer to go. Are you ready?"

The girl nodded. "I guess as ready as I can be," she said. "I'm pretty excited. Is this your first baby?"

"Yes," Barbara replied, rubbing the space over her navel. "My husband and I have been trying to start our family since we got married three years ago. We finally got lucky. I was worried we would end up old and childless."

The girl looked at her skeptically. "May I ask how old you are?"

"Twenty-three," Barbara answered. "I know that doesn't sound old, but we only have so much time, and I don't think I would want to have a baby after twenty-eight. I think that would just be so hard on the body. And how old are you?"

"Nineteen," the girl answered. "I guess I have a lot of time to have more babies." Now she started rubbing her belly. "The baby must have woken up. She's kicking like a Rockette!"

Barbara smiled. "You want a girl?"

"I do," the girl answered. "I would be okay with a boy, but it would be so wonderful to have a little girl, with the cute clothes and all. And I could teach her how to cook, and sew, and all the things that my mother taught me."

"Does your husband want a boy?" Barbara asked.

The girl looked down at her boots. "I don't have a husband." She looked up at Barbara. "I had a boyfriend, but when I told him I was pregnant, his first response was to tell me to make it go away. When I said no, he picked up a glass vase from my parents' counter and threw it at a wall. There was glass, water, and bits of flowers everywhere. It was scary. Some glass even landed on my foot, but luckily I didn't get cut. My father came running in and kicked him out of the house. I haven't seen him since. I hope I never do. If he showed his face at our house again, I think my father would punch his lights out. He never liked him anyways." She sighed. "No, I'm in this all by myself. My parents will help some, but I'm gonna be the mom. I'm going to take the best care of my baby."

Barbara looked at her. She felt a wave of sympathy. Just earlier, she was feeling sorry for herself because her husband, Reggie, wasn't able to accompany her to this appointment due to work, even though she had given him a lot of notice. Now, comparing her situation to this young girl's, she felt relief and affection toward Reggie. Reggie wanted this baby. This baby had been planned.

Barbara stuck her hand out toward the girl. "My name is Barbara," she said. "Barbara Feinman."

The girl took her hand and shook it lightly. "I'm Victoria Lester."

"Nice to meet you, Victoria," Barbara said. "Do people call you Vicky?"

Victoria shook her head. "Oh, no," she said. "Not if they don't want an earful from me. It's Victoria. Not Vicky, not Tory. Some of my friends call me Vee, and that's okay."

"Are your friends excited about your baby?" Barbara wondered.

Victoria frowned. "A lot of my friends have gone to college. I was going to junior college, but now I'm taking time off. I'm just going to focus on getting my real estate license so I can work and support me and the baby and get our own place someday. But my other friends, some are okay, but some have really shied away from me. I don't think their parents really approve of them being friends with an unwed teen mother. It's hard to believe people still feel that way in 1968, what with all the peace and love stuff going on, and all the boys dying in Vietnam, but they still do. So I basically just hang around with my mom and dad most of the time."

Barbara thought about it. "Do you live in Eastboro?"

"Yes," Victoria answered. "We live on the east side of Carson Lake. My father's a product manager at Aries Corps."

Barbara smiled. "We live over by the lake, too," she said. "Reggie's an underwriter at an investment company that's affiliated with Aries. Small world! I bet our babies will end up in school together someday. Maybe we can get together after the babies come and have them play together."

Victoria looked at Barbara hopefully. "Really?" she asked. "I would love that! But your husband won't mind, what with me being unmarried?"

Barbara waved that off with a laugh. "No, Reggie won't care about that at all," she said. "And he's at work all day anyway, so he won't even be around."

She struggled to her feet and walked over to the reception area to request a piece of paper and a pencil. She wrote her name and telephone number on the top half, then tore the paper in two. "Victoria," she said, "what's your parents' phone number?"

Victoria had a girl on February twenty-eighth. She named her Kim. Not Kimberly, but Kim, because that's what she wanted to call her. Barbara came to visit her in the hospital and met Victoria's mother, Susan Lester. She held baby Kim and longed for her own baby to arrive.

Barbara had her baby on May eighteenth, and she and Reggie named her Darlene Renee Feinman. Victoria came to see her in the hospital along with baby Kim, and Barbara marveled at how large the two-and-a-half-month-old baby looked beside her tiny newborn. They took their first photos together and deemed their daughters to already be best friends.

BABIES AREN'T EASY

Reggie was different after the baby arrived. He had been so anxious to start their family, but now he seemed disinterested in doing anything to participate in her care. Barbara had imagined them learning to care for their daughter together: giving her her first bath, taking her on carriage rides to Twin Bridges Park, changing her into her puffy pink dress with a white collar to go visit her grandparents . . . but Reggie declined. He was either too tired from work, or too busy reading his newspaper or watching the news. He did not get up at night to get the baby so Barbara could nurse her, so Barbara spent her nights and days in an exhausted fog. Her friends told her that their husbands were useless at helping with the babies, but at least they seemed interested. Reggie acted like the baby had disrupted his routine, and he resented it. It was as if he had liked the idea of a baby, but when a real one arrived, it wasn't at all what he thought he had ordered. Barbara had thought that they would start to work on conceiving baby number two quite quickly after Darlene was born, but Reggie didn't seem very interested in that either. It was like he didn't find her attractive anymore, and he would leave the room when she was nursing. There were days that went by when the only human contact Barbara experienced was holding and feeding her baby. She felt isolated and worried. But she was afraid to bring it up with Reggie.

She started calling Victoria more, and Victoria welcomed her calls. Victoria was feeling overwhelmed herself. Kim was a sweet and cuddly baby, but she had a scream that could pierce her mother's eardrums. And she just wouldn't go to sleep! Victoria was tired and worn out, but she didn't want to complain. Many people had thought she couldn't raise a child on her own, but she was showing them that she could. And she was taking classes to get her real estate license. Her mother watched the baby when she went to class. Sometimes, she felt herself drifting off to sleep during class time, and she had to rouse herself and try twice as hard to listen. Some nights, while Kim finally slept, Victoria would cry herself to sleep.

They found solace with each other. Visits gave them reasons to shower, get dressed, and put on makeup, even on days when they didn't need to. They would take the babies to the park, or to the diner for lunch, or just sit on the floor in each other's living rooms with the babies and talk. Sometimes, they would talk about their problems, but mostly, they gossiped about celebrities and other mothers.

"Did you see that hat that Carla was wearing at the park yesterday?" Barbara said to Victoria as they both dangled squeaky toys over the faces of their infants. "I think she's trying to look like Jackie Kennedy, but she really doesn't."

Victoria laughed. "No, she looked more like Jackie Gleason!" she said, and Barbara almost spit out her gum laughing.

The two mothers watched each other's babies for short periods of time so they could get their hair done or do other small chores. One afternoon in August, Victoria kept Darlene so Barbara could get her hair styled into a fancy beehive and buy a new dress. Her mother would be taking Darlene for the night so Barbara could cook dinner for Reggie and hopefully have a night of romance without the wails of a three-month-old baby as their background music. When Barbara came back to the Lester home, Victoria raved about her hair, and gave her some tips on makeup. Barbara modeled her new dress.

"Oh, Barbara," Victoria said, clapping her hands together and entwining her fingers. "You look like a movie star! Your figure is so lovely! No one would even know to look at you that you just had a baby! Reggie will find you stunning!"

Barbara blushed. "Do you really think so?" she asked, looking at herself from every possible angle in the mirror. "I always feel so awkward in my own body, with nursing and just not having time to take care of myself. But maybe now Reggie will see I'm still the woman he married, and I still take care in how I look for him."

Victoria smiled at her friend. "Barb, any man would be lucky to have you for his wife. I hope Reggie knows he won the jackpot when he married you. He's a lucky man!"

Later that night, Barbara fussed over the stove making homemade mashed potatoes to go with the steak she was waiting to put under the broiler. She had cut the ends off of fresh string beans and had a pot of water on the burner waiting to boil. Once almost everything was ready to go, she went to her bedroom and put on her new dress. She sat at her vanity and applied her makeup carefully, just as Victoria had shown her. At a quarter to six, she went back to the kitchen and turned on the broiler. Then she put the steak in the oven. Reggie would be home soon.

At six-thirty, the potatoes were getting cold and the beans, soggy. Barbara sighed and stood up to address the food. She heard the door open, and Reggie came into the kitchen.

"What's for dinner?" he asked by way of a greeting. He took off his suit coat and threw it on the back of a chair, and then loosened his tie.

Barbara attempted to smile. "Remember, Reggie?" she told him. "I made a special dinner for us tonight, but it was ready at six, so it might not be quite as fresh. Why are you late?"

Reggie shot her a look. "Late? It's six-thirty. That's hardly late. And where's the baby?" He looked around.

"She's at my mother's house for the night, remember?" Barbara said through partially gritted teeth. "So we could have some time to ourselves."

"Oh," Reggie said, turning back to look at her. "Well, good. It will be nice to get a good night's sleep for once without all of that hollering at two in the morning. Who can sleep through all that crying?"

He sat down, waiting for her to serve him.

"Mr. Finch wanted me to have a glass of scotch with him in his office before I left tonight, so I stayed behind for a few minutes. That's how you know they're looking at you for a promotion over there. When they start to take an interest in you after hours. I couldn't say no."

He looked up at Barbara as she placed a plate of food in front of him. "What's that all over your face?" he said critically.

Barbara's hand went to her cheek. "Did I get some mashed potatoes on me?"

"No," Reggie said, squinting at her. "It looks like some kind of makeup, but it looks like you did it wrong."

"What?" Barbara asked in disbelief.

"And you got a new dress. How much did that set me back?"

Barbara took a deep breath. "I bought it with money I saved from my grocery allowance," she told him. "And it was on sale. What do you think?" She did a twirl for him.

Reggie shrugged. "It's a nice dress, but don't you think you should wait until you lose the pregnancy weight before you wear something like that? It's not very flattering. It's like putting a tutu on a hippopotamus." Reggie started laughing and went back to his steak.

Barbara felt like she had been hit by a truck. She was about to say something in her defense when Reggie spoke again. "This steak is dry and cold, and the potatoes are lumpy."

Tears and anger rose up in her chest. She looked at Reggie, and then turned on her heels and ran to her bedroom and slammed the door. She threw herself down on the bed and sobbed. Reggie had never spoken to her like this before the baby, even when he did have a bit to drink. His words were hurtful and stabbing. And why? He thought he knew what it was like to be awakened every night to a hungry, crying baby? Who did Reggie think got up every night to attend to that baby, to quiet her so he could sleep, only to return later to his loud snores in their bed? Barbara was exhausted, and yet she still made an effort for them, for their marriage. But Reggie was changing.

She remembered the loving, amicable, adventurous Reggie she had met at a party at a mutual friend's house four years earlier. That Reggie was up for anything. He liked to hike, cross country ski, take long rides in the country where all they did was talk. And he loved to take her to bed, to please her, and show her how special she was to him. They talked of having children, of going on epic journeys across the country in a recreational vehicle, seeing the Grand Canyon and Old Faithful. But now their first child had arrived, and Reggie was preoccupied with his work and ignored his wife and daughter. And tonight, he was downright rude and insulting.

Barbara sat up and dabbed her eyes with a tissue. She would go back out there. She would eat her dinner with dignity, and Reggie would apologize for the way he spoke to her. Then they would talk and figure out what was going on. And everything would be okay again.

She went to the bathroom and washed the tears off her face, and with it, her carefully applied makeup. She patted her skin dry, smiled at the mirror, and then made her way to the kitchen. Reggie had already left the room to watch the news. He had left his empty plate on the table for her to clean up.

Barbara fixed a plate for herself, and then sat down to eat. Reggie came into the room, and Barbara waited for him to speak. He looked at her.

"Oh good," he said. "You took off that awful makeup. So you could see how it made you look like a clown, too." He went to the refrigerator, grabbed a bottle of beer, and walked back out of the room.

Barbara sat in a stunned silence. Then, she calmly ate the rest of her dinner, cleaned the kitchen, and went to her room. She came out with an overnight bag. She approached Reggie in front of the TV.

"I'm going to my mother's house," she told him. "I need to be with Darlene. I'll be back in the morning with the baby."

"Now you made me miss the end of that story," Reggie complained, trying to look around her. He sighed. "I'm playing golf with Mr. Finch tomorrow morning at City Club. Then we're having lunch. I may not be home until late."

"Good night, Reggie," Barbara said. She was going to kiss him on the cheek and then thought better of it. He didn't look up as she walked toward the door, left the house, and drove off in her car to her mother's house.

SOUR MILK

The apology never came. The behavior didn't change. Barbara stopped trying to get Reggie's attention. Reggie stayed later at work, and as he predicted, he got promoted with a significant pay raise soon after. Then he made more trips to the City Club with his cronies to play golf, eat endless lunches, and smoke cigars while drinking scotch. Reggie didn't even like Scotch.

Barbara decided to spend her time and energy focusing on other things. She attended to Darlene and brought her to a play group of babies her own age. She encouraged Victoria to come with Kim when she was not in class. She volunteered to assist with neighborhood events and activities and became treasurer of the Aries Corps Wives Charity Club. She and Victoria spent more time together with their daughters, walking through department stores, going to parks, or just playing in their homes when the weather got colder. They focused on talking about the unfortunate clothing choices of the other women they knew and stories they had overheard. Barbara rarely spoke about Reggie anymore.

Soon, it was Christmas time, and Aries was having its annual Christmas Banquet. It was on the same evening as the Lester family's holiday extravaganza, and Barbara wanted to go to that instead. Reggie didn't want to show up at his work function without his wife, as it just didn't fit the image of the family man he was trying to portray to his superiors. Barbara refused to go.

"It's that Lester girl, isn't it?" Reggie hissed at her. "She's putting all these hippy ideas and notions in your head. For God's sake, you're even trying to look like her now. Take that ridiculous headband out of your hair, would you? You're not a beatnik! You're a twenty-four-year-old mother, not a nineteen-year-old slut with a bastard baby!"

Barbara recoiled as if she had been slapped. "You take that back, Reginald Feinman," she said in her calmest voice, but with her fists clenched.

Reggie's face turned red. "I will not!" he exclaimed. "I said what I said. She's a no-good junior college dropout, and I wouldn't be surprised if that ragamuffin of hers ends up with a drug addiction and her picture on the centerfold of a men's magazine."

He looked at her as if daring her to make a rebuttal. Instead, Barbara took several deep breaths, released her fists, and went to pick up her baby.

"Get the hell out of here," she said to him through her teeth. "I can't even look at you. Just get out. I don't care where you go, but just leave. Did you hear me? I said *get out of here*!"

For the first time, Reggie appeared uncertain as to what to do next. Then he nodded. "Okay," he said, "I'll go. I'll spend the night at my parents' house. But I'm coming back tomorrow."

"You'll come back tomorrow to pack your things," Barbara told him. "Enough until we figure out what to do next. But I won't be here. If you do come back, I expect you to be gone again by three, understand?"

Reggie looked at her with no expression. "Okay," he said calmly. "I understand. I'll go now." He walked backward for a few steps, turned around, grabbed his coat, and was gone.

It was only then that Barbara noticed that the baby in her arms was red-faced and screaming. And that her own tears had been falling in Darlene's face. She rushed to the sofa, pulled up her shirt, and started to nurse her daughter. The baby quickly calmed and grabbed onto her hair. Suddenly she realized that Reggie had not said a word about the baby the whole time they were arguing, and when he left, he didn't tell her goodbye, or even glance at her at all. All that Barbara could think at that very moment was that she was a terrible mother, because she was feeding her baby sour milk.